# THE ADDRESS BOOK

## Other Books by Michael Levine

*A Branded World*

*Guerilla PR Wired*

*Guerilla PR*

*Lessons at the Halfway Point*

*Take It From Me*

*Selling Goodness*

*Raise Your Social I.Q.*

*The Princess and the Package*

*The Corporate Address Book*

*The Music Address Book*

*The Environmental Address Book*

*The Kid's Address Book*

# THE ADDRESS BOOK

**HOW TO REACH ANYONE WHO IS ANYONE**

**Michael Levine**

NEW MILLENNIUM PRESS
*Beverly Hills*

Every effort has been made to provide the most current mailing addresses. Addresses, however, do change, and neither the publisher nor the author is responsible for misdirected or returned mail.


Cover design: Sonia Fiore
Text design: Kerry DeAngelis, KL Design



First printing: December 2003
New Millennium Entertainment, Inc.
301 North Canon Drive
Suite 214
Beverly Hills CA 90210

Library of Congress in-Publication Data available upon request.
ISBN: 1-893224-78-3

Printed in the United States of America
www.NewMillenniumPress.com

10 9 8 7 6 5 4 3 2 1

# ACKNOWLEDGMENTS

I'm lucky. I get to say publicly to the special people in my life how much they mean to me. To each of them, my appreciation for their help with this book and, most of all, their unwavering friendship and love.

My literary agent, Craig Nelson.

My special friends, Adam Christing, Cable Neuhaus, and Alyse Reynolds.

Special thanks to Tara Griggs for commitment to excellence in the researching of this book.

To my staff, Paul Armstrong, Clarissa Clarke, Phil Foord, and Dawn Miller.


---

Interns interested in working in Mr. Levine's Los Angeles office should contact:


Intern Coordinator
Levine Communications Office
10333 Ashton Avenue
Los Angeles, CA 90024
www.levinepr.com

# INTRODUCTION

A couple of years ago, I proudly accepted an invitation to deliver a speech at the Harvard Business School. Never having visited an Ivy League school, I wasn't quite sure what to expect.

The audience of America's best and brightest took me completely by surprise—and damn near gave the faculty a collective heart attack—when they stood and cheered my concluding observation: "Some ideas are so stupid, only intellectuals can believe them."

I came to appreciate the truism about twenty years ago when I first approached New York's publishing elite with my admittedly simple idea to create a series of address books. One by one, they peered down from their thrones, rejecting the idea as "far too simple," and suggesting that in this hurry-up world, only fools would be naïve enough to write to people they didn't know.

Finally, Putnam saw its worth, and today, it is estimated over 4,000,000 letters have been successfully delivered, thanks to this best-selling series of address books.

I've heard from desperate medical patients who have received help from blood donors thanks to the book, from lost loves reunited, from consumers battling and beating corporate villains, and, of course, from fans hearing from their heroes.

By the way, a few years ago I visited the White House, and never in my life did I feel prouder than when I saw *The Address Book* on the desks in several executive offices.

Yes, the address book was a simple idea; an idea that works. But, how can you make it work for you?

* How can you make sure the notable receives your letter? The number-one reason mail to notables is left unanswered is that it is addressed improperly and never reaches its intended destination. A letter addressed simply to "Barbara Streisand, Hollywood, California" will find its way only to the dead-letter file of the post office. The complete, accurate addresses in this book will get your mail to the offices, agents, studios, managers, or even homes of the addressees, and I have been unable to find one notable, no matter how busy or important, who doesn't personally read some of his or her mail—even the President of the United States. That doesn't mean notables read and answer every single piece, but it should offer encouragement to people who write to them.

* Politicians have a standard rule of thumb: for every letter they receive, they estimate that one hundred people who didn't take the time to write are thinking the same thought as the letter expresses. So you can calculate the effect of your single letter by multiplying it by one hundred! And all entertainment figures keep a close watch on their mail. It is a real indication of what people are thinking and feeling. Often, the notable is surrounded by a small group of associates who tend to isolate the star from the public. Your letter helps break down this barrier. Amazing things have been accomplished with letters as long as they have the proper mailing address.

* Here are several important things to remember when writing notables: Always include a self-addressed stamped envelope. This is the single most important factor in writing a letter if you want a response. Because of the unusually high volume of mail notable people receive, anything you can do to make it easier for them to respond is going to work in your favor. Keep your letters short and to the point. Notables are usually extremely busy people, and long letters tend to be set aside for "future" considerations. For instance, if you want an autographed picture of your favorite TV

personality, don't write three pages of prose to explain your request.

* Make your letters as easy to read as possible. This means type it or, at the very least, handwrite it very neatly. Avoid crayons, markers, or even pencils. And don't forget to leave some margins on the paper.

* Be sure to include your name and address (even on all materials that you include with your letter) in the event the materials are separated from your letter. You would be amazed how many people write letters without return addresses and then wonder why they never hear from the person to whom they wrote.

* Never send food to notables. Due to spillage and security matters, it cannot be eaten anyway. (Would you eat a box of homemade brownies given to you by a complete stranger?) If you send gifts, don't wrap them in large boxes with yards of paper, string, and tape around them. (They may not have a crowbar on hand.) Again, don't forget to include your name and address on all material you send. Of course, don't send—or ask for—money.

* In writing to corporation heads, remember most of them rose to their lofty positions because they were better problem solvers than their company peers. Good corporation heads are zealous about finding solutions to written complaints (especially if you have sent copies of your complaint letters to consumer organizations.) A recent survey of corporation heads showed that 88 percent of all letters of complaint were resolved. Therefore, the old adage, "When you have a problem, go to the top," appears to be accurate. Likewise, corporation executives greatly appreciate hearing good news (satisfaction, extra service, helpful employees, and so forth.)

But nowhere is it written that mail should only be filled with praise and congratulations. You may enjoy shaking a fist at your favorite villain, so I have included infamous people in my book.

Most people are usually very kind and sincere in their letters. They write what they would say or ask if they had the opportunity to do so in person. This is especially true of children, who are extremely honest. On the other hand, infamous people and others who are out of favor with the public predictably receive hostile and angry letters.

Most of the people, famous and infamous, listed in *The Address Book* are movers and shakers, and thus highly transient, changing their addresses far more often than the average person. Their mail is usually forwarded to them, but occasionally a letter may be returned to the sender. If this should happen to your letter, first check to make sure that you have copied the address correctly. If you wish to locate another address for the person to whom you are writing, begin your search by writing to him or her in care of the company or association with which they may have been most recently associated. For example, if a musician or singer has last recorded an album with a specific record company, write in care of that company; a sports figure might be contacted through the last team he or she was associated with; an author through his or her most recent publisher; and so forth.

According to statistics, about 90 million pieces of mail land in the dead letter pile because the carrier couldn't make out the address, so write clearly.

Remember, *a person who writes to another makes more impact than ten thousand who are silent.*

—Michael Levine
Los Angeles, CA
michael@levinepr.com

| | |
|---|---|
| **Kim John Il**<br>President of North Korea<br>351 Phelps Drive<br>North Korea<br>Pyongyang North Korea | **AGE** 62<br>in power since 1994 |
| **King Kim Fahd**<br>**Crown Prince Abdullah**<br>Saudi Arabia<br>6464 W Sunset Blvd.<br>Saudi Arabia<br>Riyadh, Saudi Arabia | **AGE** 81 in power since 1982<br>**AGE** 80; in power since 1995 |
| **Saddam Hussein**<br>President of Iraq<br>*(This Leader is no longer in power.)* | **AGE** 66<br>in power since 1979 |
| **Charles Taylor**<br>President of Liberia<br>Liberia<br>Capitol Hill<br>1000 Monrovia 10 Liberia | **AGE** 56<br>in power since 1997 |
| **Than Shwe**<br>Burma<br>State Peace and Development Council<br>c/o Military Defense<br>Signal Pagoda Road<br>Yangon, Union of Myanmar | **AGE** 71<br>in power since 1992<br>**E-MAIL** Mission.myanmar@ties.itu.int |
| **Teodoro Obiang Nguema**<br>President of Equatorial Guinea<br>Equatorial Guinea<br>Malabo Equatorial Guinea | **AGE** 61<br>in power since 1979 |
| **Saparmurat Niyazov**<br>Turkmenistan | **AGE** 63<br>in power since 1990<br>**E-MAIL** turkmen@mindspring.com |
| **Muammar Al-Qaddafi**<br>Colonel of Libya<br>Office of the Prime Minister<br>Tripoli, Libya | **AGE** 61<br>in power since 1969. |

| | |
|---|---|
| **Fidel Castro**<br>President of Cuba<br>P.O. Box 1671<br>Cuba | **AGE** 77<br>in power since 1959<br>**INTERNET** www.cubaweb.cu |
| **Alexander Lukashenko**<br>President of Belarus<br>Belarus (Republic of)<br>Office of the President | **AGE** 49<br>in power since 1994<br>**INTERNET** www.president.gov.by<br>**E-MAIL** ires@president.gov.by |

## 10 MOST REQUESTED CELEBRITY EMAILS

| | |
|---|---|
| **Britney Spears** | **E-MAIL** britney@britneyspears.com |
| **Tom Cruise** | **E-MAIL** tomcruise@scientology.org |
| **Justin Timberlake** | **E-MAIL** justin@nsync.com |
| **Jennifer Aniston** | **E-MAIL** jeffr48196@aol.com |
| **Madonna** | **E-MAIL** madonna@wbr.com |
| **Michael Jordan** | **E-MAIL** mjordan@nba.com |
| **Tom Hanks** | **E-MAIL** ny122@aol.com |
| **Billy Zane** | **E-MAIL** billizane@aol.com |
| **Jennifer Lopez** | **E-MAIL** jennifer_lopez@sonymusic.com |
| **Ben Affleck** | **E-MAIL** Ben@affleck.com |

## 10 MOST POPULAR WEB SITES

| | |
|---|---|
| **Yahoo!** | **INTERNET** www.yahoo.com |
| **MSN.com** | **INTERNET** www.msn.com |
| **daum** | **INTERNET** www.daum.net |
| **Naver** | **INTERNET** www.Naver.com |
| **Google** | **INTERNET** www.google.com |
| **Passport.net** | **INTERNET** www.passport.net |
| **Yahoo! JAPAN** | **INTERNET** www.yahoo.co.jp |
| **Sayclub.com** | **INTERNET** www.sayclub.com |
| **Microsoft Corporation** | **INTERNET** www.microsoft.com |
| **Amazon** | **INTERNET** www.amazon.com |

## 10 TOP COMPANIES FOR 2003

**Wal-Mart Stores**
702 SW 8th St.
Bentonville, AR 72716
*Retail stores*

**INTERNET** www.walmart.com
S. Robson Walton, Chairman

**ExxonMobil**
5959 Las Colinas Blvd.
CEO
Irving, TX 75039

**INTERNET** www.exxon.mobile.com
Lee R. Raymond Chairman, President and

**General Motors**
300 Renaissance Center
Detroit, MI 48265
*World's #1 Maker of Cars and Trucks*

**INTERNET** www.gm.com
Rick Wagoner, CEO

| | |
|---|---|
| **Ford Motor Company**<br>One American Road<br>Dearborn, MI 48126<br>*Cars and trucks* | **INTERNET** www.ford.com<br>William C. Ford, Jr., Chairman |
| **Enron**<br>1400 Smith St.<br>Houston, TX 77002 | **INTERNET** www.enron.com |
| **General Electric**<br>3135 Easton Turnpike<br>Fairfield, CT 06431<br>*Electrical equipment company* | **INTERNET** www.ge.com<br>Jeffrey R. Immelt, CEO |
| **Citigroup**<br>153 E 53rd St.<br>New York, NY 10043 | **INTERNET** www.citigroup.com |
| **ChevronTexaco**<br>575 Market St.<br>San Francisco, CA 94105<br>*Petroleum refining* | **INTERNET** www.chevron.com<br>David O'Reilly, Chairman and CEO |
| **International Business Machines (IBM)**<br>Old Orchard Road<br>Armonk, NY 10504<br>*Maker of computer systems* | **INTERNET** www.ibm.com<br>Samuel J. Palmisano, Chairman and CEO |
| **Philip Morris U.S.A. (now Altria Group Inc.)**<br>120 Park Ave.<br>New York, NY 10017<br>*Tobacco company* | **INTERNET** www.philipmorrisusa.com<br>Louis Camilleri, President and CEO |
| **20th Century Fox**<br>P.O. Box 900<br>Beverly Hills, CA 90213<br>*Production company* | **INTERNET** www.foxmovies.com |

**Aadland, Beverly**
P.O. Box 1115
Canyon Country, CA 91350
*Actress*

BIRTHDAY 9/17/43

**Aaron, Hank**
c/o The Atlanta Braves
P.O. Box 4064
Atlanta, GA 30302
*Former baseball player*

BIRTHDAY 2/5/34

**Aaron, Tommy**
440 E Lake Dr.
Gainesville, GA 30506
*Golfer*

BIRTHDAY 2/22/37

**AARP (American Association for Retired Persons)**
601 E St. NW
Washington, D.C. 20049
*Association for Senior Citizens*

INTERNET www.aarp.org
Joseph S. Perkins, President

**Abba**
Roosendaal
Postbus 3079
The Netherlands
HOLLAND
NL-4700
*Music group*

**Abbott, Bruce**
c/o Metropolitan
4526 Wilshire Blvd.
Los Angeles, CA 90010
*Actor*

BIRTHDAY 7/28/54

**Abbott, Gregory**
Box 68
Bergenfield, NY 07621
*Singer*

**Abbott Laboratories**
100 Abbott Park Road
Abbott Park, IL 60064
*Drug manufacturer*

INTERNET www.abbott.com
E-MAIL webmaster@abbott.com
Miles D. White, Chairman and CEO

**ABC, Inc.**
500 S. Buena Vista St.
Burbank, CA 91521-4551
*Television network*

**INTERNET** www.abc.com
Robert Callahan, President

**ABC World News Tonight**
47 W. 66th St.
New York, NY 10023

**INTERNET** www.abcnews.com
**VOICE** 212-456-7777

**Abdul, Paula**
c/o American Idol
Fremantle Media Productions
2700 Colorado Ave., 4th Floor
Santa Monica, CA 90404
*Singer/Dancer/Choreographer*

**BIRTHDAY** 6/19/62

**Abdul-Jabbar, Kareem**
c/o Kareem Productions
5458 Wilshire Blvd.
Los Angeles, CA 90036
*Former basketball player*

**Abdullah, The Butcher**
2387 Fairburn Road SW
Atlanta, GA 30331
*Wrestler*

**BIRTHDAY** 1/1/36

**Ablaze Entertainment**
1040 N Las Palmas Ave.
Los Angeles, CA 90038
*Entertainment agency*

**Above the Line Agency**
9200 Sunset Blvd., #804
Los Angeles, CA 90069
Rima Greer, Agent
*Talent agency*

**Abraham, F. Murray**
40 5th Ave.
New York, NY 10011
*Actor*

**BIRTHDAY** 10/24/39

## AC/DC
46 Kensington Ct.
W8JDP London
England
UNITED KINGDOM
*Music group*

## Academy of Motion Pictures Arts and Sciences
8949 Wilshire Blvd.
Beverly Hills, CA 90210
*Film organization*

Bruce Davis, Executive Director

## Academy of Television Arts and Sciences
5220 Lankershim Blvd.
North Hollywood, CA 91601
*Television organization*

**INTERNET** www.emmyonline.org

## ACCESS: A Security Information Service
1511 K St. NW
Washington, D.C. 20065

**E-MAIL** access@4access.org

## Accuracy in Media, Inc.
4455 Connecticut Ave.
Washington, D.C. 20008
*Group concerned with fairness, balance and accuracy in news reporting*

**INTERNET** www.aim.org
Reed Irvine, Chairman

## Ace Hardware
2200 Kensington Ct.
Oak Brook, IL 60523
*Wholesalers*

**INTERNET** www.acehardware.com
**E-MAIL** webmaster@acehardware.com
David F. Hodnik, President and CEO

## Ace Of Base
c/o Arista Records
9975 Santa Monica Blvd.
Beverly Hills, CA 90212
*Music group*

**E-MAIL** aceofbase@arista.com

## Acker, Sharon
332 N Palm Dr., #401
Beverly Hills, CA 90210
*Actress*

## ACLU (American Civil Liberties Union)

125 Broad St.
New York, NY 10004
*Advocate of individual rights*

**INTERNET** www.aclu.org
**E-MAIL** aclu@aclu.org
Anthony D. Romero, Executive Director

## Actors and Others for Animals

11523 Burbank Blvd.
N. Hollywood, CA 91601
*Protection group for the welfare of animals*

**INTERNET** www.actorsandothers.com
Cathy Singleton, Executive Director

## Actor's Equity Association

165 W 46th St.
New York, NY 10036
*Stage actor's union*

**INTERNET** www.actorsequity.org
Alan Eisenberg, President

## Ad Council

261 Madison Ave., 11th Floor
New York, NY 10016
*Nonprofit volunteer organization that conducts public service advertising*

**INTERNET** www.adcouncil.org
**E-MAIL** info@adcouncil.org
Peggy Conlon, President

## Adams, Cindy

475 Park Ave., #PH N
New York, NY 10022
*Columnist*

## Adams, Don

2160 Century Park East
Los Angeles, CA 90067
*Actor/Writer*

**BIRTHDAY** 4/13/23

## Adams, Mason

570 Park Ave., #9B
New York, NY 10021
*Actor*

**BIRTHDAY** 2/26/19

## Adams, Maud

P.O. Box 10838
Beverly Hills, CA 90212
*Model/Actress*

**BIRTHDAY** 2/12/45

## Adams, Patch
c/o Gesundheit Institute
P.O. Box 268
Hillsboro, WV 24946
*Doctor portrayed by Robin Williams in Patch Adams*

**INTERNET** www.patchadams.org

## Adams, Tom
29-31 Kings Road
SW3 London
England
UNITED KINGDOM
*Actor*

## Adjani, Isabella
c/o ArtMedia
20 Ave. Rapp
75007
Paris, France
*Actress*

**BIRTHDAY** 6/27/55

## Adler, Margot
c/o NPR
635 Mass Ave.
Washington, D.C. 20001
*News correspondent*

## Advertising Age
711 3rd Ave.
New York, NY 10017
*Magazine*

**INTERNET** www.adage.com
**VOICE** 212-210-0100

## Advocacy Institute
1629 K St. NW
Washington, D.C. 20006
*Dedicated to strengthening the capacity of public interest/social and economic justice advocates to influence and change public policy*

**INTERNET** www.advocacy.org
**E-MAIL** info@advocacy.org
George A. Ramonas, President

## Advocates for Highway and Auto Safety
750 First St. NE #901
Washington, D.C. 20002
*Dedicated to traffic safety*

**INTERNET** www.saferds.org
Judith Lee Stone, President

## Advocates for Self Government

5 S Public Square, #304
Cartersville, GA 30120

**INTERNET** www.self-gov.org
**E-MAIL** advocates@self-gov.org
Marshall Fritz, Founder

*Encouraging people to encounter, evaluate and embrace the ideas of liberty and to improve communications*

## Advocates for Youth

1025 Vermont Ave. NW, #200
Washington, D.C. 20005

**INTERNET** www.advocatesforyouth.org
**E-MAIL** info@advocatesforyouth.org
James Wagoner, President

*Creates programs and promotes policies that help young people make informed and responsible decisions about their sexual and reproductive health*

## Adweek

770 Broadway
New York, NY 10003

**INTERNET** www.adweek.com
**VOICE** 212-764-7300

## Aerosmith

P.O. Box 882494
San Francisco, CA 94188
*Music group*

**E-MAIL** aerosmith@aerosmith.com

## Aetna Inc.

151 Farmington Ave.
Hartford, CT 06156
*Health and life insurance*

**INTERNET** www.aetna.com
John Rowe, Chairman and CEO

## Affleck, Ben

10100 Santa Monica Blvd.
Los Angeles, CA 90067
*Actor*

**BIRTHDAY** 8/15/72
**E-MAIL** ben@affleck.com

## Afghanistan

United Nations
405 E. 42nd St.
New York, NY 10017

**INTERNET** www.un.org

## AFLAC

1932 Wynnton Road
Columbus, GA 31999
*Health and life insurance*

**INTERNET** www.aflac.com
Daniel P. Amos, Chairman and CEO

## African America Institute

**INTERNET** www.aaionline.org
Mora McClean, President

380 Lexington Ave.
New York, NY 10168

*A nonprofit, multiracial, multiethnic organization whose mission is to promote African development primarily through education and training*

## Africa Action

**INTERNET** www.africaaction.org
Salih Bosker, Executive Director

50 Broad St., #711
New York, NY 10004

*Works for a positive U.S. policy toward Africa and supports human rights, democracy and development*

## Agassi, Andre

**BIRTHDAY** 4/29/70

8921 Andre Dr.
Las Vegas, NV 89148

*Tennis player*

## AGCO

**INTERNET** www.agcocorp.com
Robert J. Ratliff, Chairman, President and CEO

4205 River Green Pkwy
Duluth, GA 30096

*Distributor of agricultural equipment*

## Agee, Marilyn

**INTERNET** www.prophecycorner.com
**E-MAIL** mjagee@pe.net

8641 Sugar Gum Road
Riverside, CA 92508

*Biblical prophecy author*

## Agency, The

1800 Ave. of the Stars, #400
Los Angeles, CA 90067

*Talent agency*

## Agency for the Performing Arts

9200 Sunset Blvd., #900
Los Angeles, CA 90069

*Entertainment agency*

## Agency for the Performing Arts

888 7th Ave.
New York, NY 10106

*Entertainment agency*

## Aiello, Danny

1000 Santa Monica Blvd., #305
Los Angeles, CA 90067

*Actor*

## Aikman, Troy
c/o Cowboys Center
1 Cowboys Pkwy
Irving, TX 75063
*Former football player*

**BIRTHDAY** 11/21/66

## Ailes, Roger
440 Park Ave. S
New York, NY 10106
CEO of Fox News

## Ainge, Danny
2910 N Central
Phoenix, AZ 95012
*Former basketball player*

## Air Products and Chemicals
7201 Hamilton Blvd.
Allentown, PA 18195
*Chemicals*

**INTERNET** www.airproducts.com
Harold A. Wagner, Chairman and CEO

## Airborne Express
3101 Western Ave.
Seattle, WA 98121
*Mail, package and freight delivery*

**INTERNET** www.airborne.com
Robert S. Cline, Chairman and CEO

## Air Supply
9200 Sunset Blvd.
Los Angeles, CA 90069
*Music group*

## Akaka, Daniel
141 Hart Senate Office
Building (D-HI)
Washington, D.C. 20510
*Senator*

**E-MAIL** senator@akaka.senate.gov

## Alabama
P.O. Box 529
Fort Wayne, AL 35967
*Country music group*

## Alamo
*Rental car agency*

**INTERNET** www.alamo.com
**VOICE** 800-462-5266
**E-MAIL** reservations@goalamo.com

**Albania**
Rexhep Kemal meiddani
President I Republikes
Office of the President
Bulevardi Deshmoret e Kornbit
Tirane
Albania

**INTERNET** http://president.gov.al
**E-MAIL** presec@presec.tirana.al

**Albano, Lou**
16 Mechanic St.
Carmel, NY 10512
*Wrestler/Manager*

**Albee, Edward**
14 Harrison St.
New York, NY 10013
*Playwright*

**Albert, Eddie**
P.O. Box 485
Pacific Palisades, CA 90272-4509
*Actor*

**BIRTHDAY** 4/22/08
**E-MAIL** eddie@eddiealbert.com

**Albertsons**
250 Parkcenter Blvd.
Boise, ID 83706
*Food and drug stores*

Lawrence R. Johnston, Chairman and CEO

**Albright, Lola**
213 N Valley, #316
Burbank, CA 91505
*Actress*

**BIRTHDAY** 7/20/25

**Alcoa**
201 Isabella St. at 7th St. Bridge
Pittsburgh, PA 15212
*Metals*

**INTERNET** www.alcoa.com
Alain J.P. Belda, Chairman and CEO

**Alda, Alan**
150 East 57th St.
New York, NY 10022-2700
*Actor*

**BIRTHDAY** 1/28/36
**E-MAIL** alda@pbs.org

## Aldrin, Dr. Buzz
10380 Wilshire Blvd.
Los Angeles, CA 90024
*Former astronaut*

## Alexander, Daniele
P.O. Box 23362
Nashville, TN 37202
*Country music singer*

## Alexander, Denise
270 N Cañon Dr.
Beverly Hills, CA 90210
*Actress*

## Alexander, Jane
**BIRTHDAY** 10/28
1100 Pennsylvania Ave. NW
Washington, D.C. 20506
*Actress*

## Alexander, Jason (Jay Scott Greenspan)
**BIRTHDAY** 9/23/59
151 El Camino Dr.
Beverly Hills, CA 90212
*Actor*

## Alexander, Lamar
**INTERNET** www.alexander.senate.gov/contact.cfm
U.S. Senate (R-TN)
Washington, D.C. 20510
*Senator*

## Alexander, Shana
156 5th Ave., #617
New York, NY 10010
*News correspondent*

## Alexis, Kim
c/o Emodel
42 W 38th St., #802
New York, NY 10018
*Supermodel*

## Alf
8660 Hayden Place
Culver City, CA 90230
*Television character*

## Alfonso, Kristian
c/o NBC Studios
3000 W Alameda Ave.
Burbank, CA 91523
*Soap opera star*

## Algeria
President Abdelaziz Bouteflika
Presidence de la Republique
Place Mohamed Seddik Benyahya
El Mouradia, 16000 Algiers
Algeria

**INTERNET** www.mae-dz.org
**E-MAIL** info@mae-dz.org

## Al Hassan, Mohammed VI Ibn
King of Morocco

**INTERNET** www.mincom.gov.ma

## Ali, Muhammad
P.O. Box 187
Berrien Springs, MI 49103
*Boxing champion*

**BIRTHDAY** 1/17/42

## Alice in Chains
c/o The Plaza
535 King Road
London SW 10 057
England
UNITED KINGDOM
*Rock band*

## All My Children cast
320 W 66th St.
New York, NY 10023
*Soap opera*

## Allard, Wayne
525 Dirksen Senate Office
Bldg. (R-CO)
Washington, D.C. 20510
*Senator*

**E-MAIL** allard.senate.gov/contactme

## Allegheny Technologies Incorporated
1000 Six PPG Place
CEO
Pittsburgh, PA 15222
*Specialty metals*

Robert R. Bozzone, Chairman, President and

**Allegience**
1430 Waukegan Road
McGaw Park, IL 60085
*Healthcare*

**INTERNET** www.allegience.net
Ronald K. Labrum, President

**Allen, Corey**
8642 Hollywood Blvd.
Los Angeles, CA 90069
*Actor/Writer/Director*

**Allen, Elizabeth**
P.O. Box 243
Lake Peekskill, NY 10537
*Actress*

**Allen, George**
204 Russell Senate Office
Bldg. (R-VA)
Washington, D.C. 20510
*Senator*

**INTERNET** allen.senate.gov/email.html

**Allen, Joan**
40 W 57th St.
New York, NY 10019
*Actress*

**Allen, Jonelle**
8730 Sunset Blvd., #480
Los Angeles, CA 90069
*Actress/Singer*

**Allen, Karen**
151 El Camino Dr.
Beverly Hills, CA 90212
*Actress*

**BIRTHDAY** 10/5/51

**Allen, Marty**
5750 Wilshire Blvd., #580
Los Angeles, CA 90036
*Comedian*

**Allen, Nancy**
9830 Wilshire Blvd.
Los Angeles, CA 90212
*Actress*

## Allen, Robert
32 Ave. of the Americas
New York, NY 10013
*Business leader*

## Allen, Tim (Timothy Allen Dick)
**BIRTHDAY** 6/13/53
7920 Sunset Blvd., #400
Los Angeles, CA 91521
*Actor*

## Allen, Woody
**BIRTHDAY** 12/01/35
48 E 92nd St.
New York, NY 10128
*Actor/Comedian/Director*

## Alley, Kirstie
**BIRTHDAY** 1/12/55
151 El Camino Dr.
Beverly Hills, CA 90212
*Actress*

## Alliance for Aging Research
2021 K St. NW, #305
Washington, D.C. 20006
**INTERNET** www.agingresearch.org
**E-MAIL** info@agingresearch.org
John L. Steffens, National Chairman
*Organization promoting medical research on aging*

## Alliance for Justice
2000 P St. NW, #712
Washington, D.C. 20036
**INTERNET** www.afj.org
**E-MAIL** alliance@afj.org
*National association of environmental, civil rights, mental health, women's, children's and consumer advocacy organizations*

## Alliance to Save Energy
1200 18th St. NW, #900
Washington, D.C. 20036
**INTERNET** www.ase.org
*A nonprofit coalition of business, government, environmental and consumer leaders promoting efficient use of energy*

## Allman, Greg
**BIRTHDAY** 12/7/47
c/o Kid Glove Enterprises
2305 Vine Ville Ave.
Macon, GA 31204
*Musician*

## Allamerica Financial
440 Lincoln St.
Worcester, MA 01653
*P & C insurance*

**INTERNET** www.allamerica.com
John F. O'Brien, President and CEO

## Allred, Gloria
6300 Wilshire Blvd., #1500
Los Angeles, CA 90048
*Attorney*

## Allstate
2775 Sanders Road
Northbrook, IL 60062
*Corporation and Allstate Insurance*

**INTERNET** www.allstate.com
Edward M. Liddy, Chairman and President

## Alltel
1 Allied Dr.
Little Rock, AR 72202
*Telecommunications*

**INTERNET** www.alltel.com
Joe T. Ford, Chairman and CEO

## Alonso, Maria Conchita
9455 Eden Place
Beverly Hills, CA 90210
*Actress*

**BIRTHDAY** 6/29/57

## Alpert, Herb
360 N La Cienega Blvd.
Los Angeles, CA 90048
*Singer*

**INTERNET** www.herbalpert.com

## Alpert, Hollis
P.O. Box 142
Shelter Island, NY 11964
*Writer*

## Alpert, Dr. Richard
Box 1558
Boulder, CO 80306
*Psychologist*

## Alt, Carol
4526 Wilshire Blvd.
Los Angeles, CA 90010
*Supermodel*

## Altman, Robert
8942 Wilshire Blvd.
Beverly Hills, CA 90211
*Writer/Producer/Director*

## Altria Group Inc.
120 Park Ave.
New York, NY 10017
*Tobacco company*

**INTERNET** www.philipmorrisusa.com
Louis Camilleri, President and CEO

## Alva, Luigi
Via Moscova 46/3
Mailand 20121
Italy
*Tenor*

## Alvin and the Chipmunks
122 E 57th St., #400
New York, NY 10003
*Animated singing group*

## Amanpour, Christiane
2 Stephen St., #100
London W1P 2PL
England
UNITED KINGDOM
*Broadcast journalist*

## Amerada Hess
1185 Ave. of the Americas
New York, NY 10036
*Petroleum refining*

**INTERNET** www.hess.com
John B. Hess, Chairman and CEO

## Ameren
1901 Chouteau Ave.
St. Louis, MO 63103
*Gas and electric utilities*

**INTERNET** www.ameren.com
Charles W. Mueller, Chairman and CEO

## America
345 N Maple Dr., #300
Beverly Hills, CA 90210
*Music group*

## American-Arab Anti-Discrimination Committee

4201 Connecticut Ave. NW, #500
Washington, D.C. 20008

**INTERNET** www.adc.org
**E-MAIL** adc@adc.org
Ziad Asali, President

*Civil rights organization committed to defending the rights of people of Arab descent and promoting their rich cultural heritage*

## American Baby

125 Park Ave.
New York, NY 10017
*Magazine*

**INTERNET** www.americanbaby.com
**VOICE** 212-645-0067

## American Bear Association

108 Enchanted Lane
Franklin, NC 28744

**INTERNET** www.americanbear.org
**E-MAIL** bears@dnet.net
Bill Lea, President

*Promotes the welfare of the black bear through a better understanding*

## American Cancer Society

1599 Clifton Road NE
Atlanta, GA 30329

**INTERNET** www.cancer.org
John R. Seffrin, PhD, CEO

## American Cinematographer

P.O. Box 2230
Hollywood, CA 90078
*Magazine*

**INTERNET** www.theasc.com
**E-MAIL** jim@theasc.com
Jim McCullaugh, Publisher

## American Civil Liberties Union

125 Broad St.
New York, NY 10004
*Advocate of individual rights*

**INTERNET** www.aclu.org
**E-MAIL** aclu@aclu.org
Anthony D. Romero, Executive Director

## American Conservative Union

1007 Cameron St.
Alexandria, VA 22314

**INTERNET** www.conservative.org
**E-MAIL** acu@conservative.org
David A. Keane, Chairman

*The nation's oldest conservative lobbying organization, ACU's purpose is to effectively communicate and advance the goals and principles of conservatism*

## American Council for Capital Formation

1750 K St. NW, #400
Washington, D.C. 20006

**INTERNET** www.accf.org
**E-MAIL** info@accf.org
Dr. Charles E. Walker, Chairman and Founder

*A nonprofit, nonpartisan organization dedicated to the advocacy of tax and environmental policies that encourage saving and investment*

## American Council on Education

1 Dupont Circle
Washington, D.C. 20036

**INTERNET** www.acenet.edu
William E. Troutt, Chairman

*ACE is dedicated to the belief that equal education opportunity and a strong higher education system are essential cornerstones of a democratic society*

## American Council on Science & Health

1995 Broadway, 16th Floor
New York, NY 10023

**INTERNET** www.acsh.org
**E-MAIL** whelan@acsh.org
Elizabeth Whelan, President

*A consumer education consortium concerned with issues related to food, nutrition, chemicals, pharmaceuticals, lifestyle, the environment and health, ACSH is an independent, nonprofit, tax exempt organization*

## American Dietetic Association

216 W Jackson Blvd.
Chicago, IL 60606

**INTERNET** www.eatright.org
**E-MAIL** shcash@msu.edu
Stella Cash, Chairman

## American Electric Power

1 Riverside Plaza
Columbus, OH 43215

**INTERNET** www.aep.com
E. Linn Draper, Jr., Chairman, President and CEO

*Gas and electric utilities*

## American Enterprise Institute for Public Policy Research

1150 17th St. NW
Washington, D.C. 20036

**INTERNET** www.aei.org
**E-MAIL** info@aei.org
Christopher C. DeMuth, President

*Dedicated to preserving and strengthening the foundations of freedom-limited government, private enterprise, vital culture and political institutions and a strong foreign policy and national defense- through scholarly research, open debate and publications*

## American Express

200 Vesey St.
New York, NY 10285

**INTERNET** www.americanexpress.com
Kenneth I. Chenault, Chairman and CEO

*Diversified financials*

## American Family Insurance Group

6000 American Pkwy
Madison, WI 53783
*Insurance*

**INTERNET** www.amfam.com
Harvey R. Pierce, Chairman and CEO

## American Farm Bureau Federations

225 Touhy Ave.
Park Ridge, IL 60068

**INTERNET** www.fb.org
**E-MAIL** bstallman@fb.org
Bob Stallman, President

*As the national voice of agriculture, AFBF's mission is to work cooperatively with the member state farm bureaus to promote the image, political influence, quality of life and profitability of the nation's farm and ranch families*

## American Federation of Government Employees

80 F St. NW
Washington, D.C. 20001

**INTERNET** www.afge.org
Bobby Harnage, National President

*The largest federal employee union representing some 600,000 federal and D.C. government workers nationwide*

## American Federation of State, County and Municipal Employees

1625 L St. NW
Washington, D.C. 20036

**INTERNET** www.afscme.org
**E-MAIL** webmaster@afscme.org
Gerald W. McEntee, International President

*AFSCME is the nation's largest public employee and health care workers' union*

## American Financial Group

1 E 4th St.
Cincinnati, OH 45202
*Insurance*

**INTERNET** www.amfnl.com
Carl H. Lindner, Chairman and CEO

## American Foreign Policy Counsel

1521 16th St. NW
Washington, D.C. 20036

**INTERNET** www.afpc.org
Herman Pirchner, President

*A nonprofit organization dedicated to bringing information to those who make or influence the foreign policy of the United States and to assisting world leaders, particularly in the former USSR, with building democracies and market economies*

## American Gas Association
400 N. Capitol St., NW
Washington, D.C. 20001
**INTERNET** www.aga.com
Lennart Selander, President
*AGA represents 181 local natural gas utilities that deliver gas to 54 million homes and businesses in all 50 states*

## American General
2929 Allen Pkwy
Houston, TX 07019
**INTERNET** www.agc.com
Rodney O. Martin, President and CEO
*Health and life insurance*

## American Home Products
5 Giralda Farms
Madison, NJ 07940
**INTERNET** www.ahp.com
John R. Stafford, Chairman, President and CEO
*Pharmaceuticals*

## American Idol
Fremantle Media
2700 Colorado Ave, 4th Floor
Santa Monica, CA 90404
**INTERNET** www.idolonfox.com
**E-MAIL** askfox@fox.com

## American International Group
70 Pine St.
New York, NY 10270
**INTERNET** www.aig.com
Maurice R. Greenberg, Chairman and CEO
*P & C insurance*

## American Jewish Congress
15 E 84th St.
New York, NY 10028
**INTERNET** www.ajcongress.org
**E-MAIL** washrep@ajcongress.org
Jack Rosen, President
*Considered the legal voice of the American Jewish Community*

## American League of Lobbyists
P.O. Box 30005
Alexandria, VA 22310
**INTERNET** www.alldc.org
**E-MAIL** info@alldc.org
Deana Galek, President
*A national organization founded in 1979 dedicated to serving government relations and public affairs professionals*

## American Legion
575 N Pennsylvania St., #325
Indianapolis, IN 46204
Richard Bisso, Commander
**INTERNET** www.legion.com
**E-MAIL** natlcomdr@legion.org
**VOICE** 317-226-7918

## American Legislative Exchange Council

910 17th St. NW, 5th Floor
Washington, D.C. 20006

**INTERNET** www.alec.org
**E-MAIL** info@alec.org
Duane Parde, Executive Director

*The nation's largest bipartisan individual membership association of state legislatures with nearly 2,400 members across America*

## American Library Association

50 E Huron St.
Chicago, IL 60611

**INTERNET** www.ala.org
**E-MAIL** ala@ala.org
Mitch Freedman, President

*The oldest, largest and most influential library association in the world. For more than a century, it has been a leader in defending intellectual freedom and promoting the highest quality library and information services*

## American Medical Association

515 N State St.
Chicago, IL 60610

**INTERNET** www.ama-assn.org
Michael D. Maves, President

*Dedicated to promoting the art and science of medicine and the betterment of public health*

## American Movie Classics

150 Crossways Park W
Woodbury, NY 11797

*Cable network*

## American Postal Workers Union

1300 L St. NW
Washington, D.C. 20005

**INTERNET** www.apwu.org
William Burrus, President

*The largest postal union representing 366,000 union members in the United States*

## American Public Health Association

800 I St. NW
Washington, D.C. 20001

**INTERNET** www.apha.org
**E-MAIL** comments@apha.org
Mohammad N. Akhter, M.D., Executive Director

*The oldest and largest organization of public health professionals in the world, representing more than 50,000 members from over 50 occupations of public health*

## American Rivers

1025 Vermont Ave., #720
Washington, D.C. 20005

**INTERNET** www.amrivers.org
**E-MAIL** amrivers@amrivers.org
Rebecca R. Wodder, President

*National river conservation organization whose mission is to protect and restore America's river systems and to foster a river stewardship ethic*

## American Security Council
1155 15th St., NW 1101
Washington, D.C. 20005

## American Society of Cinematographers
P.O. Box 2230
Hollywood, CA 90078

**INTERNET** www.cinematographer.com
**E-MAIL** editor@theasc.com
Richard Crudo, President

## American Standard
1 Centennial Ave.
Piscataway, NJ 08855
*Industrial and farm equipment*

**INTERNET** www.americanstandard.com
Frederic M. Poses, Chairman and CEO

## American Tort Reform Association
1101 Connecticut Ave. NW, #400
Washington, D.C. 20036

**INTERNET** www.atra.org
**E-MAIL** sjoyce@atra.org
Sherman Joyce, President

*Founded in 1986, a broad-based, bipartisan coalition of more than 300 businesses, corporations, municipalities, associations and professional firms who support civil justice reform*

## American Veterinary Medical Association
1931 North Meacham Road, #100
Schaumburg, IL 60173

**INTERNET** www.avma.org
**E-MAIL** help@avma.org
Joseph M. Howell, President

*The objective of the association is to advance the science and art of veterinary medicine, including the relationship to public health, biological science and agriculture*

## Americans for Democratic Action
1625 K St. NW
Washington, D.C. 20006

**INTERNET** www.adaction.org
**E-MAIL** webmaster@adaction.org

*The nation's oldest independent liberal political organization, it pioneered the development and promotion of a national liberal agenda of public policy formulation and action*

## Americans for Indian Opportunity
681 Juniper Hill Road
Bernalillo, NM 87004

**INTERNET** www.aio.org
**E-MAIL** info@aio.org
LaDonna Harris, President

## America's Funniest Home Videos

P.O. Box 4333
Hollywood, CA 90078
*Television show*

## America's Most Wanted

P.O. Box Crime TV
Washington, D.C. 20016
*TV show*

**INTERNET** www.amw.com
**E-MAIL** feedback@amw.com

## American Family Insurance Group

1 E 4th St.
Cincinnati, OH 45202
*Insurance*

**INTERNET** www.amfam.com
Dale F. Mathwich, Chairman and CEO

## American Federation of Teachers

555 New Jersey Ave. NW
Washington, D.C. 20001

**INTERNET** www.aft.org
**E-MAIL** online@aft.org
Sandra Feldman, President

## American Society of Composers, Authors and Publishers

7920 Sunset Blvd., #300
Los Angeles, CA 90046

**INTERNET** www.ascap.com

## AmeriSource Health

300 Chester Field Pkwy
Malvern, PA 19355
*Wholesale pharmaceuticals*

**INTERNET** www.amerisource.com
**E-MAIL** info@amerisource.com
R. David Yost, President and CEO

## Ameritrade

4211 S 102nd St.
Omaha, NE 68127
*On-line stock trading*

**INTERNET** www.ameritrade.com
**E-MAIL** Customerservice@ameritrade.com

## Amgen Inc.

1 Amgen Center Dr.
Thousand Oaks, CA 91320
*One of the world's largest biotechnology companies*

**INTERNET** www.amgen.com
Kevin Sharer, CEO

## Amick, Madchen
8840 Wilshire Blvd.
Beverly Hills, CA 90212
*Actress*

## Amir, Sheikh
Kuwait
**INTERNET** www.mofa.gov.kw

## Amin, Idi
Box 8948
Jidda 21492
Saudi Arabia
*Former dictator of Uganda*
**BIRTHDAY** 1/1/25

## Amnesty International, USA
322 8th Ave.
New York, NY 10001
**INTERNET** www.amnesty-usa.org
**E-MAIL** aimember@aiusa.org

*Founded in 1961, Amnesty International is a grassroots activist organization whose one million strong members are dedicated to freeing prisoners of conscience, to gaining fair trials for political prisoners, to ending torture, political killings and "disappearances"*

## Amos, Deborah
2025 M St. NW
Washington, D.C. 20016
*News correspondent*

## Amos, John
P.O. Box 587
Califon, NJ 07830
*Actor*
**BIRTHDAY** 12/27/41

## Amos, Tori (Myra Ellen Amos)
9830 Wilshire Blvd.
Beverly Hills, CA 90212
*Singer*
**BIRTHDAY** 8/22/64

## Amos, Wally 'Famous'
c/o Uncle No Name Cookie Co.
P.O. Box 897
Kailua, HI 96734
*Entrepreneur*

## AMR
4333 Amon Carter Blvd.
Fort Worth, TX 76155
*Airline*

**INTERNET** www.amrcorp.com
Donald J. Carty, Chairman and CEO

## Anderson, Bill
P.O. Box 888
Hermitage, TN 37076
*Country music singer*

## Anderson, Gillian
1122 S Robertson Blvd.
Los Angeles, CA 90035
*Actress*

**BIRTHDAY** 8/9/68

## Anderson, John B.
3300 NE 36th St., #1016
Ft. Lauderdale, FL 33308
*Former Representative*

## Anderson, John
P.O. Box 1547
Goodletville, TN 37070
*Country music singer*

## Anderson, Loni
20652 Lassen, #98
Chatsworth, CA 91311
*Actress*

## Anderson, Louie
c/o Kellogg & Anderson
14724 Ventura Blvd., 2nd Floor
Sherman Oaks, CA 91403
*Comedian*

**BIRTHDAY** 3/24/53
**E-MAIL** louie@louieanderson.com

## Anderson, Lynn
P.O. Box 90454
Charleston, NC 29410
*Singer*

**BIRTHDAY** 9/26/47

## Anderson, Richard Dean
1122 S Robertson Blvd., #15
Los Angeles, CA 90035
*Actor*

**BIRTHDAY** 1/23/50

**Anderson, Pamela**
c/o Culver Studios
9336 W Washington Blvd.
Culver City, CA 90235
*Actress/Model*

BIRTHDAY 7/01/67
INTERNET www.pamelaanderson.com

**Anderson, Terry**
50 Rockefeller Plaza
New York, NY 10020
*News correspondent*

**Andress, Ursula**
Via F. Siaci 38
Rome
I-00197
ITALY
*Actress*

BIRTHDAY 3/19/36

**Andretti, Mario**
457 Rose Inn Ave.
Nathareth, PA 18604
*Race car driver*

BIRTHDAY 2/28/40

**Andrew, HRH Prince**
Suninghill Park
Windsor
England
*Son of Queen Elizabeth*

BIRTHDAY 2/19/60

**Andrews, Julie**
P.O. Box 491668
Los Angeles, CA 90049
*Actress/Singer*

BIRTHDAY 10/1/35

**Angelou, Maya**
3240 Valley Road
Winston-Salem, NC 27109
*Author*

**Angle, Jim**
2025 M St. NW
Washington, D.C. 20036
*News correspondent*

## Anheuser-Busch
1 Busch Place
St. Louis, MO 06318
*Beverages*

**INTERNET** www.anheuser-busch.com
August A. Busch III, Chairman and President

## Aniston, Jennifer
9830 Wilshire Blvd.
Beverly Hills, CA 90212
*Actress*

**BIRTHDAY** 2/11/69
**E-MAIL** jeffr48196@aol.com

## Anixter
4711 Golf Road
Skokie, 60637
*Wire and cable wholesalers*

**INTERNET** www.anixter.com
Robert W. Grubbs, Jr., President and CEO

## Anka, Paul
10573 W Pico Blvd., #159
Los Angeles, CA 90064
*Singer/Songwriter*

**BIRTHDAY** 7/30/41

## Ann-Margret (Ann-Margret Olson)
5664 Cahuenga Blvd., #336
N Hollywood, CA 91601
*Actress*

**BIRTHDAY** 4/28/41

## Ant, Adam
503 The Chambers
Chelsea Harbor Lots Road
London SW10-OXF
England
UNITED KINGDOM
*Singer*

## Anthem Insurance
120 Monument Circle
Indianapolis, IN 46204
*Health and life insurance*

**INTERNET** www.anthem.com
Larry C. Glasscock, President

## Anthrax
15 Haldane Crescent
Piners Health
Wakefield Health
Wakefield WF1 4TE
England
*Heavy metal music group*

## Anti-Defamation League
823 United Nations Plaza
New York, NY 10017
**INTERNET** www.adl.org
**E-MAIL** webmaster@adl.org
Abraham H. Foxman, National Director
*Fights anti-Semitism through programs and services that counteract hatred, prejudice and bigotry*

## Antigua
Lester Bryant Bird, Prime Minister
Office of the Prime Minister
Queen Elizabeth Highway
Parliament Building
St. John's Antigua
Antigua and Barbuda
**INTERNET** www.antigua-barbuda.com
**E-MAIL** althea@btconnect.com

## Anwar, Gabrielle
9560 Wilshire Blvd., #560
Beverly Hills, CA 90212
*Actress*
**BIRTHDAY** 2/4/70

## Aoki, Rocky
8685 NW 53rd Terrace, #201
Miami, FL 33166
*Food entrepreneur*

## Aon
123 N Wacker Dr.
Chicago, IL 60606
*Diversified financials*
**INTERNET** www.aon.com
Patrick G. Ryan, Chairman and CEO

## Apollonia
8831 W Sunset Blvd., #304
W. Hollywood, CA 90069
*Actress*

## Apple, Fiona
509 Hartnell St.
Monterrey, CA 93940
*Singer*

## Apple Computer
1 Infinite Loop
Cupertino, CA 95014
*Computers and office equipment*
**INTERNET** www.apple.com
Stephen P. Jobs, CEO

## Applegate, Christina
9055 Hollywood Hills Road
Los Angeles, CA 90046
*Actress*

**BIRTHDAY** 11/25/72

## Applied Materials
3050 Bowers Ave.
Santa Clara, CA 95054
*Electronics and semiconductors*

**INTERNET** www.appliedmaterials.com
James C. Morgan, Chairman and CEO

## Aramark
1101 Market St.
Philadelphia, PA 19107
*Food and support services, uniforms and child care*

Joseph Neubauer, Chairman and CEO

## Archer, Anne
13201 Old Oak Lane
Los Angeles, CA 90049
*Actress*

**BIRTHDAY** 10/25/50

## Archer Daniel's Midland
4666 Faries Pkwy
Decatur, IL 62526
*One of the world's largest processors of oilseeds, corn and wheat*

**INTERNET** www.admworld.com
**E-MAIL** info@admworld.com
Dwayne O. Andreas, Chairman

## Archerd, Army
c/o Daily Variety
5700 Wilshire Blvd.
Los Angeles, CA 90036
*Columnist*

## Archie Comics

**INTERNET** www.archiecomics.com
**E-MAIL** archiecom@aol.com

## Architectural Digest
370 L'Enfant Promenade SW
Washington, D.C. 20004

**INTERNET** www.architecturaldigest.com
**E-MAIL** letters@archdigest.com
**VOICE** 202-646-7476

## Argentina
Dr. Carlos Saul Menem
Presidente de la Republic
Casa de Gobierno
Balcarce 50
1064 Buenos Aires
Argentina

**INTERNET** www.presidencia.ar

**Arkin, Adam**
Lasher-McManus-Robinson
1964 Westwood, #400
Los Angeles, CA 90025-4651
*Actor*

**Arkin, Alan**
21 E 40th St., #1705
New York, NY 10076
*Actor*
**BIRTHDAY** 3/26/34

**Armani, Giorgio**
Palazzo Durini 24
Milan 1-20122
Italy
*Fashion designer*
**BIRTHDAY** 7/11/34

**Armatrading, Joan**
2 Ramillies St.
London W1V 1DF
England
UNITED KINGDOM
*Singer/Guitarist*
**BIRTHDAY** 12/9/50

**Armenia**
Robert Kocharian, President
President House
Marshal Baghramyan Ave.
19 Yerevan
Armenia
**INTERNET** www.president.am
**E-MAIL** press@president.am

**Armstrong, Bess**
151 El Camino Blvd.
Beverly Hills, CA 90212
*Actress*

**Arness, James**
P.O. Box 49003
Los Angeles, CA 90049
*Actor*
**BIRTHDAY** 5/26/23

**Arnold, Eddy**
P.O. Box 97
Brentwood, TN 37024
*Country music singer*

## Arnold, Tom

8135 W 4th St., 2nd Floor
Los Angeles, CA 90069
*Actor*

**BIRTHDAY** 3/6/59

## Arquette, David

409 N Camden Dr.
Beverly Hills, CA 90210
*Actor*

## Arquette, Patricia

1122 S Robertson Blvd.
Los Angeles, CA 90035
*Actress*

**BIRTHDAY** 4/8/68

## Arrested Development

9380 SW 72nd St., B-220
Miami, FL 33174
*Musical group*

## Arrow Electronics

25 Hub Dr.
Melville, ME 11747
*Wholesale electronics*

**INTERNET** www.arrow.com
Stephen P. Kaufman, CEO

## Arts and Entertainment

225 E 45th St.
New York, NY 10017
*Cable network*

## As the World Turns cast

c/o CBS
524 W 57th St.
New York, NY 10019
*Soap opera*

## Ashcroft, John

U.S. Department of Justice
950 Pennsylvania Avenue, NW
Washington, DC 20530-0001

**INTERNET** www.usdoj.gov/ag/ashcroftbio.html
**E-MAIL** AskDOJ@usdoj.gov

## Ashdown, Paddy

House of Commons
London SW1A AA
England
UNITED KINGDOM
*Politician*

## ASH-Action on Smoking and Health

2013 H St. NW
Washington, D.C. 20006

**INTERNET** www.ash.org
John F. Banzhaf III, Executive Director

*ASH is the nation's oldest and largest antismoking organization and the only one that regularly takes legal action to fight smoking and protect the rights of nonsmokers*

## Asian American Journalists Association

1182 Market St., #320
San Francisco, CA 94102

**INTERNET** www.aaja.org
**E-MAIL** national@aaja.org
Rene Astudillo, Executive Director

*Seeks to increase employment of Asian American print and broadcast journalists*

## Asleep at the Wheel

P.O. Box 463
Austin, TX 78767
*Country music group*

## Asner, Ed

3556 Mound View Ave.
Studio City, CA 91604
*Actor*

**BIRTHDAY** 11/15/29
**E-MAIL** 72726.357@compuserve.com

## Assante, Armand

367 Windsor Hwy
New Windsor, NY 12553
*Actor*

**BIRTHDAY** 10/4/49

## Associated Builders and Contractors

1300 N 17th St, 8th Floor
Roslyn, VA 22209

**INTERNET** www.abc.org
Robert P. Hepner, Executive Vice President

*A national trade association representing over 21,000 contractors, subcontractors, material suppliers and related firms from across the country*

## Associated Press

50 Rockefeller Plaza
New York, NY 10020

**INTERNET** www.ap.org
**VOICE** 212-621-1500

## Associated Press

221 S Figueroa
Los Angeles, CA 90012

**INTERNET** www.ap.org
**VOICE** 213-746-1200

## Associated Press
10 S Wacker Dr., #2500
Chicago, IL 60606

**INTERNET** www.ap.org
**VOICE** 312-781-0500

## Association for Community Based Education
1805 Florida Ave. NW
Washington, D.C. 20009

*ACBE's membership is comprised of community activist organizations, including many that operate literacy projects*

## Association for the Advancement of Mexican Americans
204 Clifton
Houston, TX 77083

**INTERNET** www.neosoft.com

*Committed to advancing at-risk and disadvantaged youth and families with an array of innovative programs of excellence that provide alternative education, social services and community development*

## Association of Independent Commercial Producers
11 E 22nd St., 4th Floor
New York, NY 10010

**INTERNET** www.aicp.com
**E-MAIL** mattm@aicp.com
Matt Miller, President

*Represents commercial production companies*

## Association of Trial Lawyers of America
9830 Wilshire Blvd.
Washington, D.C. 20007

**INTERNET** www.atla.org
**E-MAIL** help@atlahq.org

## Astin, John
P.O. Box 49698
Los Angeles, CA 90049
*Actor/Writer/Director*

**BIRTHDAY** 3/30/30

## Astin, Sean
P.O. Box 57858
Sherman Oaks, CA 91413
*Actor*

**BIRTHDAY** 2/25/71

## AT&T
32 Ave. of the Americas
New York, NY 10013
*Telecommunications company*

**INTERNET** www.att.com
David W. Dorman, CEO

## Atkinson, Rowan
47 Dean St.
London W1V 5HL
England
UNITED KINGDOM
*Actor*

**BIRTHDAY** 1/6/55

## Atlanta Braves
P.O. Box 4064
Atlanta, GA 30302
*Baseball team*

**INTERNET** www.Atlantabraves.com

## Atlanta Falcons
Suwanee Road at I-85
Suwanee, GA 30174
*Football team*

**INTERNET** www.Atlantafalcons.com

## Atlanta Hawks
1 CNN Center
Atlanta, GA 30303
*Hockey team*

**INTERNET** www.hawks.com

## Atlanta Journal-Constitution
72 Marietta St. NW
Atlanta, GA 30302
*Magazine*

**INTERNET** www.ajc.com
**VOICE** 404-526-5151

## Atlantic, The
77 N Washington St.
Boston, MA 02114

**INTERNET** www.theatlantic.com
**VOICE** 617-854-7700

## AtomFilms
80 S Washington St., #103
Seattle, WA 98014
*Web content provider*

**INTERNET** www.atomfilms.com
Mika Salmi, CEO and Founder

| | |
|---|---|
| **Atomic Pop**<br>1447 Cloverfield Blvd., #201<br>Santa Monica, CA 90404<br>*E-Commerce* | **INTERNET** www.atomicpop.com<br>Al Teller, CEO and Founder |
| **Attenborough, Sir Richard**<br>Old Farms, Beaver Lodge<br>Richmond Green<br>Surrey TwW JNQ-UK<br>United Kingdom<br>*Writer/Producer* | **BIRTHDAY** 8/29/23 |
| **Auberjonois, Rene**<br>P.O. Box 16296<br>Minneapolis, MN 55416-0296<br>Actor | **BIRTHDAY** 7/1/40 |
| **Auermann, Nadja**<br>c/o Elite Models<br>111 E 22nd St.<br>New York, NY 10010<br>*Supermodel* | **BIRTHDAY** 1971 |
| **Austin, Stone Cold Steve**<br>c/o WWF, Titan Towers<br>1241 E Main St.<br>Stamford, CT 06905<br>*Wrestler* | |
| **Austin American-Statesman**<br>166 E Riverside<br>Austin, TX 78767 | **INTERNET** www.statesman.com<br>**VOICE** 512-455-3500 |
| **Austin Chronicle**<br>P.O. Box 49066<br>Austin, TX 78765 | **INTERNET** www.austinchronicle.com<br>**VOICE** 512-454-5766 |
| **Australia**<br>Hon. John Winston Howard<br>Prime Minister<br>Parliament House, #MG8<br>2600 Canberra, Australian Capital<br>Territory Australia | **INTERNET** www.pm.gov.au |

## Austria
Dr. Thomas Klestil, President
Prasidentschaftskanzlei
Hofburg, Bellariator
Ballhausplatz 2
A-1010, Wien
Austria

**INTERNET** www.hofburg.at
**E-MAIL** thomas.klestil@hofburg.at

## Autobytel.com
18872 MacArthur Blvd.
Irvine, CA 92612
*E-Commerce*

**INTERNET** www.autobytel.com
Jeffrey Schwartz, President and CEO

## Automotive News/ Autoweek
1400 Woodbridge Ave.
Detroit, MI 48207

**INTERNET** www.automotivenews.com
**VOICE** 313-446-6000

## Avery Dennison
150 N Orange Grove Blvd.
Pasadena, CA 91103
*Labels and office supplies*

**INTERNET** www.averydennison.com
Philip M. Neal, Chairman and CEO

## Avis
*Rental car agency*

**INTERNET** www.avis.com
800-230-4898

## Avon
1345 Ave. of the Americas
New York, NY 10105
Stanley C. Gault, Chairman
*Cosmetics and soaps*

**INTERNET** www.avon.com

## Aykroyd, Dan
8271 Melrose Ave., #110
Los Angeles, CA 90046
*Actor/Writer*

**BIRTHDAY** 7/1/52

## Ayn Rand Institute
The Center for Advancement of Objectivism
4640 Admiralty Way, #406
Marina del Rey, CA 90292

**INTERNET** www.aynrand.org
**E-MAIL** mail@aynrand.org
Leonard Peikoff, Founder

*Seeks to promote and expound Rand's philosophy with various resources and activities*

## Azaria, Hank
c/o Fox TV
P.O. Box 900
Beverly Hills, CA 90213
*Actor*

## Azerbaijan
**INTERNET** www.president.az
**E-MAIL** president@gov.az
Heydar Aliyev, President
Office of the President
Ulitsa Levmontova 63
Baku, Azerbaijan

## B.F. Goodrich
**INTERNET** www.bfgoodrich.com
David L. Burner, Chairman
4 Coliseum Centre
2730 W Tyvola Road
Charlotte, NC 28217
*Aerospace systems and services and specialty chemicals*

## B.J.'s Wholesale Club
**INTERNET** www.bjswholesale.com
1 Mercer Road
Natick, MA 01760
Herbert J. Zarkin, Chairman
*Membership food and drug stores*

## B-52's, The
P.O. Box 60468
Rochester, NY 14606
*Music group*

## Babcock, Barbara
c/o Fox TV- "Pasadena"
Box 900
Beverly Hills, CA 90213
*Actress*

## Bacall, Lauren
1 W 72nd St., #43
New York, NY 10023
*Actress*

## Bachelor, The
**INTERNET** www.abc.com

## Bachelorette, The
**INTERNET** www.abc.com

**Backstage**
779 Broadway
New York, NY 10003
*Magazine for actors*

**INTERNET** www.backstage.com
**E-MAIL** backstage@backstage.com
Steve Elish, Publisher

**Backstreet Boys**
7380 Sand Lake Road
Orlando , FL 32819
*Music group*

**Bacon, Kevin**
227 W 42nd St.
New York, NY 10036
*Actor*

**BIRTHDAY** 7/8/58
**E-MAIL** info@baconbros.com

**Bader, Dietrich**
131 N June St.
Los Angeles, CA 90004
*Actor*

**Badham, John**
151 El Camino Blvd.
Beverly Hills, CA 90212
*Movie director*

**Baer, Jr., Max**
P.O. Box 1831
Zephyr Cove, NV 89448
*Actor*

**Baez, Joan**
P.O. Box 1026
Menlo Park, CA 94026
*Singer*

**BIRTHDAY** 1/9/41

**Bahamas**
Rt. Hon Hubert Ingraham
Prime Minister
Sir Cecil Wallace Whitfield Centre
West Bay St.
P.O. Box CB-10980
Nassau, New Providence
Bahamas

**INTERNET** www.flamingo.bahamas.net.bs

## Bahrain

Sheikg Harnad ibn 'Isa Al Khalifah, Emir
P.O. Box 555
The Amiri Court, Rifa's Palace
Rifa
*Bahrain*

## Baldacci, John

Governor of Maine

**E-MAIL** governor@maine.gov

## Bailey, F. Lee

1400 Centre Park Blvd.
W Palm Beach, FL 33401
*Attorney*

**BIRTHDAY** 6/10/33

## Baillie and the Boys

P.O. Box 121185
Arlington, TX 76012
*Country music group*

## Baio, Scott

4333 Forman Ave.
Toluca Lake, CA 91602
*Actor*

## Baiul, Oksana

c/o Int'l Ice Skating Center
1375 Hopmeadow St.
Simsbury, CT 06070

## Baker, Carroll

P.O. Box 480589
Los Angeles, CA 90048
*Actress*

**BIRTHDAY** 5/28/31

## Baker Hughes

3900 Essex Lane
Houston, TX 77027
*Provides products and services for the global petroleum market*

**INTERNET** www.bakerhughes.com
Michael E. Wiley, Chairman, President and CEO

## Baker, Lisa

P.O. Box 294287
Boca Raton, FL 33429
*Model*

## Baker, Tom
c/o London Management
2-4 Noel St.
GB-London W1V 3RB
England
UNITED KINGDOM
*Actor*

**BIRTHDAY** 1/20/34
**INTERNET** www.officialtombakerwebsite.co.uk

## Bakker, Jim
c/o New Covenant Church
P.O. Box 94
Largo, FL 33779
*Minister*

## Bakula, Scott
11431 Ventura Blvd., #329
Sherman Oaks, CA 90048
*Actor*

**BIRTHDAY** 10/9/54

## Balaban, Bob
45 Bleeker St.
New York, NY 10012
*Producer*

## Baldry, Long John
c/o SL Feldman
1505 W Second Ave
Vancouver BC
BC V6H 3Y4
CANADA
*Blues singer*

## Baldwin, Alec
1325 Ave. of the Americas
New York, NY 10019
*Actor*

## Baldwin, Stephen
4475 Sunset Dr., #199
Los Angeles, CA 90027
*Actor*

## Baldwin, William
8500 Wilshire Blvd., #700
Beverly Hills, CA 90211
*Actor*

## Ballard, Kaye

P.O. Box 922
Rancho Mirage, CA 92270
*Singer*

**BIRTHDAY** 11/20/26

## Ballard, Robert

c/o Mystic Oceano
55 Coogan Blvd.
Mystic, CT 06355
*Marine explorer*

## Baltimore City Paper

812 Park Ave.
Baltimore, MD 21201

**INTERNET** www.citypaper.com
**VOICE** 410-523-2300

## Baltimore Gas and Electric

P.O. Box 1475
Baltimore, MD 21203
*Gas and electric utilities*

**INTERNET** www.bge.com
Mayo A. Shattuck, III, President and CEO

## Baltimore Orioles

333 W Camden St.
Baltimore, MD 21201
*Baseball team*

**INTERNET** www.orioles.mlb.com

## Baltimore Ravens

200 St. Paul Place
Baltimore, MD 21202
*Football team*

**INTERNET** www.ravenszone.net

## Baltimore Sun

100 E Broad St.
Baltimore, MD 21278

**INTERNET** www.sunspot.com
**VOICE** 410-332-6000

## Banc One Corp

100 E Broad St.
Columbus, OH 43271
*Commerical bank*

**INTERNET** www.bankone.com

## Bancroft, Anne

c/o Culver Studios
9336 W Washington Blvd.
Culver City, CA 90232
*Actress*

**Band, The**
370 City Road, Leslington
London EC1V 2QA
England
UNITED KINGDOM
*Music group*

**Banderas, Antonio**
3110 Main St., #205
Santa Monica, CA 90405
*Actor*

**BIRTHDAY** 8/10/60
**E-MAIL** anbanderas@aol.com

**Bando, Sal**
104 W Juniper Lane
Mequon, WI 53092
*Baseball player*

**Bandy, Moe**
P.O. Box 1035
Branson, MO 65616
*Musician*

**Bangladesh**
Shahabuddin Ahmed, President
Bangabhaban
1000 Dhaka, Dhaka Division
*Bangladesh*

**INTERNET** www.bangladeshgov.org

**Bank of America**
48 Wall St.
Charlotte, NC 28255
*Commerical bank*

**INTERNET** www.bankofamerica.com
Kenneth D. Lewis, Chairman and CEO

**Bank of New York Company, The**
48 Wall St.
New York, NY 10286
*Commerical bank*

**INTERNET** www.bankofny.com
J. Carter Bacot, Chairman and CEO

**Banks, Ernie**
c/o Chicago Cubs
1060 W Addison St.
Chicago, IL 60613
*Baseball player*

## Banks, Tyra
PMB 710
15030 Ventura Blvd.
Sherman Oaks, CA 90036
*Model*

**BIRTHDAY** 12/3/73

## Barbeau, Adrienne
808 S Ridgeley Dr.
Los Angeles, CA 90036
*Actress*

**BIRTHDAY** 6/11/45

## Barbieri, Paula
P.O. Box 20483
Panama City, FL 32411
*Model*

## Bardot, Brigitte
P.O. Box 691885
St Tropez
La Madrague F-83990
FRANCE
*Actress*

**BIRTHDAY** 9/28/34

## Barker, Bob
c/o The Price Is Right
7800 Beverly Blvd.
Los Angeles, CA 90036
*TV game show host*

**BIRTHDAY** 12/12/23
**E-MAIL** pir@tvc.cbs.com

## Barker, Clive
P.O. Box 691885
Los Angeles, CA 90069
Director

## Barkin, Ellen
9830 Wilshire Blvd.
Beverly Hills, CA 90212
*Actress*

**BIRTHDAY** 4/16/54

## Barkley, Charles
7615 E Vaguero Dr.
Scottsdale, AZ 85258
*Basketball player*

**Barnes, Joanna**
267 Middle Road
Santa Barbara, CA 93108
*Actress/author*

**Barnes, Priscilla**
8428-C Melrose Place
W Hollywood, CA 90069
*Actress*
BIRTHDAY 12/7/56

**Barnes & Noble**
122 5th Ave.
New York, NY 10011
*Bookseller*
INTERNET www.bn.com
Marie Toulantis, CEO

**Barney**
300 E Beethany Road
Allen, TX 75002
*Dinosaur*

**Barr, Julia**
77 W 66th St.
New York, NY 10023
*Actress*

**Barris, Chuck**
77 W 66th St.
New York, NY 10023
*Television producer*

**Barron's**
200 Liberty St.
New York, NY 10281
*Financial magazine*
INTERNET www.barrons.com
VOICE 212-416-2000

**Barrows, Sydney Biddle**
210 W 70th St.
New York, NY 10023
*Alleged Madam*

**Barry, Dave**
c/o The Miami Herald
1 Herald Plaza
Miami Beach, FL 33132
*Humorist/columnist*
E-MAIL 93314.722@compuserve.com

**Barry, Mayor Marion**
3607 Suitland Road
Washington, D.C. 20004
*Mayor, District of Columbia*

**BIRTHDAY** 3/6/36

**Barrymore, Drew**
c/o Studio Fan Mail
1122 S Robertson Blvd.
Los Angeles, CA 90035
*Actress*

**BIRTHDAY** 2/22/75

**Baryshnikov, Mikhail**
c/o Vincent & Farrell
481 8th Ave.
New York, NY 10001
*Ballet dancer/actor*

**BIRTHDAY** 1/28/48

**Basinger, Kim**
4833 Don Juan Place
Woodland Hills, CA 91367
*Actress*

**BIRTHDAY** 12/8/53

**Bassett, Angela**
9465 Wilshire Blvd.
Beverly Hills, CA 90212
*Actress*

**Bassey, Shirley**
24 Ave. Princess Grace, #1200
Monte Carlo
Monaco
*Singer*

**BIRTHDAY** 1/8/37

**Bateman, Jason**
3127 Barbara Ct.
Los Angeles, CA 90068
*Actor*

**BIRTHDAY** 1/14/69

**Bateman, Justine**
4024 Radford Ave., Bldg. 3
Studio City, CA 91604
*Actress*

**BIRTHDAY** 2/19/66

## Bates, Kathy (Kathleen Doyle Bates)
6220 Del Valle
Los Angeles, CA 90048
*Actress*

**BIRTHDAY** 6/28/48

## Baton Rouge Advocate
525 Lafayette St.
Baton Rouge, LA 70802

**INTERNET** www.theadvocate.com
**VOICE** 225-383-1111

## Battle, Kathleen
165 W 57th St.
New York, NY 10019
*Opera singer*

**BIRTHDAY** 8/13/48

## Baucus, Max
511 Hart Senate Office Bldg. (D-MT)
Washington, D.C. 20510
*Senator*

**E-MAIL** baucus.senate.gov/emailmax.html

## Baxter International
1 Baxter Pkwy
Deerfield, IL 60015
*Scientific, photo, control equipment, medical systems*

**INTERNET** www.baxter.com
Harry M. Jansen, Chairman

## Bay City Rollers
42 St. Leonardo Road
East Sussex TN40 1HP
UNITED KINGDOM
*Rock band*

## Bayh, Evan
463 Russell Senate Office Bldg. (D-IN)
Washington, D.C. 20005
*Senator*

**E-MAIL** bayh.senate.gov/webmail.html

## Bazelon Center for Mental Health Law
1101 15th St. NW, #1212
Washington, D.C. 20005
*Legal advocacy for the civil rights and human dignity of people with disabilities*

**INTERNET** www.bazelon.org
**E-MAIL** webmaster@bazelon.org
Lee Carty, Communications Director

**Beach Boys**
8942 Wilshire Blvd.
Beverly Hills, CA 90211
*Music group*

**INTERNET** www.beachboysfanclub.com

**Beals, Jennifer**
PMB 710, 15030 Ventura Blvd.
Sherman Oaks, CA 91403
*Actress*

**BIRTHDAY** 12/19/63

**Bear Stearns**
245 Park Ave.
New York, NY 10167
*Securities*

**INTERNET** www.bearstearns.com
James Cayne, Chairman

**Beard, Amanda**
212 Raft Island Dr. NW
Gig Harbor, WA 98332
*Olympic gold medal swimmer*

**Beastie Boys**
1290 Ave. of the Americas
New York, NY 10104
*Rap music group*

**INTERNET** www.beastieboys.com

**Beatrix, HM Queen**
Kasteel Drakestijn
Lage Vuursche 3744 BA
Holland
*Queen of Holland*

**Beatty, Warren (Henry Warren Beatty)**
13671 Mulholland Dr.
Beverly Hills, CA 90210-1135
*Actor*

**BIRTHDAY** 3/30/37

**Beavis & Butthead**
1515 Broadway
New York, NY 10036
*Animated characters*

**Beck, Jeff**
1801 Century Park W
Los Angeles, CA 90067
*Musician*
E-MAIL jeffbeck@arista.com

**Beck, Marilyn**
P.O. Box 11079
Beverly Hills, CA 90213
*Columnist/critic*
BIRTHDAY 12/17/28

**Becker, Boris**
Lamontstr 26
81679 Moen
GERMANY
*Tennis player*
BIRTHDAY 11/22/67

**Becton, Dickinson**
1 Becton Dr.
Franklin Lakes, NJ 07417
*Scientific, photo, control equipment, medical systems*
INTERNET www.bd.com
Edward Ludwig, Chairman, President and CEO

**Bedelia, Bonnie**
40 W 57th St.
New York, NY 10019
*Actress*

**Bee Gees, The**
P.O. Box 2429
Miami Beach, FL 33140
*Music group*
INTERNET www.beegeesfanclub.org

**Begley, Jr. Ed**
3850 Mound View Ave.
Studio City, CA 91604
BIRTHDAY 9/16/49

**Belarus**
Aleksandr Lukashenko, President
Office of the President
2200010 Minsk, Minsk oblast
Belarus
INTERNET www.president.gov.by
E-MAIL ires@president.gov.by

**Belgium**
King Albert II, Palais Royal
Rue de Brederode 16
B-1000 Bruxelles
Belgium

## Belize
Said Musa, Prime Minister
Office of the Prime Minister
New Administrative Bldg.
Belmopan
Belize

**INTERNET** www.belize.gov.bz
**E-MAIL** pmbelize@btl.net

## Bell, Archie
P.O. Box 11669
Knoxville, TN 37939
*Singer*

## Bell, Catherine
28343 Ave., Crocker Stage 1
Valencia, CA 91355
*Actress*

**E-MAIL** harrietjag@aol.com

## Bell, Darryl
1750 S Hauser Blvd.
Los Angeles, CA 90019
*Actor*

## Bell, Atlanta
1095 6th Ave.
New York, NY 10036
*Telecommunications*

**INTERNET** www.bellatlantic.com
Ivan Seidenberg, CEO

## Bellamy, Bill
9830 Wilshire Blvd.
Beverly Hills, CA 90212
*Musician*

## Bellamy Brothers
P.O. Box 801
San Antonio, TX 33576
*Country music group*

## BellSouth
1155 Peachtree St. NE
Atlanta, GA 30309
*Telecommunications*

**INTERNET** www.bellsouthcorp.policy.net
F. Duane Ackerman, Chairman and CEO

## Belushi, Jim
8942 Wilshire Blvd., #155
Beverly Hills, CA 90211
*Actor*

## Belzer, Richard
SVU
23rd St. and Hudson River
New York, NY 10011
*Comedian/actor*

## Benatar, Pat
1000 Main St. Plaza, #303
Voorhees, NJ 08043
*Singer*

**BIRTHDAY** 1/19/52

## Benedict, Dirk
P.O. Box 634
Big Fork, MT 59911
*Author*

## Beneficial
301 N Walnut St.
Wilmington, DE 19801
*Financial corporation*

**INTERNET** www.beneficial.com
Finn M.W. Caspersen, CEO

## Benin
Mathieu Kerekou, President
Place de L'Independence
Boite Postale 08 0612
Cotonou
Benin

**INTERNET** www.planben.intnet.bj

## Bening, Annette
13671 Mulholland Dr.
Beverly Hills, CA 90210-1135
*Actress*

**BIRTHDAY** 5/29/58

## Benji
242 N Canon Dr.
Beverly Hills, CA 90210
*Acting dog*

## Bennett, Robert
431 Dirksen
Senate Office Bldg. (R-UT)
Washington, D.C. 20510
*Senator*

**E-MAIL** senator@bennett.senate.gov

## Benson, Craig
Governor of New Hampshire

**INTERNET** www.state.nj.us/governor/comment.html

## Benson, George
BIRTHDAY 3/2/43

519 Next Day Hill Dr.
Englewood, NJ 07631
*Singer*

## Benson, Jodi
345 N Maple Dr., #302
Beverly Hills, CA 90210
*Actress*

## Benson, Robby (Robby Segal)
BIRTHDAY 1/21/55

4151 Prospect Ave.
Hollywood, CA 90027
*Actor/Writer/Director*

## Bentsen, Hon. Lloyd
1500 Pennsylvania Ave. NW
Washington, D.C. 20220
*Former vice presidential candidate, Former senator*

## Berenger, Tom
BIRTHDAY 5/31/50

853 7th Ave., #9C
New York, NY 10019
*Actor*

## Bergen, Candice
BIRTHDAY 5/9/46

151 El Camino Blvd.
Beverly Hills, CA 90212
*Actress*

## Bergen Brunswick
INTERNET www.bergenbrunswig.com
Robert E. Martini, Chairman

1440 Kiewit Plaza
Orange, CA 92868
*Pharmaceuticals, healthcare supplier*

## Berkshire Hathaway
INTERNET www.berkshirehathaway.com
Warren E. Buffet, Chairman and CEO

1440 Kiewit Plaza
Omaha, NE 68131
*P & C insurance*

## Bernhard, Sandra
BIRTHDAY 6/6/55

3500 W Olive Ave.
Burbank, CA 91505
*Actress/Comedian*

## Bernsen, Corbin
3500 W Olive Ave.
Burbank, CA 91505
*Actor*

**BIRTHDAY** 9/7/54

## Berra, Yogi
19 Highland Ave.
Montclair, NJ 07042
*Former baseball player*

## Berry, Chuck
Berry Park
Buckner Road
Wentzville, MO 63385
*Singer/Songwriter*

**BIRTHDAY** 10/18/26

## Berry, Halle
8721 Sunset Blvd.
Los Angeles, CA 90069
*Actress*

**E-MAIL** halleberry@studiofanmail.com

## Berry, John
P.O. Box 121162
Nashville, NJ 37212
*Country music singer*

## Berry, Ken
13911 Fenton Ave.
Sylmar, CA 91342
*Actor*

**BIRTHDAY** 11/3/33

## Berti, Chiara
*Big Brother 3 Contestant*

**BIRTHDAY** 03/27/77
**INTERNET** www.justchiara.com
**E-MAIL** bb3kiki@hotmail.com

## Berti, Joel
*Actor* Inside the Osmonds

**BIRTHDAY** 12/17/71
**E-MAIL** jberti@comcast.net

## Bertinelli, Valerie
9255 W Sunset Blvd.
West Hollywood, CA 90069
*Actress*

**BIRTHDAY** 4/23/60

## Besson, Luc

76 Oxford St.
London WIN OAX
England
UNITED KINGDOM
*Film director*

**BIRTHDAY** 3/18/59

## Best, James

P.O. Box 621027
Oviedo, FL 32762
*Actor*

**BIRTHDAY** 7/26/26

## Best Buy

700 Sylvan Ave.
Eden Prairie, MN 55344
*Specialist electronics retailers*

**INTERNET** www.bestbuy.com
Richard M. Schulze, Chairman and CEO

## Best Foods

1170 8th Ave.
Englewoods Cliffs, NJ 07632
*Food producer*

**INTERNET** www.bestfoods.com
Charles R. Shoemate, CEO

## Bethlehem Steel

1170 8th Ave.
Bethlehem, PA 18016
*Metals*

**INTERNET** www.bethsteel.com
Robert S. Miller, Chairman and CEO

## Betty Boop Fan Club

1000 Beverly Way
Buena Park, CA 90621
*Nostalgic cartoon*

## Beverly Enterprises

9641 Sunset Blvd.
Fort Smith, AR 72919
*Healthcare, nursing homes*

**INTERNET** www.beverlynet.com
David R. Banks, Chairman

## Beverly Hills Hotel

9641 Sunset Blvd.
Beverly Hills, CA 90210
*Famous hotel reknown for its celebrity clientele and home of the world famous Polo lounge*

**INTERNET** www.thebeverlyhillshotel.com

## B.F. Goodrich

4 Coliseum Center
2730 W Tyvola Road
Charlotte, NC 28217
*Fire company*

**INTERNET** www.bfgoodrich.com
William R. Floyd, Chairman, President and CEO

## B.G. Prince of Rap

c/o Allstars Music
Hundshager Weg 30
68623 Hofheim
Germany
*Rap singer*

## Bhutan

King Jigme Singye Wangchuk
Royal Palace
Thimphu
Bhutan

## Biafra, Jello (Eric Boucher)

P.O. Box 419092
San Francisco, CA 94141
*Former lead singer of the punk rock band Dead Kennedys*

## Bialik, Mayim

1529 N. Cahuenga Blvd, #19
Los Angeles, CA 90028
*Actress*

**BIRTHDAY** 12/12/75

## Biden, Joseph

221 Russell Senate Office Bldg. (D-DE)
Washington, D.C. 20510
*Senator*

**E-MAIL** senator@biden.senate.gov

## Big Brother

**INTERNET** www.cbs.com/primetime/bigbrother3

## Biggs-Dawson, Roxann

1505 10th St.
Santa Monica, CA 90401
*Actress*

## Billboard

1515 Broadway
New York, NY 10036
*Music magazine*

**INTERNET** www.billboard.com
**VOICE** 1-800-449-1402

## Bindley Western

8909 Purdue Road
Indianapolis, IN 46268
*Wholesale distributors of pharmaceuticals, health and beauty care products*

**INTERNET** www.bindley.com
William E. Bindley, Chairman, President and CEO

## Bingaman, Jeff

703 Hart Senate Office Bldg. (D-NM)
Washington, D.C. 20510
*Senator*

**E-MAIL** senator_bingaman@bingaman.senate.gov

## Birmingham News

2200 4th Ave.
Birmingham, AL 35202

**INTERNET** www.bhamnews.com
205-325-2222

## Biscayne

800-688-0721
*Travel website*

**INTERNET** www.biscayne.com

## BizRate

4053 Redwood Ave.
Los Angeles, CA 46268
*E-Commerce*

**INTERNET** www.bizrate.com
Farhad Mohit, CEO and President

## BJ's Wholesale Club

1 Mercer Road
Natick, MA 01760
*Membership food and drug stores*

**INTERNET** www.bjswholesale.com
Herbert J. Zarkin, Chairman

## Bjork

40 W 57th St.
New York, NY 10019
*Singer*

## Black, Clint

9255 Sunset Blvd., #600
Los Angeles, CA 90069
*Country singer*

## Black, Shirley Temple

8949 Wilshire Blvd.
Beverly Hills, CA 90211
*Actress*

## Black and Decker

701 E Joppa Road
Towson, MD 21286
*Tools, industrial and farm equipment*

**INTERNET** www.blackanddecker.com
Nolan D. Archibald, Chairman, President and CEO

## Black Crowes, The
9200 Sunset Blvd., #900
Los Angeles, CA 90069
*Music group*

## Black Entertainment TV
1232 31st St. NW
Washington, D.C. 20007
*Cable network*

## Blackstone, Harry
16530 Ventura Blvd.
Encino, CA 91436
*Magician*

## Blair, Linda
10061 Riverside Dr., #1003
Toluca Lake, CA 91602
*Actress*

**BIRTHDAY** 1/22/59

## Blagojevich, Rod
Governor of Illinois

**E-MAIL** governor@state.il.us

## Blake, Robert
11604 Dilling St.
N Hollywood, CA 91608
*Actor*

## Bland, Bobby "Blue"
1995 Broadway, #501
New York, NY 10023
*Singer*

## Blanda, George
78001 Lago Dr.
La Quinta, CA 92253
*Former football player*

## Bledsoe, Drew
1 Bills Dr.
Orchard Park, NY 14127
*Football player*

## Bleeth, Yasmine
9595 Wilshire Blvd., #502
Beverly Hills, CA 90212
*Actress*

## Blessed Union of Souls
700 W Pete Rose Way
Cincinnati, OH 45203
*Rock music group*

## Blind Melon
9229 W Sunset Blvd., #607
W Hollywood, CA 90069
*Rock group*

## Blitzer, Wolf
8929 Holly Leaf Ln.
Bethesda, MD 20817
*News correspondent*

## Blondee
P.O. Box 23343
Beverly Hills, CA 90212
*Model*

## Blount Lisa
2060 Paramount Dr.
Los Angeles, CA 90068
*Actress*

## Blue, Vida
P.O. Box 1449
Pleasanton, CA 94556
*Former baseball player*

## Blues Traveler
Rock music group

**INTERNET** www.bluestraveler.com
**E-MAIL** blackcatz@earthlink.net

## Blume, Judy
54 Riverside Drive
New York, NY 10023
*Author*

**BIRTHDAY** 2/12/38

## Blyth, Ann
Box 9754
Rancho Santa Fe, CA 92067
*Actress*

**BIRTHDAY** 8/16/28

**Bobek, Nicole**
P.O. Box 4534
Tequesta, FL 33469
*Figure skater*

**Bochco, Steven**
694 Amalfi Dr.
Pacific Palisades, CA 90272
*Producer/screenwriter*
BIRTHDAY 12/16/43

**Boeing**
7755 E Marginal Way S
Seattle, WA 98108
*Aerospace*
INTERNET www.boeing.com
Alan R. Mulally, Chairman and CEO

**Boggs, Wade**
6006 Windham Place
Tampa, FL 33647
*Baseball player*

**Boise Cascade**
111 W Jefferson St.
Boise, ID 83702
*Forest and paper products and office supplies*
INTERNET www.bc.com
George J. Harad, Chairman and CEO

**Bold and the Beautiful cast, The**
7800 Beverly Blvd.
Los Angeles, CA 90036
*Soap opera*

**Bolivia**
Hugo Banzer Suarez, President
Palacio de Gobiemo
Plaza Mutilo
La Paz
Bolivia
INTERNET www.congreso.gov.bo
E-MAIL mig@comunica.gov.bo

**Bologna, Joseph**
16830 Ventura Blvd., #326
Encino, CA 91436
*Actor/writer/director*
BIRTHDAY 12/30/34

**Bolton, Michael**
130 W 57th St.
New York, NY 10019
*Singer*

## Bon Appetit
6300 Wilshire Blvd.
Los Angeles, CA 90048
*Magazine*

**INTERNET** www.bonappetit.com
**VOICE** 323-965-3600

## Bon Jovi
248 W 17th St., #502
New York, NY 10107
*Rock music group*

## Bon Jovi, Jon
825 8th St.
New York, NY 10019
*Singer*

## Bonaduce, Danny
2651 La Cuesta Dr.
Los Angeles, CA 90046
*Actor/talk show host*

## Bonamy, James
15 Music Square W
Nashville, TN 37203
*Singer*

## Bond, Christopher
274 Russell Senate Office Bldg. (R-MO)
Washington, D.C. 20510
*Senator*

**E-MAIL** kit_bond@bond.senate.gov

## Bonds, Gary U.S.
1560 Broadway, #1308
New York, NY 10036
*Singer*

**BIRTHDAY** 6/6/39

## Bonet, Lisa
1511 Will Geer Road
Topanga, CA 90290
*Actress*

## Bono (Paul Hewson)
4 Windmill Lane
Dublin, 2
Ireland
*Singer/songwriter*

**BIRTHDAY** 5/10/60
**INTERNET** www.U2.com

**Bono, Chastity**
P.O. Box 57593
Sherman Oaks, CA 91403
*Sonny and Cher's daughter*
BIRTHDAY 3/4/69

**Boone, Debby**
4334 Kester Ave.
Sherman Oaks, CA 91403
*Actress/singer*

**Boone, Pat**
9200 Sunset Blvd., #1007
Los Angeles, CA 90069
*Singer*
BIRTHDAY 6/1/34

**Boosler, Elayne**
584 N Larchmont Blvd.
Los Angeles, CA 90004
*Comedienne/actress*

**Boorstin, Daniel**
c/o Library of Congress
Mail Stop 1090
101 Indiana Ave. SE
Washington, D.C. 20540

**Boothe, Powers**
P.O. Box 9242
Calabasas, CA 91372
*Actor*

**Borden**
180 E Broad St.
Columbus, OH 43215
*Specialty chemicals and consumer adhesives*
C. Robert Kidder, Chairman

**Borg, Bjorn**
1360 E 9th St., #100
Cleveland, OH 44114
*Tennis player*
BIRTHDAY 6/6/56

**Borman, Col. Frank**
250 Cotorro Ct., A
Las Cruces, NM 88005
*Astronaut*

## Bosnia and Herzegovina

Alija Izetbegovic,
Presidency of the Republic
Save Kavacevica Ulica 6
71000 Sarajevo
Bosnia and Herzegovina

**INTERNET** www.mvp.gov.ba
**E-MAIL** info@mvp.gov.ba

## Boston Bruins

Fleet Center
Boston, MA 02114
*Hockey team*

**INTERNET** www.Bostonbruins.com

## Boston Celtics

151 Merrimac St.
Boston, MA 02114
*Basketball team*

**INTERNET** www.nba.com/celtics

## Boston Globe

P.O. Box 2378
Boston, MA 02107

**INTERNET** www.Bostonglobe.com
**VOICE** 617-929-2000

## Boston Herald

1 Herald Square
Boston, MA 02107

**INTERNET** www.Bostonherald.com
**VOICE** 617-426-3000

## Boston Phoenix

126 Brookline Ave.
Boston, MA 02115

**INTERNET** www.BostonPhoenix.com
**VOICE** 617-536-5390

## Boston Public

1600 Rosecrans Ave.
Bldg. 4A, 3rd Floor
Manhattan Beach, CA 90266
Attn: Boston Public
*Television show*

## Boston Red Sox

4 Yawkey Way
Fenway Park
Boston, MA 02215
*Baseball team*

**INTERNET** www.redsox.com

## Boston Symphony Orchestra

Symphony Hall
301 Massachusetts Ave.
Boston, MA 02115

**INTERNET** www.bso.org

**Bostwick, Barry**
170 S Mountain Road
New York, NY 11956
*Actor*

**BIRTHDAY** 2/24/46

**Bosworth, Brian**
230 Park Ave.
New York, NY 10169
*Actor*

**Botswana**
Festus Mogae, President
State House
Private Bag 001
Gaborone
Botswana

**INTERNET** www.gov.bw

**Bowie, David**
76 Oxford House
London, England
UNITED KINGDOM
W1N OAX

**Bowles, Camilla Parker**
Middlewick House
Nr. Corshm, Wiltshire
England
*Longstanding companion and confidante to Prince Charles*

**Boxer, Barbara**
112 Hart Senate Office
Bldg. (D-CA)
Washington, D.C 20510.
Senator

**INTERNET** www.boxer.senate.gov/contact

**Boxleitner, Bruce**
P.O. Box 5513
Sherman Oaks, CA 91403
*Actor*

**BIRTHDAY** 5/12/50

**Boy George (George O'Dowd)**
18 Wells Road, NW3
London, England
UNITED KINGDOM
*Singer*

**BIRTHDAY** 6/14/61

## Boyle, Lara Flynn
9777 S Wilshire Blvd., #504
Beverly Hills, CA 90212
*Actress*

## Boyle, Peter
130 E 2nd Ave
New York, NY 10024
*Actor*

**BIRTHDAY** 10/18/33

## Boyz II Men
10675 Santa Monica Blvd.
Los Angeles, CA 90025
R&B music group

**INTERNET** www.boyziimen.com

## Bozo the Clown
c/o WGN Television
2501 Bradley Place
Chicago, IL 60618-4701
*Television character*

## Bracco, Lorraine
236 W 45th St.
New York, NY 10036
*Actress*

**BIRTHDAY** 10/2/54

## Bradbury, Ray
10265 Cheviot Dr.
Los Angeles, CA 90064
*Author*

## Bradlee, Benjamin
3014 N St. NW
Washington, D.C. 20007
*Journalist*

## Bradshaw, John
c/o Fan Association
518 S Eagleson Road
Houston, TX 77098
*Author and Lecturer*

## Branagh, Kenneth
Shepperton Studios
Studios Road
Middlesex
TW 170QD
England
*Actor*

**BIRTHDAY** 12/10/60

## Brandis, Jonathan
11684 Ventura Blvd. #966
Studio City, CA 91604
*Actor*

## Brando, Marlon
13828 Weddington
Van Nuys, CA 91401
*Actor*

**BIRTHDAY** 4/3/24

## Branigan, Laura
P.O. Box 3484
San Dimas, CA 91773
*Singer*

**INTERNET** www.laurabranigan.com

## Bravo
150 Crossways Park W
Woodbury, NY 11797
*Cable network*

## Braxton, Toni
14724 Ventura Blvd., #440
Sherman Oaks, CA 91403
*Singer*

**INTERNET** www.tonibraxton.com

## Brazil
Fernando Henrique Cardoso, President
Oficina do President,
Palacio do Planalto
Praca dos Tres Poderes
70.50 Brasilia
Brazil

**INTERNET** www.planalto.gov.br

**E-MAIL** protocolo@planalto.gov.br

## Bread for the World

**INTERNET** www.bread.org

1100 Wayne Ave., #1000
Silver Spring, MD 20910

*Citizens' movement seeking "justice" for the world's hungry people by lobbying our nation's decision makers*

## Breaux, John

**E-MAIL** senator@breaux.senate.gov

503 Hart Senate Office Bldg. (D-LA)
Washington, D.C. 20510

*Senator*

## Brechner Center for Freedom of Information

P.O. Box 118400
Gainesville, FL 32611

Sandra F. Chanve, Director

*A unit of the College of Journalism upon which University of Florida relies*

## Bredesen, Phil

**E-MAIL** dsundquist@mail.state.tn.us

Governor of Tennessee

## Brennan, Eileen

**BIRTHDAY** 9/3/38

974 Mission Terrace
Camarillo, CA 91310

*Actress*

## Brenneman, Amy

**BIRTHDAY** 6/22/64

9830 Wilshire Blvd.
Los Angeles, CA 90210

*Actress*

## Brenner, David

**BIRTHDAY** 2/4/45

17 E 16th St.
New York, NY 10003

*Comedian*

## Brett, George

P.O. Box 419969
Kansas City, MO 64141

*Baseball player*

## Bridges, Beau

5525 N Jed Smith Road
Hidden Hills, CA 91302

*Actor*

**Bridges, Jeff**
9560 Wilshire Blvd.
Beverly Hills, CA 90212
*Actor*

**INTERNET** www.jeffbridges.com

**Bridges, Todd**
10508 Dora St.
Sun Valley, CA 91352
*Actor*

**INTERNET** www.toddbridges.com

**Brightman, Sarah**
1 Sussex Place, W69XT
London
England
UNITED KINGDOM
*Opera singer*

**Brinkley, Christie**
1122 S Robertson Road, #15
Los Angeles, CA 90035
*Model/actress*

**BIRTHDAY** 2/2/54
**E-MAIL** christinebrinkley@studiofanmail.com

**Bristol-Meyers Squibb**
345 Park Ave.
New York, NY 10154
*Pharmaceutical manufacturer*

**INTERNET** www.bms.com
Peter Dolan, Chairman and CEO

**Broadcasting**
19345 W Olympic Blvd.
Washington, D.C. 20036

**INTERNET** www.broadcasting.com

**Broderick, Matthew**
P.O. Box 69646
Los Angeles, CA 90069
*Actor*

**Brokaw, Tom**
c/o NBC News
30 Rockefeller Plaza
New York, NY 10112
*News anchor*

**E-MAIL** nightly@nbc.com

**Brolin, James**
4526 Wilshire Blvd.
Los Angeles, CA 90010
*Actor*

## Brook, Jayne
7800 Beverly Blvd.
Los Angeles, CA 90036
*Actress*

## Brooks and Dunn
**INTERNET** www.brooks-dunn.com

P.O. Box 120669
Nashville, TN 37212
*Country music band*

## Brooks, Garth
90 Fox Run Road
Nashville, TN 37203
*Country singer*

## Brooks, Albert
**BIRTHDAY** 7/22/47

1880 Century Park Dr.
Park East #900
Los Angeles, CA 90067
*Actor/writer/director*

## Brosnan, Pierce
**BIRTHDAY** 5/16/53

23852 Pacific Coast Hwy, #007
Malibu, CA 90265
ppiercyb@hotmail.com
*Actor*

## Brosnan, James L.
23715 W Malibu Road
Beverly Hills, CA 90211
*Actor*

## Brothers, Dr. Joyce
**INTERNET** www.drjoycebrothers.com

1530 Palisades Ave.
Ft. Lee, NJ 07024
*Sex therapist*

## Brown, Clancy
**INTERNET** www.clancy-brown.com

11288 Ventura Blvd., #728
Benton Harbor, MI 49023
*Voice of Mr. Crabbs on* Sponge Bob Square Pants *television show*

**Brown, "Downtown" Julie**
250 W 57th St., #821
New York, NY 10107
*Actress*

**Brown, Helen Gurley**
959 8th Ave.
New York, NY 10019
*Magazine editor*

**Brown, Denise**
P.O. Box 3777
Monarch Bay, CA 92629
*Nicole Brown-Simpson's sister*

**Brown, James**
1217 W Medical Park Road
Augusta, GA 30909
*Singer*

**Brown, Sylvia**
35 Dillon Ave.
Campbell, VA 95008
*Psychic*

**Brownback, Sam**
303 Hart Senate Office
Bldg. (R-KS)
Washington, D.C. 20510
*Senator*

**E-MAIL** brownback.senate.gov/CMEmailme.htm

**Browne, Jackson**
35 Dillon Ave.
Studio City, CA 91604
*Singer*

**Browning, Kurt**
175 Bloor St. E
South Tower, #400
Toronto, Ontario MYW328
Canada
*Ice skater*

## Browning Ferris Industries (sub. of Allied Waste)

757 N Eldridge Road
Houston, TX 77079
*Waste management*

**INTERNET** www.bfi.com
Thomas H. Van Weelden, CEO

## Brunei

Sir Muda Hassanal Bolkia
Mu'izzadin Wassaulah
Sultan
Istana Darul Hana
Bandar Seri Begawan Brunei
Maura
Brunei

**INTERNET** www.brunei.gov.bn

## Brunswick

1 N Field Ct.
Lake Forest, IL 60045
*Transportation equipment*

## Buchanan, Pat

6862 Elm St, #210
McLean, VA 22101
P.O. Box 1919
Mernfield, VA 22116
*Presidential candidate*

## Buckley, Betty

305 W 105th St., #3B
*Actress*

**BIRTHDAY** 7/3/47
**INTERNET** www.bettybuckley.com

## Buckley, Jr., William

1212 Ave. of the Americas
New York, NY 10036
*Author/editor*

## Budget

*Rental Car Agency*

**INTERNET** www.budgetrentalcars.com
**VOICE** 1-800-527-0700

## Buffalo Bills

1 Bills Dr.
Buffalo, NY 14203

**INTERNET** www.buffalobills.com

## Buffalo Evening News
1 News Plaza
Buffalo, NY 14203

**INTERNET** www.buffalo.com
**VOICE** 716-849-4444

## Buffalo Sabres
c/o HK Mgmt
8900 Wilshire Blvd., #200
Orchard Park, NY 14127

**INTERNET** www.sabres.com

## Buffett, Jimmy
550-B Duval St.
Key West, FL 33040
*Singer*

## Bulgaria
Petar Stoyanov, President
Office of the President
Veliko Narodno Subraine
Sofia 1000
Bulgaria

**INTERNET** www.president.bg
**E-MAIL** president@president.bg

## Bulldog Reporter
5900 Hollis St., R2 Newsletter
Emeryville, CA 94608

**INTERNET** www.infocomgroup.com
**VOICE** 510-596-9300

## Bulloch, Jeremy
10 Birchwood Road
London SW179BQ
England
UNITED KINGDOM
*Actor*

## Bullock, Sandra
9830 Wilshire Blvd.
Beverly Hills, CA 90212
*Actress*

**E-MAIL** sandyb@aol.com

## Bunning, Jim
316 Hart Senate Office
Bldg. (R-KY)
Washington, D.C. 20510
*Senator*

**E-MAIL** jim_bunning@bunning.senate.gov

## Burghoff, Gary
P.O. Box 1603
Beverly Hills, CA 90212
*Actor*

**Burke, Delta**
1407 Broadway, #1615
New York, NY 10018
*Actress/former Miss Florida*

**Burke, Paul**
2217 Avenida Cabelleros
Palm Springs, CA 92262
*Actor*

**Burkina Faso**
Blaise Compaore, President
Office of the President
03 BP 7030
Ouagadougou 03
Burkina Faso

**INTERNET** www.primature.gov.bf

**Burlington N Santa Fe**
8942 Wilshire Blvd.
Fort Worth, TX 76131
*Railroads*

**INTERNET** www.bnsf.com
Robert D. Krebs, Chairman and CEO

**Burnett, Carol**
5750 Wilshire Blvd., #590
Los Angeles, CA 90036
*Comedian*

**Burns, Conrad**
187 Dirksen Senate Office Bldg. (R-MT)
Washington, D.C. 20510
*Senator*

**INTERNET** www.burns.senate.gov/index.cfm
FuseAction-Home.contact

**Burns, Ken**
Maple Grove Road
Walpole, NH 03608
*Filmmaker*

**Burstyn, Ellen**
Box 217
Palisades, NY 10964
*Actress*

**Burton, Lance**
3770 S Las Vegas Blvd.
Las Vegas, NV 89109
*Magician*

## Burundi

Pierre Buyoya, President
B.P. 1870
Office of the President
Bujumbura
Burundi

**INTERNET** www.burundi.gov.bi

## Bush, Barbara

9 W Oak Dr.
Houston, TX 77056
*Former First Lady/author*

## Bush, George

9 W Oak Dr.
Houston, TX 77056
*Former president*

## Bush, Jeb

fl_governor@myflorida.com
*Governor of Florida*

## Bush, Tim

P.O. Box 79798
Long Beach, CA 90862
*Actor*

## Business 2.0

888 16th St. NW
San Francisco, CA 94134
*Online magazine*

**INTERNET** www.business20.com
**VOICE** 415-656-8699

## Business Industry Political Action Committee

888 16th St. NW
Washington, D.C. 20006
*An independent, bipartisan organization, founded in 1963*

**INTERNET** www.bipac.org
**E-MAIL** info@bipac.org

## Business Marketing

740 Rush St.
Chicago, IL 60611

**INTERNET** www.businessmarketing.com
**VOICE** 312-649-5401

## Business Week

1221 Ave. of the Americas
New York, NY 10020

**INTERNET** www.businessweek.com
**VOICE** 212-512-2511

## Butkus, Dick
3930 Villa Costera
Malibu, CA 90265
*Former football player*

## Buttafuoco, Joey
P.O. Box 3575
Chatsworth, CA 91313
*Newsmaker*

## Butthole Surfers
315 S Coast Hwy, #100
Encinitas, CA 92024
*Rock band*

**INTERNET** www.buttholesurfers.com

## Buzzi, Ruth
2309 Malaga Road
Los Angeles, CA 90068
*Comedian*

**BIRTHDAY** 7/24/36

## Byrd, Robert
311 Hart Senate Office Bldg. (D-WV)
Washington, D.C. 20510
*Senator*

**E-MAIL** senator_byrd@byrd.senate.gov

## Byrnes, Edd
P.O. Box 1623
Beverly Hills, CA 90213
*Actor*

## Caan, James
P.O. Box 6646
Ever, CO 80206
*Actor*

## Cage, Nicholas (Nicholas Coppola)
1122 S Robertson Blvd., #15
Los Angeles, CA 90035
*Actor*

**BIRTHDAY** 1/7/64

## Cain, Dean
1122 S Robertson Blvd.
Los Angeles, CA 90035
*Actor/Host of* Ripley's Believe It or Not!

**E-MAIL** deancain@studiofanmail.com

**Caine, Sir Michael**
8942 Wilshire Blvd.
Beverly Hills, CA 90211
*Actor*

**BIRTHDAY** 3/14/33

**California Angels**
P.O. Box 2000
Anaheim, CA 92803
*Baseball team*

**INTERNET** www.angels.mlb.com

**Cambodia**
Ung Huot, First Prime Minister
Office of the Prime Minister
Phnom Penh, Phnom Penh City
Cambodia

**Cameroon**
Paul Biya, President
Office of the President
Yaounde, Centre
Cameroon

**Cameron, James**
3201 Retreat Ct.
Malibu, CA 90265
*Movie director*

**E-MAIL** james@titanicmovie.com

**Cameron, Candace**
P.O. Box 8665
Calabasas, CA 91372
*Actress*

**Cameron, Kirk**
P.O. Box 8665
Calabasas, CA 91372
*Actor*

**BIRTHDAY** 10/12/70

**Campaign for U.N. Reform**
420 7th St. SE, C
Washington, D.C. 20003

**INTERNET** www.cunr.org
**E-MAIL** cunr@cunr.org

**Campbell, Ben**
380 Russell Senate Office
Bldg. (R-CO)
Washington, D.C. 20510
*Senator*

**E-MAIL** campbell.senate.gov/email.htm

**Campbell, Naomi**
Ford Model Management
344 E 59th St.
New York, NY 10022
*Supermodel*

**Campbell, Neve**
101-1184 Denman St.
Box 119
Vancouver B.C. V6G2M9
Canada
*Actress*

**Campbell, Trisha**
5750 Wilshire Blvd., #640
Los Angeles, CA 90069
*Actress*

**Campbell, Bruce**
14432 Ventura Blvd., #120
Sherman Oaks, CA 91423
*Actor*
**E-MAIL** bcact@aol.com

**Campbell, Kenneth J.**
9150 Wilshire Blvd., #175
Beverly Hills, CA 90212
*Actor*

**Campbell, Kim**
275 Slater Road, #600
K1P 5H9
Ottawa, ON
Canada
*Former Canadian Prime Minister*

**Campbell Soup**
Campbell Place
Camden, NJ 08103
*Food manufacturer*
**INTERNET** www.campbellsoup.com
Douglas R. Conant, President and CEO

**Canada**
Jean Chretien, M.P., Prime Minister
House of Commons
P.O. Box 1103
Ottawa, Ontario K1A 0A6
Canada
**INTERNET** www.pm.gc.ca
**E-MAIL** pm@pm.gc.ca

## Canadian Associated Press
1825 K St., NW
Washington, D.C. 20006

**VOICE** 202-736-1100

## Cannon, Dyan
8306 Wilshire Blvd., #1681
Beverly Hills, CA 90211
*Actress*

**BIRTHDAY** 1/4/39

## Cannon, J.D.
45 W 60th St., #10J
New York, NY 10023
*Actor*

## Cantwell, Maria
717 Hart Senate Office Bldg. (D-WA)
Washington, D.C. 20510
*Senator*

**INTERNET** www.cantwell.senate.gov/contact/index.html

## Canyon
Encore Entertainment
P.O. Box 1259
Dallas, TX 75065
*Country music group*

## Cape Verde
Antonio Mascarenhas Montiero, President
Office of the President
Cidade de Praia
Sao Taigo, Praia Concelho
Cape Verde

## Capra, Francis
1325 Ave. of the Americas
New York, NY10019
*Actor*

## Capshaw, Kate
P.O. Box 869
Pacific Palisades, CA 90272
*Actor*

## Captain & Tennille

616 Heartline Dr.
Las Vegas, NV 89145
*Singing duo*

**INTERNET** www.captainandtennille.net

## Car and Driver Magazine

2002 Hogback Road
Ann Arbor, MI 48105
*Magazine*

**INTERNET** www.caranddriver.com
**VOICE** 734-971-3600

## Carcieri, Don

*Governor of Rhode Island*

**E-MAIL** rigov@gov.state.ri.us

## Carolyn Rhea Show, The

**INTERNET** www.carolynrhea.com

## Carper, Thomas

513 Hart Senate Office
Building (D-DE)
Washington, D.C. 20510

**INTERNET** www.carper.senate.gov/email-form.html

## CBS Television Network

51 W. 52nd St.
New York, NY 10019

**VOICE** (212) 975-4321

## CBS News

555 W. 57th St.
New York, NY 10019

**VOICE** (212) 975-4114

## Chad

Idriss Deby, President
Office of the President
of the Republic
N'Djamena
Chad

**INTERNET** www.tit.td

## Chafee, Lincoln

141A Russell Senate Office
Building (R-RI)
Washington, D.C. 20510

**INTERNET** www.chafee.senate.gov/webform.htm

## Chambliss, Saxby

United States Senate (R-GA)
Washington, D.C. 20510

**E-MAIL** saxby_chambliss@chambliss.senate.gov

## Charisse, Cyd
10724 Wilshire Blvd., #1406
Los Angeles, CA 90024
*Actress*

**BIRTHDAY** 3/3/23
**INTERNET** www.cydcharisse.net

## Charles Fan club, Ray
2107 W Washington Blvd., #200
Los Angeles, CA 90018
*Singer/songwriter*

**BIRTHDAY** 3/23/30
raysrae@aol.com

## Charleston Gazette/ Daily Mail
1001 Virginia St. SE
Charleston, WV 25301

**INTERNET** www.wvgazette.com
**VOICE** 800-982-6397

## Charles, Prince of Wales
Highgrove House
Doughton
Tetbury GL8 8TN
England
*Heir to the Throne of Great Britain*

**BIRTHDAY** 11/14/48

## Charlotte Observer
600 Tryon St.
Charlotte, NC 28232

**INTERNET** www.charlotte.com
**VOICE** 704-358-5000

## Charo
2535 Las Vegas Blvd. S
Las Vegas, NV 89109
*Actress/guitarist*

**BIRTHDAY** 3/13/41

## Chase, Chevy
P.O. Box 257
Bedford, NY 10506
*Actor/comedian*

**BIRTHDAY** 10/8/43

## Chase Manhattan Corp.
270 Park Ave.
New York, NY 10017
*Commerical bank*

**INTERNET** www.chase.com
William B. Harrison Jr., CEO

## Chateau Marmont
8221 Sunset Blvd.
Los Angeles, CA 90046
*John Belushi died at this LA hotel in 1982*

| | |
|---|---|
| **Cheap Trick International**<br>P.O. Box 7118<br>FDR Station<br>New York, NY 10150<br>*Rock band* | **INTERNET** www.cheaptrick.com<br>**E-MAIL** trickintl@aol.com |
| **Checker, Chubby**<br>c/o Twisted Entertainment<br>320 Fayette St.<br>Conshocken, PA 19428<br>*Singer* | **INTERNET** www.chubbychecker.com |
| **Cheney, Dick**<br>The White House<br>1600 Pennsylvania Avenue NW<br>Washington, D.C. 20500<br>*Vice President of the United States* | **INTERNET** www.whitehouse.gov/vicepresident/<br>**E-MAIL** Vice.president@whitehouse.gov |
| **Cher (Cherilyn Sarkisian La Piere)**<br>P.O. Box 2425<br>Milford, CT 06460<br>*Actress/singer* | **BIRTHDAY** 5/20/46<br>**E-MAIL** cher@cher.com |
| **Chestnutt, Mark**<br>1160 16th Ave. S<br>Nashville, TN 37212<br>*Country music singer* | **INTERNET** www.markchesnutt.com |
| **ChevronTexaco**<br>575 Market St.<br>San Francisco, CA 94105<br>*Petroleum refining* | **INTERNET** www.chevron.com<br>David J. O'Reilly, Chairman and CEO |
| **Chicago Bears**<br>250 N Washington Road<br>Lake Forest, IL 60045<br>*Football team* | **INTERNET** www.Chicagobears.com |
| **Chicago Blackhawks**<br>c/o United Center<br>1901 W Madison St.<br>Chicago, IL 60612<br>*Hockey team* | **INTERNET** www.Chicagoblackhawks.com |

## Chicago Bulls

1901 W Madison St.
Chicago, IL 60612
*Basketball team*

**INTERNET** www.nba.com/bulls

## Chicago Cubs

1060 W Addison St.
Chicago, IL 60613
*Baseball team*

**INTERNET** www.cubs.com

## Chicago Reader

11 E Illinois St.
Chicago, IL 60611

**INTERNET** www.Chicagoreader.com
**VOICE** 312-828-0350

## Chicago Sun Times

401 N Wabash Ave.
Chicago, IL 60611

**INTERNET** www.suntimes.com
**VOICE** 312-321-3000

## Chicago Tribune

435 N Michigan Ave.
Chicago, IL 60611

**INTERNET** www.Chicagotribune.com
**VOICE** 312-222-3232

## Chicago White Sox

333 W 35th St.
Chicago, IL 60613
*Baseball team*

**INTERNET** www.cubs.com

## Childs, Andy

P.O. Box 24563
Nashville, TN 37202
*Country music singer*

**INTERNET** www.andychilds.com

## Child Welfare League of America

440 1st St. NW, #310
Washington, D.C. 20001

**INTERNET** www.cwla.org
**E-MAIL** webmaster@cwla.org
Shay Bilchik, President

*Membership association of public and private nonprofit agencies that serve and advocate for abused, neglected, and otherwise vulnerable children*

## Chile

Ricardo Lagos, President
Palacio de la Moneda
Oficina de Presidente
Santiago
Chile

## China

Jiang Zermin Guojia Zhuxi
President of the People's
Republic of China
Beijingshi
People's Republic of China

## Chirac, M. Jacques

President de la Republique
Palais de l'Elysee
55 et 57 rue de Faubourg
Saint-Honore
75008
France

**INTERNET** www.france.diplomatie.fr

## Chopra, Deepak

948 Granvis Altamira
Palos Verdes, CA 90274
*Author*

## Chow, Amy

c/o W Valley Gymnastic School
1190 Del Ave., #1
Campbell, AZ 95008
*Gymnast*

## Chubb

15 Mountain View Road
Warren, NJ 07061
*P & C insurance*

**INTERNET** www.chubb.com
John Finnegan, CEO

## Church, Charlotte

10 Great Marlborough St.
London W1F7LP
England
UNITED KINGDOM
*Singer*

**INTERNET** www.charlottechurch.com

## Cigna

1 Liberty Place
Philadelphia, PA 19192
*Health and Life insurance*

**INTERNET** www.cigna.com
H. Edward Hanway, CEO

## Cincinnati Bengals

200 Riverfront Stadium
Cincinnati, OH 45202
*Football team*

**INTERNET** www.bengals.com

## Cincinnati Enquirer

312 Elm St.
Cincinnati, OH 45202

**VOICE** 513-768-6060

## Cincinnati Post

125 E Court St.
Cincinnati, OH 45202

**INTERNET** www.cincypost.com
**VOICE** 513-352-2000

## Cincinnati Reds

100 Cynergy Field
Cincinnati, OH 45202
*Baseball team*

**INTERNET** www.cincinnatireds.com

## Cinemax

1100 Ave. of the Americas
New York, NY 10036
*Cable network*

**INTERNET** www.cinemax.com

## Cinergy

139 E 4th St.
Cincinnati, OH 45202
*Gas and electric utilities*

**INTERNET** www.cinergy.com
James E. Rogers, Chairman

## Circuit City

9950 Maryland Dr.
Richmond, VA 23233
*The #2 U.S. retailer of major appliances and consumer electronics*

**INTERNET** www.circuitcity.com
W. Alan McCoullough, Chairman, President and CEO

## Cisco Systems

170 W Tasman Dr.
San Jose, CA 95134
*Electronics, network communications*

**INTERNET** www.cisco.com
John Chambers, President and CEO

## Citigroup

153 E 53rd St.
New York, NY 10043
*Gas and electric utilities*

**INTERNET** www.citigroup.com
Michael A. Carpenter, Chairman and CEO

## Citizen Action

1750 Rhode Island Ave. NW, #403
Washington, D.C. 20036
**INTERNET** www.fas.org

*A nationwide consumer and environmental organization that addresses issues on behalf of its members*

## Citizens Committee for the Right to Keep and Bear Arms

600 Pennsylvania Ave SE #205
Washington, D.C. 20003
**INTERNET** www.ccrkba.org
**E-MAIL** info@ccrkba.org

*Organization dedicated to preserving and protecting the Second Amendment*

## Citizens for a Sound Economy

1250 H St. NW, #700
Washington, D.C. 20005
**INTERNET** www.cse.org
Paul Beckner, President

## Citizens for Tax Justice

1311 L St. NW, #400
Washington, D.C. 20005
**INTERNET** www.ctj.org
**E-MAIL** mattg@ctj.org
Robert S. McIntyre, Director

## Citizen Information Center

380 A Ave., P.O. Box 369
Lake Oswego, OR 97034
**INTERNET** www.ci.oswego.or.us/citizen/citizen.htm

*Organization helping citizens of Lake Oswego, Oregon solve city-related problems*

## Citizens Against Government Waste

1301 Connecticut Ave. NW, #400
Washington, D.C. 20036
**INTERNET** www.cagw.org
**E-MAIL** webmaster@cagw.org

*A private, nonpartisan, nonprofit organization dedicated to educating Americans about the waste, mismanagement and inefficiency of the federal government*

## Citizens Commission on Civil Rights

2000 M St. NW, #400
Washington, D.C. 20036
**INTERNET** www.cccr.org
**E-MAIL** webmaster@cccr.org

*Established to monitor civil rights policies and practices of the federal government and to seek ways to accelerate progress in the area of civil rights*

## City Pages

P.O. Box 59138
Minneapolis, MN 55459
**INTERNET** www.citypages.com
**VOICE** 612-375-1015

## Clancy, Tom
P.O. Box 800
Huntington, MD 20639
*Author*

**E-MAIL** tomclancy@aol.com

## Clapton, Eric
46 Kensington Ct.
London NW1
England
UNITED KINGDOM
*Musician*

**E-MAIL** ericclapton@wbr.com

## Clark, Dick
3003 W Olive Ave.
Burbank, CA 91505
*Television host/producer*

**BIRTHDAY** 11/30/29
**INTERNET** www.dickclarkproductions.com

## Clark, Marcia
151 El Camino Dr.
Beverly Hills, CA 90212
*Prosecuter in the O.J. Simpson Trial*

## Clark, Mary Higgins
210 Central Park S
New York, NY 10019
*Author*

**INTERNET** www.roy-clark.com

## Clark, Roy
1800 Forest Blvd.
Tulsa, OK 74114
*Musician*

**BIRTHDAY** 8/16/33

## Clash, The
268 Camden Road
London W8 5DP
England
UNITED KINGDOM
*Music group*

## Clay, Andrew Dice
836 N La Cienaga Blvd.
Los Angeles, CA 90069
*Comedian*

## Clayderman, Richard
150 bd Haussmann
75008 Paris
France
*Musician*

**BIRTHDAY** 12/28/53

## Clean Air Trust
1625 K St. NW, #725
Washington, D.C. 20006
The Hon. Robert T. Stafford
*Environmental organization*

**INTERNET** www.cleanairtrust.org
**E-MAIL** frank@cleanairtrust.org

## Clean Water Action
4455 Connecticut Ave. NW, #A300
Washington, D.C. 20008

**INTERNET** www.cleanwateraction.org
**E-MAIL** cwa@cleanwater.org
The Hon. Robert T. Stafford, Hon. Co-Chair

*Organizes strong grassroots groups, coalitions and campaigns to protect our environment, health, economic well-being and community quality of life*

## Cleese, John
115 Hazlebury Road
London SW6 21X
England
UNITED KINGDOM
*Comedian/actor*

**BIRTHDAY** 10/27/39

## Cleveland Cavaliers
1 Center Ct.
Cleveland, OH 44115
*Basketball team*

**INTERNET** www.nba.com/cavs

## Cleveland Indians
2401 Ontario St.
Cleveland, OH 44114
*Baseball team*

**INTERNET** www.indians.mlb.com/NASApp/mlb/cle/ homepage/cle_homepage.jsp

## Cleveland Plain Dealer
1801 Superior Ave.
Cleveland, OH 44114

**INTERNET** www.cleveland.com
**VOICE** 216-999-4360

## Cleveland Sun Newspapers
5510 Cloverleaf Pkwy
Valley View, OH 44125

**INTERNET** www.sunnews.com
**VOICE** 216-986-2600

## Clinton, Hillary
476 Russell Senate Office
Bldg. (D-NY)
Washington, D.C. 20510
*Senator/former First Lady*

**INTERNET** www.clinton.senate.gov

## Clinton, Bill
15 Old House Ln.
Chappaqua, NY 10514
*Former President of the United States*

## Clooney, George
9830 Wilshire Blvd.
Beverly Hills, CA 90212
*Actor*

**E-MAIL** gclooney@aol.com

## Close, Glenn
9830 Wilshire Blvd.
Beverly Hills, CA 90212
*Actress*

**E-MAIL** alivealivealive@usa.net

## CMS Energy
Fairlane Plaza S, #1100
330 Town Center St.
Dearborn, MI 48126
*Gas and electric utilities*

**INTERNET** www.cmsenergy.com
Kenneth Whipple, CEO

## CNF, Inc.
3240 Hillview Ave.
Palo Alto, CA 94303
*Trucking*

**INTERNET** www.cnf.com
Greg Quesnel, CEO

## CNN
1 CNN Center
100 International Blvd.
Atlanta, GA 30348
*Cable network*

**INTERNET** www.cnn.com
**VOICE** 404-827-1500

## Coalition on Human Needs
1700 K St. NW, #1150
Washington, D.C.20006

**INTERNET** www.chn.org
**E-MAIL** chn@chn.org
Stuart P. Campbell, Executive Director

*An alliance of over 100 national organizations working together to promote public policies which address the needs of low-income and other vulnerable populations*

**Coastal**
9 Greenway Plaza
Houston, TX 77046
*Petroleum refining*

**INTERNET** www.coastalcorp.com

**Coca-Cola**
1 Coca-Cola Plaza
Atlanta, GA 30313
*Beverages*

**INTERNET** www.cocacola.com
Douglas N. Daft, Chairman and CEO

**Coca-Cola Enterprises**
2500 Windy Ridge Pkwy
Atlanta, GA 30339
*Beverages*

**INTERNET** www.cokecce.com
Lowry F. Kline, Chairman

**Cochran, Thad**
326 Russell Senate Office Bldg. (R-MS)
Washington, D.C. 20510
*Senator*

**E-MAIL** senator@cochran.senate.gov

**Cocker, Joe**
16830 Ventura Blvd.
Encino, CA 91436
*Singer*

**BIRTHDAY** 5/20/42

**Coe, David Allan**
P.O. Box 270188
Nashville, TN 37227
*Country music singer*

**INTERNET** www.officialdavidallancoe.com

**Coen, Joel**
9560 Wilshire Blvd., #516
Beverly Hills, CA 90212
*Film director/writer*

**Cohen, William**
The Pentagon
Rm 2E777, #1400
Washington, D.C. 20201
*Secretary of Defense*

**Cohn, Mindy**
4343 Lankershim Blvd., #100
Universal City, CA 91602
*Actress*

**BIRTHDAY** 5/20/66

## Cole, Natalie
1801 Ave. of the Stars, #1105
Los Angeles, CA 90067
*Singer*

**BIRTHDAY** 2/8/50
**INTERNET** www.nataliecole.com

## Coleman, Norm
U.S. Senate (R-MN)
Washington, D.C. 20510
*Senator*

**INTERNET** www.coleman.senate.gov/contact/index.cfm

## Coleman, Dabney
360 N Kenter
Los Angeles, CA 90049
*Actor*

## Colgate-Palmolive
300 Park Ave.
New York, NY 10022
*Soaps and cosmetics*

**INTERNET** www.colgate.com
Reuben Mark, CEO

## College Press Service
P.O. Box 2831
Orlando, FL 32802

**VOICE** 407-425-4547

## Collins, Jackie
1230 Ave. of the Americas
New York, NY 10020
*Author*

**BIRTHDAY** 10/4/41

## Collins, Joan
68 Old Brompton
London SW73L2
England
UNITED KINGDOM
*Actress*

**INTERNET** www.joancollins.net

## Collins, Phil
30 Ives St.
London SW32ND
England
UNITED KINGDOM
*Musician*

**INTERNET** www.philcollins.co.uk

**Collins, Susan**
172 Russell Senate Office
Bldg. (R-ME)
Washington, D.C. 20510
*Senator*

**E-MAIL** senator@collins.senate.gov

**Collins, Gary**
2751 Hutton Dr.
Beverly Hills, CA 90210
*Hockey player*

**Colorado Avalanche**
c/o McNicholas Sports Arena
1635 Clay St.
Denver, CO 80204
*Hockey team*

**INTERNET** www.coloradoavalanche.com

**Colorado Rockies**
13880 Dulles Corner Ln.
Denver, CO 80204
*Baseball team*

**INTERNET** www.coloradorockies.com

**Colombia (Republic of)**
Andres Pastrana Arango, Presidente
Casa de Narino, Carrera 8a. 7-26
Office of the President
Santa Fe de Bogota
Colombia

**INTERNET** www.presidencia.gov.co

**Columbia Energy Group**
13880 Dulles Corner Ln.
Herndon, VA 20171
*Gas and electric utilities*

**INTERNET** www.columbiaenergy.com

**Columbia State University**
P.O. Box 1333
Columbia, SC 29202

**VOICE** 803-771-8415

**Columbia/HCA Healthcare**
1 Park Plaza
Nashville, TN 37203
Healthcare

**Columbus Dispatch**
24 S 3rd St.
Columbus, OH 43215

**INTERNET** www.dispatch.com
**VOICE** 614-461-5000

## Colvin, Shawn
30 W 21st St., 7th Floor
New York, NY 10010
*Musician*

**BIRTHDAY** 1/10/58
**INTERNET** www.shawncolvin.com
**E-MAIL** webmaster@shawncolvin.com

## Comcast
1500 Market St.
Philadelphia, PA 19102
*Telecommunications*

**INTERNET** www.comcast.com
Ralph J. Roberts,Chairman

## Comdisco
6111 N River Road
CEO
Rosemont, IL 60018
*Computer and data services*

**INTERNET** www.comdisco.com
Ronald Mishler, Chairman, President and

## Comedy Central
1775 Broadway
New York, NY 10019
*Cable network*

## Comerica
Comerica Tower at Detroit
Center 500
Detroit, MI 48226
*Commercial bank*

**INTERNET** www.comerica.com
Ralph W. Babb, President and CEO

## Commissions on Presidential Debates
1200 New Hampshire NW
Box 445
Washington, D.C. 20036

**INTERNET** www.debates.org
**E-MAIL** webmaster@debates.org
Frank Fahrenkopf Jr., Co-Chairman

*Established in 1987 to ensure that debates, as a permanent part of every general election, provide the best possible information to viewers and listeners*

## Committee for a Responsible Federal Budget
220 1/2 E St. NE
Washington, D.C. 20002

**INTERNET** www.network-democracy.org
**E-MAIL** info@network-democracy.org

*A bipartisan, nonprofit educational organization committed to educating the public regarding the budget process and particular issues that have significant fiscal policy impact*

## Committee for Study of the American Electorate (aka Moving Ideas)

421 New Jersey SE
Washington, D.C.20003

**INTERNET** http://tap.epn.org/csae
Acacia Reed, Managing Editor

*A Washington-based, nonpartisan, nonprofit, tax-exempt research institution with a primary focus on issues surrounding citizen engagement in politics*

## Committee to Advocate Texas Sovereignty

5303 Allurn Road
Houston, TX 77045

**INTERNET** www.texassovereignty.org
**E-MAIL** jdavidson@cbjd.net
Jim Davidson, Co-Founder

*Organization that believes Texas should be sovereign and independent of the U.S.*

## Common Cause

1250 Connecticut Ave., NW
Washington, D.C. 20036

**INTERNET** www.commoncause.org
webmaster@commoncause.org
John Gardner, Founder

*A nonprofit, nonpartisan citizen's lobbying organization promoting open, honest and accountable government*

## Communications Briefings

1101 King St., #110
Alexandria, VA 22314

**INTERNET** www.combriefings.com
**VOICE** 703-548-3800

## Communications News

2500 TaMiami, Trail N.
Nokomis, FL 34275
*Newsletter*

**INTERNET** www.communicationnews.com
**VOICE** 941-966-9521

## Community Nutrition Institute

910 17th St. NW, #413
Washington, D.C. 20006

**INTERNET** www.communitynutrition.org/index,htm
**E-MAIL** rl@communitynutrition.org
Rodney E. Leonard, Founder

*A leading advocate for consumer protection food program development and management and sound federal diet and health policies*

## Community Relations Report

P.O. Box 924
Bartlesville, OK 74005
*Newsletter*

**INTERNET** www.jwcom.com
**VOICE** 918-336-2767

## Comoros
Azali Assoumani, President
Office of the President
B.P. 421
Moroni, Comoros

## Compaq Computer
20555 State Hwy, 249
Houston, TX 77070
*Computers and office equipment*
**INTERNET** www.compaq.com

## Compassion in Dying
PMB 415, 6312 SW Capitol Hwy
Portland, OR 97201
**INTERNET** www.compassionindying.org
**E-MAIL** info@compassionindying.org
Barbara Coombes- Lee, President
*An organization believing in the right to die with dignity*

## Competitive Enterprise Institute
1001 Connecticut Ave.
Washington, D.C. 20036
**INTERNET** www.cei.org
**E-MAIL** info@cei.org
Fred L. Smith, President and Founder
*A pro-market public policy group committed to advancing the principles of free enterprise and limited government*

## CompUSA
14951 N Dallas Pkwy
Dallas, TX 75240
*Computer retailers*
**INTERNET** www.compusa.com
Harold F. Compton, CEO

## Computer Associates International
1 Computer Associates Plaza
Islandia, NY 11788
*Computer software*
**INTERNET** www.cai.com
Sanjay Kumar, Chairman and CEO

## Computer Professionals for Social Responsibility
P.O. Box 717
Palo Alto, CA 94302
**INTERNET** www.cpsr.org
**E-MAIL** cpsr@cpsr.org
*A public interest alliance of computer scientists and others concerned about the impact of computer technology on society*

## Computer Sciences
2100 E Grand Ave.
El Segundo, CA 90245
*Computer and data services*
**INTERNET** www.csc.com
Van B. Honeycutt, Chairman

**Computer World**
500 Old Connecticut Path
Framingham, MA 01701
*Magazine*
**INTERNET** www.computerworld.com
**VOICE** 508-879-0700

**ConAgra**
1 ConAgra Dr.
Omaha, NE 68102
*Food producer*
**INTERNET** www.conagra.com
Bruce Rohde, President and CEO

**Concerned Women for America**
1015 15th St. NW, #1100
Washington, D.C.20005
**INTERNET** www.cwfa.org
**E-MAIL** webmaster@cwfa.org
Beverly LaHaye, Founder
*A national politically active women's organization promoting Christian values and morality in family life and public policy*

**Concord Coalition**
1819 H St. NW, #800
Washington, D.C. 20006
**INTERNET** www.concordcoalition.org
**E-MAIL** concord@concordcoalition.org
*A nonprofit, charitable organization for a strong economic future for all generations*

**Confederate Railroad**
*Country music group*
**INTERNET** www.confederaterailroad.net

**Congo**
Laurent Desire Kabila, President
Presidence de la Republique
Kinshasa
Democratic Republic of the Congo/Zaire
**INTERNET** www.rdcongo.org

**Congressional Accountability Project**
Connecticut Ave. NW, #3A
Washington, D.C.20009
**INTERNET** www.essential.org
**E-MAIL** cap@essential.org
*Congressional watchdog organization*

**Congressional Budget Office**
2nd and D St. NW
Washington, D.C. 20515
**INTERNET** www.cbo.gov
**E-MAIL** webmaster@cbo.gov
Douglas Holtz-Easker, Director
*Created by the Congressional Budget and Impoundment Control Act of 1974. CBO's mission is to provide the Congress with objective, timely, nonpartisan analyses needed for economic and budget decisions*

## Congressional Quarterly, Inc.

1414 22nd St. NW
Washington, D.C. 20037

**INTERNET** www.cq.com
**E-MAIL** webmaster@cq.com
Bob Merry, Chairman

*Congressional Quarterly is a world class provider of information on government, politics and public policy*

## Conlee, John

38 Music Square E, #117
Nashville, TN 37203
*Country music singer*

**INTERNET** www.johnconlee.com

## Conley, Earl Thomas

*Country music singer*

**INTERNET** www.earlthomasconley.com

## Combs, Sean, ("P Diddy")

1540 Broadway
New York, NY 10036
*Rapper*

## Connick Jr., Harry

323 Broadway
Cambridge, MA 02139
*Singer*

## Conrad, Robert

P.O. Box 5067
Bear Valley, CA 95223
*Actor*

**BIRTHDAY** 3/1/35

## Conrad, Kent

530 Hart Senate Office
Bldg. (D-ND)
Washington, D.C. 20510
*Senator*

**E-MAIL** senator@conrad.senate.gov

## Conseco

11825 N Pennsylvania St.
Carmel, CA 46032
*Health and Life insurance*

**INTERNET** www.conseco.com
Gary C. Wendt, Chairman and CEO

## Conservative Caucus

450 Maple Ave. E
Vienna, VA 22180

**INTERNET** www.conservativeusa.org
**E-MAIL** webmaster@conservativeusa.org
Howard Phillips, Founder and Chairman

*Dedicated to educating citizens about how we must take action to restore America to its constitutionally limited government*

## Consolidated Edison

**INTERNET** www.coned.com

4 Irving Place
New York, NY 10003
*Gas and electric utilities*

## Constantine, Kevin

**E-MAIL** coaches@mail.pittsburghpenguins.com

c/o Pittsburgh Penguins
Civic Arena, Gate 9
Pittsburgh, PA 15219
*Head coach of the Pittsburgh Penguins*

## Constantine, Michael

**BIRTHDAY** 5/22/27

1604 Bern St.
Reading, PA 19604
Actor

## Constitution Society, The

**INTERNET** www.constitution.org
**E-MAIL** webmaster@constitution.org

1731 Howe Ave., #370
Sacramento, CA 95825
*A private nonprofit organization dedicated to research and public education on the principles of constitutional republican government*

## Consumer Energy Council of America Research Foundation

**INTERNET** www.cecarf.org
**E-MAIL** webmaster@cecarf.org

2000 L St. NW, #802
Washington, D.C. 20036
CECA is committed to constructive involvement of government and private organizations in broad educational initiatives and in the creation of self-sustaining and socially responsible markets for essential services

## Consumer Federation of America

**INTERNET** www.consumerfed.org

1424 16th St. NW, #604
Washington, D.C. 20036
Founded in 1972 as a private, nonprofit, 501©(3) research and education organization to complement the work of Consumer Federation of America, the Foundation has a threefold mission: to assist state and local organizations, and to provide information to the public

## Consumer Product Safety Commission

4330 E W Hwy
Bethesda, MD 20814

## Consumers Union
101 Truman Ave.
Yonkers, NY 10703
*Its mission has been to test products, inform the public and protect consumers*

**INTERNET** www.consumersunion.org
**E-MAIL** webmaster@consumersunion.org
Jean Halwran, Director

## Contact Newsletter
500 Executive Blvd.
Ossining, NY 10562
*Newsletter*

**VOICE** 914-923-9400

## Continental Airlines
1600 Smith St., Dept. HQSEO
Columbus, OH 43228
*Airline*

**INTERNET** www.continental.com
Gordon M. Bethune, Chairman and CEO

## Coolio
6733 Sepulveda Blvd., #270
Los Angeles, CA 90045
*Rap singer*

**BIRTHDAY** 8/1/63
**E-MAIL** coolio@gangster.com

## Cooper, Alice
4135 E Keim Dr.
Paradise Valley, AZ 85253
*Rock singer*

**INTERNET** www.alicecooper.com

## Cooper Industries
600 Travis St., #5800
Houston, TX 77002
*Electronics and electrical equipment*

**INTERNET** www.cooperindustries.com
H. John Riley Jr., President and CEO

## Copperfield, David
11777 San Vincente Blvd., #601
Los Angeles, CA 90048
*Magician*

**BIRTHDAY** 9/15/56
**INTERNET** www.davidcopperfield.com

## Coppola, Francis Ford
916 Kearny St.
San Francisco, CA 94133
*Filmmaker and producer*

## Cops
2225 Colorado Blvd.
Santa Monica, CA 90404
Attn: Maria Jordon
*TV show*

**INTERNET** www.fox.com/cops

## CoreStates Financial Corporation (First Union/Wachovia)

1 First Union Center
301 S College St., #4000
Charlotte, NC 28288
*Commerical bank*

**INTERNET** www.corestates.com
Ken Thompson, Chairman and CEO

## Corgan, Billy

9830 Wilshire Blvd.
Beverly Hills, CA 90212
*Musician*

**BIRTHDAY** 3/17/67

## Corman, Roger

11611 San Vincente Blvd.
Los Angeles, CA 90049
*Country music singer*

## Cornelius, Helen

772 Parkview Dr.
Hollister, MO 65672
*Country music singer*

## Corning

1 Riverfront Plaza
Corning, NY 14831
*Building materials, glass*

**INTERNET** www.corning.com
James R. Houghton, Chairman and CEO

## Cornyn, John

Washington, D.C. 20510
U.S. Senate (R-TX)
*Senator*

**INTERNET** www.johncornyn.com

## Corporate Express

1 Environmental Way
Broomfield, CO 80021
*Specialist retailers of office products*

**INTERNET** www.corporate-express.com
Mark Hoffman, President and CEO

## Corporate Public Issues

207 Loudoun St. SE
Leesburg, VA 20175

**VOICE** 703-777-8450

## Corporation for National Service

1201 New York Ave. NW
Washington, D.C. 20525

**VOICE** 202-606-5000

**Corzine, Jon**
502 Hart Senate Office
Bldg. (D-NJ)
Washington, D.C. 20510
*Senator*

corzine.senate.gov/contact.cfm

**Cosby, Bill**
Box 808
Greenfield, MA 01301
*Comedian/actor*

**BIRTHDAY** 7/12/37

**Cosmopolitan**
224 W 57th St., 4th Floor
New York, NY10019
*Magazine*

**INTERNET** www.cosmopolitan.com
**VOICE** 212-649-2000

**Costco**
999 Lake Dr.
Issaquah, WA 98027
*Specialist retailers, warehouse*

**INTERNET** www.costco.com
Wei Ji Fu, CEO

**Costello, Elvis (Declan Patrick McManus)**
18 Green
Richmond Surrey TW91PY
England
*Musician*

**BIRTHDAY** 8/25/54
**INTERNET** www.islandrecords.com/elviscostello

**Costner, Kevin**
P.O. Box 2759
Toluca Lake, CA 91610
*Actor/director/producer*

**BIRTHDAY** 1/18/55

**Costa Rica**
Miguel Angel Rodriguez
Echeverria, President
Casa Presidencial, Oficinas Presidenciales
Apartado 520-2010 Zsapoto
San Jose
Costa Rica

**INTERNET** www.casapres.go.cr

**Council of Economic Advisers, CEA**
Room 314, Old Executive
Office Bldg.
Washington, D.C. 20501

## Council of Environmental Quality

Room 360, Old Executive Office Bldg.
Washington, D.C. 20501

## Council of State Governments

2760 Research Park Dr.
P.O. Box 11910
Lexington, KY 40578

**INTERNET** www.csg.org
**E-MAIL** web_editor@csg.org
Mike Huckabee, President

*Founded on the premise that the states are the best sources of insight and innovation, CSG provides a network for identifying and sharing ideas with state leaders*

## Council on Competitiveness

1500 K St. NW, #850
Washington, D.C. 20005

**INTERNET** www.compete.org
Deborah L. Wince-Smith, President

*Shapes the national debate on competitiveness by concentrating on a few critical issues*

## Council on Foreign Relations

58 E 68th St.
New York, NY10021

**INTERNET** www.cfr.org
Leslie H. Gelb, President

*Founded in 1921 by businessmen, bankers and lawyers determined to keep the U.S. engaged in global relations*

## Count Basie Orchestra

c/o Ted Schmidt
901 Winding River Road
Vero Beach, FL 32963

## Counting Crows

947 N La Cienega Blvd., #G
Los Angeles, CA 90069
*Music group*

**INTERNET** www.countingcrows.com

## Country Living

224 W 57th St., 2nd Floor
New York, NY 10019
*Magazine*

**INTERNET** www.countryliving.com
**VOICE** 212-649-3204

## Country Music Television

2806 Opryland Dr.
Nashville, TN 37214
*Cable channel*

**INTERNET** www.cmt.com

## Couric, Katie
NBC
30 Rockefeller Plaza
New York, NY 10122
*Broadcast journalist*

**BIRTHDAY** 1/7/57

## Court TV
600 3rd Ave., 2nd Floor
New York, NY 10016
*Cable network*

**INTERNET** www.courttv.com

## Covey, Stephen
*Author*

**INTERNET** www.franklincovey.com

## Cox, Courtney (Arquette)
400 Warner Blvd.
Burbank, CA 91522
*Actress*

## Cox, DeAnna
818 18th Ave. S
Nashville, TN 37203
*Country music singer*

## Craig, Larry
520 Hart Senate Office
Bldg. (R-ID)
Washington, D.C. 20510
*Senator*

**E-MAIL** craig.senate.gov/webform.html

## Cranberries, The
9255 Sunset Blvd., #200
Los Angeles, CA 90069
*Music group*

**INTERNET** www.cranberries.ie
**E-MAIL** cranberries@elive.ie

## Crapo, Michael
111 Russell Senate Office
Bldg. (R-ID)
Washington, D.C. 20510
*Senator*

**INTERNET** www.crapo.senate.gov

## Craven, Wes
11846 Ventura Blvd., #208
Studio City, CA 91604
*Author/film director*

**BIRTHDAY** 8/2/39

## Crawford, Cindy
1122 S Robertson Blvd., #15
Los Angeles, CA 90035
*Model/actress*

**BIRTHDAY** 2/20/66
**INTERNET** www.cindy.com

## Crawford, Michael
10 Argyle St.
London W1V 1AB
England
UNITED KINGDOM
*Singer*

**BIRTHDAY** 1/19/52

## Cray, Robert
76 Oxford St.
London WIN OAX
England
UNITED KINGDOM
*Musician*

**INTERNET** www.robertcray.com

## Creative Artists Agency
9830 Wilshire Blvd.
Beverly Hills, CA 90212
*Entertainment agency*

**INTERNET** www.caa.com

## Creative Loafing
750 Willoughby Way
Atlanta, GA 30312

**INTERNET** www.creativeloafing.com
**VOICE** 800-950-5623 x1060

## Croatia
Stipe Mesic, President
Predsjednicki dvori
Pantovcak 241
10000 Zagreb, Zagrebacka
Zupanija
Croatia

**INTERNET** www.predsjednik.hr
**INTERNET** www-admin@president.hr

## Cronkite, Walter
51 W 52nd St., #1934
New York, NY 10019
*Former news anchor*

**BIRTHDAY** 11/4/16

## Crosby, David
P.O. Box 9008
Solvang, CA 93464
*Musician*

**BIRTHDAY** 8/14/41
**INTERNET** www.crosbycpr.com

## Crosby, Norm
5750 Wilshire Blvd., #580
Los Angeles, CA 90036
*Comedian*

**BIRTHDAY** 9/15/27

## Crosby, Stills, Nash and Young
17325 Ventura Blvd., #210
Los Angeles, CA 90004
*Music group*

**INTERNET** www.csny.net

## Crow, Sheryl
10345 W Olympic Blvd., #200
Los Angeles, CA 90064
*Singer/songwriter*

**E-MAIL** sherylcrow@igamail.com

## Crowe, Cameron
9830 Wilshire Blvd.
Beverly Hills, CA 90022
*Director*

**BIRTHDAY** 7/13

## Crown, Cork and Seal
1 Crown Way
Philadelphia, PA 19106
*Metal products*

**INTERNET** www.crowncork.com
John W. Conway, Chairman and CEO

## Cruise, Tom
5555 Melrose Ave.
Hollywood, CA 90038
*Actor*

**BIRTHDAY** 7/3/62
**E-MAIL** tomcruise@scientology.org

## Crystal, Billy
860 Chautauqua Blvd.
Pacific Palisades, CA 90272
*Actor*

## CSI
c/o CBS Productions
CBS Television City
7800 Beverly Blvd., Room 18
Los Angeles, CA 90036-2165

## C-SPAN
400 N Capital St. NW
Washington, D.C. 20001
*Cable network*

**INTERNET** www.c-span.org

## Csupo, Gabor

6353 Sunset Blvd.
Hollywood, CA 90028
Rugrats *creator*

**INTERNET** www.klaskycsupo.com
**E-MAIL** recruitment@klaskycsupo.com

## CSX

James Center
901 E Cary St.
Richmond, VA 23219
*Railroads*

**INTERNET** www.csx.com
Michael J. Ward, CEO

## Cuba

Fidel Castro Ruz, President
Palacio de la Revolucion
Havana, Cuba

**INTERNET** www.cubaweb.cu

## Culinary Arts Institute of America at Greystone

2555 Main St.
St. Helena, CA 94574

**INTERNET** www.ciachef.edu
L. Timothy Ryan, President

*Offers continuing education and career development classes for food and wine professionals in highly focused formats*

## Culinary Arts Institute of Louisiana

427 Lafayette St.
Baton Rouge, LA 70802

**INTERNET** www.caila.com
Vi Harrington, Founder and Owner

## Culkin, Macaulay

9560 Wilshire Blvd., #516
Beverly Hills, CA 90212
*Actor*

**BIRTHDAY** 8/26/80
**E-MAIL** culkin@writeme.com

## Cummins Engine

500 Jackson St.
Columbus, IN 47202
*Industrial and farm equipment*

**INTERNET** www.cummins.com
Tim M. Solso, Chairman and CEO

## Curtis, Jamie Lee

1350 Ave. of the Americas
New York, NY 10019
*Actress/author*

**BIRTHDAY** 11/22/58
**E-MAIL** curtis@hotmail.com

## Curtis, Tony

P.O. Box 10397
Burbank, CA 91510
*Actor/singer*

**E-MAIL** Tony.curtis@tonycurtis.com

## Cusack, Joan
8500 Wilshire Blvd., #700
Beverly Hills, CA 90211
*Actress*

## Cusack, John
**BIRTHDAY** 6/28/66
321 N Clark St., #3400
Chicago, IL 60610
*Actor/producer*

## CVS
**INTERNET** www.cvs.com
Thomas M. Ryan, Chairman
1 CVS Dr.
Woonsocket, RI 02895
*Food and drug stores*

## Cypress Hill
**INTERNET** www.cypressonline.com
151 El Camino Road
Beverly Hills, CA 90212
*Music group*

## Cyprus
**INTERNET** www.pio.gov.cy
**E-MAIL** pioxx@cytanet.com.cy
H.E. Glafcos Clerides, President
Presidential Palace
Nicosia
Cyprus

## Cyrus, Billy Ray
**BIRTHDAY** 8/25/61
**E-MAIL** brcspirit@aol.com
P.O. Box 1206
Franklin, TN 37115
*Country music singer*

## Czech Republic
**INTERNET** www.hrad.cz
Vaclav Klaus, President
Office of the President of the C.R.
Hrad (Castle)
119 08 Praha 1
Czech Republic

## D'Abo, Maryam
9255 Sunset Blvd., #515
Los Angeles, CA 90069
*Actress*

## Dahl, Arlene
c/o Dahlmark Productions
P.O. Box 116
Sparkill, NY 10976
*Actress*

**BIRTHDAY** 8/11/28

## Daily Oklahoman
P.O. Box 25125
Oklahoma City, OK 73125

**INTERNET** www.oklahoman.com
**VOICE** 405-232-3311

## Daimler Chrysler
Epplestrasse 225
70546 Stuttgart
Germany
*Motor vehicles*

**INTERNET** www.daimlerchrysler.com
Elizabeth Wade, Sr. Vice President

## Dallas Cowboys
1 Cowboys Pkwy
Irving, TX 75063-4999
*Football team*

**INTERNET** www.dallascowboys.com

## Dallas Mavericks
c/o Reunion Arena
777 Sports St.
Dallas, TX 75207
*Basketball team*

**INTERNET** www.nba.com/mavericks

## Dallas Morning News
P.O. Box 655237
Dallas, TX 75265

**INTERNET** www.dallasnews.com
**VOICE** 1-800-925-1500

## Dallas Observer
P.O. Box 190289
Dallas, TX 75219

**INTERNET** www.dallasobserver.com
**VOICE** 214-757-9000

## Dallas Stars
211 Cowboys Pkwy
Dallas, TX 75063
*Hockey team*

**INTERNET** www.dallasstars.com

## Dalton, Lacy J.
820 Cartwright Road
Reno, NV 89511
*Country music singer*

**INTERNET** www.lacyjdalton.com

## Daltrey, Roger

18/21 Jermyn St., #300
London SW1Y 6HP
England
UNITED KINGDOM
*Musician*

**BIRTHDAY** 3/1/44

## Daly, Carson

c/o MTV
1515 Broadway
New York, NY 10036
*MTV VJ*

**E-MAIL** carson@carsondaly.com

## Damn Yankees

9977 Wilshire Blvd., #1018
Beverly Hills, CA 90212
*Music group*

## Dana

4500 Dorr St.
P.O. Box 1000
Toledo, OH 43697
*Motor vehicles and parts*

**INTERNET** www.dana.com
**E-MAIL** webmaster@dana.com
Joseph M. Magliochetti, Chairman, President and CEO

## Dana, Bill

21400 Grand Oaks Ave.
Techapi, CA 93561
*Comedian/actor*

## Danes, Claire

77 W 66th St.
New York, NY 10023
*Actress*

**E-MAIL** claire@clairedanes.com

## D'Angelo, Beverly

8033 Sunset Blvd.
Los Angeles, CA 90046
*Actress*

## Dangerfield, Rodney

10580 Wilshire Blvd., 21-E
Los Angeles, CA 90024
*Actor/comedian*

**E-MAIL** rodney@rodney.com

## Daniels, Charlie
17060 Central Pike
Lebanon, TN 37087
*Country music singer*

**E-MAIL** cdbfanclub@aol.com

## Daniels, Jeff
137 Park St.
Chelsea, MI 48118
*Actor*

## Danson, Ted
955 S Carillo Dr., #300
Los Angeles, CA 90048
*Actor*

## Danza, Tony
151 El Camino Dr.
Beverly Hills, CA 90212
*Actor*

**BIRTHDAY** 4/21/51
**INTERNET** www.tonydanza.com

## Darden Restaurants
5900 Lake Ellenor Dr.
Orlando, FL 32809
*Food producer*

**INTERNET** www.darden.com
Joe R. Lee, CEO

## Dark Horse Comics
10956 SE Main
Milwaukie, OR 97222

**INTERNET** www.dhorse.com
**E-MAIL** dhc@dhorse.com

## Daschle, Thomas
509 Hart Senate Office
Bldg. (D-SD)
Washington, D.C. 20510
*Senator*

**INTERNET** www.daschle.senate.gov/webform.html

## Dateline, NBC News
30 Rockefeller Plaza, Room 510
New York, NY 10112
*Television show*

**E-MAIL** dateline@news.nbc.com

## Dave Matthews Band
*Music group*

**INTERNET** www.davematthewsband.com
**E-MAIL** fanmail@davematthewsband.com

## Davis, Geena
9830 Wilshire Blvd.
Beverly Hills, CA 90212
*Actress*

## Davis, Gray
*Ex-Governor of California*

**INTERNET** www.gray-davis.com/
**E-MAIL** Governor@gray-davis.com

## Day, Doris
P.O. Box 223163
Carmel, CA 93922
*Performer*

## Day-Lewis, Daniel
23 E 22nd St., 3rd Floor
New York, NY 10010
*Actor*

## Days of Our Lives cast
3000 W Alameda Ave.
Burbank, CA 9152
*Soap opera*

**INTERNET** www.nbc.com/nbc/Days_of_our_Lives

## Dayton, Mark
346 Russell Senate Office Bldg. (D-MD)
Washington, D.C. 20510
*Senator*

**INTERNET** www.dayton.senate.gov/webform.html

## Dayton Daily News
45 S Ludlow St.
Dayton, OH 45402

**INTERNET** www.daytondailynews.com
**VOICE** 937-225-2000

## D.C. Comics
1700 Broadway
New York, NY 10019
*Publisher of* Superman

**INTERNET** www.DCcomics.com
**E-MAIL** DCwebsite@aol.com

## de la Hoya, Oscar
633 W 5th St., #6700
Burbank, CA 91523
*Boxer*

**INTERNET** www.oscardelahoya.com

## De Niro, Robert
c/o Tribeca Productions
375 Greenwich St.
New York, NY 10013
*Actor/producer*

**E-MAIL** robertdeniro@aol.com

## De Vito, Danny

600 N River Road
Culver City, CA 90232
*Actor*

## Dean Foods

600 N River Road
Franklin Park, IL 60131
*Food producer*

**INTERNET** www.deanfoods.com
Gregg L. Engles, CEO

## Death and Dignity Education Center

1818 N St. NW, #450
Washington, D.C. 20036
*Promotes a comprehensive humane, responsive system of care for terminally ill patients*

**INTERNET** www.deathwithdignity.org
**E-MAIL** admin@deathwithdignity.org
Robert W. Lane, Executive Director

## DeBakey, Michael

1 Baylor Plaza
Houston, TX 77030
*Heart surgeon*

## Dee, Sandra

18915 Nordhoff St., #5
Northridge, CA 91324
*Actress*

**BIRTHDAY** 4/23/42

## Deep Purple

Box 254
Sheffield S61dDF
England
*Music group*

## Deere

1 John Deere Place
Moline, IL 61265
*Industrial and farm equipment*

**INTERNET** www.deere.com
Hans W. Becherer, Chairman

## Dees, Rick

3400 W Riverside Dr.
Burbank, CA 91505
*Radio personality*

**INTERNET** www.rick.com

## Defenders of Wildlife

1101 14th St. NW, #1400
Washington, D.C. 20005

**INTERNET** www.defenders.org
**E-MAIL** webmaster@defenders.org
Winsone Dunn McIntosh, Chairman, Board of Directors

*Dedicated to the protection of all native wild animals and plants in their natural communities*

## Def Leppard

72 Chancellor's Road
London W6 9 QB
England
UNITED KINGDOM
*Music group*

**INTERNET** www.defleppard.com

## DeGeneres, Ellen

9560 Wilshire Blvd., 5th Floor
Beverly Hills, CA 90210
*Actress/comedian*

## Delaney, Kim

10201 W Pico Blvd.
Los Angeles, CA 90035
*Actress*

## Dell Computer

1 Dell Way
Round Rock, TX 78682
*Computers and office equipment*

**INTERNET** www.dell.com
Michael S. Dell, CEO

## Delta Airlines

1030 Delta Blvd.
CEO
Atlanta, GA 30320
*Airline*

**INTERNET** www.delta.com
Edward H. Budd, Chairman, President and

## Delta Car Rental

**INTERNET** www.deltacars.com
**VOICE** 1-800-423-0702

## Deluise, Dom

1186 Corsica Dr.
Pacific Palisades, CA 90272
*Actor*

**INTERNET** www.domdeluise.com

## Democratic Congressional Campaign Committee

430 S Capitol St. SE
Washington, D.C. 20003

**INTERNET** www.dccc.org
**E-MAIL** webmaster@dccc.org
Robert Matsui, Chairman

*Devoted to electing a Democratic majority in the House of Representatives*

## Democratic Freedom Caucus

P.O. Box 9466
Baltimore, MD 21228

**INTERNET** www.progress.org
**E-MAIL** romike@crosslink.net

*A "progressive libertarian" group within the Democratic Party*

## Democratic National Committee

430 S Capitol St. SE
Washington, D.C.20003

**INTERNET** www.democrats.org
**E-MAIL** webmaster@democratics.org
Terry McAuliffe, Chairman

*The national party organization for the Democratic Party of the U.S.*

## Democratic Senatorial Campaign Committee

430 S Capitol St. SE
Washington, D.C. 20003

**INTERNET** www.dscc.org
**E-MAIL** info@dscc.org
Jon S. Corzine, Chairman

*A national party committee formed by the Democratic members of the U.S. Senate to raise funds for Democratic U.S. Senate candidates throughout the country*

## DeMornay, Rebecca

1122 S Robertson Blvd.
Los Angeles, CA 90035
*Actress*

## Dench, Dame Judith

46 Albemarle St.
GB London W1X 4PP
England
UNITED KINGDOM
*Actress*

## Denmark

Queen Margrethe II
Hofmarskallatet
Det. Gule Palae
DK 1256 Copenhagen
Denmark

**INTERNET** www.kongehuset.dk

## Denver, Bob
P.O. Box 269
Princeton, WV 24740
*Actor*

**E-MAIL** bob@bobdenver.com

## Denver Broncos
13655 Broncos Pkwy
Englewood, CO 80112
*Football team*

**INTERNET** www.denverbroncos.com

## Denver Nuggets
1635 Clay St.
Denver, CO 80204
*Basketball team*

**INTERNET** www.nba.com/nuggets

## Denver Post
1560 Broadway
Denver, CO 80202

**INTERNET** www.denverpost.com
303-820-1010

## Department of Agriculture
14th St. and Independence Ave. SW
Washington, D.C. 20250

**INTERNET** www.usda.ogv
Ann Veneman, Secretary of Agriculture

## Department of Commerce
14th St. and Constitution Ave. NW
Washington, D.C. 20230

**INTERNET** www.doc.gov
Don Evans, Secretary of Commerce

## Department of Defense
The Pentagon
Washington, D.C. 20301

**INTERNET** www.defenselink.mil
Donald Rumsfeld, Secretary of Defense

## Department of Education
400 Maryland Ave. SW
Washington, D.C. 20202

**INTERNET** www.ed.gov
Ron Paige, Secretary of Education

## Department of Energy
1000 Independence Ave. SW
Washington, D.C. 20585

**INTERNET** www.doe.gov
Spencer Abraham, Secretary of Energy

## Department of Health and Human Services
200 Independence Ave. SW
Washington, D.C. 20201

**INTERNET** www.dhhs.gov
Tommy Thomson, Secretary of Health and Human Services

## Department of Housing and Urban Development

451 7th St. SW
Washington, D.C. 20410

**INTERNET** www.hud.gov
Mel Martinez, Secretary of Housing and Urban Development

## Department of Justice

950 Pennsylvania Ave. NW
Washington, D.C. 20530

**INTERNET** www.usdoj.gov
John Ashcroft, Attorney General

## Department of Labor

200 Constitution Ave. NW
Washington, D.C. 20210

**INTERNET** www.dol.gov
Elaine Chao, Secretary of Labor

## Department of the Interior

1849 C St. NW
Washington, D.C. 20240

**INTERNET** www.doi.gov
Gale Norton, Secretary of Interior

## Department of the State

2201 C St. NW
Washington, D.C. 20520

**INTERNET** www.state.gov
Colin Powell, Secretary of State

## Department of Transportation

400 7th St. SW
Washington, D.C. 20590

**INTERNET** www.dot.gov
Norman Mineta, Secretary of Transportation

## Department of the Treasury

1500 Pennsylvania Ave. NW
Washington, D.C. 20220

**INTERNET** www.ustreas.gov
John Snow, Secretary of Treasury

## Department of Veteran's Affairs

810 Vermont Ave. NW
Washington, D.C. 20420

**INTERNET** www.va.gov
Anthony Principi, Secretary of Veteran's Affairs

## Depeche Mode

P.O. Box 1281
London N1 9UX
England
UNITED KINGDOM
*Music group*

**INTERNET** www.depechemode.com

## Depp, Johnny
9560 Wilshire Blvd., #500
Beverly Hills, CA 90212
*Actor*

## Derek, Bo
3625 Roblar
Santa Ynez, CA 93460
*Model/actress*

**INTERNET** www.boderek.com

## Dern, Bruce
P.O. Box 1581
Santa Monica, CA 90406
*Actor*

## Dern, Laura
132 S Rodeo Dr., #300
Beverly Hills, CA 90212
*Actress*

**BIRTHDAY** 2/1/67

## Dershowitz, Alan
1563 Massachusetts Ave.
Cambridge, MA 02138
*Attorney*

## Des Moines Register
P.O. Box 957
Des Moines, IA 50304

**INTERNET** www.desmoinesregister.com
**VOICE** 515-284-8000

## Destiny's Child
9830 Wilshire Blvd.
Beverly Hills, CA 90212
*Music group*

**INTERNET** www.destinyschild.com
**E-MAIL** destinyschild@destinyschild.com

## Detroit Free Press
600 W Fort 321
W Lafayette Blvd.
Detroit, MI 48226

**INTERNET** www.freep.com
**VOICE** 313-222-6500

## Detroit Lions
1200 Featherstone Road
Beverly Hills, CA 90212
*Football team*

**INTERNET** www.detroitlions.com

## Detroit News
615 W Lafayette Blvd.
Detroit, MI 48226

**INTERNET** www.detnews.com
**VOICE** 313-222-2300

**Detroit Pistons**
Palace of Auburn Hills
2 Championship Dr.
Auburn Hills, MI 48057
*Basketball team*

INTERNET www.nba.com/pistons

---

**Detroit Red Wings**
600 Civic Center Dr.
Auburn Hills, MI 48057
*Hockey team*

INTERNET www.detroitredwings.com

---

**Detroit Tigers**
2121 Trumbull Ave.
Detroit, MI 48226
*Baseball team*

INTERNET www.tigers.mlb.com

---

**Deukmejian, George**
555 W 5th St.
Los Angeles, CA 90013
*Former Governor of California*

---

**Dewine, Mike**
346 Russell Senate Office Bldg. (R-OH)
Washington, D.C. 20510
*Senator*

E-MAIL senator_dewine@dewine.senate.gov

---

**Dewitt, Joyce**
101 Ocean Ave., #L-4
Santa Monica, CA 90402
*Actress*

BIRTHDAY 4/7

---

**Dey, Susan**
8942 Wilshire Blvd.
Beverly Hills, CA 90211
*Actress*

BIRTHDAY 12/10/52

---

**DeYoung, Cliff**
626 Santa Monica Blvd., #57
Santa Monica, CA 90401
*Actor*

---

**Diagnosis Murder cast**
10 Universal City Plaza
32nd Floor
Universal City, CA 91608
*Sitcom*

## Diamond, Neil
P.O. Box 3357
Los Angeles, CA 90028
*Singer*

**E-MAIL** fondclub@aol.com

## Diaz, Cameron
9465 Wilshire Blvd., #319
Beverly Hills, CA 90212
*Actress*

## DiCaprio, Leonardo
P.O. Box 7487
Burbank. CA 91510
*Actor*

**BIRTHDAY** 11/11/74
**INTERNET** www.dicaprio.com
**E-MAIL** webmaster@dicaprio.com

## Diffie, Joe
38 Music Square E., #300
Nashville, TN 37203
*Country musician*

**INTERNET** www.joediffie.com

## Digital Entertainment Network
2230 Broadway
Santa Monica, CA 90404

**INTERNET** www.den.net

## Dillards
1600 Cantrell Road
Little Rock, AR 72201
*General merchandisers*

**INTERNET** www.dillards.com
William Dillard, Chairman

## Diller, Phyllis
1635 S Rockingham Dr.
Brentwood, CA 90049
*Comedian*

## Dillon, Matt
9465 Wilshire Blvd., #419
Beverly Hills, CA 90212
*Actor*

**BIRTHDAY** 2/18/64

## Dion, Celine
4 Place Laval #500
Laval PQ H7N
Canada
Singer

**BIRTHDAY** 3/30/68
**INTERNET** www.celinedion.com

## Dior, Christian

St. Anna Platz 2
80538 Munich
Germany
*Designer*

**INTERNET** www.dior.com

## Dire Straits

72 Chancellor's Road
London W6 9RS
England
UNITED KINGDOM
*Music group*

## Direct Marketing Association

224 7th St.
Garden City, NY 11530
*Marketing website*

**VOICE** 516-746-6700

## Discount Store News

425 Park Ave.
New York, NY 10022
*Weekly online magazine*

**INTERNET** www.dsnretailingtoday.com
**VOICE** 212-371-9400

## Discovery Channel

7700 Wisconsin Ave.
Bethesda, MD 20814
*Cable network*

**INTERNET** www.discovery.com

## Disney Channel

3800 W Alameda Ave.
Burbank, CA 91505
*Cable network*

**INTERNET** www.disney.go.com

## Dixie Chicks, The

56 Lindsley Ave.
Nashville, TN 37210
*Country music group*

**INTERNET** www.dixiechicks.com

## Djibouti

Ismail Omar Guelleh, President
Presidence de la Republique
*Djibouti*

**INTERNET** http://amb-djibouti.org

## Dodd, Christopher
448 Russell Senate Office Bldg. (D-CT)
Washington, D.C. 20510
*Senator*

**INTERNET** www.Dodd.senate.gov/webmail/

## Doherty, Shannen
4000 Warner Blvd.
Burbank, CA 91522
*Actress*

## Dole, Elizabeth
U.S. Senate (R-NC)
Washington, D.C. 20510
*Senator*

**INTERNET** www.senate.gov/pagelayout/senators/one_item_and_teasers/dole.htm

## Dole Foods
1365 Oak Crest Dr.
Westlake Village 91361
*Food producer*

**INTERNET** www.dole.com
David H. Murdock, Chairman and CEO

## Dolenz, Ami
c/o Ami Dolenz Fan Club
1860 Bel Air Road
Los Angeles, CA 90077
*Actress*

**INTERNET** www.amidolenz.com

## Dolenz, Mickey
9200 Sunset Blvd., #1200
Los Angeles, CA 90069
*Musician/member of the Monkees*

**BIRTHDAY** 3/19/45

## Dollar Rent A Car
Car rental agency

**INTERNET** www.dollar.com
**VOICE** 1-800-800-4000

## Domenci, Pete
328 Hart Senate Office Bldg. (R-NM)
Washington, D.C. 20510
*Senator*

**E-MAIL** senator_domenici@domenici.senate.gov

## Dominica
Vernon Lorden Shaw, President
President's House
Roseau
Dominica

**INTERNET** www.dominica.dm

## Dominican Republic
Leonel Fernandez Reyna, President
Oficina del Presidente
Santo Domingo, Distrito Nacional
Dominican Republic

**INTERNET** www.presidencia.gov.do

## Dominion Resources Black Warrior Trust
901 Main St., 17th Floor
Dallas, TX 75202
*Gas and electric utilities*

**INTERNET** www.dom.com
Thos E. Capps, VP and Administrator

## Domino, Fats
5515 Marais St.
New Orleans, LA 70117-3340
*Musician*

## Domino's Pizza, LLC
30 Frank Lloyd Wright Dr.
P.O. Box 997
Ann Arbor, MI 48106
*Pizza*

**INTERNET** www.dominos.com
David Brandon, Chairman and CEO

## Donahue, Elinor
400 S Beverly Dr., #101
Beverly Hills, CA 90212
*Actress*

**BIRTHDAY** 4/19/37

## Donahue, Lisa
*Big Brother 3 Winner*

**INTERNET** www.cbs.com\bigbrother3

## Donaldson, Sam
425 Crest Ln.
McLean, VA 22101
*Commentator*

## Donner, Richard
9465 Wilshire Blvd.
Beverly Hills, CA 90212
*Film director*

## Doobie Brothers
15140 Sonoma Way
Glen Ellen, CA 95442
*Music group*

## Doodie.com
P.O. Box 93757
Los Angeles, CA 90093
*Tom Winkler, creator*

**INTERNET** www.doodie.com
**INTERNET** content provider

## Dorgan, Byron
713 Hart Senate Office Bldg. (D-ND)
Washington, D.C. 20510
*Senator*

**E-MAIL** senator@dorgan@senate.gov

## Dorn, Michael
9000 Sunset Blvd., #1200
Los Angeles, CA 90069
*Actor*

**BIRTHDAY** 12/19/52

## Douglas, Donna
P.O. Box 1511
Huntington Beach, CA 92647
*Actress*

**BIRTHDAY** 9/26/33

## Douglas, James
Vermont Governor
133 State St., Drawer 33
Montpelier, VT 05633-1901
*Governor of Vermont*

## Douglas, Kirk
c/o Bryna Company
151 El Camino Dr.
Beverly Hills, CA 90212
*Actor*

**BIRTHDAY** 3/17

## Douglas, Michael
P.O. Box 49054
Los Angeles, CA 90049
*Actor*

**BIRTHDAY** 9/25/44

## Dover
280 Park Ave.
New York, NY 10017
*Industrial and farm equipment*

**INTERNET** www.dovercorporation.com
Thomas L. Reece, Chairman, President and CEO

## Dow, Tony

4717 Van Nuys Blvd., #102
Sherman Oaks, CA 91403
*Actor*

## Dow Chemical Company, The

2030 Dow Center
CEO
Danbury, CT 06817
*Chemicals*

**INTERNET** www.dow.com
Bill Stauropoulos, Chairman, President and

## Downey Jr., Robert

20 Waterside Plaza, 28-D
New York, NY 10010
*Actor*

## Doyle, Jim

*Governor of Wisconsin*

**E-MAIL** wisgov@mail.state.wi.us

## Dr. Hook

9850 Sandalfoot Blvd., #458
Boca Raton, FL 33428
*Music group*

## Dramalogue

P.O. Box 38711
Hollywood, CA 90038
*Newspaper for actors*

## Dr. Phil Show

P.O. Box 1902
5482 Wilshire Blvd.
Los Angeles, CA 90036

## Dre, Dr.

10900 Wilshire Blvd., #1230
Los Angeles, CA 90024
*Musician/rapper*

**BIRTHDAY** 2/18/66

## Drescher, Fran

2400 Whitman Place
Los Angeles, CA 90068
*Actress*

## Dresser Industries
10777 Grogans Mill Road, #500
The Woodlands, TX 77380
*Industrial and farm equipment*

**INTERNET** www.dresser.com
David Norton, President and CEO

## Drew Carey Show cast
4000 Warner Blvd.
Burbank, CA 91522
*Television show*

## Dreyfuss, Richard
14820 Valley Vista Blvd.
Sherman Oaks, CA 91403
*Actor*

## Drifters, The
10 Chelsea Ct.
Neptune, NJ 07753
*Music group*

## Driver, Minnie
1122 S Robertson Blvd., #15
Los Angeles, CA 90035
*Actress*

**BIRTHDAY** 1/31/71

## Drug Policy Foundation
925 9th Ave.
New York, NY 10019
*An independent, nonprofit organization with over 20,000 members that publicizes alternatives to current drug strategies, DPF believes that the drug war is not working*

**INTERNET** www.drugpolicy.org
**E-MAIL** webfeedback@dpf.org

## Dryer, Fred
1700 W Burbank Blvd., #100
Burbank, CA 91508
*Actor/producer*

**INTERNET** www.fdprods.com

## DTE Energy
2000 2nd Ave.
Detroit, MI 48226
*Gas and electric utilities*

**INTERNET** www.dteenergy.com
Anthony F. Earley Jr., Chairman

## Duchovny, David
1122 S Robertson Blvd.
Los Angeles, CA 90035
*Actor*

**Duffy, Julia**
9255 Sunset Blvd., #1010
Los Angeles, CA 90069
*Actress*

**Dukakis, Olympia**
684 Broadway, #7-E
New York, NY 10012
*Actress*

**Dukes of Dixieland**
P.O. Box 56757
New Orleans, LA 70156
*Music group*

**Duke Energy**
422 S Church St.
Charlotte, NC 28202
*Gas and electric utilities*
**INTERNET** www.duke-energy.com
Richard B. Priory, CEO

**Dunaway, Faye**
2311 W Victory Blvd.
Burbank, CA 91506
*Actress*

**Duncan, Sandy**
61 W 90th St.
New York, NY 10024
*Actress*

**Dunne, Dominick**
155 E 49th St.
New York, NY 10024
*Author*

**Dunne, Griffin**
155 E 49th St.
New York, NY 10024
*Actor*
**BIRTHDAY** 6/8/55

**Dunst, Kirsten**
151 El Camino
Beverly Hills, CA 90212
*Actress*

## Duran Duran
9255 Sunset Blvd., #200
Los Angeles, CA 90069
*Music group*

## Durbin, Richard
332 Dirksen Senate Office
Bldg. (D-IL)
Washington, D.C. 20510
*Senator*

**E-MAIL** dick@durbin.senate.gov

## Duvall, Robert
P.O. Box 520
The Plains, VA 20198
*Actor*

**BIRTHDAY** 1/15/31

## Duvall, Shelley
Rt #1, Box 377-A
Blanc, TX 78606
*Actress/producer*

## Dylan, Bob
9200 W Sunset Blvd., #530
W Hollywood, CA 90069
*Musician*

## Dylan, Jakob
9200 W Sunset Blvd., #530
W Hollywood, CA 90069
*Musician*

## E!
5670 Wilshire Blvd.
Los Angeles, CA 90036
*Cable network*

## E.I. Du Pont de Nemours
1007 Market St.
Wilmington, DE 19898
*The largest chemical company in the U.S.*

**INTERNET** www.dupont.com
Charles O. Holliday Jr., Chairman and CEO

## Eagle Forum
316 Pennsylvania Ave., #203
Washington, D.C. 20003
*Stands for the fundamental right of parents to guide the education of their own children*

**INTERNET** www.eagleforum.org
**E-MAIL** eagle@eagleforum.org

## Eagles, The

9200 Sunset Blvd., #1000
Los Angeles, CA 90069
*Music group*

## Eagleton Institute on Politics

**INTERNET** www.rci.rutgers.edu
**E-MAIL** eagleton@rci.rutgers.edu

191 Ryders Ln.
New Brunswick, NJ 08901
*Develops new knowledge and understanding of emerging topics and themes in American Politics and government in order to encourage more responsive and effective leadership*

## Eakin, Thomas C.

**BIRTHDAY** 12/16/33

2728 Shelley Road
Shaker Heights, OH 44122
*Sports promotion executive*

## Earle, Steve

10355 16th Ave. S, #200
Nashville, TN 37212
*Country music singer*

## East Bay Express

**INTERNET** www.eastbayexpress.com
510-540-7400

P.O. Box 3198
Berkeley, CA 94703

## Eastman Chemical

**INTERNET** www.eastman.com
Brian Ferguson, CEO

100 N Eastman Road
Kingsport, TN 37660
*Chemicals*

## Eastman Kodak

**INTERNET** www.kodak.com
Daniel A. Carp, CEO

343 State St.
Rochester, NY 14650
*Scientific and photography equipment*

## Easton, Sheena

**BIRTHDAY** 4/29/59
**INTERNET** www.sheenaeaston.com
**E-MAIL** webmaster@sheenaeaston.com

3000 Paradise Road
Las Vegas, NV 89109
*Singer/actress*

## East Timor

Sergio Viera de Mello, Special Rep. of the Secretary
General for the East Timor
UNTAET/UN Transitional
Administration for East Timor Dili
East Timor

**INTERNET** www.un.org

## East-West Center

1601 E W Road
Honolulu, HI 96848

**INTERNET** www.ewc.hawaii.edu
**E-MAIL** ewcinfo@eastwestcenter.org
Dr. Charles Morrison, President

*The East-West Center is an internationally recognized education and research organization established by the U.S. Congress to strengthen understanding and relations between the U.S. and the countries of the Asia Pacific region*

## Eastwood, Clint

4000 Warner Blvd.
Burbank, CA 91523
*Actor*

## Eaton

Eaton Center
Cleveland, OH 44114

**INTERNET** www.eaton.com
Alexander M. Cutler, President and CEO

*Electrical power distribution and control equipment*

## Eban, Abba

P.O. Box 394
Hertzelia, Israel
*Israel Politician and Foreign Minister*

## Ebert, Roger

P.O. Box 146366
Carmel, CA 93921
*Movie critic*

## Ebony

P.O. Box 690
Johnson Publishing
Chicago, IL 60690
*Magazine*

**INTERNET** www.ebony.com
**VOICE** 312-322-9250

## E-Business

P.O. Box 429002
San Diego, CA 92142

**INTERNET** www.advisor.com
**VOICE** 858-278-5600

## Economic Policy Institute

1660 L St. NW, #1200
Washington, D.C. 20036
*A nonprofit, nonpartisan think tank that seeks to broaden the public debate about strategies to achieve a prosperous and fair economy*

**INTERNET** www.epinet.org
**E-MAIL** epi@epinet.org
Jeff Faux, President

## Ecuador

Gustavo Naboa, President
Palacio Nacional
Garcia Moreno 1043
Quito, Ecuador

**INTERNET** www.mmrree.gov.ec
**E-MAIL** webmast@mmrree.gov.ec

## Eden, Barbara

9816 Denbigh
Beverly Hills, CA 90210
*Actress*

**BIRTHDAY** 8/22/34

## Edge, The

30-32 Sir John Rogersons Quay
IRELAND
*Musician, member of U2*

## Edison International

2244 Walnut Grove Ave.
Rosemead, CA 91770
*Gas and electric utilities*

**INTERNET** www.edisonx.com
John E. Bryson, Chairman, President and CEO

## Edwards, Anthony

15260 Ventura Blvd., #1420
Sherman Oaks, CA 91403
*Actor*

## Edwards, John

225 Dirksen Senate Office Bldg. (D-NC)
Washington, D.C. 20510
*Senator*

**E-MAIL** edwards@senate.gov/contact.html

## Edwards, Blake

P.O. Box 491668
Los Angeles, CA 90049
*Director and producer*

## Eggar, Samantha
345 N Maple Dr., #302
Beverly Hills, 90210
*Actress*

## Eggert, Nicole
11360 Brill Dr.
Studio City, CA 91604
*Actress*

## Egypt
Mohammed Hosni Mubarak, President
Presidential Palace
Abdeen
Cairo, Egypt

**INTERNET** www.presidency.gov.eg
**E-MAIL** webmaster@presidency.gov.eg

## Ehrlich, Robert
Maryland Governor
State House
100 State Circle
Annapolis, MD 21401

## Eichhorn, Lisa
1501 Broadway, #2600
New York, NY 10036
*Actress*

**BIRTHDAY** 2/4/52

## Eisner, Michael
500 S Buena Vista St.
Burbank, CA 91521
*Entertainment executive*

**BIRTHDAY** 3/7/42

## Ekland, Britt
280 S Beverly Dr., #300
Beverly Hills, CA 90212
*Actress*

## Electra, Carmen
1122 S Robertson Blvd., #15
Los Angeles, CA 90035
*Actress*

## El Paso Natural Gas

1001 Louisiana St.
Houston, TX 77002
William A. Wise, Chairman
*Pipelines*

**INTERNET** www.elpaso.com

## Electric Light Orchestra

297-101 Kinderkamack Road, #128
Oradell, NJ 07649
*Music group*

## Electronic Data Systems

5400 Legacy Dr.
Plano, TX 75024
*Computer and data services*

**INTERNET** www.eds.com
Michael H. Jordan, Chairman and CEO

## Electronic Frontier Foundation

1550 Bryant, #725
San Francisco, CA 94117

**INTERNET** www.eff.org
**E-MAIL** eff@eff.org
Brad Templeton, Executive Director

*A nonprofit, nonpartisan organization working in the public interest to protect fundamental civil liberties, including privacy and freedom of expression in the arena of computers and the internet.*

## Electronic News

350 Hudson St., 4th Floor
New York, NY 10014

**INTERNET** www.electronicnews.com
**VOICE** 212-519-7685

## Elfman, Jenna

1608 N Cahuenga Blvd., #1271
Los Angeles, CA 90028
*Actress*

## Eli Lilly

7920 Sunset Blvd.
Indianapolis, IN 46285
*Pharmaceuticals*

**INTERNET** www.lilly.com
Sidney Taurel, Chairman, President and CEO

## Elizabeth II HM Queen

Buckingham Palace
c/o Private Secretary
SW1A 1AA London
England
UNITED KINGDOM
Queen of England

**INTERNET** www.royal.gov.uk

## Elizondo, Hector
15030 Ventura Blvd., #751
Sherman Oaks, CA 91403
*Actor*

## Elle
1633 Broadway
New York, NY 10019
*Fashion magazine*

**INTERNET** www.elle.com
**VOICE** 212-767-5800

## Elliott, Chris
151 El Camino Dr.
Beverly Hills, CA 90212
*Actor*

## Elliott, David James
28343 Ave. Crocker, Stage 1
Valencia, CA 91355
*Actor*

## Elliott, Sam
151 El Camino Dr.
Beverly Hills, CA 90212
*Actor*

## Ellison, Harlan
P.O. Box 55548
Sherman Oaks, CA 91423
*Science-fiction author*

## Elmo
1 Lincoln Plaza
New York, NY 10023
Sesame Street *character*

## El Salvador
Francisco Guillermo Flores Perez, President
Oficina del Presidente
San Salvador
El Salvador

**INTERNET** www.casapres.gob.sv
**E-MAIL** webmaster@casapres.gob.sv

## Elvira (Cassandra Peterson)
15030 Ventura Blvd., #1-710
Sherman Oaks, CA 91403
*Television personality*

## Elway, John
13655 E Dove Valley
Englewood, CO 80112
*Football player*

## Ely, Joe
P.O. Box 91479
Austin, TX 78709
*Country music singer*

## EMC
**INTERNET** www.emc.com
Mike Ruettgers, Chairman
35 Parkwood Dr.
Hopkinton, MA 01748
*Computer peripherals*

## Emerson Electric
**INTERNET** www.gotoemerson.com
David N. Farr, Chairman and CEO
8000 W Florissant Ave.
St. Louis, MO 63136
*Electronics and electrical equipment*

## Eminem
Shady Records
270 Lafayette St., #805
New York, NY 10012
*Rapper*

## Empower America
**INTERNET** www.empower.org
**E-MAIL** jeffk@empower.org
William J. Bennett, Co-Director
1701 Pennsylvania Ave. NW
Washington, D.C.20006
*Encourages public policy solutions that maximize free markets and individual responsibility*

## Encore
5445 DTC Pkwy, #600
Englewood, CO 80111
*Cable network*

## Energizer Holdings, Inc.
**INTERNET** www.energizer.com
J. Patrick Mulcahy, CEO
800 Chouteau Ave.
St. Louis, MO 63134
*The #2 battery maker in the U.S.*

## Engelhard
**INTERNET** www.engelhard.com
Barry W. Perry, Chairman and CEO
101 Wood Ave.
Iselin, NJ 08830
*Surface chemical company*

## England, Tyler
38 Music Square E, #300
Nashville, TN 37203
*Musician*

## Ensign, John
364 Russell Senate Office Bldg. (R-NV)
Washington, D.C. 20510
*Senator*

**INTERNET** www.ensign.senate.gov/contact_john/364 Russellcontactjohn_email.html

## Entergy
639 Loyola Ave.
New Orleans, LA 70113
*Gas and electric utilities*

**INTERNET** www.entergy.com
Robert V.D. Luft, Chairman

## Enterprise
*Car rental agency*

**INTERNET** www.enterprise.com
**VOICE** 1-800-325-8007

## Entertainment Media Ventures
828 Monraga Dr., 2nd Floor
Los Angeles, CA 90049
*Venture capital*

**INTERNET** www.emventures.com
Sanford R Climan, Founder

## Entertainment PR Newsletter
5928 Lindley Ave.
Encino, CA 91316

**INTERNET** www.westcoastpr.com
**VOICE** 1-888-WCPR-NEWS

## Entertainment Tonight
5555 Melrose Ave.
Los Angeles, CA 90038

**INTERNET** www.et.com
**VOICE** 213-956-4900

## Entertainment Weekly
1271 Ave. of the Americas
New York, NY 10020-1300

**INTERNET** www.entertainmentweekly.com
**VOICE** 212-522-1212

## Entrepreneur
2392 Morse Ave.
Irvine, CA 92714
*Online business magazine*

**INTERNET** www.entrepreneur.com
**VOICE** 949-261-2325

## Entwhistle, Vicky
Granada TV-Quay St.
Manchester M60 9EA
UNITED KINGDOM
*Actress*

---

## Environmental Defense Fund
257 Park Ave. S
New York, NY 10010

**INTERNET** www.edf.org
**E-MAIL** contact@environmentaldefense.org
Fred Krupp, Executive Director

*Representing 300,000 members, EDF combines science, economics and law to find economically sustainable solutions to environmental problems*

---

## Environmental Health Center-Dallas
8345 Walnut Hill Ln., #220
Dallas, TX 75231

**INTERNET** www.ehcd.com
**E-MAIL** cg@ehcd.com

*Diagnosis/treatment for individuals with allergy and environmental related illnesses*

---

## Environmental Law Institute
1616 P St. NW, #200
Washington, D.C. 20036

**INTERNET** www.eli.org
**E-MAIL** webmaster@eli.org
J. William Futrell, President

*Working to advance environmental protection by improving law, policy and management*

---

## Environmental Protection Agency
401 M St. SW
Washington, D.C. 20460

---

## Enzi, Michael
290 Russell Senate Office Bldg. (R-WY)
Washington, D.C. 20510
*Senator*

**E-MAIL** senator@enzi.senate.gov

---

## Equal Employment Opportunity Commission
1801 L St. NW
Washington, D.C. 20507

---

## Equatorial Guinea
Teodor Obiang Nguema
Mbasogo, President
Oficina del Presidente
Malabo, Equatorial Guinea

## ER cast
4000 Warner Blvd.
Burbank, CA 91522
*Television show*

## Eritrea Issalas Afwerki, President
Office of the President
P.O. Box 257
Asmara
Eritrea

**INTERNET** www.netafrica.org

## Ernesto, Zedillo
Ponce de Leon
*President of Mexico*

**INTERNET** www.presidencia.gob.mx

## Erving, Dr. J. (Julius)
P.O. Box 914100
Longwood, FL 32791
*Former basketball player*

## ESPN
935 Middle St.
Bristol, CT 06010
*Cable network*

## Esquire
1790 Broadway
New York, NY 10019
*Men's magazine*

**INTERNET** www.esquire.com
**VOICE** 212-459-7500

## Essence
1500 Broadway
New York, NY 10036
*Women's magazine*

**INTERNET** www.essence.com
**VOICE** 212-642-0700

## Estee Lauder
767 5th Ave.
New York, NY 10153
*Beauty products*

**INTERNET** www.elcompanies.com
Leonard A. Lauder, CEO

## Estefan, Gloria

555 Jefferson Ave.
Miami, FL 33139
*Singer*

## Estevez, Emilio

15030 Ventura Blvd.
Sherman Oaks, CA 91403
*Actor*

## Estonia

Lennart Meri, President
Weizenbergi 39, 15050
Office of the President
EE0100 Tallinn
Estonia

**INTERNET** www.president.ee
**E-MAIL** sekretar@vpk.ee

## Eszterhas, Joe

8942 Wilshire Blvd.
Beverly Hills, CA 90211
*Screenwriter*

## Etheridge, Melissa

1700 Broadway
New York, NY 10019
*Singer*

**BIRTHDAY** 5/29/61

## Ethics and Public Policy Center

1015 15th St. NW, #900
Washington, D.C. 20005

**INTERNET** www.eppc.org
**E-MAIL** ethics@eppc.org
Hillel G. Fradkin, President

*Studies the interconnections between religious faith, political practice and social values*

## Ethiopia

Dr. Nagaso Gidada, President
Office of the President
P.O. Box 1031
Addis Ababa
Ethiopia

## Eubanks, Bob

11365 Ventura Blvd., #100
Studio City, CA 91604
*Television game show host*

**BIRTHDAY** 1/8/38

## Eubanks, Kevin
c/o Tonight Show
NBC Entertainment
3000 W Alameda Ave.
Burbank, CA 91527
*Jay Leno's bandleader*

## Eure, Wesley
P.O. Box 69405
Los Angeles, CA 90069
*Actor*

## Eurythmics
19 Music #32 Ransomes
35-37 Parkgate
London SW11 4NP
England
UNITED KINGDOM
*Music group*

## Euthanasia Research and Guidance Organization
24829 Norris Ln.
Junction City, OR 97448
**INTERNET** www.finalexit.com
**E-MAIL** ergo@efn.org
John Neel, Producer
*Organization that believes in the right to die*

## Evangelista, Linda
2640 Carmen Crest Dr.
Los Angeles, CA 90068
*Model*

## Evans, Dwight
3 Jordan Road
Lynnfield, MA 01940
*Former baseball player*

## Evans, Linda
6714 Villa Madera Dr. SW
Tacoma, WA 98499
*Actress*

## Everett, Jim
P.O. Box 609609
San Diego, CA 92160
*Football player*

## Everhart, Angie
9000 Sunset Blvd., #506
West Hollywood, CA 90069
*Actress*

## Everly Brothers
P.O. Box 56
Dunmore, KY 42339
*Music duo*

## Evert, Chris
500 NE 25th St.
Wilton Manors, FL 33305
*Tennis player*

## Everybody Loves Raymond
CBS-TV
7800 Beverly Blvd.
Los Angeles, CA 90036
*TV show*

## Ewing, Patrick
2 Magic Place
8701 Maitland Summit Blvd.
Maitland, FL 32810
*Former basketball player*

## Exxon Mobil Corporation
5959 Las Colinas Blvd.
Irving, TX 75039

**INTERNET** www.exxon.mobil.com
Lee R. Raymond, President and CEO

## F.E.A.R.
P.O. Box 33985.
Washington, D.C. 20033

**INTERNET** www.fear.org
**E-MAIL** powerhit@fli.net
Robert Bauman, Member Board of Directors

*Forfeiture Endangers American Rights is a national nonprofit organization dedicated to the reform of federal and state asset forfeiture laws to restore due process and protect the property rights of innocent citizens*

## Fabares, Shelley
P.O. Box 6010 - 909
Beverly Hills, CA 90212
*Actress*

**BIRTHDAY** 1/19/42

## Fabio
6464 Sunset Blvd.
Hollywood, CA 90028
*Actor*

## Fahey, Jeff
8306 Wilshire Blvd., #438
Beverly Hills, CA 90211
*Actor*

## Fairchild, Morgan
**BIRTHDAY** 2/30/50
P.O. Box 57593
Sherman Oaks, CA 91403
*Actress*

## Falk, Peter
**BIRTHDAY** 9/26/27
100 Universal City Plaza
Universal City, CA 91608
*Actor*

## Falwell, Rev. Jerry
P.O. Box 6004
Forest, VA 24551
*Minister/Founder of the Moral Majority and Liberty University*

## Family Guy
4705 Laurel Canyon, 3rd Floor
Valley Village, CA 91607
*Television show*

## Fannie Mae
**INTERNET** www.fanniemae.com
Franklin D. Raines,Chairman and CEO
3900 Wisconsin Ave. NW
Washington, D.C. 20016
*The world's largest diversified financial company and the nation's largest source of home mortgage funds*

## Fargo, Donna
**BIRTHDAY** 11/10/45
P.O. Box 150527
Nashville, TN 37215
*Country music singer*

## Farina, Dennis
955 S Carrillo Dr., #300
Los Angeles, CA 90048
*Actor*

## Farm Credit Administration

1501 Farm Credit Dr.
McLean, VA 22102

## Farmland Industries

3315 N Farmland Trafficway
Kansas City, MO 64116
*Food producer*

**INTERNET** www.farmland.com
Albert J. Shivley, Chairman

## Fast Company

77 North Washington St.
Boston, MA 02114
*Magazine*

**INTERNET** www.fastcompany.com
**VOICE** 617-973-0300

## FasTV

5670 Wilshire Blvd., #1550
Los Angeles, CA 90036
*Interactive television*

**INTERNET** www.fastv.com
Prince Khaled Al-Nehyen, Chairman

## Favre, Brett

3071 Gothic Ct.
Green Bay, WI 54313
*Football player*

## Fawcett, Farrah

8271 Melrose Ave., #110
Los Angeles, CA 90046
*Actress*

## Federal Bureau of Investigation

935 Pennsylvania Ave. NW
Washington, D.C. 20535

**INTERNET** www.fbi.gov
**E-MAIL** webmaster@fbi.gov
Louis J. Freeh, Director of the FBI

## Federal Deposit Insurance Corporation

550 17th St. NW
Washington, D.C. 20429

## Federal Election Commission

999 E St. NW
Washington, D.C. 20463

**INTERNET** www.fec.gov
**E-MAIL** webmaster@fec.gov
Scott E. Thomas, Inspector General

*Administers and enforces the Federal Election Campaign Act*

## Federal Home Loan Mortgage

8200 Jones Branch Dr.
McLean, VA 22102

**INTERNET** www.freddimac.com
Leland C. Brendsel, Chairman and CEO

*A stockholder-owned corporation chartered by Congress in 1970 to create a continuous flow of funds to mortgage lenders in support of homeownership and rental housing*

## Federalist Society, The

1015 18th St. NW, #425
Washington, D.C. 20036

**INTERNET** www.fed-soc.org
**E-MAIL** fedsoc@radix.net
Eugene B. Myer, National Co-chair

*A group of conservatives and libertarians interested in the current state of the legal order*

## Federal Maritime Commission

800 N Capitol St. NW
Washington, D.C. 20573

## Federal Mediation and Conciliation Service

2100 K St. NW
Washington, D.C. 20551

## Federal Reserve System (FRS), Board of Governors

20th St. & Constitution Ave. NW
Washington, D.C. 20551

## Federal Trade Commission

Pennsylvania Ave. at 6th St. NW
Washington, D.C. 20580

## Federated Department Stores

7 W 7th St.
Cincinnati, OH 45202

**INTERNET** www.federated-fds.com
James M. Zimmerman, Chairman and CEO

*General merchandisers*

## Federation for American Immigration Reform

1666 Connecticut Ave. NW, #400
Washington, D.C. 20009

**INTERNET** www.fairus.org
**E-MAIL** info@fairus.org
Sharon Barnes, Chairman, Board of Directors

*A national, membership-based educational organization with 70,000 members across the country working to help the American public understand that our nation's immigration laws must be reformed*

**FedEx**
6075 Poplar Ave., #300
CEO
Memphis, TN 38119
*Mail, package and freight delivery*

**INTERNET** www.fedexcorp.com
Sharon Barnes, Chairman, President and

---

**Feiffer, Jules**
325 W End Ave., #12A
New York, NY 10023
*Political cartoonist*

---

**Feingold, Russell**
506 Hart Senate Office
Bldg. (D-WI)
Washington, D.C. 20510
*Senator*

**E-MAIL** russell_feingold@feingold.senate.gov

---

**Feinstein, Dianne**
331 Hart Senate Office
Bldg. (D-CA)
Washington, D.C. 20510
*Senator*

**E-MAIL** feinstein.senate.gov/email.html

---

**Felder, Don**
P.O. Box 6051
Malibu, CA 90265
*Musician*

---

**Feldman, Corey**
9100 Wilshire Blvd., #503E
Beverly Hills, CA 90212
*Actor*

---

**Felix the Cat**
12020 Chandler Blvd., #200
N Hollywood, CA 91607
*Cartoon cat*

---

**Fender, Freddie**
P.O. Box 530
Bel Aire, OH 43906
*Country music singer*

---

**Ferrell, Will**
30 Rockefeller Plaza
New York, NY 10112
*Actor/comedian*

## Ferrigno, Lou
P.O. Box 1671
Santa Monica, CA 90402
*Actor*

## Fields, Sally
12307 7th Helena Dr.
Los Angeles, CA 90049
*Actress*

**BIRTHDAY** 11/6/46

## Fierstein, Harvey
250 W 52nd St.
New York, NY 10019
*Actor*

## Fiji
Kamisese Mara, President
Office of the President
Government House
Suva
Fiji

## Finland
Paavo Lipponen, Prime Minister
Eduskunta
00102 Helsinki
Finland

**INTERNET** www.eduskunta.fin

## FirstData
5660 New Northside Dr., #1400
Atlanta, GA 30328
*Computer and data services*

**INTERNET** www.firstdatacorp.com
Charles E. Fote, Chairman and CEO

## FirstEnergy
76 S Main St.
Akron, OH 44308
*Gas and electric utilities*

**INTERNET** www.firstenergycorp.com
H. Peter Burg, Chairman and CEO

## Fishburne, Laurence
10100 Santa Monica Blvd.,
25th Floor
Los Angeles, CA 90067
*Actor/playwright*

**BIRTHDAY** 7/30/61

## Fishel, Danielle
2040 Ave. of the Stars
Los Angeles, CA 90064
*Actress*

**BIRTHDAY** 5/5/81

## Fisher, Amy
92-G-1794
3595 State School Road
Albion, NY 14411
*Newsmaker "Lolita"*

## Fisher, Carrie
1700 Coldwater Canyon
Los Angeles, CA 90212
*Actress/writer*

## Fisher, Frances
8730 Sunset Blvd., #490
Los Angeles, CA 90069
*Actress*

## Fisher, Joely
9171 Wilshire Blvd., #406
Beverly Hills, CA 90210
*Actress/singer*

## Fitzgerald, Peter
555 Dirksen Senate Office Bldg. (R-IL)
Washington, D.C. 20510
*Senator*

**INTERNET** www.fitzgerald.senate.gov/contact/contact_email.htm

## Flack, Roberta
1 W 72nd St.
New York, NY 10022
*Singer*

**BIRTHDAY** 2/10/39

## Flanery, Sean Patrick
8383 Wilshire Blvd., #444
Beverly Hills, CA 90211
*Actor*

**BIRTHDAY** 10/11/65

## Fleet Boston Financial Group
1 Federal St.
Boston, MA 02110
*Commercial bank*

**INTERNET** www.fleet.com
Charles K. Gifford, Chairman and CEO

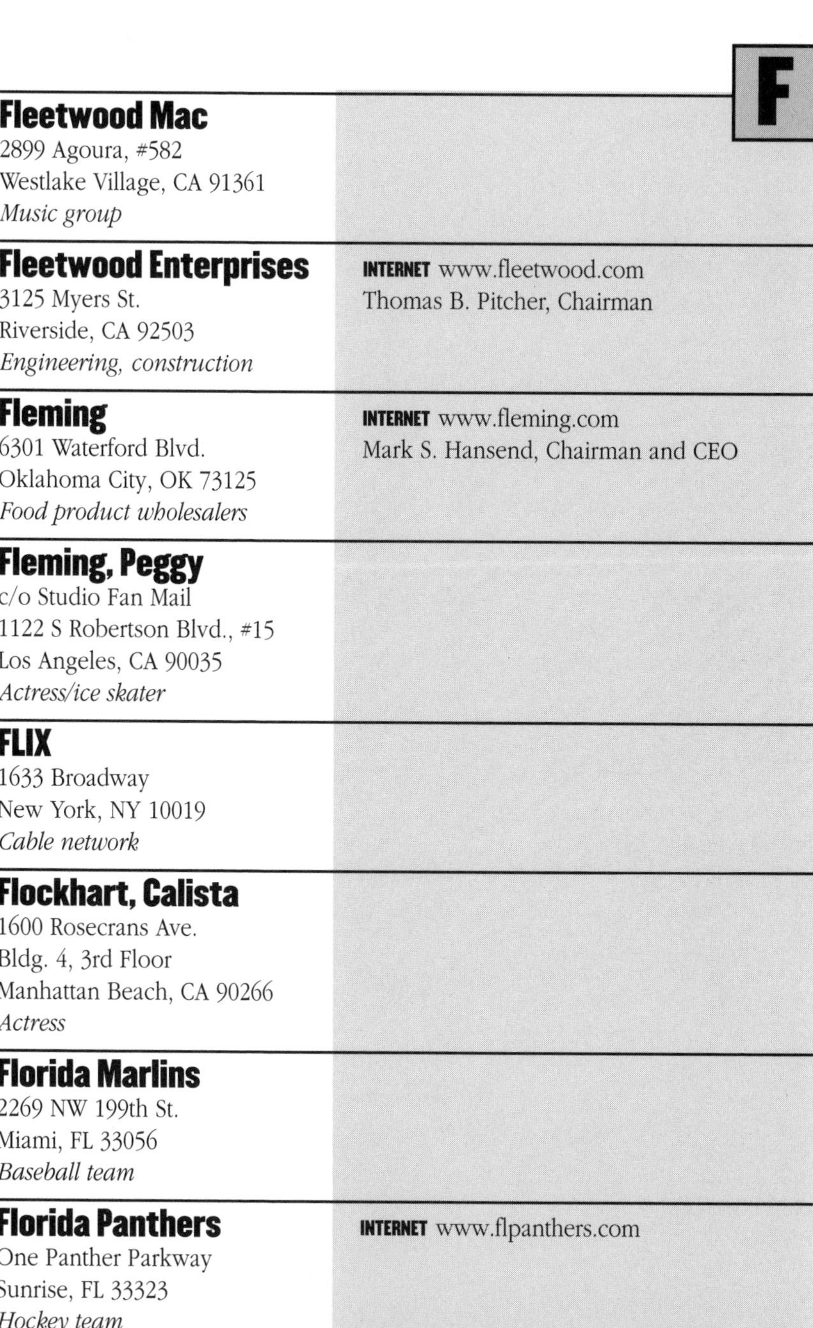

## Fleetwood Mac
2899 Agoura, #582
Westlake Village, CA 91361
*Music group*

## Fleetwood Enterprises
3125 Myers St.
Riverside, CA 92503
*Engineering, construction*

**INTERNET** www.fleetwood.com
Thomas B. Pitcher, Chairman

## Fleming
6301 Waterford Blvd.
Oklahoma City, OK 73125
*Food product wholesalers*

**INTERNET** www.fleming.com
Mark S. Hansend, Chairman and CEO

## Fleming, Peggy
c/o Studio Fan Mail
1122 S Robertson Blvd., #15
Los Angeles, CA 90035
*Actress/ice skater*

## FLIX
1633 Broadway
New York, NY 10019
*Cable network*

## Flockhart, Calista
1600 Rosecrans Ave.
Bldg. 4, 3rd Floor
Manhattan Beach, CA 90266
*Actress*

## Florida Marlins
2269 NW 199th St.
Miami, FL 33056
*Baseball team*

## Florida Panthers
One Panther Parkway
Sunrise, FL 33323
*Hockey team*

**INTERNET** www.flpanthers.com

## Florida Progress Energy
1 Progress Place
St. Petersburg, FL 33701
*Gas and electric utilities*

**INTERNET** www.progress-energy.com
William Cavanaugh III, Chairman, President and CEO

## Fonda, Jane

1050 Techwood Dr. NW
Atlanta, GA 30318
*Actress/fitness instructor*

## Fonda, Peter

RR #38
P.O. Box 2024
Livingston, MT 59047
*Actor*

## Fontaine, Joan

P.O. Box 222600
Carmel, CA 93922
*Actress*

## Foo Fighters

370 City Road
Islington
London EC1 V2QA
England
UNITED KINGDOM
*Music group*

## Food Research and Action Center

**INTERNET** www.frac.org
**E-MAIL** webmaster@frac.org

1875 Connecticut Ave. NW, #540
Washington, D.C. 20009
*Working to improve public policies to eradicate hunger and undernutrition in the U.S.*

## Forbes

**INTERNET** www.forbes.com
**VOICE** 212-620-2200

60 5th Ave.
New York, NY 10011
*Business magazine*

## Ford, Betty

P.O. 927
Rancho Mirage, CA 92270
*Former First Lady/founder Betty Ford Center*

## Ford, Faith

**BIRTHDAY** 9/14/64

9465 Wilshire Blvd., #820
Beverly Hills, CA 90212
*Actress*

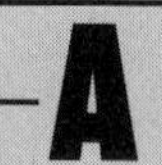

## Ford, Gerald
P.O. Box 927
Rancho Mirage, CA 92270
*Former President*

## Ford, Harrison
**BIRTHDAY** 7/13/42
P.O. Box 49344
Los Angeles, CA 90049
*Actor*

## Ford, Whitey
38 Schoolhouse Ln.
Lake Success, NY 11020
*Former baseball player*

## Ford Foundation
**INTERNET** www.fordfound.org
webmaster@fordfound.org
Paul A. Allaire, Chairman
320 E 43rd St.
New York, NY 10017
*Grant organization that supports activities that "strengthen democratic values, reduce poverty and injustice, promote international cooperation and advance human achievement"*

## Ford James Corp.
**INTERNET** www.fortjames.com
Miles L. Marsh, Chairman and CEO
1650 Lake Corp
Deerfield, IL 60015
*Forest and paper products*

## Ford Motor Company
**INTERNET** www.ford.com
William C. Ford, Chairman
1 American Road
Dearborn, MI 48126
*Cars and trucks*

## Foreman, George
4402 Waltham Ct.
Kingswood, TX 77345
*Boxer*

## Foster, Jodie
**BIRTHDAY** 11/19/62
8942 Wilshire Blvd.
Beverly Hills, CA 90211
*Actress/director*

## Fort Lauderdale Sun Sentinel
**INTERNET** www.sunsentinel.com
**VOICE** 954-356-4000
200 E Las Olas Blvd.
Ft. Lauderdale, FL 33301

## Florida Times-Union
1 Riverside Ave.
Jacksonville, FL 32202

**INTERNET** www.jacksonville.com
**VOICE** 904-359-4111

## Flowers, Gennifer
4859 Cedar Springs, #241
Dallas, TX 75219
*Newsmaker in relation to Bill Clinton*

## Fluor
1 Enterprise Dr.
Aliso Viejo, CA 92656
*Engineering, construction*

**INTERNET** www.fluor.com
Alan L. Boeckmann, Chairman and CEO

## Flynt, Larry
9211 Robin Dr.
Los Angeles, CA 90069
*Editor and creator of Hustler magazine*

## FMC
200 E Randolph Dr.
Chicago, IL 60601
*Chemicals*

**INTERNET** www.fmc.com
William G. Walter, Chairman and CEO

## Foch, Nina (Nina Consuelo Maud Fock)
P.O. Box 1884
Beverly Hills, CA 90213
*Actress*

**BIRTHDAY** 4/20/24

## Fogelberg, Dan
550 Madison Ave., 17th Floor
New York, NY 10022
*Singer*

**BIRTHDAY** 8/31/51

## Fogerty, John
7009 Penbroke Dr.
Franklin, TN 37069
*Singer/songwriter*

## Fonda, Bridget
9560 Wilshire Blvd., #500
Beverly Hills, CA 90212
*Actress*

## Fort Wayne Journal Gazette
600 W Main St.
Fort Wayne, IN 46802

**INTERNET** www.journalgazette.net
**VOICE** 219-461-8333

## Fort Worth Star Telegram
400 W 7th St.
Ft. Worth, TX 76102

**INTERNET** www.startelegram.com

## Fortune
Time Life Building
New York, NY 10020
*Business magazine*

**INTERNET** www.fortune.com
**VOICE** 212-522-1212

## Fortune Brands
300 Tower Pkwy
Lincolnshire, IL 60069

**INTERNET** www.fortunebrands.com
Norman H. Wesley, Chairman and CEO

*Leading U.S. producer of distilled products*

## Foster Wheeler
Perryville Corporate Park
Clinton, NJ 08809
*Engineering, construction*

**INTERNET** www.fwc.com
Raymond J. Milchovich, Chairman, President and CEO

## Foster Jr., Murphy J. "Mike"
*Governor of Louisiana*

**INTERNET** www.gov.state.la.us/contact2.htm

## Foundation for Biomedical Research
818 Connecticut Ave. NW, #303
Washington, D.C. 20006

**INTERNET** www.fbresearch.org
**E-MAIL** info@fbresearch.org
Michael E. Debakey, Chairman

*A nonprofit organization that focuses on the proper use of animals in medical research*

## Foundation for Economic Education
30 S Broadway
Irvington-on-Hudson, NY 10533

**INTERNET** www.fee.org
**E-MAIL** freeman@fee.org
Dr. Donald J. Boudreaux, President

*Nonpolitical, educational champion of private property, the free market and limited government*

## FOX
211 Ave. of the Americas
New York, NY 10036
*Television network*

Brian C. Mulligan, Chairman and CEO

## Fox Broadcasting Co.

**INTERNET** www.foxnews.com
310-203-3442

## Fox & Company, Inc.

34 Dale Road
Avon, CT 06001
*Marketing consultants*

**INTERNET** www.foxandcompany.com

## FOX Kids

P.O. Box 900
Beverly Hills, CA 90213

**INTERNET** www.foxkids.com

## Fox, Michael J.

9100 Wilshire Blvd., Floor 6W
Beverly Hills, CA 90212
*Actor*

**BIRTHDAY** 6/9/61
**INTERNET** www.michaeljfox.org

## Fox, Samantha

110-112 Disraeli Road
London SW1S 2DX
England
UNITED KINGDOM
*Singer*

## FPL Group

700 Universe Blvd.
Juno Beach, FL 33408
*Gas and electric utilities*

**INTERNET** www.fplgroup.com
James L. Cameron, Chairman and CEO

## France

M. Jacques Chirac, President de la Republique
Palais d'Elysees
55 et 57 rue de Faubourg
Saint-Honore
75008 Paris
France

**INTERNET** www.france.diplomatie.fr

## Franklin, Aretha

16919 Stansbury
Detroit, MI 48235
*Singer*

## Franz, Dennis

10201 W Pico Blvd., Bldg. 1
Los Angeles, CA 90035
*Actor*

## Frasier
c/o Paramount TV
5555 Melrose Ave.
Lucille Ball, Room 101
Hollywood, CA 90038
*TV show*

## Fred Meyer, Inc.
3800 SE 22nd Ave.
Portland, OR 97202
*Food and drug stores*

**INTERNET** www.fredmeyer.com
Susan M. Phillips, Chairman

## Freedom Forum
1101 Wilson Blvd.
Arlington, VA 22209

**INTERNET** www.freedomforum.org
**E-MAIL** news@freedomforum.org
Charles L. Overby, Chairman and CEO

*A nonpartisan, international foundation dedicated to free press, free speech and free spirit for all people; its mission is to help the public and the news media to better understand one another*

## Freedom Forum Media Studies Center
580 Madison Ave., 42nd Floor
New York, NY 10022

**INTERNET** www.mediastudies.org
Robert H. Giles, Director

*The Media Studies Center is the nation's premier media think tank devoted to improving the press and public's understanding of media issues*

## Fresno Bee
1626 E St.
Fresno, CA 93786

**INTERNET** www.fresnobee.com
**VOICE** 559-441-6111

## Freudenthal, Dave
*Governor of Wyoming*

governor@missc.state.wyus

## Friends
c/o Studio Fan Mail
1122 S. Robertson Blvd. #15
Los Angeles, CA 90035
*Television show*

## Friends Committee on National Legislation
245 2nd St. NE
Washington, D.C. 20002

**INTERNET** www.fcnl.org
**E-MAIL** fcnl@fcnl.org
Joanne Rains Warner, Chairperson

*A nationwide network of thousands of Quakers bringing the testimonies of "Friends" to bear on national legislation regarding peace and social justice issues*

## Friends of the Earth

1025 Vermont Ave. NW
Washington, D.C. 20005

**INTERNET** www.foe.org
**E-MAIL** foe@foe.org
Brent Blackwalder, Executive Director

*The largest international network of environmental groups in the world, representing 52 countries*

## Frist, Bill

416 Russell Senate Office Bldg. (R-TN)
Washington, D.C. 20510
*Senator*

frist.senate.gov/contact.cfm

## Fuel Cells 2000

1625 K St. NW, #725
Washington, D.C. 20006

**INTERNET** www.fuelcells.org

*A private, nonprofit, educational organization providing information to policy makers, the media and the public and supporting the early utilization of fuel cells by such means as pilot projects and government purchases*

## Fuentes, Daisy

12333 W Olympic Blvd.
Los Angeles, CA 90064
*MTV VJ*

## Fully Informed Jury Association

P.O. Box 59
Helmville, MT 59843

**INTERNET** www.fija.org
**E-MAIL** webforeman@fija.org

*A nonprofit association dedicated to the education of all Americans about their rights, powers and responsibilities as trial jurors*

## Fund for Animals

200 W 57th St.
New York, NY 10019
*Animal activist organization*

**INTERNET** www.fund.org
**E-MAIL** fundinfo@fund.org
Marion Probst, Chairman

## Fuhrman, Mark

P.O. Box 141
Sandpoint, ID 83864
*Criminal investigator/author*

## Funicello, Annette

16102 Sandy Ln.
Encino, CA 91416
*Actress/singer*

## Future of Freedom Foundation

11350 Random Hills Road, #800
Fairfax, VA 22030

**INTERNET** www.fff.org
**E-MAIL** freedom@fff.org
Jacob G. Hornberger, President

*Advances the libertarian philosophy by providing an uncompromising moral and economic case for individual liberty, free markets, private property and limited government*

## FX

P.O. Box 900
Beverly Hills, CA 90213
*Cable network*

## G, Kenny

9830 Wilshire Blvd.
Beverly Hills, CA 90212
*Musician*

## Gabon

El Hajd Omar Bongo, President
Presidence de la Republique
B.P. 546
Libreville
Gabon

**INTERNET** www.presidence-gabon.com

## Gabor, Zsa Zsa

1001 Bel Air Road
Burbank, CA 91505
*Actress*

## Gabriel, Peter

Box 35
Corsham
Wilshire London SW13 8SZ
England
UNITED KINGDOM
*Musician*

## Galavision

605 3rd Ave., 12th Floor
New York, NY 10158
*Cable network*

## Gambia
Yahya Jammeh, President
Office of the President
State House
Banjul
Gambia

**INTERNET** www.gambia.com

## Game Show Network
10202 W. Washington Blvd.
Culver City, CA 90232

John Calley, President

## Gannett
1100 Wilson Blvd.
Arlington, VA 22234
*Publishing and printing*

**INTERNET** www.gannett.com
Douglas H. McCorkindale, CEO

## Gap
1 Harrison St.
San Francisco, CA 94105
*Clothing retailer*

**INTERNET** www.gap.com
Paul S. Pressler, Chairman

## Garcia, Andy
1122 S Robertson Blvd., #15
Los Angeles, CA 90035
*Actor*

## Garner, James
33 Oakmont Dr.
Los Angeles, CA 90049
*Actor*

## Garner, Jennifer
4151 Prospect Ave.
Hollywood, CA 90027
*Actress*

**E-MAIL** jennifergarner@studiofanmail.com

## Garr, Teri
9150 Wilshire Blvd., #350
Beverly Hills, CA 90212
*Actress*

## Gates, Bill
1 Microsoft Way
Los Angeles, CA 90069
*Microsoft chairman*

## Gateway
4545 Towne Center Ct.
San Diego, CA 92121
*Computers, office equipment*

**INTERNET** www.gateway.com
Theodore W. Waitt, Chairman

## Gatlin Brothers, The
5100 Harris Ave.
Kansas City, MO 64133
*Music group*

## Gayle, Crystal
51 Music Square E
Nashville, TN 37203
*Singer*

## Gaynor, Gloria
P.O. Box 4172
Warren, NJ 07059
*Singer*

**BIRTHDAY** 9/7/48

## Gayoom, Maumoon Abdul
Maldives
*His Excellency the President*

**INTERNET** www.maldives-info.com
**E-MAIL** admin@foreign.gov.mv

## Gellar, Sarah Michelle
1122 S Robertson
Los Angeles, CA 90035
*Actress*

**BIRTHDAY** 4/14/77

## GenAmerica Corporation
700 Market St.
St. Louis, MO 63101
*Health and Life insurance*

**INTERNET** www.genamerica.com

## General Dynamics
3190 Fairview Park Dr.
Falls Church, VA 22042
*Aerospace*

Nicholas D. Chabraja, Chairman and CEO

## General Electric
3135 Easton Turnpike
Fairfield, CT 06451
*Electrical equipment company*

**INTERNET** www.ge.com
Jeffrey I. Immelt, Chairman and CEO

## General Mills
1 General Mills Blvd.
Minneapolis, MN 55426
*Food producer*

**INTERNET** www.generalmills.com

## General Services Administration
General Services Bldg.
18th & F St. NW
Washington, D.C. 20405

## Gentleman's Quarterly (GQ)
350 Madison Ave.
New York, NY 10017
*Men's fashion magazine*

**INTERNET** www.gq.com
**VOICE** 212-880-7901

## Genuine Parts
2999 Circle 75 Pkwy
Atlanta, GA 30339
*Automobile parts wholesalers*

**INTERNET** www.genpt.com
Larry L. Prince, Chairman and CEO

## Georgia
Eduard Shevardnadze,
Chairman, State Council
Plekhanova 103
Tbilisi 880064
Georgia

**INTERNET** www.presidpress.gov.ge

## Georgia-Pacific
133 Peachtree St. NE
Atlanta, GA 30303
*Forest and paper products*

**INTERNET** www.gp.com
A.D. Correll, Chairman, President and CEO

## Germany
Johannes Rau
Bundespraesident
Bundespraesidialamt
Schloss Believue, Spreeweg 1
10557 Berlin
Germany

**INTERNET** www.bundespraesident.de

## Germond, Jack
1627 K St. NW, #1100
Washington, D.C. 20006
*Newspaper columnist*

G

## GeRue, Gene "Bumpy"
HC78, Box 1105
Zanoni, MO 65784
*Author*

**INTERNET** www.ruralize.com
**E-MAIL** genegerue@ruralize.com

## Ghana
Jerry Rawlings, President
Office of the Head of State
The Castle
Accra, Greater Accra
Ghana

**INTERNET** www.ghana.gov.gh

## Giant Food
6300 Sheriff Road
Landover, MD 20785
*Food and drug stores*

**INTERNET** www.giantfood.com
Richard Baird, Chairman, President and CEO

## Gibbons, Leeza
1760 Courtney Ave.
Los Angeles, CA 90046
*Talk show host*

## Gibson, Debbie
254 W 54th St.
New York, NY 10019
*Singer/Broadway performer*

## Gibson, Mel
8942 Wilshire Blvd., #219
Los Angeles, CA 90211-1934
*Actor*

## Gilbert, Melissa
P.O. Box 57593
Sherman Oaks, CA 91413
*Actress*

## Gill, Vince
9 Music Sq., #214
Nashville, TN 37203
*Country music singer*

## Gillette
Prudential Tower Bldg.
Boston, MA 02199
*Metal products*

James M. Kilts, Chairman and CEO

| | |
|---|---|
| **Gilmore, Jim**<br>*Governor of Virginia* | **INTERNET** www.state.va.us/<br>governor/govmail.htm |
| **Gin Blossoms**<br>151 El Camino Dr.<br>Beverly Hills, CA 90212<br>*Music group* | |
| **Glover, Danny**<br>5555 Melrose Ave., #114<br>San Francisco, CA 94104 - 4903<br>*Actor* | |
| **Goldberg, Whoopi**<br>9171 Wilshire Blvd., #300<br>Beverly Hills, CA 90210<br>*Actress/comedian* | |
| **Golden West Financial Corp**<br>1901 Harrison St.<br>Oakland, CA 94612<br>*Savings institute* | **INTERNET** www.worldsavings.com<br>Herbert M. Sandler, Co-Chairman and Co-CEO |
| **Golf Channel, The**<br>7580 Commerce Dr.<br>Orlando, FL 32819<br>*Cable network* | |
| **Good Morning America**<br>1965 Broadway<br>New York, NY 10023 | **INTERNET** www.abcnews.com<br>**VOICE** 212-496-4803 |
| **Goodman, John**<br>15030 Ventura Blvd.<br>Sherman Oaks, CA 91403<br>*Actor* | |
| **Goodyear Tire and Rubber**<br>1144 E Market St.<br>Akron, OH 44316<br>*Rubber and plastic products* | **INTERNET** www.goodyear.com<br>Samir G. Gibara, Chairman, President and CEO |

## Gottfried, Gilbert
1230 Ave. of the Americas
New York, NY 10020
*Comedian*

## Gourmet
4 Times Square
New York, NY 10036
*Magazine*

**INTERNET** www.gourmet.com
**VOICE** 212-371-1330

## Grace Company, The
829 Langdon Ct.
Rochester Hills, MI 48307
*Entertainment agency*

## Graham, Bob
524 Hart Senate Office Bldg. (D-FL)
Washington, D.C. 20510
*Senator*

**E-MAIL** bob_graham@graham.senate.gov

## Graham, Lindsey
U.S. Senate (R-SC)
Washington, D.C. 20510
*Senator*

**INTERNET** www.lgraham.senate.gov/email/email.htm

## Grand Rapids Press
155 Michigan St. NW
Grand Rapids, MI 49503

**INTERNET** www.mlive.com
**VOICE** 616-459-1400

## Granholm, Jennifer
*Governor of Michigan*

**INTERNET** www.migov.state.mi.us/gov/contactgovernor.shtm

## Grant, Amy
c/o Friends Of Amy
9 Music Square, #214
Nashville, TN 37203 - 3203
*Singer*

**E-MAIL** lorimc4foa@aol.com

## Grassley, Chuck
135 Hart Senate Office Bldg. (R-IA)
Washington, D.C. 20510
*Senator*

**INTERNET** www.grassley.senate.gov/webform.htm

## Graves, Peter
9777 Wilshire Blvd., #815
Beverly Hills, CA 90212
*Actor*

## Gray, Erin
11288 Ventura Blvd.
Studio City, CA 91604
*Actress*

## Gray, Linda
1680 N Vine St., #617
Hollywood, CA 90028
*Actress*

## Gray Panthers
733 15th St. NW, #437
Washington, D.C. 20005
*Founded in 1970 by social activist Maggie Kuhn, Gray Panthers believe that all Americans should benefit from our country's abundance*

**INTERNET** www.graypanthers.org

## Graybar Electric
34 N Meramec Ave.
St. Louis, MO 63105
*Wholesaler*

Carl L. Hall, President and CEO

## Greece
Mr. Constantinos Stephanopoulos, President
Presidential Mansion
7 Vas. Georgious St.
106 74 Athens
Greece

## Greenday
5337 College Ave., #555
Oakland, CA 94618
*Music group*

## Greenland
Prime Minister
Gronlands Hjemmestyre
Post Box 1015
DK-3900 Nuuk/godthab
Greenland

**INTERNET** www.gh.gl
**E-MAIL** homerule@gh.gl

## Greenpeace

702 H St. NW
Washington, D.C. 20001
*Worldwide environmental group*

**INTERNET** www.greenpeaceusa.org

## Greens/Green Party Usa

P.O. Box 1134
Lawrence, MA 01842
*Environmental political party*

**INTERNET** www.greenparty.org
**E-MAIL** andyg@greens.org

## Gregg, Judd

393 Russell Senate Office
Bldg. (R-NH)
Washington, D.C. 20510
*Senator*

**E-MAIL** mailbox@gregg.senate.gov

## Grenada

Keith Mitchell, Prime Minister
Parliament
St. George's
Grenada

## Griffith, Melanie

201 S Rockingham Ave.
Los Angeles, CA 90049
*Actress*

## Grisham, John

P.O. Box 2400
Oxford, MS 38655
*Author*

## Grossman Larry & Assoc.

211 S Beverly Dr., #206
Beverly Hills, CA 90212
*Literary agency*

## Guardian Life Insurance Co. of America

7 Hanover Square
New York, NY 10004
*Health and Life insurance*

**INTERNET** www.glic.com

## Guatemala

Alfonso Portillo Cabrera, President
Palacio Nacional, Nivel 2
6 Calle entre 6 y 7 Avenida
Zona 1
01001 Guatemala Ciudad
Guatemala

**INTERNET** www.concyt.gob.gt

## Guccione, Bob

11 Penn Plaza, 12th Floor
New York, NY 10001
*Magazine publisher*

## Guess Who

1808 W End Ave., #1009
Nashville, TN 37203
*Music group*

## Guinea

Lansana Conte, President
Brigadeer General
Office du President
State House
Conakry
Guinea

**INTERNET** www.guinea.gov.gn

## Guinn, Kenny

*Governor of Nevada*

**INTERNET** www.state.nv.us/gov/mailgov.htm

## Gun Owners of America

8001 Forbes Place, #102
Springfield, VA 22151
*Group devoted to protecting the Second Amendment*

**INTERNET** www.gunowners.org
**E-MAIL** goamail@gunowners.org

## Guns 'N Roses

63 Main St.
Cold Springs, NY 10518
*Music group*

## Guttenberg, Steve

15237 Sunset Blvd., #48
Pacific Palisades, CA 90272
*Actor/producer*

## Guyana
Bharrat Jagdeo, President
Office of the President
New Garden St. and South Road
Georgetown
Guyana

## H. John Heinz III Center for Science, Economics and the Environment
1001 Pennsylvania Ave. NW, #735 S
Washington, D.C. 20004
*A nonprofit organization devoted to collaborative research on environmental problems*

**INTERNET** www.heinzctr.org
**E-MAIL** info@heinzctr.org
Thomas E. Lovejoy, President

## H.J. Heinz
600 Grant St.
Pittsburgh, PA 15219
*Food producer*

**INTERNET** www.heinz.com
William R. Johnson, President and CEO

## Hackman, Gene
118 S Beverly Dr., #1201
Beverly Hills, CA 90212
*Actor*

**BIRTHDAY** 1/30/30

## Hagar, Sammy
P.O. Box 5395
Novato, CA 94948
*Musician*

## Hagel, Chuck
248 Russell Senate Office Bldg. (R-NE)
Washington, D.C. 20510
*Senator*

**E-MAIL** chuck_hagel@hagel.senate.gov

## Haiti
Rene Preval, President
Palais National, Champ de Mars
Port au France
Haiti

**INTERNET** www.haitifocus.com

## Halliburton
3600 Lincoln Plaza
Dallas, TX 75201
*The world's #1 provider of oil field services*

**INTERNET** www.halliburton.com
Robert L. Crandall, Chairman

**Hamill, Mark**
10635 Santa Monica Blvd., #130
Los Angeles, CA 90025
*Actor*

**Hamilton, George**
139 S Beverly Dr., #330
Beverly Hills, CA 90212
*Actor*

**Hamilton, Scott**
20 1st St.
Colorado Springs, CO 80909
*Figure skater*

**Handgun Control, Inc.**
1225 Eye St. NW, #1100
Washington, D.C. 20005
*Gun control organization*
**INTERNET** www.handguncontrol.org
**E-MAIL** webmaster@handguncontrol.org
Sarah Brady, Chairman

**Hanks, Tom**
9830 Wilshire Blvd.
Beverly Hills, CA 90212
*Actor*
**E-MAIL** ny122@aol.com

**Hannaford Bros. (subsidiary of Delhaize America)**
145 Pleasant Hill Road
Scarborough, ME 04074
*Food and drug stores*
**INTERNET** www.hannaford.com
Hugh Farrington, Chairman

**Hannah, Daryl**
1465 Lindacrest Dr.
Beverly Hills, CA 90211
*Actress*

**Harald V**
*King of Norway*
**INTERNET** www.kongehuset.no

**Harcourt Education**
6277 Sea Harbor Dr.
Orlando, FL 32887
*Educational Publishers*

## Harkin, Tom
731 Hart Senate Office
Bldg. (D-IA)
Washington, D.C. 20510
*Senator*

**E-MAIL** tom_harkin@harkin.senate.gov

## Harnischfeger Ind. (subsidiary of Joy Global)
3600 S Lake Dr.
St. Francis, WI 53235
*Industrial and farm equipment*

**INTERNET** www.harnischfeger.com
John N. Hanson, CEO

## HarperCollins Publishers
10 E 53rd St.
New York, NY 10022
*Book publisher*

**INTERNET** www.harpercollins.com

## Harper's Bazaar
1700 Broadway
New York, NY 10019

**INTERNET** www.harpersbazaar.com
**VOICE** 212-903-5000

## Harrelson, Woody
9830 Wilshire Blvd.
Beverly Hills, CA 90212
*Actor*

## Harris
1025 W NASA Blvd.
Melbourne, FL 31919
*Electronics and electrical equipment*

**INTERNET** www.harris.com
Howard L. Lance, Chairman, President and CEO

## Harrisburg Patriot-News
P.O. Box 2265
Harrisburg, PA 17105

**INTERNET** www.patriot-news.com
**VOICE** 717-255-8100

## Hartford Courant
285 Broad St.
Hartford, CT 06115

**INTERNET** www.ctnow.com
**VOICE** 860-525-2525

## Hartford Financial Services
Hartford Plaza
Hartford, CT 06115
*P & C insurance*

**INTERNET** www.thehartford.com
Ramani Ayer, CEO

**Hasbro**
1027 Newport Ave.
Pawtucket, RI 02862
*The #2 toy maker in the U.S.*

**INTERNET** www.hasbro.com
Alan G. Hassenfeld, Chairman and CEO

**Hatch, Orrin**
104 Hart Senate Office Bldg. (R-UT)
Washington, D.C. 20510
*Senator*

**INTERNET** www.senate.gov/~hatch/

**Hatcher, Teri**
10100 Santa Monica Blvd., #410
Los Angeles, CA 90067
*Actress*

**Hauer, Rutger**
9560 Wilshire Blvd., #516
Beverly Hills, CA 90212
*Actor*

**Hauser, Ritchie**
223 E 48th St.
New York, NY 10017
*Musician*

**Hawn, Goldie**
9171 Wilshire Blvd., #300
Beverly Hills, CA 90210
*Actress*

**Hayek, Salma**
P.O. Box 57593
Sherman Oaks, CA 91402
*Actress*

**HBO**
1100 Ave. of the Americas
New York, NY 10036
*Cable network*

**Headline News**
1 CNN Center
P.O. Box 105366
Atlanta, GA 30348
*Cable network*

## Health Insurance Association of America

555 13th St. NW, #600E
Washington, D.C. 20004
*A national trade association based in Washington, D.C.*

**INTERNET** www.hiaa.org
Ben Cutler, Chairman

## Health Net

21600 Oxnard St.
Woodland Hills, CA 91367
*Healthcare*

**INTERNET** www.health.net
Richard W. Hanselman, Chairman

## Healthcare PR and Marketing News

1201 Seven Locks Road, #300
Potomac, MD 20854
*Newsletter*

**INTERNET** www.phillips.com
**VOICE** 301-340-1520

## HealthSouth

1 HealthSouth Pkwy
Birmingham, AL 35243
*Healthcare*

**INTERNET** www.healthsouth.net
Richard M. Scrushy, Chairman and CEO

## Heche, Anne

211 State St.
Madison, WI 53703
*Actress*

## Hemingway, Mariel

P.O. Box 2249
Ketchum, ID 83340
*Actress*

## Hefner, Hugh

10236 Charring Cross Road
Los Angeles, CA 90077
*Founder of Playboy*

**BIRTHDAY** 4/9/26

## Hemlock Society

P.O. Box 101810
Denver, CO 80250
*A right to die organization*

**INTERNET** www.hemlock.org
**E-MAIL** hemlock@privatel.com
Faye Girsh, Vice President

## Henry, Brad

*Governor of Oklahoma*

**E-MAIL** governor@gov.state.ok.us

## Hepburn, Katharine

350 5th Ave., #5019
New York, NY 10017
*Actress*

## Herman, Richard Talent Agency

124 Lasky Dr., 2nd Floor
Beverly Hills, CA 90212

## Hershey Food

100 Crystal A Dr.
Hershey, PA 17033
*Food producer/chocolate maker*

**INTERNET** www.hersheys.com
Richard H. Lenny, Chairman and CEO

## Hertz

*Rental car agency*

**INTERNET** www.hertz.com
**VOICE** 1-800-654-3131

## Heston, Charlton

2859 Coldwater Canyon
Beverly Hills, CA 90210
*Actor*

## Hewlett Packard

3000 Hanover St.
Palo Alto, CA 94304
*Computers and office equipment*

**INTERNET** www.hp.com
Carleton S. Fiorina, Chairman

## High Frontier

2800 Shirlington Road, #405A
Arlington, VA 22206

**INTERNET** www.highfrontier.org
**E-MAIL** hifront@erols.com
Lt. General Daniel O. Graham, Chairman of the Board

*Its mission is to ensure the nation is protected against ballistic missile attack*

## High Tech Hot Wire

99 Brookwood Road, #7
Orinda, CA 94563
*Newsletter*

**INTERNET** www.media-mark.com
**VOICE** 925-253-7862

## Highlights for Children

803 Church St.
Honesdale, PA 18431
*Magazine for kids*

## Hilton Hotels
9336 Civic Center Dr.
Beverly Hills, CA 90210
*Hotels, resorts, casinos*

**INTERNET** www.hilton.com
Stephen F. Bollenbach, President and CEO

## History Channel, The
225 E 45th St.
New York, NY 10017
*Cable network*

## Hoffman, Dustin
11661 San Vicente Blvd., #222
Los Angeles, CA 90048
*Actor*

## Holden, Bob
Missouri Capitol Bldg., Room 216
Jefferson City, MO 65102
*Governor of Missouri*

mogov@mail.state.mo.us

## Hollings, Ernest
125 Russell Senate Office Bldg. (D-SC)
Washington, D.C. 20510
*Senator*

**INTERNET** www.hollings.senate.gov/email.html

## Holly, Lauren
955 S Carrillo Dr., #300
Los Angeles, CA 90048
*Actress*

**BIRTHDAY** 10/28/63

## Hollywood Reporter
5055 Wilshire Blvd., 6th Floor
Los Angeles, CA 90036
*Trade newspaper*

## Hollywood Stock Exchange
225 Arizona Ave., #250
Santa Monica, CA 90401
*Internet content provider*

**INTERNET** www.hsx.com
Max Keiser, Co-Founder and Chairman

## Home and Garden TV
9701 Madison Ave.
Knoxville, TN 37932
*Cable network*

## Home Depot
2455 Paces Ferry Road NW
Atlanta, GA 30339
*Specialist retailers, hardware*

**INTERNET** www.homedepot.com
Bob Nardelli, President and CEO

## Home Shopping Network
1529 US Rt. 19 S
Clearwater, FL 33546
*Cable network*

## Homestore.com
225 W Hillcrest Dr., #100
Thousand Oaks, CA 91360
*Online home rentals*

**INTERNET** www.homestore.com
W. Michael Lang, Chairman and CEO

## Honduras
Carlos Roberto Flores Facusse
Presidente Constitucional
Casa de Govierno, Centro Civico-Gubernamental, Miraflores Casa Presid.
Tegucigalpa, Honduras

**INTERNET** www.sre.hn

## Honeywell
101 Columbia Road
P.O. Box 2245
Morristown, NJ 07962
*Scientific, photo, control equipment*

**INTERNET** www.honeywell.com
David M. Cote, Chairman and CEO

## Hootie & The Blowfish
P.O. Box 5656
Columbia, SC 29250
*Music group*

## Hoover Institution
Stanford University
Palo Alto, CA 94305
*The vision of the Institution's founder encompassed the principles of individual, economic and political freedom, private enterprise and representative government*

**INTERNET** www.hoover.org
Peyton M. Lake, Chairman

## Hopper, Dennis
330 Indiana Ave.
Venice, CA 90291
*Actor*

## Hormel Foods
1 Hormel Place
Austin, MN 55912
*Food maker*

**INTERNET** www.hormel.com
Joel W. Johnson, Chairman and CEO

## Horne, Lena
23 E 74th St.
New York, NY 10021
*Singer*

## House Beautiful
1700 Broadway
New York, NY 10019
*Magazine*

**INTERNET** www.housebeautiful.com
**VOICE** 212-903-5084

## Household Financial
2700 Sanders Road
Prospect Heights, IL 60070
*Diversified financials*

**INTERNET** www.household.com
William F. Aldinger III, Chairman and CEO

## Houston Chronicle
801 Texas Ave.
Houston, TX 77002

**INTERNET** www.houstonchronicle.com
**VOICE** 713-220-7171

## Houston, Whitney
*Singer*

**E-MAIL** whitneyhouston@arista.com

## Howard, Ron
9830 Wilshire Blvd.
Beverly Hills, CA 90212
*Actor/Director*

**BIRTHDAY** 3/1/54

## Huckabee, Mike
*Governor of Arkansas*

**INTERNET** www.state.ar.us/governon/gems/eletter/commentform.html

## Hudson Institute
5395 Emerson Way
Indianapolis, ID 46226

**INTERNET** www.hudson.org
**E-MAIL** webmaster@hudson.org
John Clark, Senior Research Fellow

## Human Rights Campaign
1101 14th St. NW, #200
Washington, D.C. 20005

**INTERNET** www.hrcusa.org
**E-MAIL** hrc@hrc.org
Elizabeth Birch, Director

*The largest full time lobbying team in the nation devoted to issues of fairness for lesbian and gay Americans*

**Humana**
500 W Main St.
Louisville, KY 40201
*Healthcare*

**INTERNET** www.humans.com
David A. Jones, Chairman

**Humperdinck, Engelbert**
8942 Wilshire Blvd.
Beverly Hills, CA 90211
*Singer*

**BIRTHDAY** 5/2/36

**Hungary**
Ferenc Madl
President
Kossuth Ljos ter 3-5
Office of the President
1055 Budapest, Budapest Fovaros
Hungary

**Hunt, Helen**
9830 Wilshire Blvd.
Beverly Hills, CA 90212
*Actress*

**BIRTHDAY** 6/15/63

**Hunt, James**
*Governor of North Carolina*

**E-MAIL** governor@state.nc.us

**Hunter, Holly**
9460 Wilshire Blvd., 7th Floor
Beverly Hills, CA 90212
*Actress*

**BIRTHDAY** 3/20/58

**Hunter, Rachel**
1122 S Robertson Blvd., #15
Los Angeles, CA 90035
*Supermodel*

**E-MAIL** rachelhunter@studiofanmail.com

**Hurley, Elizabeth**
3 Cromwell Place
Londow, SW 2JE UK
*Model/Actress*

**Hurt, William**
132 S Rodeo Dr., #300
Beverly Hills, CA 90212
*Actor*

## Hutchinson, Kay
284 Russell Senate Office Bldg (R-TX)
Washington, D.C. 20510
*Senator*

**INTERNET** www.hutchinson.senate.gov/e-mail.htm

## Hutton, Timothy
9830 Wilshire Blvd.
Beverly Hills, CA 90212
*Actor*

## IBM
Old Orchard Road
Armonk, NY 10504
*Maker of computer systems*

**INTERNET** www.ibm.com
Samuel J. Palmisano, Chairman and CEO

## IBP
800 Stevens Port Dr.
Dakota Dunes, SD 57049
*Food producer*

**INTERNET** www.ibpinc.com
Robert L. Peterson, Chairman and CEO

## Iceland
Olafur Ragnar Grimsson, President
Office of the President
Stadastad, Soleyjargata 1
101 Reylgavik
Iceland

## Idealab
Bill Gross, Chair and Founder
*Venture capital*

**INTERNET** www.idealab.com

## Idol, Billy
8209 Melrose Ave.
Los Angeles, CA 90046
*Singer*

## IEG Sponsorship Report
640 N LaSalle St., #600
Chicago, IL 60610
*Newsletter*

**INTERNET** www.sponsorship.com
**VOICE** 312-944-1727

## iFilm Network
400 Pacific Ave. and 3rd Ave.
San Francisco, CA 94133
*Online film guide*

**INTERNET** www.ifilm.net
Rodger Radereman, Co-Chairman and Founder

## Ikon Office Solutions

70 Valley Stream Pkwy
CEO
Valley Forge, PA 19482

**INTERNET** www.ikon.com
James J. Forese, Chairman, President and

## Illinois Tool Works

3600 W Lake Ave.
Glenview, IL 60025
*Metal products*

**INTERNET** www.itwinc.com
W. James Farrell, CEO

## IMC Global

2100 Sanders Road
Northbrook, IL 06062
*Chemicals, fertilizer*

**INTERNET** www.imcglobal.com
Douglas A. Pertz, Chairman

## Inc. Magazine

38 Commercial Wharf
Boston, MA 02210
*Business magazine*

**INTERNET** www.inc.com
617-248-8000

## India

Kocheril Raman Narayanan, President
Rashtrapati Bhavan
110004 New Delhi
India

**INTERNET** www.http://alfa.nic.in

## Indianapolis Star News

P.O. Box 145
Indianapolis, IN 46206

**INTERNET** www.indystar.com
**VOICE** 317-444-6300

## Indonesia

Abduraman Wahid, President
Office of the President
15 Jalan Merdeka Utara
Jakarta
Indonesia

**INTERNET** www.dfa-deplu.go.id

## Industry Standard

398 5th St.
San Francisco, CA 94107

**INTERNET** www.industrystandard.com

## Info World

155 Bovet Road, #800
San Mateo, CA 94402
*Online news magazine*

**INTERNET** www.infoworld.com
**VOICE** 650-572-7341

## Information Infrastructure Project
Harvard University
79 John F. Kennedy St.
Cambridge, MA 02138

---

## Information Week
600 Community Dr.
Manhassett, NY 11030

**INTERNET** www.informationweek.com
**VOICE** 516-562-5000

---

## Ingersoll-Rand
200 Chestnut Ridge Road
Woodcliff Lake, NJ 07675
*Industrial and farm equipment*

**INTERNET** www.ingersoll-rand.com
Herbert L. Henkel, Chairman, President and CEO

---

## Ingram Micro
1600 E St. Andrew Place
Santa Ana, CA 92705
*Wholesalers, computer technology*

**INTERNET** www.ingrammicro.com
Kent B. Foster, Chairman

---

## Inhofe, James
453 Russell Senate Office Bldg. (R-OK)
Washington, D.C. 20510
*Senator*

**INTERNET** www.inhofe.senate.gov/contactus.htm

---

## Inouye, Daniel
722 Hart Senate Office Bldg. (D-HI)
Washington, D.C. 20510
*Senator*

**INTERNET** www.inouye.senate.gov/webforms.html

---

## Inside PR
310 Madison Ave., #2005
New York, NY 10017
*Newsletter*

**INTERNET** www.ragan.com
**VOICE** 212-818-0288

---

## Institute for Contemporary Studies
1611 Telegraph Ave., #902
Oakland, CA 94612

**INTERNET** www.icspress.com
**E-MAIL** webmaster@icspress.com
Robert B. Hawkins Jr., President and CEO

*A nonprofit, nonpartisan policy research institute promoting self-governance and entrepreneurial ways of life*

## Institute for Food and Development Policy

398 60th St.
Oakland, CA 94618

**INTERNET** www.foodfirst.org
**E-MAIL** foodfirst@igc.apc.org
Peter Rosset, PhD, Executive Director

*Purpose is to eliminate the injustices that cause hunger*

## Institute for Humane Studies at George Mason University

3401 N Fairfax Dr.
Arlington, VA 22201

*A unique organization of graduate students who have a special interest in individual liberty*

## Institute for International Economics

11 DuPont Circle NW, #620
Washington, D.C. 20036

**INTERNET** www.iie.com
Peter G. Peterson,Director

*A private, nonprofit, nonpartisan research institute devoted to the study of international economic policy*

## Intel

2200 Mission College Blvd.
Santa Clara, CA 95052

**INTERNET** www.intel.com
Craig Barrett, Chairman Emeritus

*Computer peripherals and chip maker*

## Interactive Public Relations

316 N Michigan Ave., #300
Chicago, IL 60601

**INTERNET** www.ragan.com
**VOICE** 312-960-4100

*Newsletter*

## International Association of Laryngectomees

P.O. Box 2664
Newport News, VA 23609

**INTERNET** www.larynxlink.com

*A nonprofit voluntary organization comprised of approximately 250 member clubs and recognized organizations*

## International Bone Marrow Transplant Registry

8701 Watertown Plank Road
P.O. Box 26509
Milwaukee, WI 53226

**INTERNET** www.ibmtr.org

*The IBMTR, an ABMTR registry, aims at improving the success rate of allogeneic and autologous blood and bone marrow transplantation*

## International Dyslexia Association

8600 LaSalle Road
Baltimore, MD 21286

**INTERNET** www.interdys.org

## International Ghost Hunters Society

12885 SW N Rim Road
Crooked River Ranch, OR 97760

**INTERNET** www.ghostweb.com

*A worldwide paranormal research organization dedicated to the study of ghosts and poltergeist phenomena known as the spirits of the dead*

## International Paper

2 Manhattanville Road
Purchase, NY 10577
*Forest and paper products*

**INTERNET** www.internationalpaper.com
John T. Dillon, Chairman and CEO

## International Public Relations Review

Cardinal House
7 Wolsey Road
London KT89EL
England
UNITED KINGDOM

**VOICE** 44-181-481-7634

## Internet Magazine

Hampton Ct.
Angel House
338 Goswell Road
London EC1V7QP
England
UNITED KINGDOM

**INTERNET** www.internetmagazine.com
**VOICE** 020-7880-7438

## Interpublic Group

1271 Ave. of the Americas
New York, NY 10020
*Advertising and marketing*

**INTERNET** www.interpublic.com
John J. Dooner, Jr., Chairman and CEO

## Interstate Bakeries

12 E Armour Blvd.
Kansas City, MO 64111
*Food producers*

Charles A. Sullivan, CEO

## Intertainer

10950 Washington Blvd.
Culver City, CA 90232
*Web portal*

**INTERNET** www.intertainer.com
Jonathan Taplin, Co-Chairman and CEO

## Investigative Reporters and Editors

UMC School of Journalism
University of Missouri
Columbia, MO 65211

**INTERNET** www.ire.org

## Investor Relations Business

11th Floor
New York, NY 10019
*Newsletter*

**VOICE** 212-765-5311

## Investor Relations Newsletter

1 Kennedy Place, Rt. 12
Fitzwilliam, NH 03447

**INTERNET** www.kennedyinfo.com
**VOICE** 603-585-3101

## Investor Relations Update

716 S Brandywine St.
West Chester, PA 19382
*Newsletter*

**INTERNET** www.niri.org
**VOICE** 610-430-7057

## INXS

P.O. Box 591
Milsons Pt. NSW 1565
Australia
*Music group*

## Iraq

United Nations
405 E 42nd St.
New York, NY 10017

**INTERNET** www.un.org

## Ireland

**INTERNET** www.irlgov.ie

Mary McAleese, President
Office of the President
Phoenix Park
Dublin 8
Ireland

## Ireland, Kathy

1122 S Robertson Blvd., #15
Los Angeles, CA 90067
*Supermodel*

## Iron Butterfly

8860 Corbin Ave., #212
Northridge, CA 91324
*Music group*

## Iron Maiden

535 Kings Road
The Plaza
London SW100S
England
UNITED KINGDOM
*Music group*

## Irons, Jeremy

200 Fulham Road
London SW5
England
UNITED KINGDOM
*Actor*

## Isaak, Chris

9200 Sunset Blvd., #530
Los Angeles, CA 90069
*Musician*

## Israel

**INTERNET** www.israel-mfa.gov.il

Moshe Katzav, President
Office of the President
3 Hanassi St.
92188 Jerusalem
Israel

## Isthmus
P.O. Box 3198
Madison, WI 53703

**INTERNET** www.isthmus.com
**VOICE** 608-251-5627

## Italy
Carlo Azeglio Ciamp, President
Palazzo del Quirinale
00187 Rome
Italy

## ITT Industries
4 W Red Oak Ln.
White Plains, NY 10604
*Global engineering company*

**INTERNET** www.ittind.com
Louis J. Guiliano, Chairman and CEO

## Ivory Coast
Robert Guei, President
Presidence de la Republique
Abidjan
Boulevard Clozel
Ivory Coast

**INTERNET** www.lacotedivoire.com

## Izetbegovic, Alijaz
Bosnia and Herzegovina
Presidency of the Republic

**INTERNET** www.mvp.gov.ba

## J. P. Morgan
60 Wall St.
New York, NY 10260
*Commercial bank*

**INTERNET** www.jpmorgan.com
Bill Harrison, Chairman and CEO

## Jackson, Clarion-Ledger
311 E Pearl St.
Jackson, MS 39205

**INTERNET** www.clarion-ledger.com
**VOICE** 601-961-7000

## Jackson, Janet
338 N Foothill Road
Beverly Hills, CA 90210
*Singer*

## Jackson, Michael
c/o Neverland Ranch
Los Olivos, CA 91403
*Singer*

## Jagger, Mick
304 W 81st St.
New York, NY 10019
*Singer*

## Jamaica
Percival John Patterson,
Prime Minister
Jamaica House
6 Kingston
Jamaica

**INTERNET** www.jis.gov.jm
**E-MAIL** jis@jis.gov.jm

## James, Sonny
818 18th Ave. S
Nashville, TN 37203
*Country music singer*

## Japan
Emperor Skihito
Imperial Household Agency
11 Chiyoda, Chiyoda-ku
100 Tokyo
Japan

## JC Penney
6501 Legacy Dr.
Plano, TX 75024
*General merchandisers*

**INTERNET** www.jcpenney.com
Allen Questrom, Chairman and CEO

## Jeffords, James
728 Hart Senate Office
Bldg. (I-VT)
Washington, D.C. 20510
*Senator*

**E-MAIL** vermont@jeffords.senate.gov

## Jennings, Peter
ABC News
47 W. 66th St.
New York, NY 10023
*News anchor*

**INTERNET** www.abcnews.com

## Jethro Tull
12 Stratford Place
W1N9AF
England
UNITED KINGDOM

## Jeter, Derek
Yankee Stadium
Bronx, NY 10451
*Baseball player*

## Jett, Joan
1633 Broadway
New York, NY 10019
*Musician*

## Jewel
P.O. Box 33494
San Diego, CA 92163
*Singer*

## Jewish Defense League
P.O. Box 480370
Los Angeles, CA 90048

**INTERNET** www.jdl.org
**E-MAIL** jdljdl@aol.com

## Joel, Billy
280 Elm St., 2nd Floor
South Hampton, NY 11968
*Singer*

## Johanns, Mike
*Governor of Nebraska*

**E-MAIL** mjohanns@notes.state.ne.us

## John, Elton
P.O. Box 17139
Beverly Hills, CA 90209
*Singer*

## John, Olivia Newton
P.O. Box 110
Malibu, CA 90265
*Singer*

## John Hancock Financial Services
John Hancock Place
Boston, MA 02117
*Insurance, annuities and mutual funds*

**INTERNET** www.johnhancock.com
David F. D'Alessandro, CEO

## John Paul II the Pope
Vatican City
Rome
Italy
*His Holiness*

**INTERNET** www.vatican.va

## Johnson, Tim
324 Hart Senate Office
Bldg. (D-SD)
Washington, D.C. 20510
*Senator*

**E-MAIL** tim@johnson.senate.gov

## Johnson & Johnson
1 J&J Plaza
New Brunswick, NJ 08933
*Pharmaceuticals*

**INTERNET** www.jnj.com
William C. Weldon, Chairman and CEO

## Johnson Controls
5757 N Green Bay Ave.
Milwaukee, WI 53209
*Motor vehicles and parts*

**INTERNET** www.jci.com
James H. Keyes, Chairman and CEO

## Jones, Shirley
4531 Noeline Way
Encino, CA 91436
*Actress/Singer*

## Jones, Tom
10100 Santa Monica Blvd., #225
Los Angeles, CA 90067
*Singer*

## Jones, Tommy Lee
P.O. Box 966
San Saba, TX 76877
*Actor*

## Jordan
Ali Abu Ragheb
Prime Minister
P.O. Box 80
352 Amman
Jordan

**Jordan, Michael**
2102 W Monroe
Chicago, IL 60612
*Basketball player*

**E-MAIL** mjordan@nba.com

**Jordan, Robert**
175 5th Ave.
New York, NY 10010
*Author*

**Journal of Business Communications**
Dept. of Speech
17 Lexington Ave.
New York, NY 10010

**VOICE** 212-387-1655

**Journal of Communications**
Oxford University Press
2001 Evans Road
Cary, NC 27513

**INTERNET** www.oup.co.uk/jnlcom
**VOICE** 1-800-852-7323

**Journal of Employee Communications Management**
316 N Michigan Ave., #300
Chicago, IL 60601

**INTERNET** www.ragan.com
**VOICE** 312-960-4100

**Journey**
63 Main St.
Cold Springs, NY 10516
*Music group*

**Judas Priest**
12 Oval Road
Camden
London NW17DH
England
UNITED KINGDOM
*Music group*

**INTERNET** www.judaspriest.com

**Judd, Ashley**
151 El Camino Dr.
Beverly Hills, CA 90212
*Actress*

**BIRTHDAY** 4/19/68

**Judd, Naomi**
P.O. Box 68168
Nashville, TN 37068
*Country music singer*

**Judd, Wynona**
P.O. Box 68168
Nashville, TN 37068
*Country music singer*

**Kadrey, Richard**
*Science-fiction author*
**E-MAIL** kadrey@well.com

**Kane, Carol**
8205 Santa Monica Blvd., #1426
W Hollywood, CA 90046
*Actress*
**BIRTHDAY** 6/18/52

**Kansas City Star**
1729 Grand Ave.
Kansas City, KS 64108
**INTERNET** www.kcstar.com
**VOICE** 816-234-7900

**Kasem, Casey**
14958 Ventura Blvd.
Sherman Oaks, CA 91403
*Radio and television host*

**Kazakhstan**
Office of the Prime Minister
Republic Square
480091 Almaty
Kazakhstan

**Keaton, Michael**
10866 Wilshire Blvd., 10th Floor
Los Angeles, CA 90024
*Actor*

**Kehoe, Brendan**
*Author*
**INTERNET** www.zen.org
**E-MAIL** brendan@zen.org

**Kellner, Mark**
*Writer*
**INTERNET** www.markkellner.com
**E-MAIL** mark@kellner2000.com

## Kellogg

1 Kellogg Square
Battle Creek, MI 49016
*Food producer*

**INTERNET** www.kelloggs.com
Carlos Gutierrez, CEO

## Kelly Services

999 W Big Beaver Road
Troy, MI 48084
*Temporary employment services*

**INTERNET** www.kellyservices.com
Terence E. Adderley, Chairman, President and CEO

## Kempthorne, Dirk

*Governor of Idaho*

**INTERNET** www2.state.id.us/gov/

## Kennedy, Edward

317 Russell Senate Office Bldg. (D-MA)
Washington, D.C. 20510
*Senator*

**E-MAIL** senator@kennedy.senate.gov

## Kenny, Anthony

*Prime Minister of Saint Lucia*

**INTERNET** www.stlucia.gov.lc
**E-MAIL** pmoffice@candw.lc

## Kenya

Daniel arap Moi, President
Harambee House, Office of the President
P.O. Box 30510
Nairobi
Kenya

**INTERNET** www.kenyaweb.com

## Kerr, Deborah

Wyhergut
The Klosters
7250 Grisons
Switzerland
*Performer*

**BIRTHDAY** 9/30/21

## Kerry, John

304 Russell Senate Office Bldg. (D-MA)
Washington, D.C. 20510
*Senator*

**E-MAIL** john_kerry@kerry.senate.gov

## Kevorkian, Dr. Jack
327 E 4th St.
Royal Oak, MI 48067
*Doctor who assisted suicides*

## KeyCorp
127 Public Square
Cleveland, OH 44114
*Commercial bank*

**INTERNET** www.keybank.com
Henry L. Meyer, III, Chairman and CEO

## Kidman, Nicole
9830 Wilshire Blvd.
Beverly Hills, CA 90212
*Actress*

## Kilmer, Val
151 El Camino Dr.
Beverly Hills, CA 90212
*Actor*

## Kimberly-Clark
351 Phelps Dr.
Irving, TX 75038
*Forest and paper products*

**INTERNET** www.kimberly-clark.com
Wayne R. Sanders, Chairman and CEO

## King, B. B.
P.O. Box 26867
Las Vegas, NV 89126
*Singer*

## King, Carole
509 Hartnell St.
Monterey, CA 93940
*Singer/songwriter*

## King of Queens, The
c/o Columbia Tristar TV/
CBS Productions
10202 W. Washington Blvd.
David Lean Building, Suite 400
Culver City, CA 90232
*TV series*

## King, Rodney

9100 Wilshire Blvd., #250W
Beverly Hills, CA 90212
*Los Angeles riots newsmaker*

**INTERNET** www.rodneyking.com

## King, Stephen

47 W Broadway
Bangor, ME 04401
*Author*

## King Albert II

Belgium (Kingdom of)
Palais Royal

**INTERNET** www.http://belgium.fgov.be

## King of the Hill

P.O. Box 900
Beverly Hills, CA 90213
*Television show*

## Kinsella, W.P.

P.O. Box 2162
Blaine, WA 98231
*Author*

## Kinski, Nastassja

9830 Wilshire Blvd.
Beverly Hills, CA 90212
*Actress/model*

## Kiribati

Teburoror Tito, President
Office of the President
P.O. Box 68, Bairiki
Tarawa
Kiribati

## KISS

8730 Sunset Blvd., #175
Los Angeles, CA 90069
*Music group*

**INTERNET** www.kissonline.com

## Klestil, Dr. Thomas

1600 Varick St.
Austria (Republic of)
*President*

**INTERNET** www.hofburg.au
**E-MAIL** thomas.klestil@hofburg.at

## Klugman, Jack
22548 Pacific Coast Hwy
Malibu, CA 90265
*Actor*

## Klum, Heidi
304 Park Ave. S
Penthouse N
New York, NY 10010
*Model*

## Kmart
3100 W Big Beaver Road
Troy, MI 48084
*General merchandisers*

**INTERNET** www.kmart.com
James Adamson, Chairman and CEO

## Knight-Ridder
50 W San Fernando St.
San Jose, CA 95113
*Publishing, printing*

**INTERNET** www.kri.com
P. Anthony Ridder, Chairman and CEO

## Knot, The
*The Internet's leading wedding resource*

**INTERNET** www.theknot.com

## Knoxville News-Sentinel
208 W Church Ave.
Knoxville, TN 37950

**INTERNET** www.knoxnews.com
**VOICE** 615-523-3131

## Kohl, Herb
330 Hart Senate Office Bldg. (D-WI)
Washington, D.C. 20510
*Senator*

**E-MAIL** senator_kohl@kohl.senate.gov

## Kohl's
N 56 W 17000 Ridgewood Dr.
Menomonee Falls, WI 53051
*General merchandisers*

**INTERNET** www.kohls.com
Larry Montgomery, CEO

## Koontz, Dean
P.O. Box 9529
Newport Beach, CA 92658
*Author*

## Kosovo
Hashim Thaci, Prime Minister

**INTERNET** www.kosovo.org

## Kroger
1014 Vine St.
Cincinnati, OH 45202
*Food and drug stores*

**INTERNET** www.kroger.com
Joseph A. Pichler, President and CEO

## Kroft, Sid & Marty
7710 Woodrow Wilson Dr.
Los Angeles, CA 90046
*Producers of classic children's television shows*

## Kudrow, Lisa
1122 S Robertson Blvd.
Los Angeles, CA 90035
*Actress*

## Kulongoski, Ted
*Governor of Oregon*

**INTERNET** www.governor.state.or.us/governor/mail/mailform.html

## Kuwait
H.H. Jaber Al-Ahmed Al-Jaber Al-Sabah
Amir Sheikh
Amiri Diwan
P.O. Box 799
13008 Safat
Kuwait

**INTERNET** www.mofa.gov.kw

## Kwan, Michelle
P.O. Box 939
480 Cottage Grove Road
Lake Arrowhead, CA 92352
*Figure skater*

## Kwan, Nancy
P.O. Box 50747
Santa Barbara, CA 93150
*Actress*

## Kyl, Jon
730 Hart Senate Office Bldg. (R-AZ)
Washington, D.C. 20510
*Senator*

**INTERNET** www.kyl.senate.gov/con_form.htm

## Kyrgyzstan

Askar Akayev, President
Office of the President
Ulitsa Kirova 205
Bishkek
Kyrgyzstan

**INTERNET** www.http://gov.bishkek.su

## Laos

Kanthay Siphandon, President
Office of the President
Lane Xang Ave.
Viangchan
Laos

## Latvia

Vaira Vike-Freiberga
President of the State
Chancery of the President, Pils
Laukurns 3
LV-1900 Riga
Latvia

**INTERNET** www.president.lv
**E-MAIL** chancery@president.lv

## LA Weekly

P.O. Box 4315
Los Angeles, CA 90078

**INTERNET** www.laweekly.com
**VOICE** 323-465-9909

## Labelle, Patti

1212 Grennox Road
Wynnewood, PA 19096
*Singer*

**BIRTHDAY** 10/4/44

## Lacayo, Arnoldo Aleman

*Nicaragua Presidente*

**INTERNET** www.presidencia.gob.ni

## Ladd, Cheryl

P.O. Box 1329
Santa Ynez, CA 93460
*Actress*

**BIRTHDAY** 7/2/51

## Ladies' Home Journal

125 Park Ave.
New York, NY 10017
*Women's Magazine*

**INTERNET** www.lhj.com
**VOICE** 1-800-374-4545

**Lahti, Christine**
c/o Studio Fan Mail
1122 S Robertson Blvd.
Los Angeles, CA 90035
*Actress*

**Laine, Frankie**
P.O. Box 6910
San Diego, CA 92166
*Singer*

**Lake, Ricki**
226 W 26th St.
New York, NY 10001
*Talk show host*

**Laker, Freddie**
138 Cheapside
EC2V6BL, London
England
UNITED KINGDOM
*Founder of original Laker Airways*

**Lakin, Christine**
**BIRTHDAY** 1/25/79
8369 Sausalito Ave.
Los Angeles, CA 91304
Actress

**LaLanne, Jack**
**INTERNET** www.jacklalanne.com
430 Quintana Road
Morro Bay, CA 93442
*Fitness guru*

**Lama, Dalai**
McLeod Ganj 176219
Himachal Pradesh
INDIA
*Humanitarian*

**Lamas, Lorenzo**
**BIRTHDAY** 1/20/58
3727 W Magnolia Blvd.
Burbank, CA 91505
*Actor*

## Lambert, Christopher
9100 Wilshire Blvd., #305
Beverly Hills, CA 90212
*Actor*

**BIRTHDAY** 3/29/57

## Lancaster New Era
8 W King St.
P.O. Box 1328
Lancaster, PA 17603
*Online newspaper*

**VOICE** 717-291-8734

## Landers, Audrey
4048 Las Palmas Dr.
Sarasota, FL 34238
*Actress*

**BIRTHDAY** 7/18/59

## Landers, Judy
3933 Losillas Dr.
Sarasota, FL
34238-4537
*Actress*

**BIRTHDAY** 10/7/61

## Lando, Joe
151 El Camino Blvd.
Beverly Hills, CA 90212
*Actor*

**BIRTHDAY** 12/9/61

## Landon Jr., Michael
3736 Calle Jazmin
Calabasas, CA 91302
*Actor/Son of Michael Landon*

## Landrieu, Mary
724 Hart Senate Office Bldg. (D-LA)
Washington, D.C. 20510
*Senator*

**INTERNET** www.landrieu.senate.gov/webform.html

## Lane, Diane
25 Sea Colony Dr.
Santa Monica, CA 90405-5321
*Actress*

**BIRTHDAY** 1/22/65

**Lane, Nathan**
P.O. Box 1249
White River Junction, VT 05001
*Actor*

**Lang, K.D.**
P.O. Box 33800
Station D
Vancouver, BC V6J 5C7
Canada
*Singer*

**BIRTHDAY** 11/2/61

**Lange, Jessica**
9333 Wilshire Blvd.
Beverly Hills, CA 90210
*Actress*

**Lange, Hope**
1801 Ave. of the Stars, #902
Los Angeles, CA 90067
*Actress*

**Lange, Ted**
6950 McLennan Ave.
Van Nuys, CA 91406
*Actor*

**Langella, Frank**
151 El Camino Blvd.
Beverly Hills, CA 90212
*Actor*

**BIRTHDAY** 1/1/40

**Langenkamp, Heather**
156 F St. SE
Washington, D.C. 20003
*Actress*

**Lansbury, Angela**
635 N Bonhill Road
Los Angeles, CA 90049
*Actress*

**LaPaglia, Anthony**
8942 Wilshire Blvd.
Beverly Hills, CA 90212
*Actor*

## Lapinski, Tara
888 Dennison Ct.
Bloomfield Hills, MI 48302
*Gymnast*

## Larroquette, John
15332 Antioch St.
Pacific Palisades, CA 90272
*Actor*

## Larry King Live
820 1st St. NE
Washington, D.C. 20002
*News television show*

**INTERNET** www.cnn.com
**VOICE** 202-898-7983

## Larson, Gary
Box 36A
Denver, CO 80236
*Cartoonist*

## La Salle, Eriq
P.O. Box 2396
Beverly Hills, CA 90213
*Actor*

## Lasorda, Tommy
1473 W Maxzim Ave.
Los Angeles, CA 92633
*Former L.A. Dodgers manager*

## Lassie
16133 Soledad Canyon Road
Canyon Country, CA 91351
*Acting dog*

## Late Night with David Letterman
30 Rockefeller Plaza
New York, NY 10112

**INTERNET** www.cbs.com/lateshow
**VOICE** 212-664-5908

## Latifah, Queen
155 Morgan St.
Jersey City, NJ 07302
*Actress/singer*

## Lauder, Estee
767 5th Ave.
New York, NY 10153
*Cosmetics*

## Lauer, Matt
30 Rockefeller Plaza
New York, NY 10112
*Broadcast journalist*

## Lauper, Cyndi
2211 Broadway, #1
New York, NY 10024 - 6200
*Singer*

## Lauren, Ralph
1107 5th Ave.
New York, NY 10128
*Fashion designer*

## Laurents, Arthur
Box 582
New York, NY 11959
*Director*

## Laurie, Piper
3130 Oakshire Dr.
Santa Monica, CA 90068-1743
*Actress*

## Lautenberg, Frank
Hart Senate Office
Bldg. (D-NJ)
Washington, D.C. 20510
*Senator*

**INTERNET** www.lautenberg.senate.gov/webform.html

## Laver, Rod
P.O. Box 4798
Hilton Head Island, SC 29928
*Tennis player*

**BIRTHDAY** 8/9/38

## Lavin, Linda
321 Front St.
Wilmington, NC 28401
*Actress*

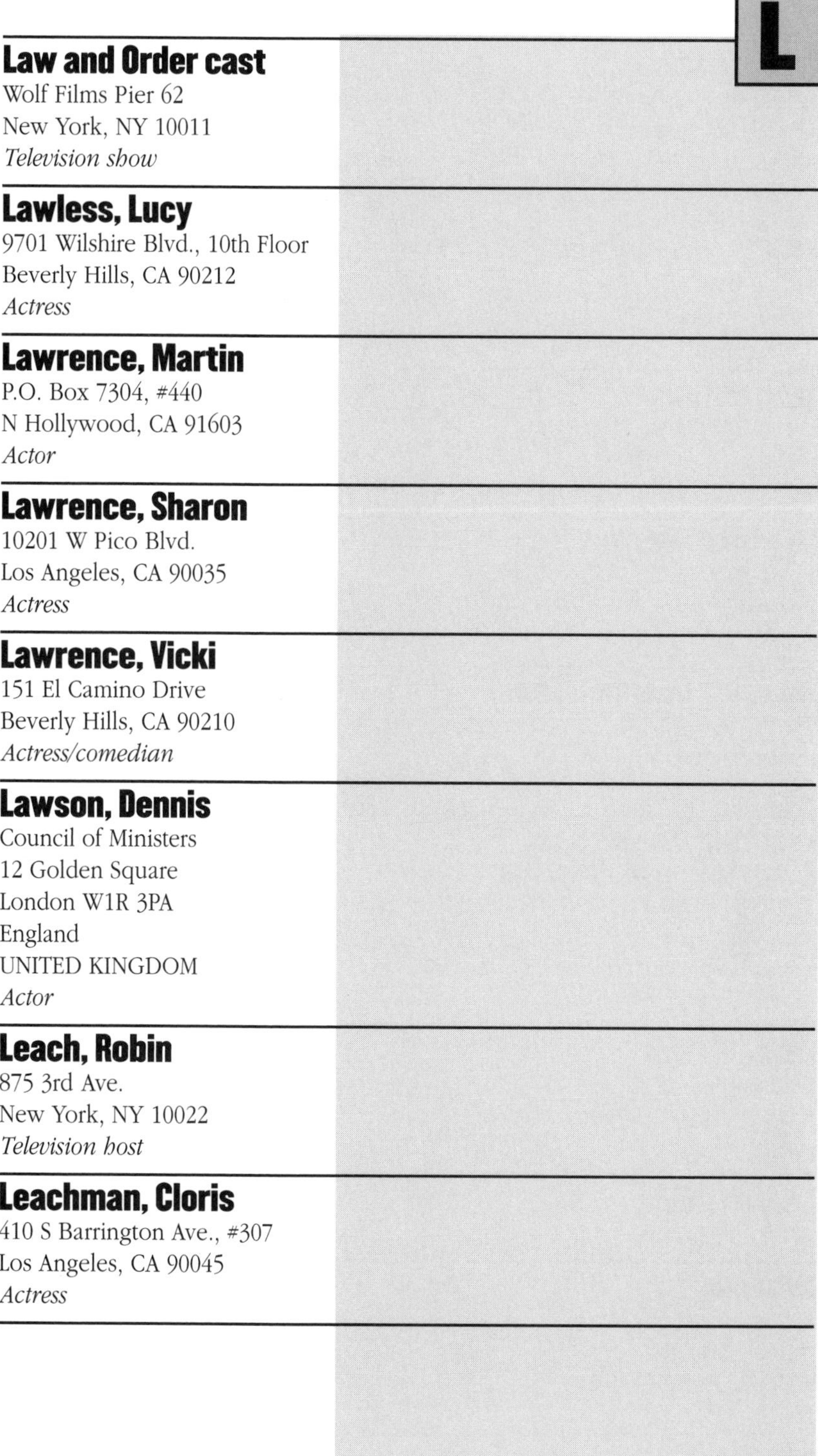

L

## Law and Order cast
Wolf Films Pier 62
New York, NY 10011
*Television show*

## Lawless, Lucy
9701 Wilshire Blvd., 10th Floor
Beverly Hills, CA 90212
*Actress*

## Lawrence, Martin
P.O. Box 7304, #440
N Hollywood, CA 91603
*Actor*

## Lawrence, Sharon
10201 W Pico Blvd.
Los Angeles, CA 90035
*Actress*

## Lawrence, Vicki
151 El Camino Drive
Beverly Hills, CA 90210
*Actress/comedian*

## Lawson, Dennis
Council of Ministers
12 Golden Square
London W1R 3PA
England
UNITED KINGDOM
*Actor*

## Leach, Robin
875 3rd Ave.
New York, NY 10022
*Television host*

## Leachman, Cloris
410 S Barrington Ave., #307
Los Angeles, CA 90045
*Actress*

## Leahy, Patrick
433 Russell Senate Office
Bldg. (D-VT)
Washington, D.C. 20510
*Senator*

**E-MAIL** senator_leahy@leahy.senate.gov

## Lear
21557 Telegraph Road
Southfield, MI 48086
*Motor vehicles and parts*

**INTERNET** www.lear.com
Robert E. Rossiter, CEO

## Lear, Norman
1911 Westridge Road
Los Angeles, CA 90049
*Television producer*

## Learned, Michael
127 E 23rd St.
New York, NY 10010
*Actress*

## Learning Channel, The
7700 Wisconsin Ave.
Bethesda, MD 20814
*Cable network*

## Learning Disabilities Association of America
**INTERNET** www.ldanatl.org

7700 Wisconsin Ave.
Pittsburgh, PA 15234
*The only national organization devoted to defining and finding solutions to the broad spectrum of learning disabilities*

## Leary, Denis
9560 Wilshire Blvd., #50
Beverly Hills, CA 90212
*Comedian*

## Leavitt, Mike
*Governor of Utah*

**E-MAIL** governor@gov.state.ut.us

## Lebanon
Emile Lahoud, President
Baabda Palace
Office of the President
Beirut
Lebanon

**INTERNET** www.presidency.gov.lb

**LeBlanc, Matt**
1122 S Robertson Blvd.
Los Angeles, CA 90035
*Actor*

**LeBrock, Kelly**
P.O. Box 57593
Sherman Oaks, CA 91402
*Actress/model*

**Lee, Brenda**
2175 Carson St.
Nashville, TN 37211
*Singer*
**BIRTHDAY** 12/11/44

**Lee, Christopher**
2-4 Noel St.
London WLV 3RB
England
UNITED KINGDOM
*Actor*

**Lee, Kathy**
204 River Edge Ln.
Seiverville, TN 37862
*Singer*

**Lee, Spike**
124 DeKalb
New York, NY 11217
*Film director*

**Lee, Stan**
387 Park Ave. S
New York, NY 10016
*Spiderman publisher*

**Lee, Tommy**
No. 1 Leggett Road
31341 Mulholland Hwy
Malibu, CA 90265
*Singer*

**Leggett and Platt**
3 World Financial Center
Carthage, MO 64836
*Furniture*
**INTERNET** www.regionalstock.com
Felix E. Wright, Chairman

## Lehman Brothers Holdings
745 Seventh Ave.
New York, NY 10019
*Securities*

**INTERNET** www.lehman.com
J. Wayne Leonard, Chairman and CEO

## Leigh, Janet
1625 Summit Ridge Dr.
Beverly Hills, CA 90210
*Actress*

## Leigh, Jennifer Jason
2400 Whitman Place
Los Angeles, CA 90068
*Actress*

## Leisure, David
8428-C Melrose Place
Los Angeles, CA 90046
*Actor*

**BIRTHDAY** 11/16/50

## Leno, Jay
c/o Big Dog Productions
P.O. Box 7885
Burbank, CA 91510
*Host of* The Tonight Show

**BIRTHDAY** 4/20/50

## Leonard, Robert Sean
P.O. Box 103
Waldwick, NJ 07463
*Actor*

## Leonard, Sugar Ray
4401 E W Hwy
Baltimore, MD 20914
*Former boxer*

## Leonel Fernandez Reyna
*President of the Dominican Republic*

**INTERNET** www.presidencia.gov.do
**E-MAIL** correspondencias@presidencia.gov.do

## Leoni, Tea
2300 W Victory Blvd., #384
Burbank, CA 91506
*Actress*

## Lesotho
Letsie III, King
Royal Palace
Maseru
Lesotho

## Letterboxing.org
**INTERNET** www.letterboxing.org

*Organization dedicated to the hobby of letterboxing*

## Letterman, David
c/o Worldwide Pants Inc.
1697 Broadway
New York, NY 10019
*Host of* The Late Show

## Levin, Carl
**E-MAIL** senator@levin.senate.gov

269 Russell Senate
Office Bldg. (D-MI)
Washington, D.C. 20510
*Senator*

## Levine, Michael
**BIRTHDAY** 4/17/54
**E-MAIL** michael@levinepr.com

Levine Communications
10333 Ashton Ave.
Los Angeles, CA 90024
*Public relations executive/media expert*

## Lewinksy, Monica
P.O. Box 819
1224 Darlington
Los Angeles, CA 90049
*Infamous White House intern/reality TV show hostess*

## Lewis, Al
612 Lighthouse Ave., PMB 220
Pacific Grove, CA 93951
*Actor*

## Lewis, Carl
1801 Ocean Blvd., #112
Santa Monica, CA 90405
*Track and field Olympian*

## Lewis, Huey
P.O. Box 819
Mill Valley, CA 94942
*Singer*

## Lewis, Jerry
3160 W Sahara Ave., #C16
Las Vegas, NV 89102
*Actor/comedian*

## Lewis, Jerry Lee
P.O. Box 384
Nashville, TN 38103
*Singer*

## Lewis, Juliette
1122 S Robertson Blvd.
Los Angeles, CA 90035
*Actress*

## LG & B
220 W Main St.
Louisville, KY 40232
*Gas and electric utilities*

**INTERNET** www.lgenergy.com
Roger W. Hale, Chairman and CEO

## Liberia
Dr. Charles Ghankay Taylor, President
Office of the President, Capitol Hill
1000 Monrovia 10
Liberia

## Liberty Mutual Insurance Group
175 Berkeley St.
Boston, MA 02117
*P & C insurance*

Edmund F. Kelly, CEO

## Libya
Muammar al-Qaddafi, Colonel
Office of the President
Tripoli
Libya

## Liddy, G. Gordon
P.O. Box 3649
Washington, D.C. 20007
*Watergate conspirator*

## Lieberman, Joseph
706 Hart Senate
Office Bldg. (D-CT)
Washington, D.C. 20510
*Senator*

**INTERNET** www.lieberman.senate.gov/webform.html

## Liechtenstein
H.S.H Prince Hans Adam II
Schloss
FL-9490 Vaduz
*Liechtenstein*

**INTERNET** www.firstlink.li

## Lien, Jennifer
1700 Varilla Dr.
W Covina, CA 91792
*Actress*

## Lifetime
309 W 49th St.
New York, NY 10019
*Cable network*

## Limbaugh, Rush
E1B Bldg., 17th Floor
2 Penn Plaza
New York, NY 10121
*Author and radio show host*

**E-MAIL** rush@eibnet.com

## Limited
3 Limited Way
Columbus, OH 43430
*Specialist retailers, women's clothing*

**INTERNET** www.limited.com
Leslie H. Wexner, CEO

## Lincoln, Blanche
355 Dirksen Senate
Office Bldg. (D-AR)
Washington, D.C. 20510
*Senator*

**INTERNET** www.lincoln.senate.gov/webform.html

## Lincoln National
1500 Market St., #3900
Philadelphia, PA 19012
*Health and Life insurance*

**INTERNET** www.lfg.co
Jon A. Boscia, President and CEO

**Linden, Hal**
254 W 54th St.
New York, NY 10019
*Actor*

BIRTHDAY 3/20/31

**Lindsay, George**
P.O. Box 110225
Nashville, TN 37222
*Country music singer*

**Lingle, Linda**
1290 Ala Moana Blvd.
Honolulu, HI 96814
*Governor of Hawaii*

**Linux Magazine**
c/o Grey Agency
P.O. Box 55731
Boulder, CO 80323

INTERNET www.linux-mag.com
VOICE 1-800-950-1974

**Lipnicki, Jonathan**
9100 Wilshire Blvd., 6th Floor
Beverly Hills, CA 90212
*Actor*

BIRTHDAY 10/22/90

**Lithuania**
Valdas Adamkus, President
Gedimino pr. 5
Office of the President
2026 Vilnius
Lithuania

INTERNET www.president.lt
E-MAIL info@president.lt

**Litton Industries**
21240 Burbank Blvd.
Woodland Hills, CA 91367
*Electronics, electrical equipment*

INTERNET www.littoncorp.com
Michael R. Brown, Chairman Emeritus

**Liu, Lucy**
c/o Media Five Entertainment
P.O. Box 900
Beverly Hills, CA 90213
*Actress*

**Live**
P.O. Box 20266
Lehigh Valley, PA 18002
*Music group*

## Live with Regis and Kelly
7 Lincoln Square
New York, NY 10023
*Talk show*

**INTERNET** www.regisandkelly.com

## LL Cool J
405 Park Ave., #1500
New York, NY 10022
*Rap singer*

## Lloyd, Christopher
P.O. Box 491246
Los Angeles, CA 90049
*Actor*

## Lobo, Rebecca
P.O. Box 385
Medford, MA 02052
*Basketball player*

## Locke, Gary
*Governor of Washington*

**INTERNET** www.governor.wa.gov/contact/govemail.htm

## Locke, Sondra
7465 Hillside Ave.
Los Angeles, CA 90046
*Actress*

**BIRTHDAY** 5/28/48

## Lockhart, June
P.O. Box 3027
Santa Monica, CA 90402
*Actress*

## Lockheed Martin
6801 Rockledge Dr.
Bethesda, MD 20817
*Aerospace*

**INTERNET** www.lockheedmartin.com
Vance D. Coffman, CEO

## Locklear, Heather
1863 Courtney Terrace
Los Angeles, CA 90046
*Actress*

## Loeb, Lisa
3575 Cahuenga Blvd., #450
Los Angeles, CA 90068
*Singer*

**Loews**
667 Madison Ave.
New York, NY 10021
*P & C insurance*

**INTERNET** www.loews.com
Laurence A. Tisch, Co-Chairman

**Lollobrigida, Gina**
Via Appia Antica 223
I-00178
Italy
*Actress*

**BIRTHDAY** 7/4/27

**Lom, Herbert**
2-4 Noel St.
London W1V 3RB
England
UNITED KINGDOM
*Performer*

**Long, Shelley**
15237 Sunset Blvd.
Pacific Palisades, CA 90272
*Actress*

**BIRTHDAY** 8/23/49

**Long Island Power Authority**
333 Earle Ovington Blvd.
Uniondale, NY 11553
*Gas and electric utilities*

**INTERNET** www.lipower.org
Richard M. Kessel, Chairman

**Longs Drug Stores**
141 N Civic Dr.
Walnut Creek, CA 94596
*Food and drug stores*

**INTERNET** www.longs.com
Warren F. Bryant, Chairman

**Lopez, Jennifer**
P.O. Box 57593
Sherman Oaks, CA 91403
*Actress/singer*

**E-MAIL** jennifer_lopez@sonymusic.com

**Lords, Traci**
345 N Maple Dr., #375
Beverly Hills, CA 90210
*Actress*

**BIRTHDAY** 5/7/68

## Loren, Sophia
1151 Hidden Valley Road
Thousand Oaks, CA 91361
*Actress*

**BIRTHDAY** 9/20/34

## Los Angeles Clippers
c/o Los Angeles Sports Arena
3939 S Figueroa
Los Angeles, CA 90037
*Basketball team*

## Los Angeles Daily News
21221 Oxnard St.
Woodland Hills, CA 91367

**INTERNET** www.dailynews.com
**VOICE** 818-713-3636

## Los Angeles Dodgers
100 Elysian Park Ave.
Los Angeles, CA 90012
*Baseball team*

## Los Angeles Kings
1111 S. Figueroa St.
Los Angeles, CA 90015
*Hockey team*

## Los Angeles Lakers
1111 S. Figueroa St.
Los Angeles, CA 90015
*Basketball team*

## Los Lobos
P.O. Box 128037
Nashville, TN 37212
*Music group*

## Lott, Trent
487 Russell Senate
Office Bldg. (R-MS)
Washington, D.C. 20510
*Senator*

**E-MAIL** senatorlott@lott.senate.gov

## Louis-Dreyfus, Julia
535 Alma Real Dr.
Pacific Palisades, CA 90272
*Actress*

## Louise, Tina
310 E 46th St., #18T
New York, NY 10017
*Actress*

## Louisville Courier-Journal
525 W Broadway
Louisville, KY 40202

**INTERNET** www.courier-journal.com
**VOICE** 502-582-4011

## Love, Courtney
150 E 58th St., #1900
New York, NY 10155
*Singer*

## Love-Hewitt, Jennifer
11601 Wilshire Blvd., #1900
Los Angeles, CA 90025
*Actress/singer*

## Loveless, Patty
P.O. Box 1423
White House, GA 37188
*Singer*

## Lovett, Lyle
P.O. Box 11206
Spring, TX 77391
*Singer*

## Lowe, Chad
1505 10th St.
Santa Monica, CA 90401
*Actor*

## Lowe, Rob
15030 Ventura Blvd.
Sherman Oaks, CA 91403
*Actor*

**BIRTHDAY** 3/1764

## Lowe's
1605 Curtis Bridge Road
Wilesboro, NC 28697
*Specialist retailer*

**INTERNET** www.lowes.com
Robert L. Tillman, Chairman, President and CEO

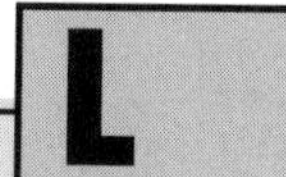

## LTV

200 Public Square
Cleveland, OH 44114
*Metal producer*

**INTERNET** www.ltvsteel.com
Bill Bricker, Chairman, President and CEO

## Lucci, Susan

P.O. Box 621
Quogue, NY 10019
*Soap opera star*

## Lucent Technologies

600 Mountain Ave.
Murray Hill, NJ 07974

**INTERNET** www.lucent.com
Richard A. McGinn, Chairman and CEO

## Lugar, Richard

306 Hart Senate Office Bldg. (R-IN)
Washington, D.C. 20510
*Senator*

**E-MAIL** senator_lugar@lugar.senate.gov

## Lukashenko, Aleksandr

President of the Republic of Belarus

**INTERNET** www.president.gov.by
**E-MAIL** ires@president.gov.by

## LULAC National Education Service Center

221 N Kansas, #1200
El Paso, TX 79901
*League of United Latin American Citizens*

**INTERNET** www.lulac.org
Brent Wilkes, Executive Director

## Lumbly, Carl

8730 Sunset Blvd., #480
Los Angeles, CA 90067
*Actor*

## Lunden, Joan

15821 Ventura Blvd., #320
Encino, VA 91436
*Author*

## Lundgren, Dolph

1122 S Robertson Blvd., #15
Los Angeles, CA 90035
*Actor*

**BIRTHDAY** 10/18/59

## Lundy, Jessica
151 El Camino Dr.
Beverly Hills, CA 90212
*Actress*

## Lutheran Brotherhood
625 4th Ave. S
Minneapolis, MN 55415

Rolf F. Bjelland, Chairman

## Luxembourg
Jean Benoit D'Aviano,
Grand Duke
Grand Ducal Place
2013
Luxembourg

## Lynch, David
P.O. Box 931567
Los Angeles, CA 90093-1567
*Director*

## Lynley, Carol
612 Lighthouse Ave.
Pacific Grove, CA 93951
*Actress*

**BIRTHDAY** 2/13/42

## Lynyrd Skynyrd
Sanctuary Records
5226 Greens Dairy Rd.
Raleigh, NC 27616-4612
*Music group*

**INTERNET** www.lynyrdskynyrd.com

## Lyondell Petrochemical
1221 McKinney St.
Houston, TX 77253
*Chemicals*

**INTERNET** www.lyondell.com
Dan Smith, Chairman

## Macchi, Luis Angel Gonzales
*President of Paraguay*

**INTERNET** www.presidencia.gov.py

## Macdonald, Norm
9150 Wilshire Blvd.
Beverly Hills, CA 90212-3427
*Comedian/actor*

## MacDowell, Andie
8942 Wilshire Blvd.
Beverly Hills, CA 90211
*Actress*

## Macedonia
Boris Trajkovski, President
Office of the President
11 Oktomvril b.b.
91000 Skopje
Macedonia

## MacGraw, Ali
**BIRTHDAY** 4/1/38
10345 W. Olympic Blvd.
Los Angeles, CA 90064
*Actress*

## Mackie, Bob
1400 Broadway
New York, NY 10018
*Fashion designer*

## MacLaine, Shirley
**E-MAIL** info@shirleymaclaine.com
25200 Malibu Road, #4
Malibu, CA 90265
*Actress*

## MacPherson, Elle
6 E 68th St.
New York, NY 10021
*Model*

## Macnee, Patrick
**BIRTHDAY** 2/6/22
P.O. Box 1853
Rancho Mirage, CA 92270
*Actor*

## Madagascar
**INTERNET** www.an.online.mg
Didier Ratsiraka, President
Presidence de la Republique
Ambohitsirohitra 101
Antananarivo
Madagascar

## Mad Magazine

1700 Broadway
New York, NY 10019
*Comedic magazine*

**INTERNET** www.dccomics.com

## Madonna

9348 Civic Center Dr., 1st Floor
Beverly Hills, CA 90210
*Singer/songwriter*

**E-MAIL** madonna@wbr.com

## Maher, Bill

7800 Beverly Blvd.
Los Angeles, CA 90036
*Host of* Real Time With Bill Maher
*comedian/author*

## Maine Times

P.O. Box 2129
Bangor, ME 04402

**INTERNET** www.mainetimes.com
**VOICE** 1-800-439-8866

## Majors, Lee

2877 S Paradise Road, #903
Las Vegas, NV 89109
*Actor*

## Malawi

Regional Administrator
Private Bag 32
Lilongwe 3, Central Region
Malawi

## Malaysia

Paramount Ruler Sultan Tuanku
Salehuddin Abdul Aziz Shah
Istana Negara
Kuala Lumpur, Malaysia

## Malcolm in the Middle

4024 Radford Ave., Office S
Studio City, CA 91604
*Television show*

## Malden, Karl

1845 Mandeville Canyon Road
Los Angeles, CA 90049
*Actor*

## Maldives

Maumoon Abdul Gayoom,
His Excellency the President
Office of the President
Marine Dr.
Male 20-05
Maldives

**INTERNET** www.maldives-info.com
**E-MAIL** admin@foreign.gov.mv

## Mali

Alpha Oumar Konare, President
Presidence, Koulouba
Barnako
Mali

## Malta

Dr. Guido Demarco, President
The Palace
Office of the President
CMR 02, Valletta
Malta

**INTERNET** www.magnet.mt
**E-MAIL** info@magnet.int

## Majorino, Tina

1640 S Sepulveda
PMB 530
Los Angeles, CA 90025
*Actress*

## Malkovich, John

P.O. Box 5106
Westport, CT 06881-5106
*Actor*

**BIRTHDAY** 12/9/53

## Mamas & The Papas, The

805 3rd Ave.
New York, NY 10022
*Music group*

**E-MAIL** emailhowie@aol.com

## Mandel, Howie

23679 Calabasas Road
Calabasas, CA 91302
*Comedian/actor*

## Mandrell, Barbara

P.O. Box 620
Hendersonville, TN 37077
*Singer*

## Mandrell, Louise
P.O. Box 620
Hendersonville, TN 37077
*Singer*

## Manhattan Institute
52 Vanderbilt Ave.
New York, NY 10017

**INTERNET** www.manhattan-institute.org
**E-MAIL** barreiro@manhattan-institute.org
Lawrence Mone, President

*A think tank whose mission is to develop and disseminate new ideas that foster greater economic choice and individual responsibility*

## Manhattan Transfer
141 Dunbar Ave.
Fords, NJ 08863
*Music group*

## Manheim, Camryn
10201 W Pico Blvd.
Los Angeles, CA 90035
*Actress*

## Manheim Steamroller
9120 Mormon Bridge Road
Omaha, NE 68512
*Music group*

## Manilow, Barry
6 W 57th St.
New York, NY 10019
*Musician*

## Manners, Miss
1651 Harvard Sq. NW
Washington, D.C. 20009
*Etiquette specialist*

## Manpower
5301 N Ironwood Road
Milwaukee, WI 53217
*Temporary employment services*

**INTERNET** www.manpower.com
Jeff Joerres, Chairman

## Manson, Charles
c/o Pinnacle
B33920, Corcoran State Prison
Corcoran, CA 93212
*Convicted serial killer/cult leader*

## Manson, Marilyn
7336 Santa Monica Blvd., #730
W Hollywood, CA 90046
*Musician*

## Mantegna, Joe
P.O. Box 7304, #103
N Hollywood, CA 91603
*Actor*

## Maples, Marla
725 5th Ave.
New York, NY 10022
*Ex-wife of Donald Trump*

## March, Jane
5 Jubilee Place
London SW3 3TD
England
UNITED KINGDOM
*Actress*

## Marcos, Imelda
Leyte Providencia Dept.
Tolosa, Leyte
Philippines
*Former First Lady*

## Margolin, Stuart
9255 Sunset Blvd., #404
Los Angeles, CA 90069
*Actor*

## Margolis, Cindy
345 N Maple Dr.
Beverly Hills, CA 90210
*Model/actress*

**INTERNET** www.cindymargolis.com

## Margulies, Julianna
9465 Wilshire Blvd., #212
Beverly Hills, CA 90212
*Actress*

## Marjanovi, Mirko
Yugoslavia Prime Minister

**INTERNET** www.vlda.cg.yu
**E-MAIL** vlada@cg.yu

**Marriott International**
10400 Fernwood Road
Bethesda, MD 20817
*Hotels, resorts, and casinos*

**INTERNET** www.marriott.com
J. Willard Marriott, Jr., CEO

**Marsalis, Branford**
9520 Cedarbrook Dr.
Beverly Hills, CA 90210
*Musician*

**Marsalis, Wynton**
33 W 60th St.
New York, NY 10023
*Musician*

**Marshall Islands**
Kessai Note, President
Capitol Bldg.
96960 Majuro
*Marshall Islands*

**Marshall, Penny**
9465 Wilshire Blvd.
Beverly Hills, CA 90212
*Actress/director*

**Marshall, Peter**
16714 Oakview Dr.
Encino, CA 91316
*Television game show host*

**BIRTHDAY** 3/20/27

**Marsh and McLennan**
1166 Ave. of the Americas
New York, NY 10036
*Diversified financials*

**INTERNET** www.marshmac.com
Ernest M. Asaff, Chairman, President and CEO

**Martin, Dick**
30765 Pacific Coast Hwy, #103
Malibu, CA 90265
*Actor/Television personality*

**Martin, Pamela Sue**
13755A Mono Way, #220
Sonora, CT 95370
*Actress*

**BIRTHDAY** 1/5/54

## Martin, Ricky
9560 Wilshire Blvd., #500
Beverly Hills, CA 90212
*Singer*

## Martin, Steve
P.O. Box 929
Beverly Hills, CA 90213
*Actor/comedian*

## Martindale, Wink
5744 New Castle
Calabasas, CA 91302
*Television game show host*

**BIRTHDAY** 12/4/34

## Martz, Judy
*Governor of Montana*

**INTERNET** www.state.mt.us/gov2/css/staff/contact.asp

## Marvel Comics
387 Park Ave. S
New York, NY 10016
*Producer of comics*

**INTERNET** www.marvel.com
**E-MAIL** pgitter@marvel.com
Eric Ellenbogen, CEO

## Marx, Richard
15250 Ventura Blvd.
Sherman Oaks, CA 91403
*Musician*

## Masterson, Mary Stuart
P.O. Box 1249
White River, VT 05001
*Actress*

## Matchbox Twenty
9830 Wilshire Blvd.
Beverly Hills, CA 90212
*Music group*

## Mathers, Jerry
10100 Santa Monica Blvd., #2490
Los Angeles, CA 90067
*Actor*

## Matheson, Tim
1187 Coast Village Road, #504
Santa Barbara, CA 93108
*Actor*

**BIRTHDAY** 12/31/48

**Mathis, Johnny**
3500 W Olive Ave., #750
Burbank, CA 91505
*Singer*

**Mattea, Kathy**
P.O. Box 158482
Nashville, TN 37215
*Singer/songwriter*

**Matthews, Dave**
509 Hartnell St.
Monterey, CA 93940
*Musician*

**Mattingly, Don**
12641 Brown Road
Evansville, IN 47711
*Baseball player*

**Mauritania**
Maaouya Ould Sidi Ahmed Taya, President
Presidence de la Republique
B.P. 184
Nouakchott
Mauritania

**INTERNET** www.mauritania.mt

**Mauritius**
Cassam Uteem, President
Government House
Port Louis
Mauritius

**INTERNET** http://ncb.intnet.mu

**Maven, Max**
7095 Hollywood Blvd.
Hollywood, CA 90028
*Mentalist/magician*

**INTERNET** www.maxmaven.com
**E-MAIL** maxmaven@aol.com

**Mavericks, The**
P.O. Box 23329
Nashville, TN 37202
*Music group*

## May Dept. Store, The
207B Westport Road, #202
St. Louis, MO 63101
*General merchandisers*

**INTERNET** www.mayco.com

## Mays, Willie
51 Mount Yernin Ln.
Atherton, CA 94025
*Former baseball player*

**BIRTHDAY** 5/6/31

## Maytag
403 W 4th St. N
Newton, IA 50208
*Electronics, electrical equipment*

**INTERNET** www.maytagcorp.com
Leonard Hadley, Chairman and CEO

## MBNA
1100 N King St.
Wilmington, DE 19884
*Commercial bank*

**INTERNET** www.mbnainternational.com
Charles Cawley, Chairman and CEO

## McAleese, Mary
*President of Ireland*

**INTERNET** www.irlgov.ie
**E-MAIL** webmaster@aras.irlgov.ie

## McBride, Martina
406-68 Water St.
Vancouver
British Columbia
V6B 1A4
*Country music singer*

## McCallister, Dawson
P.O. Box 8123
Irving, TX 75016
*Christian talk show host*

## McCain, John
241 Russell Senate
Office Bldg. (R-AZ)
Washington, D.C. 20510
*Senator*

**E-MAIL** john_mccain@mccain.senate.gov

## McCarthy, Andrew
10345 W Olympic Blvd.
Los Angeles, CA 90064
*Actor*

**BIRTHDAY** 11/29/62

## McCarthy, Jenny

8424A Santa Monica Blvd., #804
West Hollywod, CA 90069
*1994 Playboy Playmate of the Year*
*Former MTV game show host*

**BIRTHDAY** 11/2/72

## McCartney, Sir Paul

1 Soho Square
London WI
England
UNITED KINGDOM
*Musician*

## McCartney, Stella

429 W 14th St.
New York, NY 10014
*Fashion designer*

## McCaughey, Kenny & Bobbi

615 N 1st St.
Carlisle, IA 50047-7709
*Parents of Septuplets*

## McClanahan, Rue

1185 Ave. of the Americas
New York, NY 10036
*Actress*

**BIRTHDAY** 2/21/34

## McClintock, Jessica

1400 16th St.
San Francisco, CA 94103
*Formalwear designer*

## McConaughey, Matthew

1888 Century Park E
Los Angeles, CA 90067
*Actor*

## McConnell, Mitch

361-A Russell Senate
Office Bldg. (R-KY)
Washington, D.C. 20510
*Senator*

**E-MAIL** senator@mcconnell.senate.gov

**McCord, Kent**
15301 Ventura Blvd., #345
Sherman Oaks, CA 91403
*Actor*

**McCormick, Maureen**
22817 Pera Road, #M
Woodland Hills, CA 91364
*Actress*

**McCormick, Pat**
12121 La Maida St., #7
N Hollywood, CA 91607
*Comedian/writer*

**McCoy, Matt**
4526 Wilshire Blvd.
Los Angeles, CA 90010
*Actor*

**McCoy, Neal**
3878 Oak Lawn Ave.
Dallas, TX 75219
*Country music singer*

**McCracken, Jeff**
15760 Ventura Blvd.
Encino, CA 91436
*Singer/songwriter*

**INTERNET** www.countryjoe.com

**McCullough, Julie**
612 Lighthouse Ave.
Pacific Grove, CA 93951
*Actress*

**McDaniel, Mel**
P.O. Box 2285
Hendersonville, TN 37077
*Country music singer*

**McDermott, Dylan**
P.O. Box 25516
Los Angeles, CA 90025
*Actor*

**McDonald's**
McDonald's Plaza
Oak Brook, IL 60523
*Food services*

**INTERNET** www.mcdonalds.com
Donald Washburn, Chairman and CEO

**McDormand, Frances**
79 E 4th St.
New York, NY 10003
*Actor*

**McDowell, Malcolm**
10100 Santa Monica Blvd., 25th Floor
Los Angeles, CA 90067
*Actor*

**BIRTHDAY** 6/19/43

**McDowell, Ronnie**
P.O. Box 268
Russellville, AL 35653
*Country music singer*

**BIRTHDAY** 2/28/55

**McEnroe, John**
23712 Malibu Colony Road
Malibu, CA 90265
*Tennis player*

**McEntyre, Reba**
10210 W Pico Blvd.
Los Angeles, CA 90025
*Country music singer*

**McFadden, Gates**
5555 Melrose Blvd.
Los Angeles, CA 90038
*Actress*

**BIRTHDAY** 8/28/49

**McFerrin, Bobby**
826 Broadway
New York, NY 10003
*Singer*

**McGavin, Darren**
P.O. Box 2939
Beverly Hills, CA 90210
*Actor*

## McGinley, Ted
14951 Alva Dr.
Pacific Palisades, CA 90272
*Actor*

**BIRTHDAY** 5/30/58

## McGovern, Elizabeth
17319 Magnolia Blvd.
Encino, CA 91316
*Actress*

## McGovern, George
P.O. Box 3339
Washington, D.C. 20033
*Ex-Senator/former presidential candidate*

## McGovern, Maureen
163 Amsterdam Ave.
New York, NY 10023-5001
*Singer*

**INTERNET** www.maureenmcgovern.com

## McGraw, Tim
3310 W End Ave., #500
Nashville, TN 37203
*Country music singer*

## McGraw-Hill
1221 Ave. of the Americas
New York, NY 10020
*Publishing, printing*

**INTERNET** www.mcgraw-hill.com
Harold W. McGraw, III, Chairman, President and CEO

## McGregor, Ewan
503/504 Lotts Road
The Cambers
Chelsea Harbour SQ1O OXF
England
UNITED KINGDOM
*Actor*

**BIRTHDAY** 3/31/71

## McGwire, Toby
250 Stadium Plaza
St. Louis, MO 63102
*Baseball player*

## McKeon, Nancy
P.O. Box 6778
Burbank, CA 91510
*Actress*

**BIRTHDAY** 4/4/66

**McKesson HBOC, Inc.**
1 Post St.
San Francisco, CA 94104
*Wholesalers*

**INTERNET** www.mckesson.com
John Hammergren, Chairman

**McLachlan, Sarah**
1650 W 2nd Ave.
BC V67 4R3
British Columbia
Canada
*Singer*

**McMurtry, Larry**
Box 552
Archer City, TX 76351
*Author*

**McMurtry, Tom**
P.O. Box 273
Edwards AFB, CA 93523
*Test pilot*

**McNeil, Robert Duncan**
5555 Melrose Ave.
Los Angeles, CA 90038
*Actor*

**McNichol, Kristy**
151 El Camino Dr.
Beverly Hills, CA 90212
*Actress*

**Mead**
Courthouse Plaza NE
Dayton, OH 45463
*Forest and paper products*

**INTERNET** www.mead.com
John A. Luke, Jr., President and CEO

**Meadows, Audrey**
350 Trousdale Ave.
Beverly Hills, CA 90210
*Actress*

**Meadows, Jayne**
16185 Woodvale Road
Encino, CA 91430
*Actress*

## Meadows, Kristen
13576 Cheltenham Dr.
Sherman Oaks, CA 91423
*Actress*

## Meat Loaf
9255 Sunset Blvd., #200
Los Angeles, CA 90069
*Singer*

**BIRTHDAY** 9/27/51

## Medeiros, Glenn
P.O. Box 8
Kauai, HI 96765
*Singer*

## Media Industry Newsletter
305 Madison Ave., #4417
New York, NY 10165

**INTERNET** www.philips.com
**VOICE** 212-983-5170

## Media Access
950 18th St. NW, #220
Washington, D.C. 20006

**INTERNET** www.mediaacess.org
Andrew Jay Schwartzman, President and CEO

## Media Matters
18 E 41st St., #1806
New York, NY 10017
*Newsletter*

**INTERNET** www.mediadynamicsinc.com
**VOICE** 212-683-7895

## Media Research Center
325 S Patrick St.
Alexandria, VA 22314

**INTERNET** www.mediaresearch.org
**E-MAIL** mrc@mediaresearch.org
L. Brent Bozell III, Founder and Chairman

## Mediascope
12711 Ventura Blvd., #280
Studio City, CA 91604
*Media consultants*

**INTERNET** www.mediascope.org
Hubert D. Jessup, President

## Media Week
1515 Broadway, 12th Floor
New York, NY 10036
*Newsletter*

**INTERNET** www.mediaweek.com
**VOICE** 212-536-5336

## Megadeth
1750 N Vine St.
Hollywood, CA 90028
*Music group*

## Meidani
Albania
Tirane Albania
President I Republikes

**INTERNET** http://president.gov.al

## Mellencamp, John
P.O. Box 6777
Bloomington, IN 47408
*Singer*

## Mellon Bank Corporation
1 Mellon Bank Center
Pittsburgh, PA 15258
*Commercial bank*

**INTERNET** www.mellon.coma
Frank Cahouet, Chairman and CEO

## Memphis Commercial Appeal
**INTERNET** www.gomemphis.com
**VOICE** 901-529-2211

## Menem, Dr. Carlos Saul
Argentina
*Presidente de la Republic*

**INTERNET** www.presidencia.ar

## Mercantile Bank Corporation
216 N Division Ave.
Grand Rapids, MI 49503
*Banking*

Gerald R. Johnson Jr., Chairman

## Merck
1 Merck Dr.
Whitehouse Station, NJ 08889
*Pharmaceuticals*

**INTERNET** www.merck.com
Raymond V. Gilmartin, Chairman and CEO

## Merchant, Natalie
9830 Wilshire Blvd.
Beverly Hills, CA 90212
*Singer*

## Meri, Lennart
*President of Estonia*

**INTERNET** www.presidnet.ee
**E-MAIL** sekretar@vpk.ee

## Merisel
200 Connecticut Blvd.
El Segundo CA 90245
*Computer wholesalers*

**INTERNET** www.merisel.com
Timothy N. Jenson, President, CEO and COO

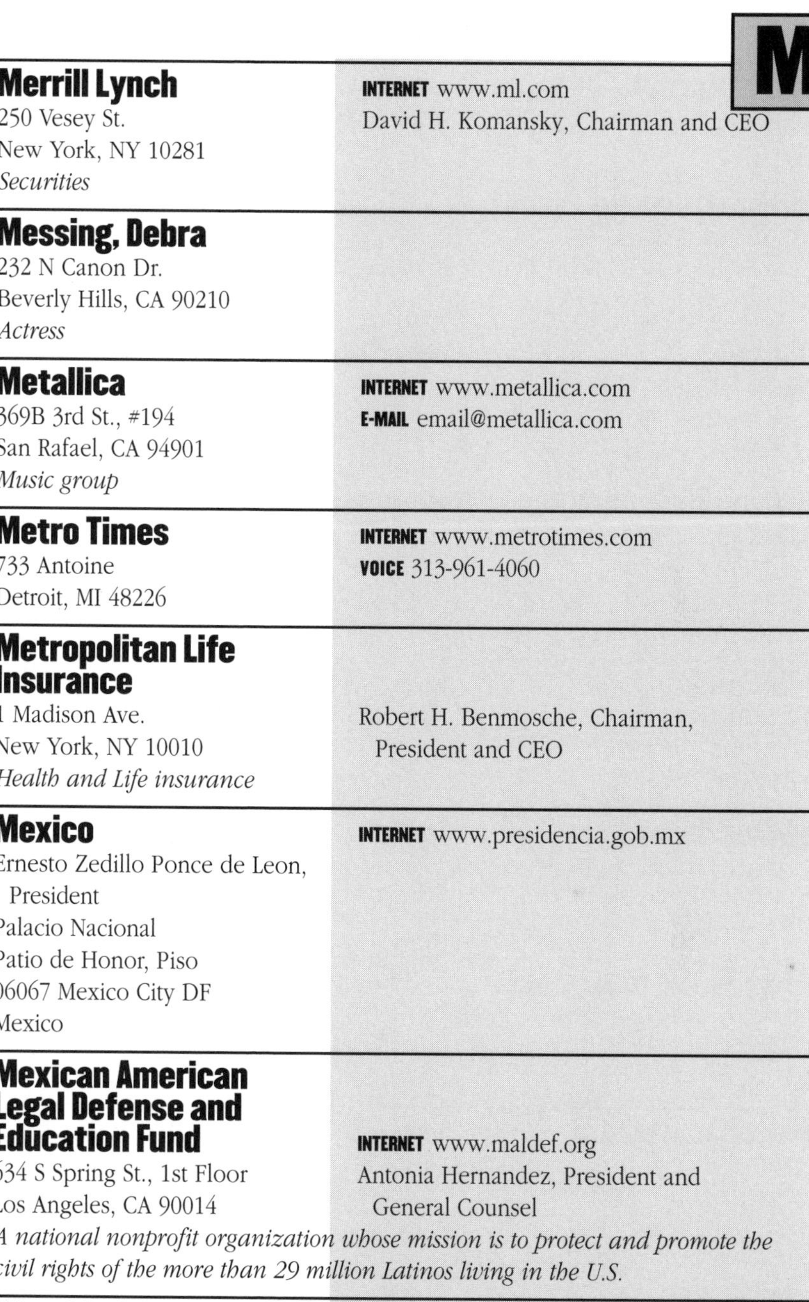

## Merrill Lynch
250 Vesey St.
New York, NY 10281
*Securities*

**INTERNET** www.ml.com
David H. Komansky, Chairman and CEO

## Messing, Debra
232 N Canon Dr.
Beverly Hills, CA 90210
*Actress*

## Metallica
369B 3rd St., #194
San Rafael, CA 94901
*Music group*

**INTERNET** www.metallica.com
**E-MAIL** email@metallica.com

## Metro Times
733 Antoine
Detroit, MI 48226

**INTERNET** www.metrotimes.com
**VOICE** 313-961-4060

## Metropolitan Life Insurance
1 Madison Ave.
New York, NY 10010
*Health and Life insurance*

Robert H. Benmosche, Chairman, President and CEO

## Mexico
Ernesto Zedillo Ponce de Leon, President
Palacio Nacional
Patio de Honor, Piso
06067 Mexico City DF
Mexico

**INTERNET** www.presidencia.gob.mx

## Mexican American Legal Defense and Education Fund
634 S Spring St., 1st Floor
Los Angeles, CA 90014

**INTERNET** www.maldef.org
Antonia Hernandez, President and General Counsel

*A national nonprofit organization whose mission is to protect and promote the civil rights of the more than 29 million Latinos living in the U.S.*

## Miami Dolphins
c/o Miami Arena
2269 NW 199th St.
Miami, FL 33056
*Football team*

## Miami Herald
1 Herald Plaza
Miami, FL 33132

**INTERNET** www.Miami.com
**VOICE** 305-350-2111

## Michael, George
338 N Foothill Road
Beverly Hills, CA 90210
*Singer*

## MicroAge
2400 S MicroAge Way
Tempe, AZ 85282
*Computer wholesalers*

**INTERNET** www.microage.com
Jeffrey D. McKeever, Chairman and CEO

## Micron Technology
8000 S Federal Way
CEO
Boise, ID 83707
*Electronics, electrical equipment*

**INTERNET** www.micron.com
Steve R. Appleton, Chairman, President and

## Microsoft
1 Microsoft Way
Redmond, WA 98052
*Computer software*

**INTERNET** www.microsoft.com
Steven A. Ballmer, President and CEO

## Midler, Bette
1222 16th Ave. S, 3rd Floor
Nashville, TN 37212
*Actress/singer*

**BIRTHDAY** 12/1/45

## Mike & The Mechanics
9200 Sunset Blvd.
Los Angeles, CA 90069
*Music group*

## Mikulski, Barbara
709 Hart Senate
Office Bldg. (D-MD)
Washington, D.C. 20510
*Senator*

**E-MAIL** senator@mikulski.senate.gov

## Milano, Alyssa
P.O. Box 1326
Torrance, CA 90505
*Actress*

**BIRTHDAY** 12/19/73

**Miles, Vera**
P.O. Box 1599
Palm Desert, CA 92261
*Actress*

**BIRTHDAY** 8/23/29

**Miller, Arthur**
Tophet Road
Box 320, R #1
Roxbury, CT 06783
*Playwright*

**Miller, Zell**
257 Dirksen Senate
Office Bldg. (D-GA)
Washington, D.C. 20510
*Senator*

**INTERNET** www.miller.senate.gov/email.htm

**Miller, Dennis**
7800 Beverly Blvd.
Los Angeles, CA 90036
*Television host/comedian/actor*

**BIRTHDAY** 11/3/53

**Mills, Donna**
253 26th St., #269
Santa Monica, CA 90402
*Actress*

**Mills, Hayley**
81 High St.
Hampton Middlesex
England
UNITED KINGDOM
*Actress*

**Mills, Sir John**
Hill House
Denham Village
GB-Buckinghamshire
England
UNITED KINGDOM
*Actor*

**BIRTHDAY** 2/22/08

**Milsap, Ronnie**
P.O. Box 40655
Nashville, TN 37203
*Country music singer*

## Milwaukee Brewers
P.O. Box 3099
Milwaukee, WI 53214
*Baseball team*

## Milwaukee Bucks
1001 N 4th St.
Milwaukee, WI 53203
*Basketball team*

## Milwaukee Journal
333 W State St.
Milwaukee, WI 53201

**INTERNET** www.jsonline.com
**VOICE** 414-224-2000

## Minghella, Anthony
2 St. Charles Place
London W10 6EG
England
UNITED KINGDOM
*Film director*

## Minnelli, Liza
150 E 69th St., #21-G
New York, NY 10021
*Actress*

**BIRTHDAY** 3/12/46

## Minnesota Mining and Manufacturing
3M Center
St. Paul, MN 55144
*Scientific, photo, control equipment*

**INTERNET** www.mmm.com
W. James McNerney, Jr., Chairman and CEO

## Minnesota Timberwolves
600 First Ave N
Minneapolis, MN 55403
*Basketball team*

## Minnesota Twins
34 Kirby Puckett Place
Minneapolis, MN 55415
*Baseball team*

## Minnesota Vikings
9520 Viking Dr.
Minneapolis, MN 55344
*Football team*

## Miss America Pageant
1325 Boardwalk
Atlantic City, NJ 08401

**INTERNET** www.missamerica.org
Robert Renneisen Jr., President and CEO

## Miss Piggy
1 Lincoln Plaza
New York, NY 10022
*Star of The Muppets*

## Miss Teen USA
c/o Rubenstein Public Relations
1345 Ave. of the Americas
New York, NY 10105

**INTERNET** www.missteenusa.com

## Miro, Muhammad Mustafa
Office of the President
Syria
Damascus Syria
*Prime Minister*

## Mitchell, George
8280 Greensboro Dr.
McLean, VA 22102
*Former Senator*

## Mitchell, Joni
1505 W 2nd Ave., #200
Vancouver, BC V6H 3Y4
Canada
*Singer*

## Moceanu, Dominique
17911 Fall River Circle
Houston, TX 77090
*Olympic gymnast*

## Modern Bride
249 W 17th St.
New York, NY 10011

**INTERNET** www.modernbride.com
**VOICE** 212-462-3600

**Modern Health**
740 N Rush St.
Chicago, IL 60611

INTERNET www.modernhealthcare.com
VOICE 312-280-3173

---

**Modine, Matthew**
8942 Wilshire Blvd.
Beverly Hills, CA 90211
*Actor*

BIRTHDAY 3/22/59

---

**Mohamad, Dr. Dato Seri Mahathir**
*Malaysia Prime Minister*

INTERNET www.smpke.jpm.my

---

**Moldova**
Petru Lucinschi, President
Office of the President
154, Stefan cel Mara Blvd.
Chisinau
Moldova

INTERNET www.moldova.md

---

**Moll, Richard**
1119 N Amalfi Dr.
Pacific Palisades, CA 90272
*Actor*

BIRTHDAY 1/13/43

---

**Molne, M.I. Sr. Marc Forne**
Cap de Govern
Carrer Prat de la Geu 62
Andorra la Vella
Andorra

INTERNET www.andorra.ad/govern

---

**Monaco**
Prince Rainer II
Palais de Monaco
Boit Postal 518
98015 Monte Carlo
Monaco

---

**Money, Eddie**
P.O. Box 1994
San Francisco, CA 94142
*Singer*

---

**Money**
1271 Ave. of the Americas
New York, NY 10020
*Magazine*

INTERNET www.money.com
VOICE 212-522-1212

## Mongolia

**INTERNET** www.pmis.gov.mn

Natsagryn Bagabandi, President
State House
12 Ulaanbaatar
Mongolia

## Monkees, The

16035 Santa Monica Blvd.
Los Angeles, CA 90025
*Music group*

## Monsanto

**INTERNET** www.monsanto.com
Robert B. Shapiro, President and CEO

800 N Lindbergh Blvd.
St. Louis, MO 63167
*Chemicals*

## Montana, Joe

21515 Hawthorne Blvd.
Torrance, CA 90503-6503
*Former football player*

## Montel Williams Show, The

**INTERNET** www.montelshow.com

## Montiero, Antonio Mascarenahas

Office of the President
520 Latimer Road
Sao Taigo, Praia Concelho
Cidade de Praia Cape Verdi
*President*

## Montreal Canadians

Montreal Forum
2313 St. Catherine St. W
Montreal, PQ H3H 1N2
Canada
*Hockey team*

## Montreal Expos

**INTERNET** www.montrealexpos.com

P.O. Box 500, Station M
Montreal, Quebec H1V 3P2
Canada
*Baseball team*

**Monty Python**
68-A Delancey St.
Camdentown, London NW170W
England
UNITED KINGDOM

**Moody Blues, The**
Rt. 1, Box 57
Belvedere, NC 27919
*Music group*

**Moore, Demi**
9830 Wilshire Blvd.
Beverly Hills, CA 90212
*Actress*

**Moore, Julianne**
9830 Wilshire Blvd.
Beverly Hills, 90212
*Actress*

**Moore, Mary Tyler**
*Actress*
BIRTHDAY 12/29/36
E-MAIL mtmpix@aol.com

**Moore, Sir Roger**
889 Beverly Blvd., #713
Los Angeles, CA 90048
*Actor*
BIRTHDAY 10/14/27

**Moran, Erin**
P.O. Box 3261
Quartz Hill, CA 93586
*Actress*
BIRTHDAY 10/18/61

**Moranis, Rick**
101 Central Park W, #12-B
New York, NY 10023
*Actor*

**Morauta, Hon. Mekere**
*Papua New Guinea Prime Minister*
INTERNET www.pm.gov.pg

## Morgan, Stanley, Dean Witter and Co.

1585 Broadway
New York, NY 10036
*Securities*

**INTERNET** www.deanwitterdiscover.com
Richard Martini, CEO

## Morissette, Alanis

75 Rockefeller Plaza
New York, NY 10019
*Singer/songwriter*

## Morita, Noriyuki 'Pat'

2705 Cricket Hollow Ct.
Henderson, NV 89014
*Actor*

**BIRTHDAY** 6/28/30

## Morocco

King Mohammed VI Ibn Al Hassan
Palais Royal
Rabat
Morocco

**INTERNET** www.mincom.gov.ma

## Morris, Gary

2829 Dogwood Place
Nashville, TN 37204
*Singer/songwriter*

## Morrison, Van

59 Oxford Road S
Cheswick, London W43DD
England
UNITED KINGDOM
*Singer*

**BIRTHDAY** 8/31/45

## Moscosco, Mireya Elisa

*Panama President*

**INTERNET** www.presidencia.gob.pa

## Moss, Kate

5 Jubilee Place, 1st Floor
London SW3 3TD
England
UNITED KINGDOM
*Model*

**BIRTHDAY** 1/16/74

## Mother Jones
731 Market St., 6th Floor
San Francisco, CA 94103

**INTERNET** www.motherjones.com
**VOICE** 415-665-6637

## Motley Crue
9255 Sunset Blvd., #200
Los Angeles, CA 90069
*Music group*

## Motorola
1303 E Algonquin Road
Schaumburg, IL 60196
*Electronics, electrical equipment*

**INTERNET** www.mot.com
Christopher B. Galvin, Chairman and CEO

## Mottola, Thomas D.
550 Madison Ave.
New York, NY 10022
*Music producer*

## Movie Channel, The
1633 Broadway
New York, NY 10019
*Cable network*

## Mozambique
His Excellency Joaquim Alberto Chissano, President
Avenida Julius Nyerere 2000
Caixa Postal 285
Maputo
Mozambique

**INTERNET** www.mozambique.com

## MSNBC
2200 Fletcher Ave.
Fort Lee, NJ 07024
*Cable network*

## Mswati III
King of Swaziland

**INTERNET** http://home.swazi.com/government
**E-MAIL** ppcu@realnet.co.sz

## MTV
1515 Broadway
New York, NY 10036
*Cable network*

**INTERNET** www.mtv.com
Olle Langenius, Chairman and CEO

## Mubarak, Mohammed Hosni
*President of Egypt*

**INTERNET** www.presidency.gov.eg
**E-MAIL** webmaster@presidency.gov.eg

## Mulgrew, Kate
5555 Melrose Ave.
Los Angeles, CA 90038
*Actress*

**BIRTHDAY** 4/29/55

## Multinational PR Report
P.O. Box 39244
Washington, D.C. 20016
*Newsletter*

**VOICE** 202-244-2580

## Muppets
P.O. Box 20750
New York, NY 10023
*Television show*

## Murkowski, Frank
*Governor of Alaska*

**INTERNET** www.gov.state.ak.us/emailform.html

## Murkowski, Lisa
322 Hart Senate
Office Bldg. (R-AK)
Washington, D.C. 20510
*Senator*

**INTERNET** www.murkowski.senate.gov

## Murphey, Michael Martin
9830 Wilshire Blvd.
Beverly Hills, CA 90212
*Country music singer*

## Murphy, Eddie
1740 Broadway, 15th Floor
New York, NY 10019
*Actor/comedian*

**BIRTHDAY** 4/3/61

## Murray, Anne
4950 Yonge St., #2400
Toronto, Ontario
Canada M2N 6K1
*Singer*

**INTERNET** www.annemurray.com

## Murray, Bill
9830 Wilshire Blvd.
Beverly Hills, CA 90212
*Actor/comedian*

**BIRTHDAY** 9/21/50

## Murray, Patty
173 Russell Senate
Office Bldg. (D-WA)
Washington, D.C. 20510
*Senator*

**E-MAIL** senator_murray@murray.senate.gov

## Musgrove, Ronnie
*Governor of Mississippi*

**E-MAIL** governor@governor.state.ms.us

## Myanmar
Than Shwa, Chairman
State Peace and
Development Council
Ministry of Defense
Signal Pagoda Road
Yangon Myanmar

## Myers, Mike
9150 Wilshire Blvd.
Beverly Hills, CA 90212
*Actor*

## Nabors, Jim
P.O. Box 10364
Honolulu, HI 96816
*Actor/singer*

## Nader, Ralph
1600 20th St. NW
Washington, D.C. 20009
*Green Party former presidential candidate*

## Namibia
San Nujoma, President
State House, Robert Mugabe Ave.
Private Bag 13339
Windhoek, Namibia

**INTERNET** www.republicofnamibia.com

## Napolitano, Janet
*Governor of Arizona*

**INTERNET** www.governor.state.az.us
/post/feedback.cfm

## Nash, Graham
230 E Union St.
Pasadena, CA 91101
*Musician*

**INTERNET** www.grahamnash.com

## Nashville Network, The
2806 Opryland Dr.
Nashville, TN 37214
*Cable network*

## Nashville Tennessean
1100 Broadway
Nashville, TN 37202

**INTERNET** www.tennessean.com
**VOICE** 615-259-8000

## National
*Car rental agency*

**INTERNET** www.nationalrentalcars.com
**VOICE** 1-800-227-7368

## National Aeronautics and Space Administration (NASA)
300 E St. SW
Washington, D.C. 20546

**INTERNET** www.nasa.org

## National Alliance for the Mentally Ill
2107 Wilson Blvd., #300
Arlington, VA 22201

**INTERNET** www.nami.org
Bob Beall, Executive Director

*An organization working with and for persons with mental illnesses and their families*

## National Aphasia Association
814 Thayer Ave.
New York, NY 10010

**INTERNET** www.aphasia.com

*An organization dedicated to promoting the care, welfare and rehabilitation of those with aphasia through public education and support of research*

## National Association of the Deaf
246 Sycamore St., #100
Silver Spring, MD 20910

**INTERNET** www.nad.org

*The oldest and largest organization representing people with hearing disabilities in the U.S.*

## National Black Deaf Advocates
1200 W Harrison St., #2010
Decatur, GA 30030

**INTERNET** www.nbda.org

## National Council on Stuttering

4245 E Ave.
Chicago, IL 60607

*Provides information about the prevention and treatment of stuttering*

## National Cued Speech Association

**INTERNET** www.cuedspeech.org

6931 Arlington Road
Rochester, NY 14618

*Cued Speech is a sound-based visual communication system*

## National Cystic Fibrosis Foundation

**INTERNET** www.cff.org

230 W Monroe St., #1800
Bethesda, MD 20814

*Assures the development of the means to cure and control cystic fibrosis and to improve the quality of life for those with the disease*

## National Enquirer

**INTERNET** www.nationalenquirer.com
**VOICE** 561-997-7733

5401 NW Broken Sound
Boca Raton, FL 33487

## National Foundation on the Arts and Humanities

1100 Pennsylvania Ave. NW
Washington, D.C. 20506

## National Labor Relations Board (NLRB)

1099 14th St. NW
Washington, D.C. 20570

## National Mediation Board

1301 K St. NW, #250 East
Washington, D.C. 20572

## National Multiple Sclerosis Society

**INTERNET** www.nmss.org

733 3rd Ave., 6th Floor
New York, NY 10017

## National Parkinson's Disease Foundation

**INTERNET** www.parkinson.org

1501 NW 9th Ave.
Miami, FL 33136
*Its goal is to find the cause and cure for Parkinson's Disease*

## National Science Foundation (NSF)

4201 Wilson Blvd.
Washington, D.C. 22230

## National Security Council (NSC)

Old Executive Office Bldg.
Washington, D.C. 20503

## National Spasmodic Dysphonia Association, Inc.

**INTERNET** www.dysphonia-foundation.org

5100 E La Palma Ave., #208
Chicago, IL 60601
*A nonprofit organization whose main focus is to promote public awareness of Spasmodic Dysphonia*

## National Stuttering Project

**INTERNET** www.nsastutter.org

1 E Wacker Dr., #2430
Anaheim Hills, CA 92807
*A network of more than 75 active local support groups and programs collaborating to meet the needs of children and adults who stutter*

## National Transportation Safety Board

490 L'Enfant Plaza SW
Washington, D.C. 20594

## Nauru

Bernard Dowiyogo, President
Parliament House
Yaren District
Nauru-Central Pacific

## Nazarbayev, Nursultan

President of Kazakhstan
480091 Almaty Kazakhstan

## NBC Nightly News

**INTERNET** www.nbc.com
**VOICE** 212-664-4444

## Neal, Patricia

45 E End Ave.
New York, NY 10028
*Actress*

**BIRTHDAY** 1/20/26

## Neeson, Liam

245 W 52nd St.
New York, NY 10019
*Actor*

## Nelson, Willie

P.O. Box 91659
Austin, TX 78749
*Singer/songwriter*

**BIRTHDAY** 4/30/33

## Nelson, Bill

716 Hart Senate
Office Bldg. (D-FL)
Washington, D.C. 20510
*Senator*

**INTERNET** www.billnelson.senate.gov/contact/index.cfm#email

## Nelson, Ben

720 Hart Senate
Office Bldg. (D-NE)
Washington, D.C. 20510
*Senator*

**INTERNET** www.bennelson.senate.gov/email.html

## Nelson, Craig T.

28872 Boniface Dr.
Malibu, CA 90265
*Actor*

## Nepal

King Birendra Bir Bikram
Shah Dev
Narayanhity Royal Palace
Kathmandu
Nepal

## Netherlands
Willem Kok, Prime Minister
Binnenhof 20, 2513 AA
Post Bus 20001, 2500EA
The Hague, Netherlands

**INTERNET** www.postbus51.nl

## Neville, Aaron
P.O. Box 750187
New Orleans, LA 70175
*Singer*

## New England Patriots
Gillette Stadium
One Patriot Place
Foxboro, MA 02035-1388
*Football team*

## New Haven Register
40 Sargent Dr.
New Haven, CT 06511

**INTERNET** www.nhregister.com
**VOICE** 203-789-5200

## New Jersey Devils
P.O. Box 504
East Rutherford, NJ 07073
*Hockey team*

## New Jersey Nets
405 Murray Hill Pkwy
East Rutherford, NJ 07073
*Basketball team*

## New Millennium Entertainment
301 N. Canon Dr., Suite 214
Beverly Hills, CA 90210
*Publishers*

**INTERNET** www.nmaudio.com
**VOICE** 310-273-7722
Michael Viner, CEO

## New Orleans Hornets
1501 Girod St.
New Orleans, LA 70113
*Basketball team*

**INTERNET** www.nba.com/hornets

## New Orleans Saints
1500 Poydras St.
Metairie, LA 70003
*Football team*

## New Times
P.O. Box 2510
Phoenix, AZ 85002

**INTERNET** www.Phoenixtimesnews.com
**VOICE** 602-271-0040

## New York Daily News
415 W 33rd St.
New York, NY 10001

**INTERNET** www.nydailynews.com
**VOICE** 212-210-2100

## New York Giants
c/o Nassau Coliseum
East Rutherford, NJ 07073
*Football team*

## New York Islanders
c/o Nassau Coliseum
Uniondale, NY 11533
*Hockey team*

## New York Jets
1000 Fulton Ave.
Hempstead, NY 11550-1099
*Football team*

## New York Knicks
2 Pennsylvania Plaza
New York, NY 10121
*Basketball team*

## New York Life Insurance
51 Madison Ave.
New York, NY 10010
*Health and Life insurance*

Seymour G. Stemberg, Chairman, President and CEO

## New York Magazine
444 Madison Ave., 14th Floor
New York, NY 10022

**INTERNET** www.newyorkmag.com
**VOICE** 212-560-2001

## New York Mets
c/o Shea Stadium
123-01 Roosevelt Ave.
Flushing, NY 11368
*Baseball team*

## New York Post
1211 Ave. of the Americas
New York, NY 10036

**INTERNET** www.nypostonline.com
**VOICE** 212-930-8000

## New York Rangers
4 Pennsylvania Ave.
New York, NY 10001
*Hockey team*

## New York Yankees
c/o Yankee Stadium
161st St. and River Ave.
Bronx, NY 10451
*Baseball team*

## New Yorker
4 Times Square
New York, NY 10036

**INTERNET** www.newyorker.com
**VOICE** 212-840-3800

## New Zealand
Helen Clark, Prime Minister
Prime Minister's Office
Parliament House, Executive Wing
Wellington, New Zealand

**INTERNET** www.executive.govt.nz/minister/pm/index.html
**E-MAIL** pm@ministers.govt.nz

## Newell Rubbermaid Inc.
29 E Stephenson St.
Freeport, IL 61032
*Metal products*

**INTERNET** www.newellco.com
Joe Gallie, CEO

## Newhart, Bob
420 Anapolo Dr.
Los Angeles, CA 90077
*Actor*

## Newman, Paul
555 Long Wharf Dr.
New Haven, CT 06511
*Actor/philanthropist*

## NewsRadio cast
9150 Wilshire Blvd.
Beverly Hills, CA 90212
*Television show*

## Newsweek
251 W 57th St.
New York, NY 10019

**INTERNET** www.newsweek.com
**VOICE** 212-445-4000

## Newton, Wayne

3422 Happy Ln.
Las Vegas, NV 89120
*Singer*

## Niagara Mohawk Holdings, Inc.

300 Erie Blvd. W
Syracuse, NY 13202
*Gas and electric utilities*

**INTERNET** www.nimo.com
William E. Davis, CEO

## Nicaragua

Amoldo Aleman Lacayo,
Presidente
Casa de la Presidencia
Avenida Bolivar y Dupla Sur
Managua
Nicaragua

**INTERNET** www.presidencia.gob.ni

## Nichols, Nichelle

22647 Ventura Blvd.
Woodland Hills, CA 91364
*Actress*

**E-MAIL** nichelle@uhura.com

## Nicholson, Jack

11500 W Olympic Blvd., #510
Los Angeles, CA 90064
*Actor*

**BIRTHDAY** 4/22/37

## Nickelodeon

1515 Broadway
New York, NY 10036
*Cable network*

## Nicklaus, Jack

1170 US Highway 1
North Palm Beach, FL 33408
*Professional golfer*

**BIRTHDAY** 1/21/40

## Nickles, Don

133 Hart Senate
Office Bldg. (R-OK)
Washington, D.C. 20510
*Senator*

**E-MAIL** senator@nickles.senate.gov

## Nicks, Stevie

P.O. Box 112083
Carrollton, TX 75011
*Singer*

## Nielsen, Brigitte

P.O. Box 57593
Sherman Oaks, CA 91403
*Actress*

**BIRTHDAY** 7/15/63

## Nielsen, Leslie

1622 Viewmont Dr.
Los Angeles, CA 90069
*Actor*

## Niger

President de la Communaute
Urbain
BP 258
Niarney
Niger

## Nigeria

Olusegun Obasanjo, President
Presidential Villa
State House, Aso Rock
Abuja
Nigeria

**INTERNET** www.nigeriagov.org
**E-MAIL** president.obasanjo@nigeriagov.org

## Nightline

47 W 66th St.
New York, NY 10023

**INTERNET** www.abc.com
**VOICE** 212-887-4995

## Nike

1 Bowerman Dr.
Beaverton, OR 97005
*Apparel/footwear*

**INTERNET** www.nike.com
Philip H. Knight, Chairman, President and CEO

## Nimoy, Leonard

2300 W Victory Blvd., #C-384
Burbank, CA 91506
*Actor*

**BIRTHDAY** 3/26/31

## Nine Inch Nails

83 Riverside Dr.
New York, NY 10019
*Music group*

## Nintendo of America, Inc.

4820 150th Ave. NE
Redmond, WA 98052

**INTERNET** www.nintendo.com
Howard Lincoln, President

## No Doubt

P.O. Box 8899
Anaheim, CA 92812
*Music group*

## Nolte, Nick

c/o Kingsgate Films
6153 Bonsall Dr.
Malibu, CA 90265
*Actor*

## Nordstrom

617 6th Ave.
Seattle, WA 98101
*General merchandisers*

**INTERNET** www.nordstrom.com
Bruce Nordstrom, Chairman

## Norfolk Southern

3 Commercial Place
CEO
Norfolk, VA 23510
*Railroads*

**INTERNET** www.nscorp.com
David R. Goode, Chairman, President and

## Norris, Chuck

18653 Ventura Blvd., #751
Tarzana, CA 91356
*Actor*

**BIRTHDAY** 3/10/40

## North Cyprus

H.E. Raul Denktas, President
The Office of the President
Mersin 10
Lefkosa
N Cyprus, Turkey

**INTERNET** www.kktc.pubinfo.gov.nc.tr

## North Korea

Kim Jong Il
President, Standing Committee
Supreme People's Assembly
Pyongyang
North Korea

## North, Oliver

22570 Markey Cove, #240
Dulles, VA 20166
*Military leader/politician*

## Northeast Utilities

174 Brush Hill Ave.
W Springfield, MA 01090
*Gas and electric utilities*

**INTERNET** www.nu.com
Michael G. Morris, CEO

## Northrop Grumman

1840 Century Park E
Los Angeles, CA 90067
*Aerospace*

**INTERNET** www.northgrum.com
Ronald D. Sugar, Chairman, President and
CEO

## Northwest Airlines

5101 Northwest Dr.
St. Paul, MN 55111
*Airline*

**INTERNET** www.nwa.com
Gary L. Wilson, Chairman

## Northwestern Mutual Life Insurance

720 E Wisconsin Ave.
Milwaukee, WI 53202
*Health and Life insurance*

**INTERNET** www.northwesternmutual.com
Edward J. Zore, Chairman and CEO

## Norway

King Harald V
Royal Palace
Det. Kgl. Slott, Drammensveien 1
N-0010 Oslo
Norway

**INTERNET** www.kongehuset.no

## Norwest Venture Capital

80 S 8th St.
Minneapolis, MN 55402
*Venture capital*

**INTERNET** www.norwestvc.com
John E. Lindahl, Managing General Partner

### *NSYNC
7380 St. Lake Road, #350
Orlando, FL 32819
*Music group*

### Nuclear Energy Institute
1776 I St. NW, #400
Washington, D.C. 20006
**INTERNET** www.nei.org
Marvin Fertel, Sr. Vice President
*The nuclear energy industry's Washington-based policy organization*

### Nuclear Information and Resource Service
1424 16th St. NW, #601
Washington, D.C. 20036
**INTERNET** www.nirs.org
Michael Mariotte, Chair
*Organization concerned with nuclear power, radioactive waste, radiation and sustainable energy issues*

### Nuclear Regulatory Commission (NRC)
11555 Rockville Plaza
Rockville, MD 20852

### Nucor
2100 Rexford Road
Charlotte, NC 28211
**INTERNET** www.nucor.com
Dan DiMicco, Chairman, President and CEO
*Metals*

### Nye 'The Science Guy', Bill
401 Mercer St.
Seattle, WA 98109
*"The Science Guy"*

### O Magazine
1700 Broadway
New York, NY 10012
**INTERNET** www.oprah.com
**VOICE** 212-925-3180

### Oak Ridge Boys
88 New Schackle Road
Hendersonville, TN 37075
*Country music group*

### Oakland Athletics
c/o Oakland Alameda Coliseum
7677 Oakport St.
Oakland, CA 94621
*Baseball team*

### Oakland Raiders

c/o Oakland Alameda Coliseum
Oakland, CA 94621
*Football team*

### Oasis

54 Linhope St.
London NW1 6HL
England
UNITED KINGDOM
*Music group*

**E-MAIL** thefans@oasisnet.com

### O'Bannon, Frank

*Governor of Indiana*

**E-MAIL** fobannon@state.in.us

### O'Brien, Conan

c/o Late Night
30 Rockefeller Plaza
New York, NY 10012
*Host of* Late Night with Conan O'Brien

### Occidental Petroleum

10889 Wilshire Blvd.
Los Angeles, CA 90024
*Chemicals*

**INTERNET** www.oxy.com
Ray R. Irani, Chairman and CEO

### O'Connor, Carroll Fan club

c/o Twentieth Television
30826 Broad Beach Road
Malibu, CA 90265
*Actor*

### O'Dell, Nancy

P.O. Box 900
Beverly Hills, CA 90213
*Entertainment Talk Show Host*

### O'Donnell, Chris

2029 Central Park E, #500
Los Angeles, CA 90067
*Actor*

### O'Donnell, Rosie

1271 Ave. of the Americas
New York, NY 10020
*Comedian/actress*

## O'Dwyer's Marketplace

271 Madison Ave., #600
New York, NY 10016
*Newsletter*

**INTERNET** www.odwyerpr.com
**VOICE** 212-679-2471

## Office Depot

2200 Old Germantown Road
Delray Beach, FL 33445
*Specialist retailer*

**INTERNET** www.officedepot.com
Bruce Nelson, Chairman

## Office Max

3605 Warrensville Center Road
Shaker Heights, OH 44122
*Specialist retailer*

**INTERNET** www.officemax.com
Peter Shaw, Chairman and CEO

## Office of Administration

Old Executive Office Bldg., #725
Washington, D.C. 20503

## Office of Management and Budget

Executive Office Bldg.
Washington, D.C. 20503

## Office of National Drug Control Policy

Executive Office of The President
Washington, D.C. 20502

## Office of Personnel Management

1900 E St. NW
Washington, D.C. 20415

## Office of the United States Trade Representative

600 17th St. NW
Washington, D.C. 20508

## O'Hara, Maureen

Box 1400
St. Croix, VT 00820
*Actress*

**BIRTHDAY** 8/17/20

## OIC International

240 W Tulpehocken St.
Philadelphia, PA 19144
*The international arm of Rev. Leon H. Sullivan's self-help work skills training movement and job education programs, serving Africa and developing nations worldwide*

**INTERNET** www.oicinternational.org

## Olajuwon, Hakeem

2 Greenway Plaza, #400
Houston, TX 77046
*Basketball player*

## Olmos, Edward James

2020 Ave. of the Stars, #500
Los Angeles, CA 90067
*Actor*

**BIRTHDAY** 2/24/47

## Olsen, Ashley

1801 Century Park E., 12th Floor
Los Angeles, CA 90067
*Actress*

## Olsen, Mary Kate

1801 Century Park E., 12th Floor
Los Angeles, CA 90067
*Actress*

## Olsten

175 Broad Hollow Road
Melville, NY 11747
*Temporary employment services*

**INTERNET** www.olsten.com
Edward Blechschmidt, CEO

## Omaha World Herald

1334 Dodge St.
Omaha, NE 68102

**INTERNET** www.omaha.com
**VOICE** 402-444-1000

## Oman

Qabus bin said Al said
Sultan
The Palace
Muscat
Oman

**INTERNET** www.om.zest.co.ae

## Omnicom

437 Madison Ave.
New York, NY 10022
*Advertising, marketing*

Roger Nguyen, President and CEO

## O'Neal, Ryan

21368 Pacific Coast Hwy
Los Angeles, CA 90265
*Actor*

## O'Neal, Shaquille

P.O. Box 951840
Lake Mary, FL 32795
*Basketball player*

## O'Neal, Tatum

300 Central Park W
New York, NY 10024
*Actress*

## Ono, Yoko

1 W 72nd St.
New York, NY 10023
*Wife of the late John Lennon*

## Opportunity

73 Spring St.
New York, NY 10012
*Magazine*

**INTERNET** www.opportunitymag.com
**VOICE** 212-925-3180

## Oprah Winfrey Show, The

110 N Carpenter
Chicago, IL 60607

**INTERNET** www.oprah.com
**VOICE** 312-633-0808

## Oracle

500 Oracle Pkwy
Redwood City, CA 94065
*Computer software*

**INTERNET** www.oracle.com
Lawrence J. Ellison, Chairman and CEO

## Orange County Register

625 N Grand Ave.
Santa Ana, CA 92711

**INTERNET** www.ocregister.com
**VOICE** 714-835-1234

## Orlando Magic
8701 Maitland Summit Blvd.
Orlando, FL 32810
*Basketball team*

## Orlando Sentinel
633 N Orange Ave.
Orlando, FL 32801

**INTERNET** www.orlandosentinel.com
**VOICE** 407-420-5000

## Ormond, Julia
9465 Wilshire Blvd., #517
Beverly Hills, CA 90212
*Actress*

**BIRTHDAY** 1/4/65

## Osborne, Jeffrey
1325 Ave. of the Americas
New York, NY 10019
*Singer*

## Osbourne, Ozzy
P.O. Box 5249
Beverly Hills, CA 90209
Singer

## Osmond, Donny & Marie
51 W Center, #424
Orem, UT 84057
*Singers/performers*

## Osmond, Marie
3325 N University, #375
Provo, UT 84605
*Singer*

**BIRTHDAY** 10/13/59

## Oteri, Cheri
30 Rockefeller Plaza
New York, NY 10112
*Actress/comedian*

## Outdoor Life
2 Park Ave.
New York, NY 10016
*Magazine*

**INTERNET** www.outdoorlife.com

**Overture.com**
140 W Union St.
Pasadena, CA 91103
*Web portal*

INTERNET www.goto.com
Ted Meisel, CEO

**Owens, Buck**
3223 Sillect Ave.
Bakersfield, CA 93308
*Country music singer*

**Owens and Minor**
4800 Cox Road
Glen Allen, VA 23060
*Wholesalers*

INTERNET www.owens-minor.com
David T. Brown, Chairman and CEO

**Owens-Corning**
1 Owens Corning Pkwy
Toledo, OH 43659
*Building materials, glass*

INTERNET www.owenscorning.com
Glen H. Hiner, Chairman and CEO

**Owens-Illinois**
1 Sea Gate
Toledo, OH 43666
*Building materials, glass*

Joseph H. Lemieux, Chairman and CEO

**Owens, Bill**
136 State Capitol
Denver, CO 80203
*Governor of Colorado*

E-MAIL governorowens@state.co.us

**Oxford Health Plans**
48 Monroe Tpke
Trumbull, CT 06611
*Healthcare*

INTERNET www.oxhp.com
Norman C. Payson, Chairman and CEO

**Oz, Frank**
P.O. Box 20726
New York, NY 10023
*Puppeteer*

**PACCAR**
777 106th Ave. NE
Bellevue, WA 98009
*Motor vehicles and parts*

INTERNET www.paccar.com
Mark Pigott, Chairman Emeritus

## Pacific Life Insurance
700 Newport Center Dr.
Newport Beach, CA 92660
*Health and Life insurance*

**INTERNET** www.pacificlife.com
Thomas C. Sutton, Chairman and CEO

## PacifiCare Health Systems
3120 W Lake Center Dr.
Santa Ana, CA 92704
Brad A. Bowlus, Chairman
*Healthcare*

**INTERNET** www.pacificare.com

## Pacificorp
700 NE Multnomah St.
Portland, OR 97232
*Gas and electric utilities*

**INTERNET** www.pacificorp.com
Judi Johansen, President and CEO

## Pacino, Al
350 Park Ave., #900
New York, NY 10022
*Actor*

**BIRTHDAY** 4/25/40

## Pakistan
Muhammad Rafiq Tarar, President
Office of the President
Constitution Ave.
Islamabad
Pakistan

## Palau
Kumiuro Nakamura, President
Office of the President
P.O. Box 100
Koro
Palau (Pacific Ocean)

## Palestine
Yassir Arafat, President
Palestinian National Authority
Abu Khadra Bldg.
Omar al-Mukhtar St.
Gaza, via Israel

**INTERNET** www.pna.org

## Palmer, Arnold

9000 Bay Hill Road
Orlando, FL 32819
*Golfer*

## Palmer, Robert

c/o Tribeca Productions
2-A Chelsea Manor
SW3
England
UNITED KINGDOM
*Singer*

## Paltrow, Gwyneth

8500 Wilshire Blvd., #700
Beverly Hills, CA 90211
*Actress*

## Panama

Mireya Elisa Moscoso de Arias
President
Palacio de las Garzas
Panama City
Panama

**INTERNET** www.presidencia.gob.pa

## Papua New Guinea

The Hon. Mekere Morauta,
Prime Minister
Protocol Office, Dept. of
The Prime Minister
P.O. Box 6605
Morauta House
NCD, Boroko
Papua New Guinea

**INTERNET** www.pm.gov.pg

## Parade

711 3rd Ave.
New York, NY 10017

**INTERNET** www.parade.com

## Parent's Magazine

**INTERNET** www.parentsmagazine.com
**E-MAIL** pmmcustserv@cdsfulfillment.com

## Parker, Andrea

121 N San Vincente Blvd.
Beverly Hills, CA 90211
*Actress*

## Parker, Mary Louise

151 El Camino Dr.
Beverly Hills, CA 90212
*Actress*

**BIRTHDAY** 8/2/64

## Parker, Sarah Jessica

P.O. Box 69646
Los Angeles, CA 90069
*Actress*

**BIRTHDAY** 3/25/66

## Parker Hannifin

6035 Parkland Blvd.
Cleveland, OH 44124
*Industrial and farm equipment*

**INTERNET** www.parker.com
Duane E. Collins, Chairman, President and CEO

## Parnell, Lee Roy

1227 17th Ave. S
Nashville, TN 37212
*Country music singer*

## Partnership for a Drug-Free America

405 Lexington Ave.
New York, NY 10174
*The Partnership for a Drug-Free America is a private, nonprofit, nonpartisan coalition of professionals from the communications industry*

**INTERNET** www.drugfreeamerica.org

## Parton, Dolly

Attn: Dunice Eledg
700 Dollywood Pkwy
Pigeon Forge, TN 37863
*Country music singer/actress*

## Partyline

1040 First Ave., #340
New York, NY 10022
*Newsletter*

**INTERNET** www.partylinepublishing.com

## Passions cast

3000 W Alameda Ave.
Burbank, CA 91523
*Soap opera*

**Pataki, George E.**
State Capitol
Albany, NY 12224
*Governor of New York*

**Patterson, Floyd**
P.O. Box 336
New Paltz, NY 12561
*Former boxer*

**Patterson, Percival John**
*Prime Minister of Jamaica*
**INTERNET** www.jis.gov.jm
**E-MAIL** jis@jis.gov.jm

**Patti, Sandy**
P.O. Box 2940
Anderson, IN 46018
*Religious music singer*

**Patton, Paul E.**
*Governor of Kentucky*
**E-MAIL** governor@mail.state.ky.us

**Pauley, Jane**
271 Central Park W
New York, NY 10024
*Journalist/talk show host*

**Pavarotti, Luciano**
941 Via Giardini 41040
Saliceta S. Guiliano
Modena
Italy

**Pawlenty, Tim**
*Governor of Minnesota*
**INTERNET** www.mainserver.state.mn.us/governor/feedback_from_constituents.html

**Paxton, Bill**
151 El Camino Dr.
Beverly Hills, CA 90212
*Actor/director*
**BIRTHDAY** 5/17/55

**Payless Car Rental**
*Rental car agency*
**INTERNET** www.paylesscarrental.com
**VOICE** 1-800-729-5377

**PBS**
1320 Braddock Place
Alexandria, VA 22314
*Broadcast network*

## PC Magazine
650 Townsend St.
San Francisco, CA 94103

**INTERNET** www.pcmag.com
**VOICE** 415-551-4800

## PC World
501 2nd St.
San Francisco, CA 94107

**INTERNET** www.pcworld.com
**VOICE** 415-243-0500

## Peck, Gregory
P.O. Box 837
Beverly Hills, CA 90213
*Actor*

**BIRTHDAY** 4/5/16

## PECO Energy
2301 Market St.
Philadelphia, PA 19103
*Gas and electric utilities*

**INTERNET** www.peco.com
Corbin A. McNeill Jr., Chairman, President and CEO

## Pele
c/o Minist. Extraordinario de Esporte
Praca dos tres Poderes
70150-900 Brasilia D.F.
Brasalia
*Former soccer player*

**BIRTHDAY** 10/21/40

## Peniston, Ce Ce
250 W 57th St.
New York, NY 10107
*Performer*

## Penn, Sean
2049 Century Park E
Los Angeles, CA 90067
*Actor*

## Penn & Teller
4132 S Rainbow Blvd., #377
Las Vegas, NV 89103
*Magicians*

**INTERNET** www.sincity.com

## Penn Traffic
1200 State Fair Blvd.
Syracuse, NY 13221
*Food and drug stores*

Joseph V. Fisher, President and CEO

## People
1271 Ave. of the Americas
New York, NY 10020
*Magazine*

**INTERNET** www.people.com
**VOICE** 212-350-1212

## PepsiCo
700 Anderson Hill Road
Purchase, NY 10577
*Beverages*

**INTERNET** www.pepsico.com
Steve Reinemund, Chairman and CEO

## Perdue, Frank
P.O. Box 1656
Horsham, PA 19044
*Businessman*

## Perdue, Sonny
*Governor of Georgia*

**INTERNET** www.gagovernor.org/governor/contact.html

## Perez, Rosie
111 W 44th St.
New York, NY 10036
*Actress*

## Perlman, Rhea
275 S Beverly Dr., #215
Beverly Hills, CA 90212
*Actress*

## Perot, Ross
2300 W Plano Dr.
Plano, TX 75075
*Businessman/former presidential candidate*

## Perrine, Valerie
Via Toscana 1
Rome
1-00187
Italy
*Actress*

## Perry, Luke
1122 S Robertson Blvd., #15
Los Angeles, CA 90035
*Actor*

**BIRTHDAY** 10/11/65

## Perry, Rick
*Governor of Texas*

INTERNET www.governor.state.tx.us/acgPERRY2001/e-mail.html

## Perry, Matthew
1122 S Robertson Blvd., #15
Los Angeles, CA 90035
*Actor*

E-MAIL matthewperry@studiofanmail.com

## Peru
Alberto Fujomori Kenyo, President
Ministerio de la Presidencia
Av. Paseo de la Republico 4297
Surquillo
Lima
Peru

INTERNET www.pres.gob.pe
E-MAIL postmaster@pres.gob.pe

## Pesci, Joe
P.O. Box 6
Lavallette, NJ 08735
*Actor*

## Peter Kiewit Sons
1000 Kiewit Plaza
Omaha, NE 68131
*Engineering, construction*

Kenneth E. Stinson, Chairman and CEO

## Peter, Paul & Mary
121 Mr. Herman Way
Ocean Grove, NJ 07756
*Music group*

## Peters, Bernadette
323 W 80th St.
New York, NY 10024
*Actress*

BIRTHDAY 2/28/48

## Petersen, Wolfgang
9830 Wilshire Blvd.
Beverly Hills, CA 90212
*Director*

BIRTHDAY 3/14/41

## Petrenko, Viktor
1375 Hopmeadow St.,
P.O. Box 5773
Simsbury, CT 06070
*Ice skater*

## Petty, Tom

Official Fan Club
1926 Contra Costa Blvd.
Pleasant Hill, CA 94523
*Singer*

**INTERNET** www.tompetty.com

## Petty, Lori

400 W Alameda Ave.
Burbank, CA 90049
*Actress*

## Petty, Richard

311 Bronson Mill Road
Randleman, NC 27317
*Race car driver*

## Pfeiffer, Michelle

3727 Magnolia, #300
Burbank, CA 91505
*Actress/singer*

## Pfizer

235 E 42nd St.
New York, NY 10017
*Pharmaceuticals*

**INTERNET** www.pfizer.com
Henry McKinnell, Chairman and CEO

## PG&E

1 Market St.
San Francisco, CA 94105
*Gas and electric utilities*

**INTERNET** www.pge.com

## Pharmacia Corporation

100 Rt. 206 N
Peapack, NJ 07977
*Pharmaceuticals*

**INTERNET** www.pnu.com
Fred Hassan, President and CEO

## Phelps Dodge

2600 N Central Ave.
Phoenix, AZ 85004
*Metals*

**INTERNET** www.phelpsdodge.com
Stephen Whisler, Chairman

## Philadelphia 76ers

P.O. Box 25040
Philadelphia, PA 19147
*Basketball team*

## Philadelphia City Paper
123 Chestnut St., 3rd Floor
Philadelphia, PA 19147

**INTERNET** www.citypaper.net
**VOICE** 215-735-8535

## Philadelphia Eagles
c/o Corestates Spectrum
Broad St. and Pattison Ave.
Philadelphia, PA 19148
*Football team*

## Philadelphia Flyers
3601 S Broad St.
Philadelphia, PA 19148
*Hockey team*

## Philadelphia Inquirer/ Daily News
400 N Broad St.
Philadelphia, PA 19101

**INTERNET** www.philly.com
**VOICE** 215-854-2000

## Philadelphia Phillies
c/o Live 7
P.O. Box 7575
Philadelphia, PA 19101
*Baseball team*

## Philbin, Regis
Lincoln Square, 5th Floor
New York, NY 10023
*Talk show host*

## Philip Morris U.S.A. (now Altria Group Inc.)
120 Park Ave.
New York, NY 10017
*Tobacco company*

**INTERNET** www.philipmorrisusa.com
Louis Camilleri, President and CEO

## Philippines
Joseph Estrada, President
Malacanang Palace
Jose P. Laurel St.
Manial
Philippines

**INTERNET** www.erap.com
**E-MAIL** erap@erap.com

## Phillips, Stone
30 Rockefeller Plaza
New York, NY 10122
*News correspondent*

## Phillips, Julianne
1999 Ave. of Stars, #2830
Los Angeles, CA 90049
*Actress/model*

## Phillips Petroleum
Phillips Bldg.
Bartlesville, OK 74004
*Petroleum refining*

**INTERNET** www.phillips66.com
Norman R. Augustine, Chairman and CEO

## Phoenix Coyotes
2 N Central
Phoenix, AZ 85004
*Hockey team*

## Phoenix Home Life Mutual Insurance
1 American Row
Hartford, CT 06115
*Health and Life insurance*

Robert W. Fiondella, Chairman and CEO

## Phoenix Suns
201 E Jefferson
Phoenix, AZ 85004
*Basketball team*

## Pietz, Amy
P.O. Box 81
Oak Creek, WI 53154
*Actress*

## Pink Floyd
43 Portland Road
London W11
England
UNITED KINGDOM
*Music group*

## Pinkett-Smith, Jada
9560 Wilshire Blvd., #516
Beverly Hills, CA 90212
*Actress*

## Pippen, Scottie
1 Center Ct., #200
Portland, OR 97227
*Basketball player*

## Pitney Bowes
1 Elmcroft Road
Stamford, CT 06926
*Computers, office equipment*

**INTERNET** www.pitneybowes.com
Michael J. Critelli, Chairman

## Pitt, Brad
9830 Wilshire Blvd.
Beverly Hills, CA 90212
*Actor*

## Pittsburgh Penguins
66 Mario Lemieux Place
Pittsburgh, PA 15219
*Hockey team*

## Pittsburgh Pirates
600 Stadium Circle
Pittsburgh, PA 15212
*Baseball team*

## Pittsburgh Post Gazette
50 Blvd. of the Allies
Pittsburgh, PA 15230

**INTERNET** www.post-gazette.com
**VOICE** 412-263-1100

## Pittsburgh Steelers
300 Stadium Circle
Pittsburgh, PA 15212
*Football team*

## Pittston Minerals Group
448 NE Main St.
Lebanon, VA 24266
*Mining*

**INTERNET** www.pittstonminerals.com
Michael Brinks, President and CEO

## Platters, The

525 Kensington Road
Southington, CT 06489
*Music group*

## Playboy

680 N Lake Shore Dr.
Chicago, IL 60611
*Magazine*

**INTERNET** www.playboy.com
**VOICE** 312-751-8000

## Pleasant Company-American Girl Co.

8400 Fairway Place
Middletown, WI 53562
*Makers of American Girl dolls*

**INTERNET** www.americangirl.com
Pleasant Rowland, Founder

## Plumb, Eve

280 S Beverly Dr., #400
Beverly Hills, CA 90212
*Actress*

## Plummer, Christopher

49 Wampum Hill Road
Weston, CT 06883
*Actor*

## PNC Financial Services Group, Inc., The

1 PNC Plaza
249 5th Ave.
Pittsburgh, PA 15222
*Commercial bank*

**INTERNET** www.pncbank.com
James Rohr, President and CEO

## Poland

Aleksander Kwasniewski, President
Kancelaria Prezydenta RP
Ul. Wiejska 10
00-902 Warsaw
Poland

**INTERNET** www.president.pl.or
**E-MAIL** listy@prezydent.pl

## Poitier, Sydney

9830 Wilshire Blvd.
Beverly Hills, CA 90212
*Actor*

**BIRTHDAY** 2/20/27

## Popular Mechanics
810 7th Ave.
New York, NY 10019

**INTERNET** www.popularmechanics.com
**VOICE** 212-649-2000

## Popular Science
2 Park Ave.
New York, NY 10016

**INTERNET** www.popularscience.com
**VOICE** 212-481-8062

## Porizkova, Paulina
304 Park Ave. S, 12th Floor
New York, NY 10010
*Model*

## Portland Oregonian
1320 SW Broadway
Portland, OR 97201

**INTERNET** www.oregonlive.com
**VOICE** 503-221-8327

## Portman, Natalie
15030 Ventura Blvd., #1-170
Sherman Oaks, CA 91403
*Actress*

## Portugal
Jorge Sampaio, President
Presidentia da Republica
Palacio de Belem
1300 Lisboa
Portugal

**INTERNET** www.prmerio-ministro.gov.pt

## Post, Markie
10153 Riverside Dr., #333
Toluca Lake, CA 90049
*Actress*

**BIRTHDAY** 11/4/50

## Poston, Tom
10375 Wilshire Blvd., #5B
Los Angeles, CA 90024
*Actor*

**BIRTHDAY** 10/17

## Poundstone, Paula
1223 Broadway, #162
Santa Monica, CA 90404
*Comedian*

## Povich, Maury

15 Penn Plaza
New York, NY 10001
*Talk show host*

## Powell, Colin

U.S. Department of State
2201 C Street NW
Washington, DC 20520
*Secretary of State/former military leader*

**INTERNET** www.state.gov/secretary/

## Powers, Stefanie

P.O. Box 5087
Sherman Oaks, CA 91403
*Actress*

**BIRTHDAY** 11/2/42

## Powter, Susan

6250 Ridgewood Road
St. Cloud, MN 56395
*Fitness guru*

## PP&L Industries

2 N 9th St.
Allentown, PA 18101
*Gas and electric utilities*

William F. Hecht, Chairman, President and CEO

## PPG Industries

1 PPG Place
Pittsburgh, PA 15272
Chemicals

**INTERNET** www.ppg.com
Raymond W. LeBoeuf, CEO

## PR Chicago

30 N Michigan Ave., #508
Chicago, IL 60602
*Newsletter*

**VOICE** 312-372-7744

## PR News Publisher

1201 Seven Locks Road, #300
Potomac, MD 20854
*Newsletter*

**INTERNET** www.prandmarketing.com
**VOICE** 301-354-1761

## PR Reporter

14 Front St.
P.O. Box 60
Exeter, NH 03833
*Newsletter*

**INTERNET** www.prpublishing.com
**VOICE** 603-778-0514

## PR Watch
3318 Gregory St.
Madison, WI 53711
*Newsletter*

**VOICE** 608-233-3346

## PR Week
250 5th Ave.
New York, NY 10001
*Newsletter*

**INTERNET** www.prweek.us.com
**VOICE** 212-532-9200

## Praxair
39 Old Ridgebury Road
Danbury, CT 06810
*Chemicals*

**INTERNET** www.praxair.com
Dennis H. Reilly, Chairman

## Premiere
1633 Broadway
New York, NY 10016
*Magazine*

**INTERNET** www.premiere.com
**VOICE** 212-767-5400

## Presley, Lisa-Marie
1167 Summit Dr.
Beverly Hills, CA 90210
*Singer*

## Presley, Priscilla
1167 Summit Dr.
Beverly Hills, CA 90210
*Actress*

**BIRTHDAY** 5/24/45

## Preston, Kelly
15030 Ventura Blvd., #710
Sherman Oaks, CA 91403
*Actress*

**BIRTHDAY** 10/13/62

## Pretenders, The
3 E 54th St.
New York, NY 10022
*Music group*

## Prevention
1901 Bell Ave.
Des Moines, IA 50315

**INTERNET** www.prevention.com
**VOICE** 1-800-813-8070

## Price, Ray
1722 S Glenstone Ave., #UU
Springfield, MO 65804
*Singer*

## Priestley, Jason
9560 Wilshire Blvd., #316
Beverly Hills, CA 90212
*Actor*

## Prince
7801 Audubon Road
Chanhassen, MN 55317
*Singer*

## Prince Andrew
Buckingham Palace
London SW1A 1AA
England
UNITED KINGDOM

## Princess Caroline
80 Ave. Foch
F-75016
Paris, France

## Princess Stephanie of Monaco
Maison Clas St. Martin F
Paris, France

## Principal, Victoria
120 S Spalding Dr.
Beverly Hills, CA 90212
*Actress*

## Principal Financial Group
711 High St.
Des Moines, IA 50392
*Health and Life insurance*

**INTERNET** www.principal.com
J. Barry Griswell, President and CEO

## Prinze, Jr., Freddie
9830 Wilshire Blvd.
Beverly Hills, CA 90212
*Actor*

## Procter and Gamble
1 P&G Plaza
Cincinnati, OH 45202
*Soaps, cosmetics*

**INTERNET** www.pg.com
Alan G. Lafley, President and CEO

## Prodigy
17-19 Alma Road
XW18 1AA
England
UNITED KINGDOM

## Progress Energy Carolinas, Inc.
411 Fayetteville St.
Raleigh, NC 27602
*Gas and electric utilities*

**INTERNET** www.Progress-energy.com
William Cavanaugh, III, Chairman, CEO

## Progressive Co.
6300 Wilson Mills Road
Mayfield Village, OH 44143
*P & C insurance*

**INTERNET** www.progressive.com
Rob Glaser, Chairman, President and CEO

## Prosky, Robert
306 9th Ave.
Washington, D.C. 20003
*Actor*

## Providence Journal Bulletin
75 Fountain St.
Providence, RI 02902

**INTERNET** www.projo.com
**VOICE** 401-277-7000

## Provident Financial Group, Inc.
1 E 4th St.
CEO
Cincinnati, OH 45202
*Commercial bank*

**INTERNET** www.provident-bank.com
Craig Blunden, Chairman, President and

## Prowse, David
P.O. Box 1181
Croyden CR9 7BQ
England
UNITED KINGDOM
*Actor*

## Prudential Insurance Company of America
751 Broad St.
Newark, NJ 07102
*Health and Life insurance*

**INTERNET** www.prudential.com
Vivian Banta, Chairman and CEO

## Prudhomme Chef

2424 Chartres
New Orleans, LA 70117
*Louisiana Chef*

**INTERNET** www.chefpaul.com

## Pruett, Jeanne

1906 Chet Atkins P1, #502
Nashville, TN 37212
*Country music singer*

## Prussia, Guido

Guido Prussioa Res
Campo 602
Segrate
Milano
Italy
*Italian television journalist*

## Pryor, Mark

U.S. Senate (D-AR)
Washington, D.C. 20510
*Senator*

**INTERNET** www.pryor.senate.gov/email_webform.htm

## Public Service Enterprise Group

80 Park Plaza
Newark, NJ 07101
*Gas and electric utilities*

**INTERNET** www.pseg.com
E. James Ferland, Chairman, President and CEO

## Public Broadcasting Service (PBS)

1320 Braddock Place
Alexandria, VA 22314

**INTERNET** www.pbs.org
310-203-3442

## Public Relations Quarterly

44 W Market St.
P.O. Box 311
Rhinebeck, NY 12572

**INTERNET** www.newsletter-clearinghouse.com
**VOICE** 914-876-2081

## Public Relations Review

JAI Press
10606 Mantz Road
Silver Springs, MD 20903-1247

**INTERNET** www.jaipress.com
**VOICE** 301-445-3231

**Public Relations Tactics, PRSA**
33 Irving Place, 3rd Floor
New York, NY 10003
*Newsletter*

**INTERNET** www.prsa.org
**VOICE** 212-995-2230

**Publishing News**
P.O. Box 9642
Scottsdale, AZ 85252

**INTERNET** www.bookzonepro.com

**Publix Super Markets**
1936 George Jenkins Blvd.
Lakeland, FL 33815
*Food and drug stores*

Charlie H. Jenkins, Chairman and CEO

**Pullman, Bill**
2599 Glen Green
Los Angeles, CA 90068
*Actor/producer*

**BIRTHDAY** 12/17/54

**Putin, President**
Krsnopresenskaya 2
Moscow Russia

**Quaker Oats Co., The**
321 N Clark St.
Chicago, IL 60610
*Food producer*

**INTERNET** www.quakeroats.com
Robert S. Morrison, Chairman, President and CEO

**Quaid, Dennis**
8942 Wilshire Blvd.
Beverly Hills, CA 90211
*Actor*

**Quaid, Randy**
P.O. Box 17572
Beverly Hills, CA 90209
*Actor*

**Quantum**
500 McCarthy Blvd.
Milpitas, CA 95035
*Computer peripherals*

**INTERNET** www.quantum.com
Michael A. Brown, Chairman and CEO

## Quayle, Dan

815 Warren St., Box 856
Huntington, IN 46750
*Former Vice President*

**BIRTHDAY** 2/4/47

## Qatar

Sheik Hamad bin Khalifa al_thani
Emir
The Royal Palace
P.O. Box 923
Doha
Qatar

**INTERNET** www.mofa.gov.qa

## Queen Mary Hotel

P.O. Box 8
Long Beach, CA 90802
*Former cruise ship turned hotel and tourist attraction*

**INTERNET** www.queenmary.com

## Quiet Riot

P.O. Box 24455
New Orleans, LA 70184
*Music group*

## Quinn, Anthony Tyler

8949 Sunset Blvd., #201
Los Angeles, CA 90069
*Actor*

## Quivers, Robin

40 W 57th St., 14th Floor
New York, NY 10019
*Radio personality*

## QVC

1365 Enterprise Dr.
West Chester, PA 19380
*Cable network*

## R.E.M.

P.O. Box 8032
Athens, GA 30603
*Music group*

## R.R. Donnelley and Sons
77 W Wacker Dr.
Chicago, IL 60601
*Publishing, printing*
**INTERNET** www.rrdonnelley.com
William L. Davis, Chairman and CEO

## Rabbani
Afghanistan
Kabul Afghanistan
*Chairman of the Ruling Council*

## Rabbitt, Eddie
P.O. Box 35286
Cleveland, OH 91604
*Singer*

## Rachins, Alan
10474 Santa Monica Blvd., #380
Los Angeles, CA 90025
*Actor*

## Radcliffe, Ted
501 E 32nd St., #1105
Chicago, IL 60616
*Baseball player*

## Radio-Television News Directors Association
1000 Connecticut Ave. NW, #615
Washington, D.C. 20036
*The world's largest professional organization devoted exclusively to electronic journalism*
**INTERNET** www.rtnda.org

## Ragan's Annual Report Review
316 N Michigan Ave., #300
Chicago, IL 60601
*Newsletter*
**INTERNET** www.ragan.com
**VOICE** 312-960-4100

## Rage Against the Machine
5550 Wilshire Blvd., #302
Los Angeles, CA 90036
*Music group*

## Ragheb, Ali Abu
*Jordan Prime Minister*
**INTERNET** www.nic.gov.jo
**E-MAIL** info@nic.gov.jo

## Rainbow/Push Coalition, The

321 N Clark St.
Chicago, IL 60615

**INTERNET** www.rainbowpush.org

*A multi-racial, multi-issue international membership organization founded by Rev. Jesse L. Jackson, Sr.*

## Raitt, Bonnie

15030 Ventura Blvd., #710
Sherman Oaks, CA 91403
*Singer*

## Raleigh News and Observer

215 S McDowell St.
Raleigh, NC 27601

**INTERNET** www.newsobserver.com
**VOICE** 919-829-4500

## Ralston Purina Company

Checkerboard Square
St. Louis, MO 63164
*Pet food producer*

**INTERNET** www.ralston.com
J. Patrick Mulcahy, President and CEO

## Rand

1700 Main St.
P.O. Box 2138
Santa Monica, CA 90407

**INTERNET** www.rand.org
James A. Thomson, Chairman

*A nonprofit institution that helps improve policy and decision-making through research and analysis*

## Randall, Tony

1 W 81st St., #6D
New York, NY 10024
*Performer*

## Randolph, Boots

4798 Lickton Park
Whites Creek, TN 37189
*Musician*

## Raphael, Sally Jesse

15 Penn Plaza, OF2
New York, NY 10001
*Talk show host*

## Rappaport, Michael
1610 Broadway
Santa Monica, CA 90404
*Actor*

## Rather, Dan
524 W 57th St.
New York, NY 10019
*News anchor*

## Ratzenberger, John
**BIRTHDAY** 4/16/47
P.O. Box 8189
Calabasas, CA 91372
*Actor*

## Raven, Eddie
1071 Bradley Road
Gallatin, TN 37066
*Country music singer*

## Ray, Jimmy
10 Great Marlborough St.
Reno, NV 89505
*Country music singer*

## Raye, Collin
P.O. Box 530
Reno, NV 89509
*Country music singer*

## Reader's Digest Assoc.
**INTERNET** www.readersdigest.com
James P. Schadt, Chairman and CEO
Reader's Digest Road
Pleasantville, NY 10570
*Publishing, printing*

## Reading is Fundamental
600 Maryland Ave. SW, #600
Washington, D.C. 20024
*America's largest children's literary organization helps children grow up reading by offering them activities that make reading appealing and by giving them books*

## Reagan, Ronald and Nancy
2121 Ave. of the Stars, #34
Los Angeles, CA 90067
*Former President and First Lady*

## Reason Foundation

3415 S Sepulveda Blvd., #400
Los Angeles, CA 90034

**INTERNET** www.reason.org
Lynn Scarlett, CEO

*A national research and educational organization that explores and promotes the twin values of rationality and freedom as the basic underpinnings of a good society.*

## Red Hot Chili Peppers

1116 Aqua Vista #339
N Hollywood, CA 91693
*Music group*

## Redbook

224 W 57th St., 5th Floor
New York, NY 10019
*Women's magazine*

**INTERNET** www.redbook.woman.com/rb
**VOICE** 212-649-3330

## Reddy, Helen

2029 Century Park E, #600
Los Angeles, CA 90067
*Singer*

## Redford, Robert

1101 East Montana Avenue
Santa Monica, CA 90403
*Actor/film director*

**BIRTHDAY** 8/18/37

## Reebok

100 Technology Center Dr.
CEO
Stoughton, MA 02072
*Athletic apparel/footwear*

**INTERNET** www.reebok.com
Paul B. Fireman, Chairman, President and

## Reece, Gabrielle

P.O. Box 2246
Malibu, CA 90265
*Volleyball player/model*

## Reed, Jack

320 Hart Senate Office Bldg. (D-RI)
Washington, D.C. 20510
*Senator*

**E-MAIL** jack@reed.senate.gov

## Reed, Jerry

153 Rue De Grande
Brentwood, TN 37027
*Musician*

**Reed, Pamela**
1505 10th St.
Santa Monica, CA 90404
*Actress*

**Reese, Della**
55 W 800 St.
Salt Lake City, UT 37021
*Actress*

**Reeve, Christopher**
c/o American Paralysis Assoc.
500 Morris Ave.
Springfield, NJ 07081
*Actor*
BIRTHDAY 9/25/52

**Reeves, Keanu**
9460 Wilshire Blvd., #700
Beverly Hills, CA 90212
*Actor*
BIRTHDAY 9/4/64

**Reeves, Ronna**
P.O. Box 80424
Midland, TX 79709
*Country music singer*

**Reid, Harry**
528 Hart Senate
Office Bldg. (D-NV)
Washington, D.C 20510
*Senator*
INTERNET www.reid.senate.gov/email_form.cfm

**Reilly, Charles Nelson**
2341 Gloaming Way
Beverly Hills, CA 90212
*Actor*
BIRTHDAY 1/13/31

**Reiner, Carl**
714 N Rodeo Dr.
Beverly Hills, CA 90210
*Actor/writer*
BIRTHDAY 3/20/22

**Reiner, Rob**
23704 Malibu Colony Road
Malibu, CA 90265
*Director*
BIRTHDAY 3/16/45
FAX 310-205-2721

## Reiser, Paul

11845 W Olympic Blvd.
Los Angeles, CA 90064
*Actor*

## Reliance Group Holdings

55 E 52nd St.
New York, NY 10055
*P & C insurance*

**INTERNET** www.rgh.com
George R. Baker, Chairman

## Rendell, Ed

Forum Bldg., #439
Commonwealth Ave. & Walnut St.
Harrisburg, PA 17120
*Governor of Pennsylvania*

**INTERNET** www.governor.state.pa.us/

## Renfro, Brad

9560 Wilshire Blvd., #5
Beverly Hills, CA 90212
*Actor*

**BIRTHDAY** 7/25/82

## Reno, Janet

15495 Eagle Nest Ln.
Miami Lakes, FL 33014
*Former Attorney General*

## REO Speedwagon

3500 W Olive Ave., #600
Burbank, CA 91505
*Music group*

## Republican Liberty Caucus (RLC)

611 Pennsylvania Ave. SE, #370
Washington, D.C. 20003

**INTERNET** www.rlc.org
Clifford Thies, Chairman

*The primary objective of the RLC is to help elect libertarian-leaning Republicans to public office at all levels of government*

## Republican National Committee

310 1st St. NE
Washington, D.C. 20003=

Gov. Marc Racicot, Chairman

## Retton, Mary Lou

114 White Ave.
Fairmont, WV 26554
*Gymnast*

R

## Reynolds, Burt
P.O. Box 3288
Tequesta, FL 33469
*Actor*

## Reynolds, Debbie
6415 Lankershim Blvd.
N Hollywood, CA 91606
*Actress*

**BIRTHDAY** 4/1/32

## Reynolds Metals
6601 W Broad St.
c/o Cheryl Snider
Richmond, VA 23230
*Metals*

**INTERNET** www.rmc.com
Jeremiah J. Sheehan, Chairman and CEO

## Rhys-Davies, John
24 Poland St.
London WV1 3DD
England
UNITED KINGDOM
*Actor*

## Ricci, Christina
8942 Wilshire Blvd.
Beverly Hills, CA 90211
*Actress*

## Rice, Anne
1239 First St.
New Orleans, LA 70130
*Author*

## Richard, Cliff
Queen Anne House
Way Bridge
Surrey
UNITED KINGDOM
*Actor/singer*

## Richard, Little
8401 Sunset Blvd.
Los Angeles, CA 90069
*Singer*

## Richards, Denise
1100 Glendon Ave., #1000
Los Angeles, CA 90024
*Actress*

## Richardson, Bill
*Governor of New Mexico*

**INTERNET** www.governor.state.nm.us/Constituentserv/contactform.htm

## Richardson, Patricia
253A 26th St.
Santa Monica, CA 90402
*Actress*

## Richmond News Leader/Times
300 E Franklin St.
Richmond, VA 23293

**INTERNET** www.timesdispatch.com
804-649-6000

## Ridge, Tom
*Secretary of Homeland Security*

**INTERNET** www.Dhs.gov

## Righteous Brothers
151 El Camino Dr.
Beverly Hills, CA 90212
*Music group*

## Riley, Bob
P.O. Box 59541
Birmingham, AL 32559
*Governor of Alabama*

**INTERNET** www.governor.state.al.us/office/email/email.html

## Riley, Jeannie C.
906 Granville Road
Franklin, TN 37064
*Country music singer*

## Rimes, LeAnn
1801 Whitehall
Garland, TX 75043
*Country music singer*

## Ringwald, Molly
9454 Wilshire Blvd.
Beverly Hills, CA 90212
*Actress*

## Rinna, Lisa
3000 W Alameda Ave.
Burbank, CA 91523
*Actress*

## Ripken Jr., Cal
333 W Camden St.
Baltimore, MD 21201
*Baseball player*

## Ripon Society
501 Capitol Ct. NE, #300
Washington, D.C. 22000
**INTERNET** www.riponsoc.org
*A moderate Republican research and policy organization dedicated to a commonsense, pragmatic system of governance*

## Rite Aid
30 Hunter Land
Camp Hill, PA 17011
*Food and drug stores*
**INTERNET** www.riteaid.com
Robert G. Milles, President and COO

## Rivera, Geraldo
1211 Ave. of the Americas
New York, NY 10036
*News correspondent*

## Riverfront Times
6358 Delmar Blvd., #200
St. Louis, MO 63130
**INTERNET** www.riverfronttimes.com
**VOICE** 314-615-6666

## Rivers, Joan
P.O. Box 49774
Los Angeles, CA 90049
*Television personality/comedian*

## Rivers, Johnny
12358 Ventura Blvd., #342
Studio City, CA 91604
*Singer*

**Rizzuto, Phil**
912 Westminster Ave.
Hillside, NJ 07205
*Baseball player/announcer*

**RJR Nabisco**
7 Campus Dr.
Parsippany, NJ 07054
*Food producer*
**INTERNET** www.nabisco.com
James R. Johnston, President and CEO

**Robbins, Tim**
40 W 57th St.
New York, NY 10019
*Actor*

**Robert, Guei**
*Ivory Coast President*
**INTERNET** www.lacotedivoire.com

**Roberts, Julia**
40 W 57th St.
New York, NY 10019
*Actress*
**BIRTHDAY** 10/28/67

**Roberts, Pat**
302 Hart Senate
Office Bldg. (R-KS)
Washington, D.C. 20510
*Senator*
**INTERNET** www.roberts.senate.gov/email.htm

**Roberts, Tanya**
1122 S Robertson Blvd., #15
Los Angeles, CA 90035
*Actress*
**E-MAIL** tanyaroberts@studiofanmail.com

**Robinson, Arthur**
*President of Trinidad and Tobago*
**INTERNET** www.nisc.gov.tt
presoftt@carib-link.net

**Robinson, Brooks**
P.O. Box 1168
Baltimore, MD 21203
*Baseball player*

**Robinson, Smokey**
14724 Ventura Blvd., #410
Sherman Oaks, CA 91403
*Musician*

## Rock, Chris
151 El Camino Blvd.
Beverly Hills, CA 90212
*Actor/comedian*

## Rockefeller, John
**E-MAIL** senator@rockefeller.senate.gov

531 Hart Senate
Office Bldg. (D-WV)
Washington, D.C. 20510
*Senator*

## Rockefeller Foundation, The
**INTERNET** www.rockfound.org

420 5th Ave.
New York, NY 10018
*Grant organization for arts, the humanities, equal opportunity, school reform, and international science-based development*

## Rockwell International
**INTERNET** www.rockwell.com

777 E Wisconsin Ave., #1400
Milwaukee, WI 53202
*Electronics, electrical equipment*

## Rocky Mountain News
**INTERNET** www.rockymoutainnews.com
**VOICE** 303-892-5000

400 W Colfax Ave.
Denver, CO 80204

## Rodriguez, Chi Chi
3916 Clock Point Trail
Stow, OH 44224
*Golfer*

## Rodriguez, Johnny
P.O. Box 23162
Nashville, TN 37202
*Country music singer*

## Roe, Tommy
P.O. Box 26037
Minneapolis, MN 55426
*Singer/songwriter*

## Rogers, Kenny
**BIRTHDAY** 8/21/38

P.O. Box 100, Route #1
Colbert, GA 30628
*Singer/songwriter*

## Rogers, Mimi
11693 San Vincente Blvd.
Los Angeles, CA 90049
*Actress*

## Roker, Al
*Television weatherman*

**E-MAIL** mailbag@roker.com

## Rolling Stone Magazine
1290 Ave. of the Americas
New York, NY 10104

**INTERNET** www.rollingstone.com
**VOICE** 212-484-1616

## Rolling Stones, The
8900 Wilshire Blvd., #200
Beverly Hills, CA 90211
*Music group*

## Romania
Emile Constantinescu, President
Palatul Cotroceni
Bd. Geniului 1
Bucharest, Romania

**INTERNET** www.presidency.ro

## Romney, Mitt
Governor of Massachusetts
153 Alewife Brook Pkwy
Cambridge, MA 02140

## Ronald Reagan Presidential Library
40 Presidential Dr.
Simi Valley, CA 93065

**INTERNET** www.reaganlibrary.net
Mark Burson, Executive Director

## Rooney, Andy
254 Rowayton Ave.
Rowayton, CT 06853
*Journalist*

## Rooney, Jack
926 River Ave.
Indianapolis, IN 46221
*Actor*

## Rooney, Mickey
1400 Red Sail Circle
Westlake Village, CA 91361
*Actor*

## Roper Center for Public Opinion Research

University of Connecticut,
U-164 Bldg.
341 Mansfield Road
Storrs, CT 06269

**INTERNET** www.ropercenter.uconn.edu
Lisa Parmelee, Associate Director

*The leading nonprofit center for the study of public opinion, maintaining the world's largest archive of public opinion data*

## Rose, Charlie

499 Park Ave., 15th Floor
New York, NY 10022
*Journalist*

## Rose, Pete

8144 Glades Road
Boca Raton, FL 33434
*Baseball player*

## Roseanne

5 Crest Road
Rolling Hills, CA 90274
*Actress*

## Ross, Diana

P.O. Box 11059
Glenville Station
Greenwich, CT 06813
*Singer*

## Ross, Marion

20947 Ventura Blvd., #144
Woodland Hills, CA 91364
*Actress*

**BIRTHDAY** 10/25/28

## Rounds, Mike

*Governor of South Dakota*

**E-MAIL** sdgov@state.sd.us

## Rourke, Mickey

9150 Wilshire Blvd., #350
Beverly Hills, CA 90212
*Actor*

## Rowland, John G.

*Governor of Connecticut*

**E-MAIL** governor.rowland@po.state.ct.us

**Royal Rent A Car**
*Rental car agency*

**INTERNET** www.royalrentacar.com
**VOICE** 1-800-314-8616

**Ruehl, Mercedes**
177 MacDougal St.
New York, NY 10014
*Actress*

**BIRTHDAY** 2/28/48

**Rugrats**
1258 N Highland Ave.
Hollywood, CA 90038
*Television cartoon*

**Rumsfeld, Donald**
The White House
1600 Pennsylvania Avenue NW
Washington, DC 20500

**INTERNET** www.whitehouse.gov/government/rumsfeld-bio.html

**Rush**
189 Carlton St.
M5A 2K7
Ontario, Canada
*Music group*

**Rushdie, Salman**
c/o Gillon Aitken
29 Fernshaw Road
London SW10 OTG
England
UNITED KINGDOM
*Author*

**Russell, Kurt**
500 S Buena Vista, #10-D-06
Burbank, CA 91521
*Actor*

**Russell, Nipsey**
1650 Broadway
New York, NY 10019
*Comedian*

**Russia**
Vladimir Vladimirovich Putin, President
The Kremlin
Moscow, Russia

**INTERNET** www.gov.ru
**E-MAIL** president@gov.ru

### Rwanda
Paul Kagame, President
Presidence de la Republique
Kigali
Rwanda

### Ryan, Meg
151 El Camino Dr.
Beverly Hills, CA 90212
*Actress*

### Ryan, Nolan
P.O. Box 670
Alvin, TX 77512
*Former baseball player*

### Ryan, Tim
30 Rockefeller Plaza
New York, NY 140112
*Sports broadcaster*

### Ryder, Winona
350 Park Ave., #900
New York, NY 10022
*Actress*

**BIRTHDAY** 10/29/71

### Ryder Systems
3600 NW 82nd Ave.
Miami, FL 33166
*Truck leasing*

**INTERNET** www.ryder.com
M. Anthony Burns, Chairman and CEO

### Sabato, Jr., Antonio
P.O. Box 12073
Marina Del Rey, CA 90295
*Actor*

### Sacramento Bee
2100 Q St.
Sacremento, CA 95852

**INTERNET** www.sacbee.com
**VOICE** 916-321-1000

### Sacramento Kings
1 Sports Pkwy
Sacramento, CA 95834
*Hockey team*

## Safeco

Safeco Plaza
Seattle, WA 98185
*P & C insurance*

**INTERNET** www.safeco.com
Bob Dickey, President

## Saint Kitts and Nevis

The Hon. Dr Denzil Douglas,
Prime Minister
Office of the Prime Minster
Government Headquarters
Basseterre
Saint Kitts and Nevis

**INTERNET** www.stkittsnevis.net

## Saint Lucia

Kenny Anthony, Prime Minister
Office of the Prime Minister
Government Headquarters
Castries
Saint Lucia

**INTERNET** www.stlucia.gov.lc
**E-MAIL** pmoffice@candw.lc

## Saint Patrick's Cathedral

460 Madison Ave.
New York, NY 10022
*The largest Roman Catholic church in the U.S.*

Msgr. Anthony Dalla Villa

## Saint Vincent and the Grenadines

Rt. Hon James Fitz-Allen Mitchell
Prime Minister
Office of the Prime Minister
Government Headquarters
Kingstown
Saint Vincent and the Grenadines

## Sajak, Pat

10202 W Washington Blvd.
Culver City, CA 90232
*Television game show host*

## Sales, Soupy

c/o Harold Ober Assoc.
245 E 35th St.
New York, NY 10016
*Actor*

## Salinger, J.D.
425 Madison Ave.
New York, NY 10017
*Author*

## Salt 'n Pepa
250 W 57th St., #821
New York, NY 10107
*Music group*

## San Antonio Spurs
100 Montana St.
San Antonio, TX 78203
*Basketball team*

## San Diego Chargers
9449 Friars Road
San Diego, CA 92108
*Football team*

## San Diego Chicken
6549 Mission Gorge Road
San Diego, CA 92120
*Sports mascot*

## San Diego Padres
P.O. Box 2000
San Diego, CA 92120
*Baseball team*

## San Diego Reader
P.O. Box 85803
San Diego, CA 92186

**INTERNET** www.sandiegoreader.com
**VOICE** 619-235-3000

## San Diego Union/Tribune
350 Camino de la Reina
San Diego, CA 92112

**INTERNET** www.signonsandiego.com
**VOICE** 619-299-3131

## San Francisco 49ers
4949 Centennial Blvd.
San Francisco, CA 95054
*Football team*

## San Francisco Bay Guardian
520 Hampshire
San Francisco, CA 94110

**INTERNET** www.sfbg.com
**VOICE** 415-255-3100

## San Francisco Chronicle
901 Mission
San Francisco, CA 94103

**INTERNET** www.sfgate.com
**VOICE** 415-777-1111

## San Francisco Giants
3 Com Park
San Francisco, CA 94124
*Baseball team*

## San Jose Sharks
525 W Santa Clara St.
San Jose, CA 95113
*Hockey team*

## San Marino-Italy
Secretary of State, Political Affairs
San Marino
San Marino-Italy

**INTERNET** http://inthenet.sm/cultur.htm

## Sanches, Stacey
9242 Beverly Blvd.
Beverly Hills, CA 90212
*Performer*

## Sandler, Adam
9701 Wilshire Blvd.
Beverly Hills, CA 90212
*Actor/comedian*

**E-MAIL** sandler@cris.com

## Sanford, Mark
*Governor of South Carolina*

**E-MAIL** governor@govoepp.state.sc.us

## Santa Barbara Independent
1221 State St.
Santa Barbara, CA 93101

**INTERNET** www.independent.com
**VOICE** 805-965-5518

## Santana, Carlos
121 Jordan St.
San Rafael, CA 94901
*Musician*

## Sao Tome and Principe
Miguel Trovoada, President
Office of the President
CP 38
Sao Tome
Sao Tome and Principe

## Santorum, Rick
120 Russell Senate
Office Bldg. (R-PA)
Washington, D.C. 20510
*Senator*

**INTERNET** www.santorum.senate.gov/email.htm

## Sara, Mia
130 W 42nd St., #1804
New York, NY 10036
*Actress*

## Sara Lee
3 First National Plaza
Chicago, IL 60602
*Food producer*

**INTERNET** www.saralee.com

## Sarandon, Susan
40 W 57th St.
New York, NY 10019
*Actress*

**BIRTHDAY** 10/4/46

## Sarbanes, Paul
309 Hart Senate
Office Bldg. (D-MD)
Washington, D.C. 20510
*Senator*

**INTERNET** www.sarbanes.senate.gov/pages/email.html

## Sassoon, Vidal
1163 Calle Vista
Beverly Hills, CA 90210
*Hairstylist to the Stars*

## Saturday Evening Post
1100 Waterway Blvd.
Indianapolis, IN 46202

**INTERNET** www.saturdayeveningpost.com
**VOICE** 317-636-8881

**Saturday Night Live cast**
c/o Studio Fan Mail
30 Rockefeller Plaza
New York, NY 10020
*Live comedic television show*

**Saudi Arabia**
King Fahd Bin Abdulaziz Al Saud
Royal Diwan
Riyadh
Saudi Arabia
**VOICE** 966-1-488-2222

**Savage, Fred**
1122 S Robertson Blvd.
Los Angeles, CA 90035
*Actor*
**E-MAIL** fredsavage@studiofanmail.com

**Saved By The Bell: The New Class cast**
330 Bob Hope Dr.
Burbank, CA 91523
*Television show*

**SBC Communications**
175 E Houston
San Antonio, TX 78205
*Telecommunications*
**INTERNET** www.sbc.com
Keith Cambron, Chairman and CEO

**Schaech, Jonathan**
1122 S Roxbury Dr.
Los Angeles, CA 90035
*Actor*
**BIRTHDAY** 9/10/69

**Schafer, Edward T.**
*Governor of North Dakota*
**E-MAIL** governor@state.nd.us

**Scheider, Roy**
P.O. Box 364
Sagaponack, NY 11962
*Actor*
**BIRTHDAY** 11/10/32

**Scheindlin, Judge Judy**
5042 Sunset Blvd., #303
Hollywood, CA 90028
*Television judge*

## Schering-Plough

1 Giralda Farms
Madison, NJ 07940
*Pharmaceuticals*

**INTERNET** www.sch-plough.com
Richard Jay Kogan, Chairman and CEO

## Schiffer, Claudia

342 Madison Ave., #1900
New York, NY 10173
*Model*

## Schlessinger, Dr. Laura

610 S Ardmore Ave.
Los Angeles, CA 90005
*Psychologist*

## Schroeder, Rick

10201 W Pico Blvd.
Los Angeles, CA 90035
*Actor*

## Schumer, Charles

313 Hart Senate
Office Bldg. (D-NY)
Washington, D.C. 20510
*Senator*

**INTERNET** www.schumer.senate.gov/webforms.html

## Schwarzenegger, Arnold

State Capitol Building
Sacramento, CA 95814
*Governor of California*

**INTERNET** www.governor.ca.gov/state/newgov/govsite/gov_homepage.jsp
**E-MAIL** Governor@governor.ca.gov

## Schwarzkopf, Gen. Norman

400 N Ashley Dr.
Tampa, FL 33602
*Former military leader/politician*

## Schwimmer, David

1122 S Robertson Blvd., #15
Los Angeles, CA 90035
*Actor*

## SCI Systems

2101 W Clinton Ave.
Huntsville, AL 35807
*Electronics, electrical equipment*

Jure Sola, President and CEO

## Science
1200 New York Ave. NW
Washington, D.C. 20005
*Magazine*

**INTERNET** www.science.com
**VOICE** 202-326-6400

## Scientific American
415 Madison Ave.
New York, NY 10017
*Magazine*

**INTERNET** www.scientificamerican.com
**VOICE** 212-754-0550

## Sci-Fi Channel, The
1230 Ave. of the Americas
New York, NY 10020
*Cable network*

## Scott, Tom Everett
9560 Wilshire Blvd., #516
Beverly Hills, CA 90213
*Actor*

## Scott, Gini Graham
6114 La Salle Ave., #358
Oakland, CA 94611
*Author/radio talk show host*

**INTERNET** www.giniscott.com

## Scully, Vin
1000 Elysian Park Ave.
Los Angeles, CA 90212
*Sportscaster*

## Seagal, Steven
1041 N Formosa Ave., #200
W Hollywood, CA 90046
*Actor*

## Seagate Technology
920 Disc Dr.
c/o Cite
Scotts Valley, CA 95066
*Computer peripherals, software*

**INTERNET** www.seagate.com
Stephen J. Luczo, CEO, Chairman

## Seal
3300 Warner Blvd.
Burbank, CA 91505
*Singer*

## Sears Roebuck

3333 Beverly Road
Hoffman Estates, IL 60179
*General merchandisers*

**INTERNET** www.sears.com
Allan J. Lacy, Chairman, President and CEO

## Seattle Mariners

P.O. Box 4100
Seattle, WA 98104
*Baseball team*

## Seattle Post-Intelligencer

101 Elliot Ave. W
Seattle, WA 98111

**INTERNET** www.seattlepi.com
**VOICE** 206-448-8000

## Seattle Seahawks

11220 NE 53rd St.
Seattle, WA 98033
*Hockey team*

## Seattle Supersonics

190 Queen Anne Ave. N
Seattle, WA 98109
*Basketball team*

## Seattle Times

1120 John St.
Seattle, WA 98109

**INTERNET** www.nwsource.com
**VOICE** 206-464-2111

## Seattle Weekly

1008 Western Ave., #300
Seattle, WA 98104

**INTERNET** www.seattleweekly.com
**VOICE** 206-623-0500

## Sebelius, Kathleen

*Governor of Kansas*

**E-MAIL** governor@ink.org

## Secada, Jon

2250 Coral Way
Miami, FL 33145
*Singer*

## Second Amendment Sisters

18484 Preston Road, #102
Dallas, TX 75252
*Women's advocacy group*

**INTERNET** www.sas-aim.org
Juli Bednarzyk, Director

## Securities and Exchange Commission
450 5th St. NW
Washington, D.C. 20549

## Sedaka, Neil
201 E 66th St., #3N
New York, NY 10021
*Singer/songwriter*

**BIRTHDAY** 3/13/39

## Seeger, Pete
P.O. Box 431
Duchess Junction
Beacon, NY 12508
*Singer*

## Sega of America
1750 Vine St.
San Francisco, CA 94103
*Videogame manufacturer*

**INTERNET** www.sega.com
Tetsu Kayama, President and COO

## Seger, Bob
567 Purdy
Birmingham, MI 48009
*Musician*

## Seinfeld, Jerry
211 Central Park W
New York, NY 10024
*Comedian*

**BIRTHDAY** 4/29/54

## Selective Service System (SSS)
1515 Wilson Blvd.
Arlington, VA 22209

## Seles, Monica
1 Erieview Plaza
Cleveland, OH 44114
*Tennis player*

## Seleh, Ali Abdullah
*Yemen President*

**INTERNET** www.yemeninfo.gov.ye

## Self
350 Madison Ave.
New York, NY 10017
*Magazine*

**INTERNET** www.self.com
**VOICE** 212-286-2860

## Self Help for Hard of Hearing People, Inc.
7910 Woodmont Ave., #1200
Bethesda, MD 20814
*The goal is to enhance the quality of life for people who are hard of hearing*

**INTERNET** www.shhh.org

## Sellecca, Connie
15030 Ventura Blvd.
Sherman Oaks, CA 91403
*Actress*

**BIRTHDAY** 5/25/55

## Selleck, Tom
331 Sage Ln.
Santa Monica, CA 90402 - 1119
*Actor*

## Senegal
Abdoulaye Wade, President
Office of the President
Avenue Roume, BP 168
Daker
Senegal

**INTERNET** www.primature.sn

## Service Merchandise
7100 Service Merchandise Dr.
Brentwood, TN 37027
*Specialist retailers*

**INTERNET** www.servicemerchandise.com
Raymond Zimmerman, Chairman

## ServiceMaster
1 ServiceMaster Way
Downers Grove, IL 60515
*Diversified outsourcing services*

**INTERNET** www.svm.com
Jonathan Ward, Chairman and CEO

## Sesame Street
1 Lincoln Plaza
New York, NY 10022
*Television show*

**Sessions, Jeff**
493 Russell Senate
Office Bldg. (R-AL)
Washington, D.C. 20510
*Senator*

**E-MAIL** senator@sessions.senate.gov

**Seventeen Magazine**
711 3rd Ave.
New York, NY 10017
*Magazine*

**INTERNET** www.seventeen.com

**Seychelles**
France-Albert Rene, President
The State House, P.O. Box 55
Mahe
Victoria
Seychelles

**INTERNET** www.seychelles-online.com.sc
**E-MAIL** ppo@seychelles.net

**Seymour, Jane**
70 Sabra Ave.
Oak Park, CA 91377
*Actress*

**BIRTHDAY** 2/15/51

**Seymour, Stephanie**
c/o Worldwide Pants Inc.
5415 Oberlin Road
San Diego, CA 92121
*Model*

**Sezer, Ahmet Necdet**
President of Turkey

**INTERNET** www.cankaya.gov.tr
**E-MAIL** cankaya@tccb.gov.tr

**Shaffer, Paul**
1697 Broadway
New York, NY 10019
*Music director*

**Sharon, Ariel**
Prime Minister of Israel
Israel

**INTERNET** www.pmo.gov.il
**E-MAIL** ask@israel-info.gov.il

**Sharpton, Rev. Al**
1941 Madison Ave.
New York, NY 10035

**Shatner, William**
11288 Ventura Blvd., #725
Studio City, CA 91604
*Actor*

**BIRTHDAY** 3/22/32

**Shaw Industries**
616 E Walnut Ave.
Dalton, GA 30720
*Textiles*

Robert E. Shaw, CEO

**Shearer, Harry**
1900 Pico Blvd.
Santa Monica, CA 90405
*Comedian/writer/director*

**Sheedy, Ally**
151 El Camino Dr.
Beverly Hills, CA 90212
*Actress*

**Sheen, Charlie**
15030 Ventura Blvd.
Sherman Oaks, CA 91403
*Actor*

**Sheen, Martin**
6916 Dume Dr.
Malibu, CA 90265
*Actor*

**Sheila E.**
15250 Ventura Blvd.
Sherman Oaks, CA 91403
*Singer*

**Shelby, Richard**
110 Hart Senate
Office Bldg. (R-AL)
Washington, D.C. 20510
*Senator*

**E-MAIL** senator@shelby.senate.gov

**Sheldon, Sidney**
9100 Wilshire Blvd., #1000
Beverly Hills, CA 90212
*Author*

## Shepherd, Cybill
P.O. Box 261503
Encino, CA 91426
*Actress/model*

**BIRTHDAY** 2/18/50

## Shepherd Express
413 N 2nd St.
Milwaukee, WI 53203

**INTERNET** www.shepherd-express.com
**VOICE** 414-276-2222

## Sheppard, T.G.
P.O. Box 510
Dundee, IL 60118
*Country music singer*

## Sheridan, Jamey
Pier 62 at W 23rd St.
New York, NY 10011
*Actor*

## Sherwin-Williams
101 Prospect Ave. NW
Cleveland, OH 44115
*Chemicals*

**INTERNET** www.sherwin-williams.com
John G. Breen, Chairman

## Shevardnadze, Eduard
Georgia (Republic of)
*Chairman, State Council*

**INTERNET** www.presidpress.gov.ge
**E-MAIL** office@presidpress.gov.ge

## Shields, Brooke
10061 Riverside Dr., #1013
Toluca Lake, CA 91602
*Actress*

**BIRTHDAY** 5/31/65

## Shimmerman, Armin
8730 Sunset Blvd.
Los Angeles, CA 90069
*Actor*

## Shore, Pauly
8491 Sunset Blvd., #700
W Hollywood, CA 90069
*Comedian/actor*

## Shore, Roberta
P.O. Box 71639
Salt Lake City, UT 84171
*Singer*

**Short, Martin**
760 N La Cienega Blvd., #200
Los Angeles, CA 90069
*Actor*

**BIRTHDAY** 3/26/50

**Showtime**
1633 Broadway
New York, NY 10019
*Cable network*

**Shreveport Times**
222 Lake St.
Shreveport, LA 71130

**INTERNET** www.shreveporttimes.com
**VOICE** 318-459-3200

**Shriver, Maria**
3110 Main St., #300
Santa Monica, CA 90405
*Broadcast journalist*

**BIRTHDAY** 11/6/55

**Shriver, Pam**
401 Washington Ave., #902
Baltimore, MD 21204
*Tennis player*

**Shue, Andrew**
5700 Wilshire Blvd.
Los Angeles, CA 90036
*Actor*

**Shue, Elizabeth**
5700 Wilshire Blvd.
Los Angeles, CA 90036
*Actress*

**Siegan and Wisman, LTD**
29 S La Salle
Chicago, IL 60603
*Entertainment agency*

**Siegfried & Roy**
1639 N Valley Dr.
Las Vegas, NV 89102
*Circus act*

## Sierra Club National Office

85 Second St., 2nd Floor
San Francisco, CA 94105
*A nonprofit organization that promotes conservation*

**INTERNET** www.sierraclub.org

## Sierra Leone

Ahmad Tejankabbah, President
Office of the President
State House, Tower Hill
Freetown
Sierra Leone

**INTERNET** www.sierra-leone.org

## Silicon Graphics

1600 Amphitheatre Pkwy
Mountain View, CA 94043
*Computers, office equipment*

**INTERNET** www.sgi.com
Robert R. Bishop, Chairman and CEO

## Silverman, Fred

1642 Mandeville Ln.
Los Angeles, CA 90049
*Television producer*

## Silverman, Jonathan

2255 Mountain Oaks Dr.
Los Angeles, CA 90068
*Actor*

**BIRTHDAY** 8/5/66

## Silverstone, Alicia

1122 S Robertson Blvd., #15
Los Angeles, CA 90035
*Actress*

**BIRTHDAY** 1/4/76

## Simmons, Richard

P.O. Box 5403
Beverly Hills, CA 90209
*Fitness guru*

## Simon, Neil

10745 Chalon Road
Los Angeles, CA 90077
*Playwright*

## Simon, Paul

1619 Broadway
New York, NY 10019
*Musician/songwriter*

## Simpson, O.J.
9450 SW 112th St.
Miami, FL 33176
*Former football player*

## Simpsons, The
P.O. Box 900
Beverly Hills, CA 90213
*Television cartoon*

## Sinatra, Nancy
P.O. Box 10236
Beverly Hills, CA 90210
*Actress/singer*

## Sinbad
9830 Wilshire Blvd.
Beverly Hills, CA 90024
*Comedian*

## Singapore
Sellapan Ramanathan Nathan, President
Istana
Orchard Road
238823 Singapore
Singapore

**INTERNET** www.gov.sg/istana

## Singer, Lori
1465 Lindacrest Dr.
Beverly Hills, CA 90210
*Actress*

**BIRTHDAY** 5/6/62

## Slash
5664 Cahuenga, #246
N Hollywood, CA 91601
*Musician*

## Slater, Christian
9150 Wilshire Blvd., #350
Beverly Hills, CA 90210
*Actor*

**BIRTHDAY** 8/18/69

## Slater, Kelly
510 18th Ave.
Honolulu, HI 96816
*Actress*

## Sledge, Percy
9850 Sandalfoot Blvd., #458
Boca Raton, FL 33428
*Singer*

**BIRTHDAY** 11/25/40

## Slovakia
Rudolf Schuster, President
Stefanikova 1
810 00 Bratislava
Slovakia

**INTERNET** www.prezident.sk

## Slovenia
Andrej Bajuk, Prime Minister
Gregorciceva 20
61000 Ljubljana
Slovenia

**INTERNET** www.sigov.si
**E-MAIL** alja.brglez@gov.si

## Small Business Administration
409 32nd St. SW
Washington, D.C. 20416

## Smart Computing
131 W Grand Dr.
Lincoln, NE 68521

**INTERNET** www.smartcomputing.com
**VOICE** 1-800-544-1264

## Smart, Elizabeth
**INTERNET** www.elizabethsmart.com
*Abducted child who was missing for 9 months and was found alive*

## Smashing Pumpkins
9830 Wilshire Blvd.
Beverly Hills, CA 90212
*Music group*

## Smith, Gordon
404 Russell Senate
Office Bldg. (R-OR)
Washington, D.C. 20510
*Senator*

**INTERNET** www.gsmith.senate.gov/webform.htm

## Smith, Anna Nicole
5750 Wilshire Blvd.
Los Angeles, CA 90036
*Television personality*

## Smith, Jaclyn
10398 Sunset Blvd.
Los Angeles, CA 90077
*Actress*

**BIRTHDAY** 10/26/47

## Smith, Kevin
3 Harding Road
Red Bank, NJ 07701
*Actor*

## Smith, Will
9830 Wilshire Blvd.
Beverly Hills, CA 90212
*Actor*

**BIRTHDAY** 9/25/68

## Smith and Wesson
2100 Roosevelt Ave.
Springfield, MA 01102
*Firearms*

**INTERNET** www.smith-wesson.com
Mitchell Saltz, CEO and President

## Smithfield Foods
200 Commerce St.
Smithfield, VA 23430

Joseph W. Luter, III, Chairman, President and CEO

## Smithsonian Institution
1000 Jefferson Dr. SW
Washington, D.C. 20560
*Independent trust of the U.S., holding more than 140 million artifacts and specimens in its trust for the diffusion of knowledge*

**INTERNET** www.si.edu
Robert McCadams, Secretary

## Smits, Jimmy
P.O. Box 49922
Los Angeles, CA 90049
*Actor*

**BIRTHDAY** 7/9/55

## Smurfit-Stone Container Corporation
150 N Michigan Ave.
Chicago, IL 60601
*The world's top maker of containerboard and corrugated containers and a leading wastepaper recycler*

**INTERNET** www.smurfit.com
Michael W.J. Smufit, Chairman

## Snipes, Wesley
P.O. Box 490
New York, NY 10014
*Actor*

## Snoop Doggy Dogg
250 W 57th St., #821
New York, NY 10107
*Rap singer*

## Snowe, Olympia
**E-MAIL** olympia@snowe.senate.gov

154 Russell Senate
Office Bldg. (R-ME)
Washington, D.C. 20510
*Senator*

## Snyder, Tom
7800 Beverly Blvd.
Los Angeles, CA 90036
*Talk show host*

## Soap Opera Digest
**INTERNET** www.soapoperadigest.com

45 W 25th St.
New York, NY 10010

## Software Magazine
**INTERNET** www.software.com
**VOICE** 508-366-2031

1900 W Park Dr.
Westborough, MA 01581

## Sojourners
**INTERNET** www.sojo.net

2401 15th St. NW
Washington, D.C. 20009
*Christian ministry whose mission is to proclaim and practice the biblical call to integrate spiritual renewal and social justice*

## Solar Energy Industries Association
**INTERNET** www.seia.org

1616 H St. NW, 8th Floor
Washington, D.C. 20006
*A national trade association for all solar businesses and enterprises in the fields of photovoltaics, solar electric power, solar thermal power and solar building products*

## Solectron
**INTERNET** www.solectrom.com
Mike Cannon, Chairman, President and CEO

777 Gibraltar Dr.
Milpitas, CA 95035
*Electronics, electrical equipment*

## Solomon Islands
Bartholomew Ulufa'alu
Prime Minister
Prime Minister's Office
P.O. Box G1
Honiara, Guadalcanal
Solomon Islands

## Somalia
Collective Chairmanship
National Salvation Council
Mogadishu
Somalia

## Somers, Suzanne
P.O. Box 9090
Clearwater, FL 34618
*Actress*

**BIRTHDAY** 11/5/40

## Sonoco
1 N 2nd St.
Harsville, SC 29550
*Forest and paper products*

**INTERNET** www.sonoco.com
Jack Drosdick, Chairman

## Sorbo, Kevin
P.O. Box 410
Buffalo Center, IA 50424
*Actor*

## Soros Foundation Network
888 7th Ave.
New York, NY 10606
*Grant organization supporting research that promotes an "open society"*

**INTERNET** www.soros.org
George Soros, Founder

## Sorvino, Mira
41 W 86th St.
New York, NY 10024
*Actress*

## Sorvino, Paul
232 N Canon Dr.
Beverly Hills, CA 90210
*Actor*

## Soto, Talisa
484 Madison Ave., #P-13
New York, NY 10022
*Model*

## Soul, David
863 N Beverly Glen Blvd.
Los Angeles, CA 90077
*Actor*

## Soul Asylum
8500 Wilshire Blvd., #700
Beverly Hills, CA 90211
*Music group*

## Soundgarden
207 & 1/ 2 1st Ave. S
Seattle, WA 98104
*Music group*

## South Africa
Thabo Mvuyelwa Mbeki, President
Office of the President
Private Bag X1000
Union Buildings, Government Ave.
0001 Pretoria
South Africa

**INTERNET** www.gov.za/president
**E-MAIL** president@po.gov.za

## South Korea
Kim Dae Jung, President
Office of the President
1 Sejong-ro Chongro-gu
110-050 Seoul
South Korea

**INTERNET** www.bluehous.go.kr
**E-MAIL** webmaster@cwd.go.kr

## Southern Energy
900 Ashwood Pkwy, #500
Atlanta, GA 30338
*Gas and electric utilities*

**INTERNET** www.southernco.com
S. Marie Fuller, Chairman and CEO

## Southern Living
P.O. Box 62376
Tampa, FL 33662
*Magazine*

**INTERNET** www.southernliving.com
**VOICE** 1-800-272-4101

## Southwest Airlines
2702 Love Field Dr.
Dallas, TX 75235
*Airlines*

**INTERNET** www.iflyswa.com
James Parker, Chairman, President and CEO

## Spacek, Sissy
Rt. 22
Cobham, VA 22929
*Actress*

**BIRTHDAY** 12/25/49

## Spacey, Kevin
120 W 45th St.
New York, NY 10036
*Actor*

**BIRTHDAY** 7/26/59

## Spade, David
9150 Wilshire Blvd.
Beverly Hills, CA 90212
*Actor*

## Spader, James
8942 Wilshire Blvd.
Beverly Hills, CA 90211
*Actor*

## Spain
King Juan Carlos I de
Borbon y Borbon
Palacio de la Zarzuela
28071 Madrid
Spain

**INTERNET** www.casareal.es

## Speak Easy International Foundation
233 Concord Dr.
Paramus, NJ 07652
*A supportive self-help mutual aid group for people with a stuttering condition*

## Spears, Britney
137-139 W 25th St.
New York, NY 10001
*Singer*

**BIRTHDAY** 12/2/81
**E-MAIL** britney@britneyspears.com

## Special Olympics International

1325 G St. NW, #500
Washington, D.C. 20005

**INTERNET** www.specialolympics.org
Sargent Timothy Shriver,
Chairman of the Board

*An international program of year-round sports training and athletic competition for more than one million children and adults with mental retardation*

## Specter, Arlen

711 Hart Senate Office Bldg. (R-PA)
Washington, D.C. 20510
*Senator*

**INTERNET** www.arlen_specter.senate.gov

## Speechwriter's Newsletter

316 N Michigan Ave., #300
Chicago, IL 60601

**INTERNET** www.ragan.com
**VOICE** 312-960-4100

## Spelling, Aaron

5700 Wilshire Blvd.
Los Angeles, CA 90036
*Television producer*

## Spelling, Tori

5700 Wilshire Blvd.
Los Angeles, CA 90036
*Actress*

## Spielberg, Steven

100 Universal City Plaza
Bldg. #10, 34th Floor
Universal City, CA 91608
*Producer/director*

**BIRTHDAY** 12/18/47

## SPIN

104 E 25th St.
New York, NY 10010
*Rock magazine*

**INTERNET** www.spin.com
**VOICE** 212-633-8200

## Spiner, Brent

8383 Wilshire Blvd., #550
Beverly Hills, CA 90211
*Actor*

**BIRTHDAY** 2/24/49

## Spinks, Leon

P.O. Box 88771
Carol Stream, IL 60188
*Boxer*

## Spokane Spokesman Review
W 999 Riverside Dr.
Spokane, WA 99210

**INTERNET** www.spokesmanreview.com
**VOICE** 509-459-5485

## Sports Illustrated
Time Life Bldg.
New York, NY 10020
*Magazine*

**INTERNET** www.si.com
**VOICE** 212-522-3233

## Springer, Jerry
454 N Columbus Dr.
Chicago, IL 60611
*Talk show host*

## Springfield, Rick
515 Ocean Ave.
Santa Monica, CA 90212
*Singer*

## Springfield Union
1860 Main St.
Springfield, MA 01102

**INTERNET** www.masslive.com
**VOICE** 413-788-1332

## Springsteen, Bruce
1224 Benedict Canyon
Beverly Hills, CA 90210
*Singer*

## Sprint
2330 Shawnee Mission Pkwy
Westwood, KS 66205
*Telecommunications*

**INTERNET** www.sprint.com
William T. Esrey, CEO

## Squier, Billy
P.O. Box 1251
New York, NY 10023
*Singer*

**BIRTHDAY** 5/12/50

## Sri Lanka
H.E. Chandrika Bandaranaike Kumaratunga, President
Presidential Secretarial Bldg.
Colombo, O1
Sri Lanka

**INTERNET** www.lk.

## St. Louis Cardinals

250 Stadium Plaza
St. Louis, MO 63102
*Baseball team*

## St. Paul Companies, Inc.

385 Washington St.
St. Paul, MN 55102
*P & C insurance*

**INTERNET** www.stpaul.com
Martin Hudson, Chairman and CEO

## St. Petersburg Times

490 First Ave. S
St. Petersburg, FL 33701

**INTERNET** www.sptimes.com
**VOICE** 727-893-8111

## Stabenow, Debbie

702 Hart Senate
Office Bldg. (D-MI)
Washington, D.C. 20510
*Senator*

**E-MAIL** senator@stabenow.senate.gov

## Stahl-Sullivan, Lisa

13775 A Mono Way, #220
Pacific Grove, CA 93951
*Actress*

## Stallone, Sylvester

350 Park Ave.
New York, NY 10022
*Actor*

## Stamos, John

254 W 54th St.
New York, NY 10019
*Actor*

## Staples

500 Staples Dr.
Framingham, MA 01702
*Specialist retailers*

**INTERNET** www.staples.com
Ronald L. Sargent, Chairman and CEO

## STAR

660 White Plains Road
Tarrytown, NY 10591
*Weekly tabloid newspaper*

**VOICE** 914-332-5000

## Star Trek Voyager cast
5555 Melrose Ave.
Los Angeles, CA 90038
*Television show*

## Starr, Ringo
24 Ave. Princess Grace
98000 Monte Carlo
Monaco
*Musician*

## STARZ
5445 DTC Pkwy, #600
Englewood, CO 80111
*Cable network*

## State Farm Insurance Company
1 State Farm Plaza
Bloomington, IL 61710
*P & C insurance*

Edward B. Rust Jr, Chairman and CEO

## State Street Corp
225 Franklin St.
Boston, MA 02110
*Commercial bank*

**INTERNET** www.statestreet.com
David A. Spina, Chairman

## Steele, Danielle
P.O. Box 1637
New York, NY 10156
*Author*

## Stein, Ben
602 N Crescent Dr.
Beverly Hills, CA 90210
*Comedian/actor/television game show host*

## Stern, Howard
10 E 44th St., #500
New York, NY 10017
*Radio show host*

## Stevens, Connie
426 S Robertson Blvd.
Los Angeles, CA 90069
*Actress/singer*

**BIRTHDAY** 8/8/38

**Stevens, Ray**
1708 Grand Ave.
Nashville, TN 37212
*Singer*

**BIRTHDAY** 1/24/39

**Stevens, Stella**
2180 Coldwater Canyon
Hollywood, CA 90028
*Actress*

**BIRTHDAY** 10/1/36

**Stevens, Ted**
522 Hart Senate
Office Bldg. (R-AK)
Washington, D.C. 20510
*Senator*

**INTERNET** www.stevens.senate.gov/webform.htm

**Stevenson, Parker**
4526 Wilshire Blvd.
Los Angeles, CA 90010
*Actor*

**Stewart, Martha**
11 W 42nd St.
New York, NY 10036
*Television personality*

**BIRTHDAY** 8/3/41

**Stewart, Patrick**
Oxford House
76 Oxford St.
London W1D1BS
England
UNITED KINGDOM
*Actor/writer*

**BIRTHDAY** 7/13/30

**Stewart, Rod**
1122 S Robertson Blvd., #15
Los Angeles, CA 90035
*Singer*

**BIRTHDAY** 1/10/45

**Stine, R.L.**
555 Broadway
New York, NY 10012
*Author*

**Sting (Gordon Matthew Sumner)**
2 The Grove
Highgate Village
London N6
England
UNITED KINGDOM
*Singer/songwriter*

BIRTHDAY 10/2/51

**Stockwell, Dean**
9560 Wilshire Blvd., #516
Beverly Hills, CA 90212
*Actor*

BIRTHDAY 3/5/35

**Stone, Doug**
P.O. Box 943
Springfield, TN 37172
*Country music singer*

**Stone, Oliver**
520 Broadway
Santa Monica, CA 90401
*Film director/producer*

**Stone, Sharon**
P.O. Box 7304
N Hollywood, CA 91603
*Actress*

**Stone Temple Pilots**
118 W Magnolia
Burbank, CA 91506
*Music group*

**Stowe, Madeline**
9565 Wilshire Blvd., #516
Beverly Hills, CA 90212
*Actress*

BIRTHDAY 8/18/58

**Strait, George**
1000 18th Ave. S
Nashville, TN 37212
*Country music singer*

## Streep, Meryl

**BIRTHDAY** 4/22/49

9830 Wilshire Blvd.
Beverly Hills, CA 90212
*Actress*

## Street, Picabo

P.O. Box 1640
Eagle, ID 83616
*Olympic skier*

## Streisand, Barbra

**BIRTHDAY** 4/24/42

5670 Wilshire Blvd., #2400
Los Angeles, CA 90036
*Singer/actress*

## Strug, Kerri

5670 Wilshire Blvd., #2400
Los Angeles, CA 90036
*Gymnast*

## Struthers, Sally

**BIRTHDAY** 7/28/48

8721 Sunset Blvd.
Los Angeles, CA 90046
*Actress*

## Stuart, Marty

119 17th Ave. S
Nashville, TN 37203
*Singer/songwriter*

## Stuttering Foundation of America

**INTERNET** www.stuttersfa.org

3100 Walnut Grove Road, #603
Memphis, TN 38111
*The first nonprofit, charitable association in the world to concern itself with the prevention and improved treatment of stuttering*

## Sudan

Omar Hassan Ahmed Al-Bashir, President General
Revolutionary Command Council
Khartoum
Sudan

## Sugar Ray

P.O. Box 8309
Kirkland, WA 98034
*Music group*

## Sun Microsystems
901 San Antonio Road
Palo Alto, CA 94303
*Computers, office equipment*

**INTERNET** www.sun.com
Scott G. McNealy, Chairman and CEO

## Sun Trust Bank
303 Peachtree St. NE
Atlanta, GA 30308
*Commercial bank*

**INTERNET** www.suntrust.com
James Shaw, Chairman, President and CEO

## Sunset
80 Willow Road
Menlo Park, CA 94025
*Magazine*

**INTERNET** www.sunset.com
**VOICE** 650-321-3600

## Sununu, John
Senate Russell Courtyard 4 (R-NH)
Washington, D.C. 20510
*Senator*

**E-MAIL** mailbox@sununu.senate.gov

## Superstation WTBS
1 CNN Center
Atlanta, GA 30348
*Cable network*

## Supertramp
2220 Colorado Ave.
Santa Monica, CA 90404
*Music group*

## Supervalu
11840 Valley View Road
Eden Prairie, MN 55344
*Wholesaler*

**INTERNET** www.supervalu.com
Jeffrey Noddle, Chairman and CEO

## Suriname
Jules Adjodhia, Prime Minister
Nationala Assemblee
Wulfingstraat
Paramaribo
Suriname

## Survivor
9830 Sandlefoot Blvd., #458
Boca Raton, FL 33428
*Music group*

## Survivor
*Reality television series*

**INTERNET** www.cbs.com

## Sutherland, Donald
9830 Wilshire Blvd.
Beverly Hills, CA 90212
*Actor*

**BIRTHDAY** 7/17/36

## Sutherland, Kiefer
132 S Rodeo Dr., #300
Beverly Hills, CA 90212
*Actor*

**BIRTHDAY** 12/18/66

## Swaggart, Jimmy
P.O. Box 262550
Baton Rouge, LA 70826
*Television evangelist*

## Swank, Hilary
9100 Wilshire Blvd. W, #600
Beverly Hills, CA 90212
*Actress*

## Swayze, Patrick
132 S Rodeo Dr.
Beverly Hills, CA 90212
*Actor/singer*

**BIRTHDAY** 8/18/52

## Swaziland
King Mswati III
Royal Palace
Mbabane
Swaziland

## Sweden
King Carl XVI Gustaf
Royal Palace
Kungliga Slottet
S-111 30 Stockholm
Sweden

**INTERNET** www.royalcourt.se

## Switzerland
Adolf Ogi
President de la Confederation
Bundeshaus Wet
Ch-3003 Bern
Switzerland

**INTERNET** www.admin.ch

## Syracuse Herald-Journal
Clinton Square
Syracuse, NY 13221

**INTERNET** www.syracuse.com
**VOICE** 315-470-2265

## Syria
Bashar al-Assad, President
Presidential Palace
Abu Rumana al-Rashid St.
Damascus
Syria

## Sysco
1390 Enclave Pkwy
Houston, TX 77077
*Food wholesalers*

**INTERNET** www.sysco.com
Keith D. Shapiro, Senior Chairman

## Taft, Bob
*Governor of Ohio*

**E-MAIL** governor.taft@das.state.oh.us

## Taiwan
Chen Shui-bian
President
Office of the President
Chiehshou Hall
122 Chungking S Road, Sec 1
10036 T'aipei
Taiwan

## Tajikistan
Imamali Rakhmanov, President
Office of the President
Prospekt Lenina 42
Dushanbe
Tajikistan

## Takei, George
419 Larchmont Blvd.
Los Angeles, CA 90004
*Actor*

## Talent, James
U.S. Senate (R-MO)
Washington, D.C. 20510
*Senator*

## Tampa Bay Buccaneers
1 Buccaneers Place
Tampa Bay, FL 33607
*Football team*

## Tandy Brands Accessories, Inc.
90 E Lamar Blvd., #200
Arlington, TX 76011
*Leather goods manufacturer*

**INTERNET** www.tandybrands.com
J.S. Britt Jenkins, President and CEO

## Tanzania
Benjamin Mkapa, President
State House
P.O. Box 9120, Magogoni Rd
Dar es Salaam
Tanzania

## Tarantino, Quentin
12400 Wilshire Blvd.
Los Angeles, CA 90025
*Director*

**BIRTHDAY** 3/27/63

## Tarar, Muhammad Rafiq
c/o Marie Ambrosino
*President of Pakistan*

**INTERNET** www.pak.gov.pk
**E-MAIL** ce@pak.gov.pk

## TASH
P.O. Box 6
Baltimore, MD 21204

**INTERNET** www.tash.com

*An international association of people with disabilities, their family members, other advocates and professionals fighting for a society in which inclusion of all people in all aspects of society is the norm*

## Taya, Maaouya Ould Sidi Ahmed
President
Presidence de la Republique
B.P. 184
Nouakochott
Mauritania

**INTERNET** www.mauritania.mr

## Taylor, Elizabeth
P.O. Box 55995
Sherman Oaks, CA 91413-0995
*Actress*

**BIRTHDAY** 2/27/32

## Taylor, James
1250 6th St., #401
Santa Monica, CA 90401
*Singer/songwriter*

**BIRTHDAY** 3/12/48

## Taylor, Jonathan
119 Rockland Center, #251
Burbank, CA 91521
*Actor*

## Taylor, Nikki
8362 Pines Blvd., #334
Hollywood, FL 33024
*Model*

## TBS (Turner Broadcasting)
100 International Blvd. NW
Atlanta, GA 30303
*Cable network*

## Tech-Data
5350 Tech Data Dr.
Clearwater, FL 33760
*Wholesalers*

**INTERNET** www.techdata.com
Steven A. Raymond, Chairman Emeritus

## Tejankabbah, Ahmad
*President of Sierra Leone*

**INTERNET** www.sierra-leone.org/govt.html

## Teen
8490 Sunset Blvd.
Los Angeles, CA 90069
*Magazine*

**INTERNET** www.teen.com
**VOICE** 310-854-2222

## Telecommunications
1333 H St. NW
Washington, D.C. 20005
*Magazine*

**INTERNET** www.tr.com
**VOICE** 202-842-3006

## Telecommunications for the Deaf, Inc.
8630 Fenton St., #604
Silver Spring, MD 20910
*An active national advocacy organization focusing its energies and resources on addressing equal access issues in telecommunications and media for four constituencies in deafness and hearing loss*

**INTERNET** www.tdi-online.org

## Telemundo
2290 W 8th Ave.
Hialeah, FL 33010
*Cable network*

## Television Digest
2115 Ward Ct. NW
Washington, D.C. 20037

**INTERNET** www.1-news.com
**VOICE** 202-872-9200

## Temple-Inland
303 S Temple Dr.
Diboll, TX 75941
*Forest and paper products*

**INTERNET** www.templeinland.com
Kenneth M. Jastrow II, Chairman and CEO

## Temptations, The
9200 Sunset Blvd.
Los Angeles, CA 90069
*Music group*

## Tenet Healthcare
3820 State St.
Santa Barbara, CA 93105
*Healthcare*

**INTERNET** www.tenethealth.com
Jeffrey C. Barbakow, Chairman and CEO

## Tenneco Automotive, Inc.
500 N Field Dr.
Lake Forest, IL 60045
*Motor vehicles and parts*

**INTERNET** www.tenneco-automotive.com
Mark P. Frissora, Chairman and CEO

## Tennessee Valley Authority (TVA)
400 W Summit Hill Dr.
Knoxville, TN 37902

## Tesh, John
P.O. Box 6010
Sherman Oaks, CA 91413
*Musician/talk show host*

## Texaco
2000 Westchester Ave.
White Plains, NY 10650
*Petroleum refining*

**INTERNET** www.texaco.com
Peter L. Bijur, CEO

## Texas Instruments
12500 T1 Blvd.
Dallas, TX 75243
*Electronics, electrical equipment*

**INTERNET** www.ti.com
Thomas J. Engibous, Chairman, President and CEO

## Texas Rangers
P.O. Box 90111
Arlington, TX 76004
*Baseball team*

## Textron
40 Westminster
Providence, RI 02903
*Aerospace*

**INTERNET** www.textron.com
Lewis B. Campbell, Chairman and CEO

## Thailand
King Bhumibol Adulyadej
(Rama IX)
Chitralada Villa
Bangkok
Thailand

## Than, Shwa
Chairman, State of Peace and Dev. Council
Yangon, Myanmar
c/o Ministry of Defense
Signal Pagoda Road
Myanmar

## That 70's Show
4024 Radford Ave., Office S
Studio City, CA 91604
*Television show*

**INTERNET** www.that70sshow.com

## Theisman, Joe
ESPN Plaza
935 Middle St.
Bristol, CT 06010
*Sports broadcaster*

## Thermo Electron
81 Wyman St.
Waltham, MA 02254
*Scientific, photo, control equipment*

**INTERNET** www.thermo.com
Marijn E. Dekkers, Chairman, President and CEO

## Theron, Charlize
9560 Wilshire Blvd., #500
Beverly Hills, CA 90212
*Actress*

## Thicke, Alan
10505 Sarah St.
Toluca Lake, CA 91602
*Actor*

## Thiessen, Tiffani-Amber
1212 S Robertson Blvd., #15
Los Angeles, CA 90035
*Actress*

**BIRTHDAY** 1/23/74

## Thomas, B.J.
P.O. Box 120003
Arlington, TX 76012
*Singer*

## Thomas, Craig
109 Hart Senate Office Bldg (R-WY)
Washington, D.C. 20510
*Senator*

**INTERNET** www.thomas.senate.gov/html/contact.html

## Thomas, Heather
1122 S Robertson Blvd., #15
Los Angeles, CA 90035
*Actress*

**BIRTHDAY** 9/8/57
**E-MAIL** heatherthomas@studiofanmail.com

## Thomas, Irma
P.O. Box 26126
New Orleans, LA 70186
*Musician*

## Thomas, Jonathan Taylor
P.O. Box 64846
Beverly Hills, CA 90212
*Actor*

**BIRTHDAY** 9/8/81

**Thomas, Philip Michael** BIRTHDAY 5/26/49
P.O. Box 837709
Miami, FL 33283
*Actor*

**Thomas Jefferson Center for the Protection of Free Expression** INTERNET www.tjcenter.org
400 Peter Jefferson Place
Charlottesville, VA 22911
Robert M. O'Neil, Director
*A unique organization, devoted solely to the defense of free expression in all its forms*

**Thompson, Andrea**
600 3rd Ave.
New York, NY 10016
*Actress*

**Thompson, Emma**
56 Kings Road
Kingston-On-Thames
England KT2 5HF
UNITED KINGDOM
*Actress*

**Thompson, Lea** BIRTHDAY 5/31/62
7966 Woodrow Wilson Dr.
Los Angeles, CA 90046
*Actress*

**Thompson, Sada** BIRTHDAY 9/27/29
Box 490
Southbury, CT 06488
*Actress*

**Thorne-Smith, Courtney**
4024 Radford Ave.
Studio City, CA 91604
*Actress*

**Thornton, Billy Bob**
11777 San Vicente Blvd.
Los Angeles, CA 90049
*Actor*

| | |
|---|---|
| **Thurman, Uma**<br>1775 Broadway, #701<br>New York, NY 10019<br>*Actress* | |
| **TIAA-CREF**<br>730 3rd Ave.<br>New York, NY 10017<br>*Health and Life insurance* | John H. Biggs, Chairman, President and CEO |
| **Tiegs, Cheryl**<br>457 Cuesta Way<br>Los Angeles, CA 90077<br>*Model* | |
| **Tillis, Pam**<br>P.O. Box 120073<br>Nashville, TN 37212<br>*Country music singer* | |
| **Tilly, Jennifer**<br>1465 Lindacrest Dr.<br>Beverly Hills, CA 90210<br>*Actress* | **BIRTHDAY** 2/14/60 |
| **Timberlake, Justin**<br>*Singer* | **INTERNET** www.justin@nsync.com |
| **Time**<br>1271 Ave. of the Americas<br>New York, NY 10020<br>*Magazine* | **INTERNET** www.time.com<br>**VOICE** 212-522-1212 |
| **Time Warner**<br>75 Rockefeller Plaza<br>New York, NY 10019<br>*Entertainment, publishing* | **INTERNET** www.timewarner.com<br>Richard Parsons, Chairman and CEO |
| **Tito, Teburoro**<br>Office of the President<br>Tarawa, Kiribati<br>P.O. Box 68<br>*President of Bairiki Kiribati* | |

## TJFR Business News Reporter

2020 Arapahoe St.
Denver, CO 80205
*Newsletter*

**INTERNET** www.tjfr.com
**VOICE** 303-296-1200

## TJX

770 Cochituate Road
Framingham, MA 01701
*Specialist retailer*

**INTERNET** www.tjmaxx.com
Edmond J. English, Chairman

## TLC

1325 Ave. of the Americas
New York, NY 10019
*Cable network*

## TNT Network

1 CNN Center
Atlanta, GA 30348
*Cable network*

## Today Show, The

30 Rockefeller Plaza
New York, NY 10019

**INTERNET** www.today.msnbc.com
**E-MAIL** today@nbc.com
**VOICE** 212-664-4238

## Toledo Blade

541 Superior St.
Toledo, OH 43660

**INTERNET** www.theblade.com
**VOICE** 419-245-6000

## Tomas Rivera Policy Institute

1050 N Mills Ave.
Claremont, CA 91711

**INTERNET** www.trpi.org
Harry P. Pachon, President

*Freestanding, nonprofit, policy research organization which has attained a reputation as the nation's "premier Latino think tank"*

## Tomei, Marisa

120 N 45th St., #3600
New York, NY 10036
*Actress*

## Tomlin, Lily

151 El Camino Dr.
Beverly Hills, CA 90212
*Actress*

## Tonga
King Taufa'ahau Tupou IV
The Palace
P.O. Box 6
Nuku'alofa
Tonga

## Tonight Show, The
3000 W Alameda Ave.
Burbank, CA 91523

**VOICE** 818-840-2222

## Toronto Blue Jays
1 Blue Jays Way
ON- M5V 1J1
Canada
*Baseball team*

## Toronto Maple Leafs
Maple Leaf Gardens
ON- M5B 1L1
Canada
*Hockey team*

## Toronto Raptors
20 Bay St.
ON- M5J 2N8
Canada
*Basketball team*

## Tosco
72 Cummings Point Road
Stamford, CT 06902
*Petroleum refining*

**INTERNET** www.tosco.com
Thomas D. O'Malley, Chairman and CEO

## Total Acting Experience, A
20501 Ventura Blvd., #399
Woodland Hills, CA 91364
*Entertainment agency*

## Toto
34 N Palm St., #100
Ventura, CA 93001
*Music group*

## Town and Country

1700 Broadway
New York, NY 10019
*Magazine*

**VOICE** 212-903-5000

## Townshend, Pete

4 Friars Ln.
Richmond Surrey
TW9 1NL
England
UNITED KINGDOM
*Singer*

## Toys for Tots Foundation

**INTERNET** www.toysfortots.org

*Recognized fund-raising and support organization for the Marine Corps Reserve Toys for Tots program*

## Trans World Airline

1 City Center
515 N 6th St.
St. Louis, MO 63101
*Airline*

**INTERNET** www.twa.com
William F. Compton, CEO

## Transamerica

600 Montgomery St.
San Francisco, CA 94111
*Health and Life insurance*

**INTERNET** www.transamerica.com
George Foegele, Chairman

## Travel and Leisure

1120 Ave. of the Americas
New York, NY 10036

**INTERNET** www.travelandleisure.com
**VOICE** 212-382-5600

## Travel Weekly

500 Plaza Dr.
Secaucus, NJ 07094

**INTERNET** www.twcrossroads.com
**VOICE** 201-902-1500

## Travelers Property Casualty Corp

1 Tower Square
Hartford, CT 06183
*Insurance*

Robert L. Lipp, Chairman

## Travis, Randy

P.O. Box 121137
Nashville, TN 37212
*Country music singer*

**BIRTHDAY** 5/4/59

## Travolta, John

BIRTHDAY 2/18/54

P.O. Box 3560
Santa Barbara, CA 93130
*Actor*

## Trebek, Alex

10210 W Washington Blvd.
Culver City, CA 90232
*Television game show host*

## Trends Research Institute

INTERNET www.trendsresearch.com

P.O. Box 660
Rhinebeck, NY 12572
*Combines unique resources with its own trademarked methodology to help companies profit from trends*

## Tribune Company

INTERNET www.tribune.com
Dennis Fitzsimmons, Chairman, President and CEO

435 N Michigan Ave.
Chicago, IL 60611
*Newspapers, publishing, Chicago Cubs owner*

## Trinidad and Tobago

INTERNET www.nisc.gov.tt

Arthur Robinson, President
President's House
St. Ann's
Trinidad and Tobago

## Tritt, Travis

BIRTHDAY 2/9/63

830 E Hillview Dr.
Brentwood, TN 37027
*Country music singer/songwriter*

## Trovoada, Miguel

Office of the President
C.P. 38, Sao Tome
Principe Sao Tome and Principe
*President*

## Trudeau, Garry

200 Madison Ave.
New York, NY 10024
*Cartoonist*

**Trump, Donald**
725 5th Ave.
New York, NY 10022
*Real Estate mogul*
**BIRTHDAY** 6/14/46

**Trump, Ivana**
10 E 64th St.
New York, NY 10021
*Ex-wife of Donald Trump*

**Trump, Ivanka**
10 E 64th St.
New York, NY 10021
*Model*

**TruServ**
8600 W Bryn Mawr Ave.
Chicago, IL 60631
*Specialist retailers*
**INTERNET** www.truserv.com
Donald Hoye, President and CEO

**TRW**
1900 Richmond Road
Cleveland, OH 44124
*Motor vehicles and parts*
**INTERNET** www.trw.com
Ken Maciver; Chairman and CEO

**Tucker, Tanya**
330 Franklin Road, #135A-257
Brentwood, TN 37027
*Country music singer*
**BIRTHDAY** 10/10/58

**Tucson Weekly**
P.O. Box 2429
Tucson, AZ 85702
**INTERNET** www.tucsonweekly.com
**VOICE** 520-792-3630

**Tulsa Daily World**
318 S Main Mall
Tulsa, OK 74102
**INTERNET** www.tulsaworld.com
**VOICE** 918-581-8300

**Tunisia**
Zine El Abidine Ben Ali
President
Presidence de la Republique, Palais de Carthage
2016 Carthage
Tunisia
**INTERNET** www.ministeres.tn

## Turkel, Studs
850 W Castlewood
Chicago, IL 60640
*Author*

## Turkey
Ahmet Necdet Sezer, President
Cumhurbaskanligi Kosku
Cankaya
06100 Ankara
Turkey

**INTERNET** www.cankaya.gov.tr
**E-MAIL** cankaya@tccb.gov.tr

## Turkmenistan
Saparmurad Niyazov, President
Office of the President
Zdaniye Pravitel'stra
Ashkabad
Turkmenistan

## Turlington, Christy
9560 Wilshire Blvd.
Beverly Hills, CA 90212
*Model*

## Turner, Kathleen
163 Amsterdam Ave., #210
New York, NY 10023
*Actress*

## Turner, Ted
1050 Techwood Dr. NW
Atlanta, GA 30318
*Media executive*

**BIRTHDAY** 11/26/39

## Turner, Tina
9830 Wilshire Blvd.
Beverly Hills, CA 90212
*Singer*

## Turner Broadcasting Systems
1 CNN Center
Atlanta, GA 30348
*Operator of cable television networks*

**INTERNET** www.turner.com
Ted Turner, President

## Turner Classic Movies
1 CNN Center
Atlanta, GA 30348
*Cable network*

## Turner Classic Movies
901 Main St., #4900
Atlanta, GA 30348
*Cable network*

## Turner Corp.
1177 Ave. of the Americas
Dallas, TX 75202
*Engineering, construction*

**INTERNET** www.turnerconstruction.com
Bud Gravette, Chairman and CEO

## Tuvalu
Hon. Ionatana Ionatana,
Prime Minister
Government of Tuvalu
Private Mail Bag, Vaiaku
Funafuti
Tuvalu

## TV Food Network
1177 Ave. of the Americas
New York, NY 10036
*Cable network*

## TV Guide
100 Matsonford Road
Radnor, PA 19088
*Magazine*

## Twain, Shania
9 Music Square S
Nashville, TN 37203
*Singer*

## TXU Corp
1601 Bryan St.
Dallas, TX 75201
*Metal products*

**INTERNET** www.txu.com
Erie Nye, L. Dennis Kozlowski

## Tyler Moore, Mary
510 E 86th St., #21-A
New York, NY 10028
*Actress*

## Tyson, Mike

10100 Santa Monica Blvd., #1300
Los Angeles, CA 90067
*Boxer*

## Tyson Foods

2210 W Oaklawn Dr.
Springdale, AR 72762
*Food producer*

**INTERNET** www.tyson.com
Don Tyson, Chairman

## U.S. Bancorp

601 2nd Ave. S
Minneapolis, MN 55402
*Commercial bank*

**INTERNET** www.usbank.com
John F. Grundhofer, Chairman and CEO

## U.S. International Trade Commission

500 E St. SW
Washington, D.C. 20436

## U.S. Office Products

1025 T Jefferson St. NW
Washington, D.C. 20007
*Wholesalers*

**INTERNET** www.usop.com
Charles P. Pieper, Chairman

## U.S. Postal Service

475 L'Enfant Plaza W SW
Washington, D.C. 20260

## U.S. Term Limits

10 G. St. NW, #410
Washington, D.C. 20002
*Organization devoted to setting term limits for elected officials*

**INTERNET** www.termlimits.org
Howard Rich, President

## U2

119 Rockland Center, #350
Nanuet, NY 19054
*Music group*

## UAL

1200 E. Algonquin Rd.
Elkgrove Village, IL 60007
*Airlines*

**INTERNET** www.ual.com
James E. Goodwin, Chairman and CEO

## UBS Financial Services, Inc.

Mark Sutton, President of PaineWebber Group
*Securities*

**INTERNET** www.ubs.com/e/

## Uganda

Yoweri Kaguta Museveni
President
Office of the President
Parliament Bldg.
P.O. Box 7168
Kampala
Uganda

**INTERNET** www.uganda.co.ug

## Ukraine

Leonid Kuchma, President
11 Bankova St.
Office of the President
252005, Kiev
Ukraine

**E-MAIL** postmaster@ribbon.kiev.ua

## Ullman, Tracey

13555 D'este Dr. Pacific
Pacific Palisades, CA 91205
*Comedian*

## Underwood, Blair

2029 Century Park E, #1190
Los Angeles, CA 90067
*Actor*

## Unicom

10 S Dearborn St.
CEO
Chicago, IL 60603
*Gas and electric utilities*

**INTERNET** www.exelonenterprises.com
John W. Rowe, Chairman, President and

## Union of Concerned Scientists

2 Brattle Square
Cambridge, MA 2238

**INTERNET** www.ucsusa.org
Thomas Stone, Executive Director

*A nonprofit alliance of scientists and citizens working for a healthy environment and a safe world*

## Union Pacific

1416 Dodge St., #1230
Omaha, NE 68179
*Railroads*

**INTERNET** www.up.com
Richard K. Davidson, Chairman, President and CEO

## Unisource

6600 Governors Lake Pkwy
Norcross, GA 30071
*Wholesalers*

**INTERNET** www.unisourcelink.co
James Pignatelli, President

## Unisys

Unisys Way
Blue Bell, PA 19424
*Computer and data services*

**INTERNET** www.unisys.com
Lawrence A. Weinbach, Chairman, President and CEO

## United Arab Emirates

Sheikh Zaid bin Sultan Al Nahayan, President
Amiti Palace
P.O. Box 280
Abu Dhabi
United Arab Emirates

**INTERNET** www.fedfin.gov.ae

## United Kingdom

Rt. Tony Blair
Prime Minister
10 Downing St.
SQ1A 2AA London
England
UNITED KINGDOM

**INTERNET** www.number10.gov.uk

## United Healthcare

9900 Bren Road E
Minneapolis, MN 55343
*Healthcare*

**INTERNET** www.unitedhealthcare.com
Ken Burdick, CEO

## United Parcel Service (UPS)

55 Glanlake Pkwy NE
Atlanta, GA 30328

**INTERNET** www.ups.com
Michael L. Eskew, Chairman and CEO

## United Services Automobile Assn.

9800 Fredericksburg Road
USAA Bldg.
San Antonio, TX 78288
*P & C insurance*

**INTERNET** www.usaa.com

## United States Martial Arts Association, The

011 Mariposa Ave.
Citrus Heights, CA 95610

**INTERNET** www.mararts.org
Renshi Lawrence A. Emmons, Chairman

## United States of America

George W. Bush, President
The White House
1600 Pennsylvania Ave. NW
Washington, D.C. 20500
USA

**INTERNET** www.whitehouse.gov

## United States Olympic Committee

1 Olympic Plaza
Colorado Springs, CO 80909

**INTERNET** www.usoc.org
Sandy Baldwin, President

## United Talent Agency

9560 Wilshire Blvd.
Beverly Hills, CA 90212
*Talent agency*

## United Technologies Corp

1 Financial Plaza
Hartford, CT 06101
*Aerospace*

**INTERNET** www.utc.com
George David, Chairman and CEO

## Universal Tobacco

1501 N Hamilton St.
Richmond, VA 23230
*Tobacco producer*

**INTERNET** www.universalcorp.com
Henry H. Harrell; Chairman and CEO

## Univision

605 3rd Ave., 12th Floor
New York, NY 10158
*Cable network*

## Unocal
2141 Rosecrans Ave., #4000
El Segundo, CA 90505
*Mining, crude-oil production*

**INTERNET** www.unocal.com
Charles R. Williamson, Chairman and CEO

## Unser Jr., Al
7625 Central NW
Albuquerque, NM 87121
*Race car driver*

## UPN
5555 Melrose Ave., Marathon 1200
Los Angeles, CA 90038
*Cable network*

## Uruguay
Jorge Batlle, President
Av. Dr. Alberto de Herrera 3350
Edificio Libertad Presidencia
Montevideo
Uruguay

**INTERNET** www.presidencia.gub.uy

## Urban Institute
2100 M St. NW
Washington, D.C. 20037
Robert D. Reischauer, President
*A nonprofit economic, social and policy research organization*

**INTERNET** www.urban.org

## US Airways Group
2345 Crystal Dr.
Arlington, VA 22227
*Airlines*

**INTERNET** www.usairways.com
David Siegel, Chairman

## US Arms Control and Disarmament Agency
320 21st St. NW
Washington, D.C. 20451

## US Commission on Civil Rights
624 9th St. NW
Washington, D.C. 20425

## US News and World Report

1050 Thomas Jefferson NW
Washington, D.C. 20007
*Magazine*

**INTERNET** www.usnews.com
**VOICE** 202-955-2000

## USA Weekend

1000 Wilshire Blvd.
Arlington, VA 22229

**INTERNET** www.usaweekend.com
**VOICE** 1-800-487-2956

## US Weekly

1290 Ave. of the Americas
New York, NY 10104

**INTERNET** www.usmagazine.com
**VOICE** 212-484-1616

## USA Network

1230 Ave. of the Americas
New York, NY 10020
*Cable network*

**INTERNET** www.usanetwork.com
**VOICE** 212-408-9100

## USF Worldwide, Inc.

1100 Arlington Heights Road, #600
Itasca, IL 60143
*Transportation*

**INTERNET** www.usfreightways.com
Doug Christianson, President

## USG

125 S Franklin St.
P.O. Box 6721
Chicago, IL 60606
*Building materials, glass*

**INTERNET** www.usg.com
William C. Foote, Chairman, President and CEO

## USX

600 Grant St.
Pittsburgh, PA 15219
*Petroleum refining*

**INTERNET** www.usx.com
Thomas J. Usher, Chairman and CEO

## UtiliCorp United, Inc.

20 W 9th St.
Kansas City, MO 64105
*Gas and electric utilities*

**INTERNET** www.utilicorp.com
Richard C. Green, Jr., Chairman and CEO

## Uzbekistan

Islam Karimov, President
Office of the President
Akhunbabayeva 1
Tashkent
Uzbekistan

**INTERNET** www.gov.uz

## Van Damme, Jean Claude
c/o Studio Fan Mail
1122 S Robertson Blvd.
Los Angeles, CA 90035
*Actor*

## Van Dyke, Dick
23215 Mariposa De Oro
Malibu, CA 90265
*Actor*

## Van Dyke, Jerry
P.O. Box 2130
Benton, AZ 72018
*Actor*

## Van Halen, Eddie
31736 Broad Beach Road
Malibu, CA 90265
*Musician*

## Van Houten, Leslie
#W13378
Bed #1B314U
California Inst. For Women
16756 Chino Corona
Frontera, CA 91720
*Convicted Member of the Manson "Family"*

## Vancouver Canucks
GM Place
800 Griffiths Way
BC
V6B 6G1
Canada
*Hockey team*

## Vancouver Grizzlies
1414 Seabright Dr.
902 Griffiths Way
BC
V6B 6G1
Canada
*Sports team*

## Vandross, Luther
P.O. Box 5542
Beverly Hills, CA 90209
*Singer*

## Vanilla Ice
250 W 57th St., #84
New York, NY 10107
*Singer*

## Vanity Fair
4 Times Square
New York, NY 10036
*Magazine*

**INTERNET** www.vanityfair.com
**VOICE** 212-286-2860

## Vanuatu
John Bernard Bani, President
Office of the President
P.O. Box 110
Port-Vila
Vanuatu

## Vargas, Elizabeth
77 W 66th St.
New York, NY 10023
*Journalist*

## Variety
245 W 17th St.
New York, NY 10011
*Daily/weekly magazine*

**INTERNET** www.variety.com
**VOICE** 212-645-0067

## Vatican City
His Holiness John Paul II, Pope
Apostolic Palace
00120
Vatica City
Rome
Italy

**INTERNET** www.vatican.va

## Vedder, Eddie
9560 Wilshire Blvd., #516
Beverly Hills, CA 90212
*Singer/songwriter*

## Vencor

1 Vencor Place
680 S 4th St.
Louisville, KY 40202
*Healthcare*

**INTERNET** www.vencor.com
Edward L. Kunitz, President and CEO

## Venezuela

Hugo Rafael Chavez Frias, President
Oficina del Presidente
Palacio de Miraflores
Caracas
Venezuela

**INTERNET** www.venezuela.gov.ve

## Veterans of Foreign Wars

406 W 34th St.
Kansas City, MO 64111
*Organization dedicated to securing the rights and benefits of veterans*

**INTERNET** www.vfw.org

## VF

628 Green Valley Road, #50
Greensboro, NC 27408
*Apparel*

**INTERNET** www.vfc.com
Mackey J. McDonald, Chairman, President and CEO

## VH-1

1515 Broadway
New York, NY 10036
*Music television network*

## Victoria's Secret

Intimate Brands
3 Limited Pkwy
Columbus, OH 43216
*Lingerie*

**INTERNET** www.victoriassecret.com
Leslie H. Wexner, Chairman, President and CEO

## Video Magazine

460 W 34th St.
New York, NY 10001

**INTERNET** www.videomagazine.com
**VOICE** 212-947-6500

## Vietnam

Le Kha Phieu
General Secretary
Council of Ministers
Bac Thao
Hanoi
Vietnam

## Vietnam Veterans of America

8605 Cameron St., #400
Silver Spring, MD 20910
*National veterans' service organization*

**INTERNET** www.vva.org
George C. Duggins, President

## Vila, Bob

115 Kingston St., #300
Boston, MA 02111
*Television show host*

## Villenueve, Jacques

c/o Williams GP Engineering Ltd
Grove Wantage
GB Oxfordshire OX12 oDQ
England
UNITED KINGDOM
*Professional Formula 1 Driver/1997 World Cup Winner*

## Vilsack, Thomas

Iowa Governor

**INTERNET** www.state.ia.us/governor/comments/capitol_correspond/index.html

## Vince Shute Wildlife Sanctuary

P.O. Box 77
Orr, MN 55711

Kiari Lee, Co-Founder

*360 acre refuge and black bear sanctuary which experts regard as one of the best places in North America for viewing wild bears and their behavior*

## Vinton, Bobby

2701 W Hwy 76
P.O. Box 6010
Branson, MO 65616
*Singer*

**BIRTHDAY** 4/16/35

## Visitor, Nana

3252 Dewitt Dr.
Los Angeles, CA 90068
*Actress*

**BIRTHDAY** 7/26/57

## Vitale, Dick

935 Middle St.
ESPN Plaza
Bristol, CT 06010
*Sports broadcaster*

## VJ Enterprises
P.O. Box 295
Morton Grove, IL 60053
*Metaphysical tours to sacred sites*

**INTERNET** www.v-j-enterprises.com
Joshua and Vera Shapiro

## Vodafone Group PLC
The Courtyard, 2-4 London Road
Newbury, Berkshire RG14 UX
UNITED KINGDOM
*Telecommunications*

**INTERNET** www.vodafone.-airtouch-plc.com
Lord MacLaurin of Knebworth, Chairman

## Vogue
4 Times Square
New York, NY 10036

**INTERNET** www.vogue.com
212-286-2860

## Voight, Jon
9660 Oak Pass Road
Beverly Hills, CA 90210
*Actor*

## Voinovich, George
317 Hart Senate
Office Bldg. (R-OH)
Washington, D.C. 20510
*Senator*

**INTERNET** www.senator_voinovich.senate.gov

## Wachovia
1 First Union Center
Charlotte, NC 28288
*Commercial bank*

**INTERNET** www.wachovia.com
G. Kennedy “Ken” Thompson, CEO

## Wade, Virginia
Sharstead Ct.
Sittingbourne, Kent
UNITED KINGDOM
*Tennis player*

## Wagner, Robert
1500 Old Oak Road
Los Angeles, CA 90049
*Actor*

**BIRTHDAY** 2/10/30

## Wagner, Jack
1134 Alta Loma Road
West Hollywood, CA 90069
*Actor*

## Wagner, Lindsay

P.O. Box 5002
Sherman Oaks, CA 90272
*Actress*

**BIRTHDAY** 6/22/49

## Wagoner, Porter

P.O. Box 290785
Nashville, TN 37229
*Country music singer*

## Wai-hing, Emily Lau

Citibank Tower, #602
3 Garden Road
Central Hong Kong
*Hong Kong Legislator and Democracy Advocate*

## Waite, John

110 W 57th St., #300
New York, NY 10019
*Singer*

## Waits, Tom

2798 Sunset Blvd.
Los Angeles, CA 90026
*Singer/songwriter*

**BIRTHDAY** 12/7/49

## Walgreens

200 Wilmot Road
Deerfield, IL 60015
*Food and drug stores*

**INTERNET** www.walgreens.com
David Behauer, Chairman and CEO

## Walken, Christopher

142 Cedar Road
Wilton, CT 06897
*Actor*

## Walker, Ally

10390 Santa Monica Blvd., #300
Los Angeles, CA 90025
*Actress*

## Walker, Billy

P.O. Box 618
Hendersonville, TN 37077
*Country music singer*

**Walker, Clay**
P.O. Box 8125
Gallatin, TN 37066
*Country music singer*

**Walker, Olene**
Office of the Governor
210 State Capitol
Salt Lake City, UT 84114
*Governor of Utah*

**INTERNET** www.utah.gov/governor
**EMAIL** governor@utah.com

**Wallach, Eli**
90 Riverside Dr.
New York, NY 10024
*Actor*

**Wallflowers, The**
9200 Wilshire Blvd., #1
Los Angeles, CA 90069
*Music group*

**Wal-Mart**
702 SW 8th St.
Bentonville, AR 72716
*Retail stores*

**INTERNET** www.walmart.com
S. Robson Walton, Chairman

**Walston, Ray**
423 S Rexford Dr., #205
Beverly Hills, CA 90212
*Actor*

**BIRTHDAY** 11/2/24

**Walt Disney**
500 S Buena Vista St.
Burbank, CA 91521
*Entertainment*

**INTERNET** www.disney.com
Michael Eisner, Chairman and CEO

**Walters, Barbara**
77 W 66th St.
New York, NY 10023
*Television hostess*

**BIRTHDAY** 9/25/31

**Wang, Garrett**
9300 Wilshire Blvd., #410
Beverly Hills, CA 90212
*Actor*

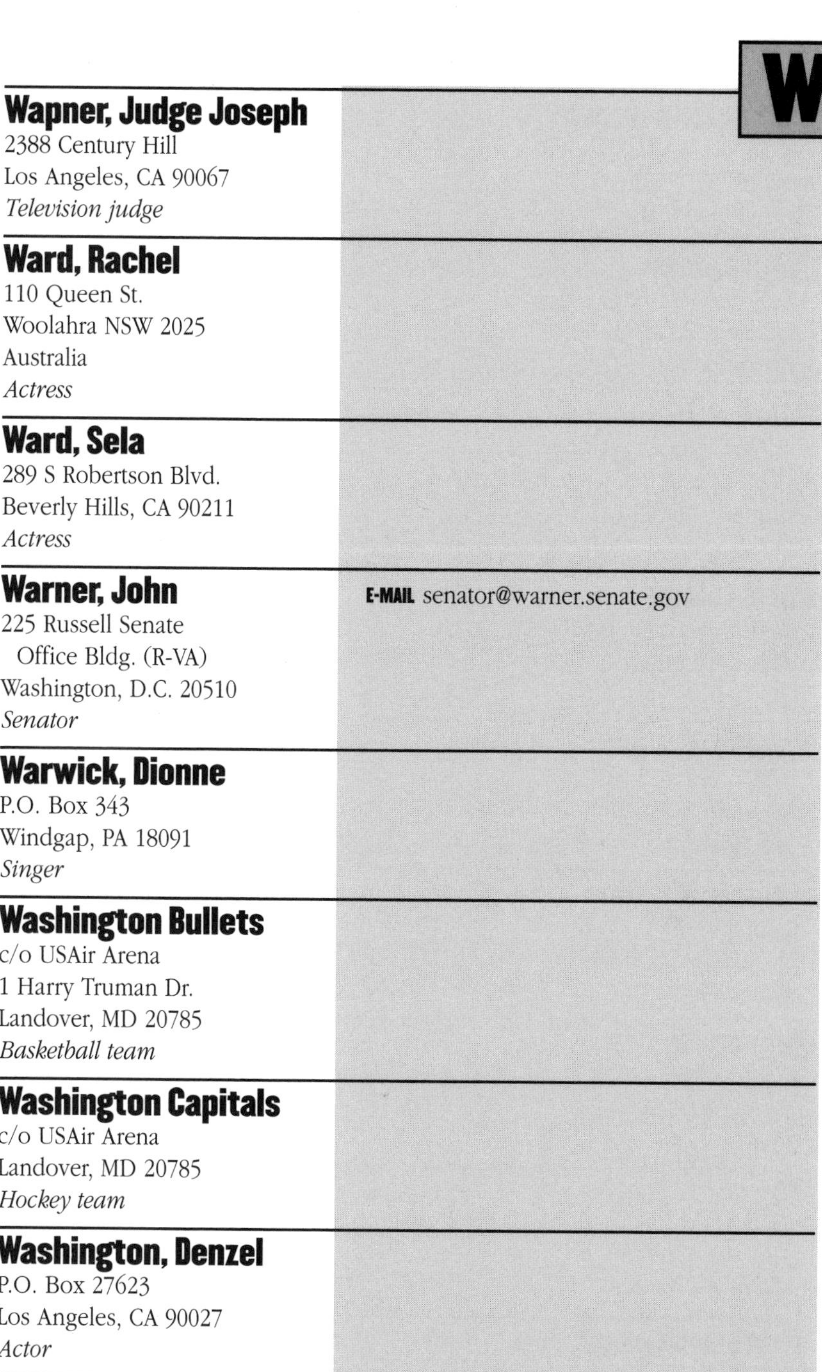

**Wapner, Judge Joseph**
2388 Century Hill
Los Angeles, CA 90067
*Television judge*

**Ward, Rachel**
110 Queen St.
Woolahra NSW 2025
Australia
*Actress*

**Ward, Sela**
289 S Robertson Blvd.
Beverly Hills, CA 90211
*Actress*

**Warner, John**
225 Russell Senate
Office Bldg. (R-VA)
Washington, D.C. 20510
*Senator*
E-MAIL senator@warner.senate.gov

**Warwick, Dionne**
P.O. Box 343
Windgap, PA 18091
*Singer*

**Washington Bullets**
c/o USAir Arena
1 Harry Truman Dr.
Landover, MD 20785
*Basketball team*

**Washington Capitals**
c/o USAir Arena
Landover, MD 20785
*Hockey team*

**Washington, Denzel**
P.O. Box 27623
Los Angeles, CA 90027
*Actor*

**Washington Redskins**
P.O. Box 17247
Washington D.C. 10002
*Football team*

## Waste Management
1001 Fannin, #4000
Houston, TX 77002
*Waste management*

**INTERNET** www.wm.com
Robert Miller, Chairman, President and CEO

## Waters, John
1100 W 36th St.
Baltimore, MD 21211
*Actor/director*

**BIRTHDAY** 4/22/49

## Waterston, Sam
Wolf Films Pier 62
Hudson River & W 23rd St.
New York, NY 10011
*Actor*

**BIRTHDAY** 11/15/40

## Watley, Jody
1700 Broadway, 5th Floor
New York, NY 10019
*Singer*

## Wayans, Damon
9220 Sunset Blvd., #320
Los Angeles, CA 90069
*Comedian/actor*

## Wayans, Marlon
9220 Sunset Blvd., #106
Los Angeles, CA 90069
*Comedian/actor*

## Wayans, Shawn
9220 Sunset Blvd., #106
Los Angeles, CA 90069
*Comedian/actor*

## WB
4000 Warner Blvd., #34R
Burbank, CA 91522
*Broadcast network*

## Weather Channel, The
2600 Cumberland Pkwy
New York, NY 30339
*Cable network*

**Weaver, Dennis**
P.O. Box 257
Ridgeway, CO 81432 - 9717
*Actor*

**Weaver, Sigourney**
40 W 57th St.
New York, NY 10019 - 3211
*Actress*

**Webber, Andrew Lloyd**
725 5th Ave.
New York, NY 10022
*Composer/producer*
**BIRTHDAY** 3/22/48

**Weber, Steven**
8942 Wilshire Blvd.
Beverly Hills, CA 90211
*Actor*

**Welch, Raquel (Racquel Tejada)**
9903 Santa Monica Blvd., #514
Beverly Hills, CA 90210
*Actress*
**BIRTHDAY** 9/5/40

**Wells, Dawn**
11684 Ventura Blvd., #985
Studio City, VA 91604
*Actress*

**Wendt, George**
9150 Wilshire Blvd.
Beverly Hills, CA 90212
*Actor*

**West, Adam**
P.O. Box 3446
Ketchum, ID 83340 - 3340
*Actor*

**West, Jerry**
P.O. Box 3463
Memphis, TN 38117
*Basketball player*

## Western Samoa

Malietoa Tanumafili II, King
Government House
Vailima
Apia
Western Samoa, South Pacific

## Westvaco

299 Park Ave.
New York, NY 10171
*Forest and paper products*

**INTERNET** www.westvaco.com
John A. Luke, Jr., Chairman

## West Wing

*TV show*

**INTERNET** www.westwingtv.com

## Westword

P.O. Box 5970
Denver, CO 80217

**INTERNET** www.westword.com
**VOICE** 303-296-7744

## Weyerhaeuser

33663 Weyerhaeuser Way S
P.O. Box 2999
Federal Way, WA 98003
*Forest and paper products*

**INTERNET** www.weyerhaeuser.com
Jack Crighton, Chairman

## WGN

1 Technology Plaza
Tulsa, OK 74136
*Cable network*

## Whirlpool

2000 N, #M-63
Benton Harbor, MI 49022
*Electronics, electrical equipment*

**INTERNET** www.whirlpool.com
David R. Whitwam, Chairman and CEO

## White, Betty

P.O. Box 491965
Los Angeles, CA 90049
*Actress*

## White, Bryan

2100 W End Ave., #1000
Nashville, TN 37203
*Country music singer*

## White House, The
1600 Pennsylvania Ave.
Washington, D.C. 20500

**INTERNET** www.whitehouse.gov

## White, Lari
1028B 18th Ave.
Nashville, TN 37212
*Country music singer*

## White, Vanna
c/o Wheel of Fortune
10202 W Washington Blvd.
Culver City, CA 90232
*Television Personality*

**BIRTHDAY** 2/8/57

## White Zombie
c/o Psychoholics Anonymous
P.O. Box 885343
San Francisco, CA 84188
*Music group*

## Whitman, Slim
2825 Blue Brick Dr.
Nashville, TN 37214
*Country music singer*

## Whitman
3501 Algonquin Road
Rolling Meadows, IL 60008
*Beverages*

**INTERNET** www.whitmancorp.com
Bruce S. Chelberg, Chairman, President and CEO

## Whose Line Is It Anyway?
c/o Hat Trick Productions
10 Livonia St Comedy Show
UNITED KINGDOM
W1V
*Comedy show*

## Who, The
12 Oval Road
London NW1 7DH
England
UNITED KINGDOM
*Music group*

## Wichita Eagle and Eagle Beacon

1 Stevenage Road
Wichita, KS 67201

**INTERNET** www.kansas.com
**VOICE** 316-268-6000

## Wilderness Society, The

1615 M St NW
Washington, D.C. 20036
*Devoted primarily to public lands protection and management issues*

**INTERNET** www.wilderness.org

## Wilder, Gene

1511 Sawtelle Blvd., #155
Los Angeles, CA 90025
*Actor*

## William, HRH Prince

Highgrove House
Glocestershire
England
UNITED KINGDOM

## Williams, Andy

2500 W Hwy 76
Branson, MO 65616
*Singer*

**BIRTHDAY** 12/3/27

## Williams, Hank Jr.

P.O. Box 850, Hwy 79E
Paris, TN 38242
*Country music singer*

## Williams, JoBeth

9465 Wilshire Blvd.
Beverly Hills, CA 90212
*Actress*

**BIRTHDAY** 12/6/48

## Williams, John

Symphony Orchestra
301 Massachusetts Ave.
Boston, MA 02115

## Williams, Robin

9830 Wilshire Blvd.
Beverly Hills, CA 90212
*Actor/comedian*

**BIRTHDAY** 7/21/52

## Williams, Serena
U.S. Tennis Association
70 W Red Oaks Ln.
White Plains, NY 10604
*Tennis player*

## Williams, Vanessa
4526 Wilshire Blvd.
Los Angeles, CA 90010
*Actress*

## Williams, Venus
U.S. Tennis Association
70 W Red Oaks Ln.
White Plains, NY 10604
*Tennis player*

## Willis, Bruce (Walter Bruce Willis)
1122 S Robertson Blvd., #15
Los Angeles, CA 90035
*Actor*

**BIRTHDAY** 3/19/55

## Wilson, Carnie
13601 Ventura Blvd.
Sherman Oaks, CA 91423
*Singer*

**BIRTHDAY** 4/29/68

## Wilson, Katharina
c/o Puzzle Publishing
P.O. Box 230023
Portland, OR 97281
*Author*

**INTERNET** www.alienjigsaw.com
**E-MAIL** webmaster@alienjigsaw.com

## Wilson, Mara
3500 W Olive Ave.
Burbank, CA 91506
*Actress*

## Wilson, Rita
P.O. Box 900
Beverly Hills, CA 90213
*Actress*

## Winfrey, Oprah
P.O. Box 909715
Chicago, IL 60690
*Talk show host/actress*

**BIRTHDAY** 1/29/54

## Winger, Debra
9830 Wilshire Blvd.
Beverly Hills, CA 90212
*Actress*

**BIRTHDAY** 5/16/55

## Wings cast
5555 Melrose Ave.
Wilder Bldg, 2nd Floor
Hollywood, CA 90038
*Television show*

## Winkler, Henry
P.O. Box 49914
Los Angeles, CA 90049
*Actor/director*

**BIRTHDAY** 10/30/45

## Winokur Agency, The
5575 North Umberland St.
Pittsburgh, PA 15217
*Entertainment agency*

## Winslet, Kate
503/504 Lotts Road
The Chambers
Chelsea Harbour
London SWIO OXF
England
UNITED KINGDOM

## Winters, Shelley
457 N Oakhurst
Beverly Hills, CA 90210
*Actress*

## Winwood, Steve
P.O. Box 261640
Encino, CA 91426
*Musician*

## Wired
660 3rd St., 1st Floor
San Francisco CA 94107
*Magazine*

**INTERNET** www.wired.com

## Wireless
135 Chestnut Ridge Road
Montrale, NJ 07645

**INTERNET** www.wbt2.com
**VOICE** 201-802-3000

## Wisconsin State Journal
1901 Fish Hatchery Road
Madison, WI 53708

**INTERNET** www.madison.com
**VOICE** 608-252-6200

## Wise, Bob
1900 Kanawha Blvd. E.
Charleston, WV 25305
*Governor of West Virginia*

## Witherspoon, Reese
9100 Wilshire Blvd., 6th Floor, #6W
Beverly Hills, CA 90210
*Actress*

## Witt, Katarina
Reichenhaner Str
D-09023
Chemnitz
Germany
*Ice skater*

## Woman's Day
1633 Broadway
New York, NY 10019

**INTERNET** www.womansday.com
**VOICE** 212-767-6418

## Woman's World
270 Sylvan Ave.
Englewood Cliffs, NJ 07632

**VOICE** 201-569-6699

## Women's Wear Daily
7 W 34th St.
New York, NY 10001

**INTERNET** www.womensweardaily.com
**VOICE** 212-630-4000

## Wonder, Stevie
4616 W Magnolia Blvd.
Burbank, CA 91505
*Musician/singer*

**Woo, John**
2500 Broad Blvd., #320
Santa Monica, CA 90405
*Film director*

**Wood, Elijah**
151 El Camino Blvd.
Beverly Hills, CA 90212
*Actor*
**BIRTHDAY** 1/28/81

**Woodard, Alfre**
602 Bay St.
Santa Monica, CA 90405
*Actor*

**Woods, Tiger**
6704 Teakwood St.
Cyprus, CA 90630
*Golf champion*

**Woodward, Joanne**
1120 5th Ave., #1C
New York, NY 10128-0144
*Actress*
**BIRTHDAY** 2/27/30

**Wopat, Tom**
P.O. Box 128031
Nashville, TN 37212
*Actor/singer*
**INTERNET** www.wopat.com

**Worcester Telegram**
20 Franklin St.
Worcester, MA 01615
**INTERNET** www.telegram.com
**VOICE** 508-793-9100

**Working Communicator, The**
316 N Michigan Ave., #300
Chicago, IL 60601
**INTERNET** www.ragan.com
**VOICE** 312-960-4100

**Working Mother**
230 Park Ave.
New York, NY 10169
**INTERNET** www.workingmother.com
**VOICE** 212-551-9500

## World Future Society
7910 Woodmont Ave., #450
Bethesda, MD 20814
*A nonprofit educational and scientific organization for people interested in how social and technological developments are shaping the future*

**INTERNET** www.wfs.org
Clement Bezold, Executive Director

## Worley, Joanne
P.O. Box 2054
Toluca Lake, CA 91610
*Actress*

## Wright, Michelle
P.O. Box 152
Morpeth, Ontario NOP 1XO
Canada
*Country music singer*

## Wright, Ann Reps.
165 W 46th St., #1105
New York, NY 10036
*Entertainment agency*

## WTBS
1 CNN Center, P.O. Box 105366
Atlanta, GA 30348
*Cable network*

## WWF
Titan Tower
1241 E Main St., P.O. Box 3857
Stamford, CT 06902
*World Wrestling Foundation*

## Wyden, Ron
516 Hart Senate Office Bldg. (D-OR)
Washington, D.C. 20510
*Senator*

**INTERNET** www.wyden.senate.gov/contact.html

## Wyle, Noah
4000 Warner Blvd.
Burbank, CA 91522
*Actor*

## Wynona
325 Bridge St.
Franklin, TN 37064
*Musician*

## Xena, Warrior Princess cast
70 Universal City Plaza
Universal City, CA 91608
*Television show*

## Xerox
800 Long Ridge Road
Stamford, CT 06904
*Computers and copiers*

**INTERNET** www.xerox.com
Anne Mulcahy, Chairman and CEO

## Yahoo Internet Life
28 E. 28th St.
New York, NY 10016-7930

**INTERNET** www.yil.com
**VOICE** 212-503-4782
Timothy Koogle, CEO

## Yankovic, 'Weird Al'
c/o Close Personal Friends of Al
8033 Sunset Blvd.
Los Angeles, CA 90046
*Musician*

**INTERNET** www.weirdal.com

## Yanni
P.O. Box 46996
Eden Prairie, MN 55344
*Musician*

## Yearwood, Trisha
3310 W End Ave.
Nashville, TN 37203
*Country music singer*

## Yellow
10990 Roe Ave.
Overland Park, KS 66211
*Trucking*

**INTERNET** www.yellowcorp.com
William D. Zollars, Chairman, President and CEO

## Yemen
Ali Abdullah Saleh, President
Office of the President
Sana
Yemen

**INTERNET** www.yemeninfo.gov.ye

## Yes
151 El Camino Blvd.
Beverly Hills, CA 90212
*Music Group*

**Yes Dear**
c/o 20th Television/
CBS Productions
4024 Radford Ave.
Bldg. 7, 2nd floor
Studio City, CA 91604
*Sitcom*

**Yothers, Tina**
280 S Beverly Dr.
Beverly Hills, CA 90212
*Actress/singer*

**Young and the Restless cast**
7800 Beverly Blvd.
Beverly Hills, CA 90036
*Soap opera*

**Young, Burt**
43 Navy St., #5305
Venice, CA 90291
*Actor*

**Young, Jesse Colin**
Box 31
Lancaster, NH 03584
*Musician*

**Young, John**
c/o NASA, Mail AC5
Houston, TX 77058
*Astronaut*

BIRTHDAY 9/24/30

**Young, Nina**
c/o Narrow Road Company
21-22 Poland St.
London W1V 3DD
England
*Actress*

**Young, Sean**
9200 Sunset Blvd.
Los Angeles, CA 90069
*Actress*

## Yugoslavia

**INTERNET** www.gov.yu

Slobodan Milosevic, Federal President
Savezna Skupstina
11000 Belgrade, Servia
Yugoslavia

## Zadora, Pia

**BIRTHDAY** 5/4/56

9560 Wilshire Blvd.
Beverly Hills, CA 90212
*Actress/singer*

## Zambia

**INTERNET** www.statehouse.gov.zm

Frederick Chiluba, President
Office of the President
Cabinet Office, Box 30208
Lusaka
Zambia

## Zane, Billy

450 N Rossmore Ave., #400
Los Angeles, CA 90067

## Zappa, Dweezil

P.O. Box 5265
N Hollywood, CA 91616
*Musician*

## Zappa, Moon Unit

**BIRTHDAY** 9/28/67

P.O. Box 5265
N Hollywood, CA 91616
*Frank Zappa's daughter*

## Zemeckis, Robert

**BIRTHDAY** 5/14/52

1880 Century Park E, #900
Los Angeles, CA 90067
*Director/producer*

## Zero Population Growth

**INTERNET** www.zpg.com
Peter Kostmayer, Executive Director

1400 16th St. NW, #320
Washington, D.C. 20036
*The nation's largest grassroots organization concerned with the impacts of rapid population growth and wasteful consumption*

## Zero to Three

National Center for Clinical Infant Programs
734 15th St. NW, #1000
Washington, D.C. 20005
*A national nonprofit dedicated to the healthy development of infants, toddlers and their families*

**INTERNET** www.zerotothree.org
Arnold Milstein, Director

## Zeta-Jones, Catherine

76 Oxford St.
Oxford House
W1N OAX
London
England
UNITED KINGDOM
*Actress*

**BIRTHDAY** 9/25/69

## Ziering, Ian

1122 S Robertson Blvd. #15
Los Angeles, CA 90035
*Actor*

## Zimbabwe

Robert Mugabe, Executive President
Office of the President
Private Batg 7700, Causeway
Harare
Zimbabwe

**INTERNET** www.gta.gov.zw

## Ziglar, Zig

2009 Chenault, #100
Carrolton, TX 75006
*Author*

## Zimbabwe

Causeway
Office of the President
Private Bag 7700
Harare, Zimbabwe

**INTERNET** www.gta.gov.zw

## Zimbalist, Stephanie

3500 W Olivier Ave., #1400
Burbank, CA 91505
*Actress*

## Zuniga, Daphne
P.O. Box 1249
White River Junction, VT 05001
*Actress*

## Zydeco, Buckwheat
P.O. Box 561
Rhinebeck, NY 12572
*Musician*

## ZZ Top
P.O. Box 19744
Houston, TX 77024
*Music group*